Henry C. Pearson

Her Opportunity

Henry C. Pearson

Her Opportunity

ISBN/EAN: 9783337287009

Printed in Europe, USA, Canada, Australia, Japan

Cover: Foto ©Andreas Hilbeck / pixelio.de

More available books at **www.hansebooks.com**

BY

HENRY CLEMENS PEARSON.

AUTHOR OF " HIS OPPORTUNITY."

BOSTON

JAMES H. EARLE, PUBLISHER,

178 WASHINGTON STREET.

1 8 8 9.

TO

THE KINDEST OF CRITICS,

My Mother,

THIS VOLUME IS AFFECTIONATELY DEDICATED.

CONTENTS.

———•———

HER OPPORTUNITY.

I.

An Adventure on the Cable Road.

MISS BELLE, daughter of Ex-Governor Pitcairn, of New York, had taken a quiet afternoon jaunt to Harlem. What impelled the young lady to go unattended from her elegant Fifth Avenue home to One Hundred and Fifty-fifth street, by the " Elevated Road," or why she still continued her way in the commodious cars of the Cable Road, would perhaps puzzle her to state. At all events, were the journey purposeless or not, she seemed to enjoy it, and quietly studied the faces and actions of the few passengers who entered at the crossings.

Nor was she unnoticed; the conductor, a diminutive blonde of two-and-twenty, twisted a backward moustache, and gazed approvingly at the "stunnin'est girl that ever rode on this car, sir"; the "grip-man" turned once, twice, thrice, even his big red face beaming with pleasure at the thought that his little Sally would in a few years be grown, and, he flattered himself, resemble that lady; a fagged-looking woman in a shawl, yellowed by sun and rain, smiled gratefully as if the sight of the fair young face refreshed her, as well it might.

Meanwhile the car was bowling along with the free-coasting motion peculiar to this kind of traction, and only the alarm-gong at the front disturbed the harmony of the ride.

Among other things that Miss Pitcairn noted, was the manner in which the burly "grip-man" handled the car. A turn of the brake-wheel, and it stopped in less than its own length; an opposite twist, the grip caught the cable, and the car was swept along as smoothly and easily as if it were a boat in the rapids.

As she watched, they approached a crossing where stood a lady, signalling with closed parasol and open anxiety. With the abandon of an old hand, the pilot released the grip and set the brake, timing it to stop at the crossing, but the car sped on. With a look of chagrin, he turned the wheel yet more, and finding that it did no good, shook it with all his strength, while the car, suddenly beyond his control, swept along faster than before, the grip-man still laboring at the wheel, and sounding the gong harshly at all teams that might by any possibility get in the way.

The little conductor, seeing that something was wrong, hastened forward and attempted to assist the grip-man, and then two of the male passengers with white faces tried to help, but all to no avail. On went the car swiftly, smoothly; by indignant pedestrians who signalled in vain for it to stop; grazing heavy teams, whose surly drivers kept the track until the last minute; on — on — the danger growing and reflecting itself in the faces of the frightened passengers.

A sudden turn in the road showed another car but a short distance ahead, stopping to let off a passenger. At sight of this, the male passengers on the runaway were struck with panic, and all of them, including the conductor, jumped off, almost tumbling over each other, in their eagerness to save themselves. The woman in the faded shawl started to follow, but a daintily gloved hand was laid on her arm, and a tremulous voice said, —

"O, pray, do not jump off! We are much safer to sit still. See, the driver remains."

"But we shall be killed! O, why do n't it stop!"

With a crash, the car struck the one in front, just as the latter got under way, and instead of upsetting or stopping, swept along, carrying the forward car with it, as easily as if it had been but another passenger. The great cable, rattling, whirring, in its narrow flume, had in some way caught the grip, and was now speeding both cars to the end of the route. What it would do there who could tell? Perhaps no harm, perhaps cause a sudden, disastrous wreck.

In the second, as in the first car, the men jumped out and saved their precious lives. There was, however, one exception, a tall, strongly built young man, who took up a position in the rear door, where Miss Pitcairn saw him, and at once her face lighted with pleasure, and her pallor was relieved by a faint color. At first, the gentleman did not notice the occupants of the car in the rear, as he was doing his best to soothe the frantic ladies that crowded toward the door of his car and insisted upon throwing themselves off, a proceeding that he refused to allow in spite of hysterical appeals and half-delirious abuse.

Meanwhile the grip-man was still at work, trying to shake off the strange hold of the cable, and to this end called to the gentleman who was but a few feet distant,—

"Say, there, lend me a hand till we break this grip!"

Closing the door and holding it with one hand, the stranger reached over and caught the wheel with the other, giving it a powerful pull that made the car rock.

"You've more muscle than me. I'll hold that door. Come over here," said the grip-man, and suiting the action to the word, he leaped over the guard, while the other vaulted lightly into his place. As he alighted on the platform, he glanced into the car, and a look of surprise flashed into his eyes.

"Miss Pitcairn here?" he said, as if to himself.

"O Mr. Buckingham, can you stop the car?" said a sweet voice as he caught the wheel with both hands, and bracing himself against the guard, put the strength of sinewy arms, broad shoulders, and generous back, into a mighty wrench. He could not answer except by a look that said most eloquently, "I'll try."

The shaft bent, the car rocked and shivered, but the cable still held. Again the young Hercules bent himself to his task, and again the steel shaft showed its splendid temper by resisting the strain. With white lips he set himself to a third and final trial, when with a crash, the cars struck a heavily loaded truck, the cable shook itself loose with a jerk that threw every car on the line from the track, and the perilous ride was at an end.

The trembling, half-fainting ladies were assisted unhurt from the cars, and stood looking in dismay at the wreck and at the rapidly gathering crowd.

"Let me show you into this office, until I can summon a carriage," Professor Buckingham had said to Miss Pitcairn; and with the lady leaning on his arm, he crossed the street, and opened a door that disclosed the neat office of a paper-box factory. A trim young woman sat at a table within the railing, making ring boxes as deftly as if she were a swift-moving, tireless automaton.

"This lady can sit here a few moments, I suppose?" said the Professor, with an unconscious touch of authority in his tones, placing a chair as he spoke.

"Yes, sir," was the reply, as the clever fingers moved on without pause.

"And could I trouble you to get her a glass of water?"

"In the corner," with a nod toward a tiny jar, crowned with a bright tin dipper.

The gentleman appeared a trifle nettled at first, that any one could so ignore his beautiful charge, yet he did not betray it except by a slight knitting of the brow, but procured the water and handed it as if from a cup of crystal.

When he had gone, Miss Pitcairn watched the rapid worker with intense interest. The flying fingers, the air of concentration, the constantly increasing pile of boxes, all opened to her a view of life entirely new. She had never before known that it was necessary for people to work so rapidly.

"I beg pardon, but may I talk to you?" she said at last. "Can you not stop a minute?"

"I can't stop very well, because I have a certain amount to do, but it won't trouble me to be talked to, one bit," said the other pleasantly.

"Do you always work like this?"

"One should work as fast as this, to earn enough to live on," was the reply.

"But I should think it would be very exhausting?" ventured Miss Pitcairn.

"It is, but starving is more so.'

"How much money can a—a young person earn at this work?" continued the visitor.

"A young person can earn from three to five dollars," smiled the box-maker.

"A day, of course?"

The worker actually stopped and glanced at the questioner to see if she were sane, and then seeing the interested look on the beautiful face, smothered an ironical reply, and said, —

"O, dear, no, miss; three dollars a week, perhaps four, is the average. I manage to get five, because I 'tend the office and help on the pay-roll, but I am obliged to make just as many boxes as the rest, all the same."

"But how can you live?" said Miss Pitcairn, in real distress.

"Me? I can live high beside the other girls. O, five dollars a week is n't to be despised, nor three dollars, either. It may be starvation wages, but it is n't starvation. There is talk, though, of this place being sold, and the work going to a Jew down town. If it does, *that* will mean starvation, sure, for some of us."

"But he will hire you just the same?"

"No, he wants none of this help. The girls are about wild over it, but what can they do? If they peep or mutter, they are turned off, and so they just work days and worry nights, all except me. When I get out of work I am going to imitate Steve Brodie, jump off the Brooklyn bridge," was the reply, with the first tinge of bitterness or recklessness that she had shown.

"Don't talk so. I'm sure you will be successful in finding employment," said the other, in a low, sad tone.

At this instant the Professor returned, and Miss Pitcairn entered the waiting carriage, and was driven to the station, where she took the cars for her home.

"Do you know," said the Professor, "you were in a building this afternoon that was formerly owned by your grandfather?"

"Indeed, how did you learn that?" wa the interested query.

"I asked a patrolman the name of the firm who own the paper-box business, and while he did not know, he was able to tell me that the building was called Van Alstyne's mill, and that it was built by Jacob Van Alstyne for a dwelling-house when he was a young man. He lived there some years and then moved into the city. Some years ago it was enlarged and made into a box factory."

"How strange! It must be still in the family, then, for grandpapa willed that none of his real estate should be sold until fifteen years after his death."

"Then there are five years more of owner ship," said the gentleman.

"And of responsibility," murmured Miss Pit-

cairn to herself, while the Professor, his eyes
keenly fixed on her face, strove to read what
was passing in her mind, and failed, as men
generally do in similar cases.

Very pleasant was the quick ride down to the
cross street that let one through from the "L"
road to the point nearest the Pitcairn residence,
for both of the young people, belonging to the
same circle, had much to talk about that was
interesting.

Professor Buckingham, although too much of a
student to be in the whirl of society life, was
one who was more than welcome, and could
make himself the most agreeable of partners.
As a junior professor in New York's most noted
college, he had already proved himself a man of
force, and aside from his success as instructor,
was making an enviable name for himself in
literature.

Added to this was the blue Buckingham
blood, a generous slice of his father's fortune, and it will be seen that he had several
reasons for being happy. He was one, however,
who took prosperity calmly, and worked steadily
at his chosen vocation, varying the "grind" by
a couple of hours daily in the gymnasium, or on
the ball field, for he was a famous athlete, and
perhaps won the hearts of the youths under him

by his excellence in field sports as well as in the dead languages.

"You will come in, Professor?" Miss Pitcairn said, when they reached her home.

"Thanks, no, I must help one of my boys on his Greek. I presume he is waiting for me now."

With a quick clasp of the hand, and a lifting of the hat, he hailed a cab and was gone.

II.

An Unfashionable Proceeding.

THE Pitcairn residence was one of the new houses of Gotham well up town, in sight of the park, and yet so situate that from its windows could be seen more than a mile of the fashionable avenue. The corner upon which the mansion stood had been purchased by the Governor when he was still a young man, and when the land was tenantless except for the motley cabins of the "squatters." With the wonderful growth of the city had grown his fortune. The modest business that he had founded had broadened and enlarged, taking in partners, gathering new clients, filling larger places, until its name was a synonym for sterling worth, as well as enterprise. In spite of the large interests involved, Governor Pitcairn, although grown gray and portly, was still actual head of the house, and managed its many details with an ease that showed him a born executive.

"Pity the Governor has no son to inherit his

business," said his friends, finding something to pity in him, as no doubt they would in the angel Gabriel. But the Governor gave no sign that both heart and ambition were not fully satisfied by his lovely daughter.

Picture him sitting in ample arm chair after dinner, the shades drawn, the room full of a mellow light, his evening paper lying unread on the rich carpet while he talks to a caller of his idol, Belle.

"Yes, the home seems but half a home with Belle away," he says, in the strong voice of a well man. "She suddenly discovered a second cousin of ours in Harlem, and accepted an invitation to spend a week there. My dear, it *was* a week, was n't it?" turning to his wife.

"Yes, James, and I rejoice in it. These cousins are estimable people, much like the old-fashioned New Englanders, with quiet tastes and no dissipations. It will be a decided change for Belle, who is weary of the fevered life of this great city."

"But I am sure she has never *looked* fagged," exclaimed Mrs. Crittenden, whose errand had been a sudden requisition for the absent one to serve on a committee for some church matter.

"Fagged," laughed her father; "she can tire me out and remain fresh as a rose; but I wish she were here, although I doubt if I should allow you to carry her off this evening, for I want her myself. She has not gone away because she is tired out, by any means. I suspect, on the contrary, it is some charitable scheme that her mother and she are prosecuting with great secrecy."

In the mean time, as has been suggested, Miss Belle was in Harlem — a thought that filled her society friends with surprise, and could they have followed her in the adventures of that memorable week, what would have been their emotions? As the readers of this tale are to be intimate rather than society friends, there is no reason why Miss Pitcairn's week in Harlem should not be to them, as it was to her, a look at an unknown world.

Miss Pitcairn's glimpse of a life of which she had heretofore known nothing — a life where young girls were obliged to strain every nerve, improve each moment, to keep soul and body together — had begotten in her a desire to see and know more of this state of affairs. With the feeling that she had a measure of ownership in the box factory, inasmuch as it had been the property of her grandfather, she did not hesitate again to visit it, and to hold converse with the busy young woman in the outer office. Her questions were so much to the point, that Miss Murdock,—for that was the worker's name,—realized that they were not dictated by idle curiosity, and answered with great freedom.

"But I can't give you any idea of how things are," she said finally. "One must see these places for themselves."

This answer sank deep into Belle's heart. By birth and breeding she felt she was different from these shop-girls, but her common sense suggested that circumstances had much to do with that. Fresh from a New England college, where the best and broadest education was given, a dazzling season in New York society had not quenched her desire to be of use in the great, troubled world. She had taken Miss Murdock partly into her confidence from the start, for she instinctively acknowledged her plain common sense, and knew she would not be swayed by petty selfishness; but the benevolent box-maker had no idea that she was talking to the daughter of Governor Pitcairn, whose name was known the length of Manhattan Island, nor that her questioner was heiress to large estates of the aristocratic Van Alstynes.

"Why could n't I spend a day or two learning to make boxes?" inquired Miss Pitcairn, hesitatingly, almost frightened at her own boldness.

"No one taken to learn for less than a week," was the reply.

At first, this seemed an insurmountable obstacle, but as the desire to see her fellow-women striving for daily bread became stronger, she at length decided to visit a long-neglected cousin and secure her co-operation. This was more difficult than was at first imagined, for she met with a decided refusal, but her eloquence and her mother's permission finally won the day. She came to Harlem, and in plain dress and calico apron, took her place at the beginners' table as a "paster." She found the work exceedingly simple, and easily learned its routine, but was also soon aware that the speed necessary to make even a poor living was the result of months of severe practice. Her acquaintance with her fellow-workers progressed slowly, for almost the only time that they could stop to converse was at noon, when they took a short half hour. At other times the owner of the business, a burly, sullen-looking man named Betteredge, emphatically discouraged what he termed "jaw work."

There seemed to be an atmosphere of fear in the factory, that certainly was not necessary, and that more than once made Miss Pitcairn thrill with indignation; and as little by little she learned more of the man who held so many helpless women in his cruel power, she came to despise him as heartily as did the rest. When out of hearing, the girls alluded to him as "the alderman," and, to her surprise and disgust, Miss Pitcairn learned that he was, indeed, one of the "city fathers," and had a strong political backing.

In place of errand-boy, the mill supported a small, ragged girl, bright and sharp beyond her years, and an object of constant irritation to Mr. Betteredge. Nothing that she did suited him, and his chief signs of disapprobation were vigorous cuffs. The little girl, Jack by name, usually "ducked" in time to evade the blows, and kept out of the way as much as possible; but despite her quickness, hardly a day passed that did not leave the traces of tears on her soiled face.

It was during Miss Pitcairn's second day in Harlem that she learned of this persecution, and to the horror of the humble sisterhood she rebelled.

It happened in this wise: Jack was sweeping, not very rapidly, for the broom was heavy, and the slender arms and wrists not over-strong, while Betteredge, lurking behind a pile of cardboard in an adjoining room, was slyly watching her, his sullen eyes full of dislike. One or more of the piece workers saw him, but dared not apprise the child of her danger. At length, when she was resting an instant, Betteredge darted up behind, and with a single blow sent her reeling half across the room. He was about to follow it up with a second blow, when he found himself confronted by a queenly young woman, whose eyes flashed such contempt that the strong man fairly quailed.

"Jack," she said, drawing the sobbing child to her, "if this wicked, cowardly man ever strikes you again, come and tell me. You have rights, little one, and it shall cost him dearly if he tramples on them."

At the word "rights" Betteredge turned pale, and, to the astonishment of the workers, muttered something about not being himself, and slunk out of the room.

"*That* was a fetcher!" said Jack, drying her eyes suddenly. "Looked azzif he'd stole sumpin', did n't he?"

Among the box-makers to whom Miss Pitcairn was especially drawn, was one who had been absent during this episode, and who, perhaps, was the only one of them all that would dare interfere. She was a plain, quiet young woman, of twenty-five years, who turned off the work as if it were play, and then helped the slower ones. In this helping she was impartial and fearless, meeting the eye of the tyrant with a firmness that caused him to let her alone. Belle, to her surprise, came in for her share of this assistance toward the end of the week.

"You must work faster than this, dear," said the helper, kindly, "or the boss won't have you round at all. You do your work very nicely, but quickness tells the tale."

"Thank you, but I am afraid I never shall be as quick as the rest," was the demure reply.

"O, yes, you will. Just pitch right in, and do your best, and the Lord will make you successful," was the bright reply.

"The Lord ain't found in box-shops," spoke up a listener whose bench was near them.

"Indeed He is, Kitty, for it's here I found Him, and I tell you, dear, your troubles would grow very light if you would but let Him bear them."

"Kate Thomas, less noise down there," interrupted the harsh voice of the owner.

"Don't forget what I say, *He* can help you," said she in a lower tone.

Mr. Betteredge must have been in a villanous mood, for he strode down to the bench, his red face inflamed with anger, and said, —

"Look here, this ain't a gospel mill, and I won't have your preachin' no longer. You just put on your things and git out!"

"But, Mr. Betteredge, there are no rules against 'piece workers' talking in any other box factories. I'm sure I have not hindered the work," said the girl, turning pale.

"Git along! I do n't need you here, and any one that do n't like my style of runnin' this place can git out."

This last was said as there was a slight show of rebellion among the girls, for Kate Thomas was a favorite. The threat of the tyrant, however, recalled them, and they bent to their tasks without a word.

"I 've been a faithful hand, sir, and it 's hard to be discharged this way," said the offender, with a faint hope that there might be some relenting, but the hard face only grew the harder, and with a sigh, she turned and left the room.

As the door closed, Miss Pitcairn rose, threw aside her apron, donned her wrap, and started to follow.

"Where are you goin'?" was the brutal question of the box manufacturer, as he stepped in front of her.

"Allow me to pass, sir," said the young heiress, drawing herself up to her full height, and bestowing such a look of scorn upon him that he moved aside in ludicrous haste, while she swept out and speedily overtook the girl so suddenly and unjustly discharged.

"You see, I've espoused your cause, and left also," said Belle brightly, stepping up beside her.

"O, why did you do that!" exclaimed Kate in dismay. "And you just learnin'? dear! dear! You'll starve before you get another place. Even old hands find it terrible hard to get work."

"There, don't worry for me. My father will not see me suffer," said Belle, cheerily.

"Is he workin'?"

"Yes," was the reply with a conscious blush, "I believe he's doing very well."

"You ought to be thankful for that, even if he don't get mor'n a dollar a day," said benevolent Kate, noting the blush, and thinking with charitable tact that perhaps "doing well" might serve to keep the wolf but a short distance from the door.

"What shall you try to do now, if I may ask?" inquired Miss Pitcairn with some hesitation.

"O, hunt, I suppose. Climb stairs, study newspapers, and starve, until I get another job. I'm just about discouraged to-night, for I wasn't fit to work to-day, but—but—'I know that my Redeemer liveth.'"

The sentence ended in a sob, for as she said, brave Kate Thomas, the helper of the weak ones, was herself weak then, and rested heavily on the Almighty arm.

"Cheer up. He will help you,—I am so sure He will," said Belle gently, taking her arm with loving pressure. "Come, you look faint; go to dinner with me."

Truth to tell, the offer was tempting, for the lunch that the girl had brought had been divided with a poorer sister. She did not object strenuously, therefore, until the door of a restaurant that certainly could not be called fashionable was approached, when she drew back in amazement.

"O, not in there!" she exclaimed.

"Why? Isn't it respectable?" was the somewhat startled query.

"Yes! yes! but the prices they charge. And the colored waiters won't look at you unless you give them a quarter. Why, they charge thirty-five cents for a plate of soup, such as one would get for five, or, at most, ten cents in any common place."

Obediently Belle allowed herself to be conducted to a modest lunch counter, where the prices had no horror in them for Miss Thomas, and both made a good meal of crackers and milk.

Before they separated, the Governor's daughter had secured the address of both Kate Thomas and Sarah Murdock, and as she returned to her Fifth Avenue home that night, it was with a firm purpose to do something to help the box-makers. Perhaps this decision was written on her face, for her father, after kissing her, held her off to admire for a minute, and said,—

"Well, well, little one! Where's the languid look,—the society indifference? What's the new idea?"

"You sharp-eyed papa! I've made up my mind to do some good in the world; but does it really show on my face?" was the genuinely feminine reply.

"Will you abandon it if it does?"

"Of course not, but, papa, if I try to help the right sort of people,—those who are trying to help themselves,—you won't make fun, but will stand by me?"

The Governor looked into her eyes, alight with earnest purpose, and said,—

"My little girl, when you get your plans matured, come to me, and I'll back you with all I have, and here's my hand on it. Do you want any money now?"

"No, papa. I'm not sure I shall want money."

"Oho, it's moral support? This is getting serious. Well, count on me — and on mother."

Mrs. Pitcairn had just come in from a drive, and said in her sweet, low voice, —

"You may promise any thing for me, James, except that Belle shall spend another week away from home. My dear child, how I have missed you!"

"To repay you, mamma mine, I will tell you, first, all of my numerous and strange adventures, and papa will have to wait for his share."

"Humph!" said the Governor in mock disgust. "Any plan that can not stand the searching analysis of the masculine intellect, will never avail to ameliorate the condition of the benighted Harlemites."

"There, mamma, he's talking Volapük again," was the only reply he received, as mother and daughter, their arms entwining each other's waists, slowly ascended the broad stair-case, followed by the Governor's look of proud affection.

III.

A Courageous Venture.

THE interest that Miss Pitcairn had so suddenly developed in the welfare of the hundreds of young women employed in the Van
Alstyne mill did not die out when she returned
to New York. Although busy with society's demands, the problem of securing to those depend-
ent ones a better enjoyment of life, and an
opportunity to be more than mere machines, was
ever before her for solution. The impulse to give
to each a sum of money, and thereafter allow
them to shift for themselves, although natural,
did not commend itself as wise, for these girls
were far from being beggars, and worked hard
enough to be gaining a little each day instead of losing. They were surely entitled to
an opportunity for earning a living, for they
were constant and willing producers, and the
young heiress was strongly impressed that her
mission would be in securing to them their just
deserts. A few words that Sarah Murdock

dropped suggested a way to do this,—a thought at first rejected as out of the question, yet so entertaining in its novelty and possibilities that it could not be forgotten.

Miss Murdock had met Belle by appointment at her cousin's in Harlem, and was discussing the affairs of the factory in her usual direct manner.

"Mr. Betteredge is heartily sick of the box business, and will certainly sell it out within a couple of weeks," she said. "I know this, because he has promised a Jew in New York that he shall have it, if a better offer does not come up during that time. He has made me promise not to tell a soul in the mill, because he says it would interfere with the finishing of the work. The Jew runs a factory, and will take the stock and the accounts, but won't hire any of the help. All that troubles Mr. Betteredge is that the three years' lease of the building will still be on his hands, and he will have to hunt up an acceptable tenant"

"Will not the Jew take the lease?"

"No; he feels that he has Mr. Betteredge at a disadvantage, and is bound to get all he can at the smallest possible cash outlay. I do n't care how much he beats him, but the thought of all the girls being thrown out of work at

once drives me distracted, and I verily believe
that the hateful old alderman is gloating over
the fact that most of us will be starving a week
after the factory stops."

"Surely he is not such a brute as that?"

"You don't know him as we do. When he
dislikes anybody there is nothing too bad for
them, and he hates every soul of us."

Soon after this conversation, Mr. Crittenden,
a prominent real estate man in New York, and
the agent of the Van Alstyne estates, received
a long letter from Miss Pitcairn that caused him
to open his eyes in astonishment, and shake his
head, and say, —

"Pity the Governor had n't a boy. Women
rarely reckon on the cost of things. Wonder
what the new whim will develop into. Well, I
certainly shall not suffer, but, on the contrary,
get a good commission, and with the wide mar-
gin given, perhaps a chance to turn an honest
penny."

Thus soliloquizing, he took a train for Harlem
to see Mr. Betteredge, but on arriving at the
factory learned that he had gone to New York,
and would be found either at his "new saloon,"
or at "Dittenhoffer's brewery." With true per-
sistence he immediately returned, determined to
find the man he was looking for. While he is

on his way down town, allow us to introduce
Mr. Dittenhoffer, intimate friend of Betteredge,
a brewer, immensely fat, red-faced, and beery-
looking.   A successful man was the brewer, if,
indeed, success ever attends that business; and
his bullet head and little, red-rimmed eyes bespoke cunning and self-satisfaction.

At the moment that Mr. Crittenden stepped off
the cars to seek Betteredge, the latter had left his
saloon and strolled over to the brewery and found
Dittenhoffer in the office with a foaming mug be
fore him, about to take a final drink and go home

"Goot evening, mein frient," he said, cordially.
"Sidt right dowun and drink mit me.   Vat's the
goot vort?"

"Oh, nothing special.   I came in for a little
advice which you can give me, if any one can."

The other bowed profoundly, and listened with
a vast smile, that began at the heavy circles under his eyes, and spread itself into wrinkles and
creases and a brewer's dozen of double chins.

"I'm bound to sell out that place of mine up
at Harlem, for it isn't much of a business by
the side of my saloon.   Now I can close it up
without loss, but the girls hate me, and take no
pains to conceal it when my back is turned, and
I want to give them a dose all around that they
will remember."

"You midt holdt back deir pay."

"No, I can't do that, for there are plenty of smart lawyers that are only too ready to jump on a fellow for a claim of that kind. I want some new scheme."

Dittenhoffer shook his head wisely, and puffed at a long German pipe, as if in deep thought. At that moment Mr. Crittenden came in, with the genuine New York hurry, and said, —

"Ah, Mr. Betteredge, I was told I should find you here. Can I see you for a few minutes?"

"Just as well here as anywhere," was the half surly reply. "I have no secrets from my friend Dittenhoffer."

"Very well," returned the caller, refusing with a slight gesture a proffered glass of beer. "I wished to ascertain if you desired to dispose of your lease of the Van Alstyne mill?"

"No, I don't know that I do, unless it is a specially good offer," was the careless reply.

"Governor Pitcairn's daughter is anxious to secure the building for some purpose which she does not divulge. You know, perhaps, it belongs to her share of the Van Alstyne property, and she would take the lease off your hands at a very fair price, I think."

"I'm not anxious to sell, but I tell you what I'll do," said the alderman, after a moment's thought. "If you can get her to take the stock and the machinery at appraisal, which is n't much, I· will give up the lease without any bonus."

"Supposing we put that in writing," suggested wily Mr. Crittenden.

It was therefore written out, read over, and approved.

"Add five hundred dollars to it, and I'll dispose of 'good will' and all," said Betteredge, jocularly.

"Very well," was the serious reply, and that clause was added, much to Mr. Crittenden's satisfaction, be it noted, for here he saw a chance for the "honest penny."

The box manufacturer looked amazed, started to remonstrate, and then let it pass, thinking that, after all, it mattered little, as the good will could be of value only to one who could use it. This business finished, and the appraiser named, Mr. Crittenden took his departure.

When the door had closed after him, Betteredge jumped to his feet and said, —

"Now I have it! That fool of a Crittenden has just let me out in a way that will give me the chance I wanted to make those box-makers squirm."

Then he sat down, drew his chair close to Dittenhoffer, and the two unworthies talked and chuckled and drank beer for another half hour before they parted. As they shook hands at the door, Dittenhoffer said, impressively, wagging a pudgy forefinger, —

"Drag it oudt. Make it last tree weeks, a month, seex weeks. You can affordt it, undt it vill be lots of fun."

"You bet your life," was the reply, as the other strode gaily away.

The following Saturday evening it was announced at the box shop that there would be no work Monday or Tuesday, but that all must be on hand Wednesday morning. Mr. Betteredge made this announcement in person, adding that he was about to secure a large contract for certain work, and that he must get ready. He stated, also, in the kindliest tones that he had ever used in the mill, that the prices on "piece work" would be raised fifty per cent. when they started up again.

To say that the girls were jubilant, would be to state it very mildly. To be sure, the thought of even two days' waiting sorely tried some of them, yet the prospect of an increase such as was promised soon dispelled even this passing cloud, and all readily agreed not to "give this away" to any one, lest the rival manufacturers learn of it and "cut prices," and a reduction be necessary.

All day Monday in their humble homes waited the box-makers, their scanty fare seasoned with hope, which was all they had in abundance. On Tuesday there came a note to each, saying, that owing to the difficulty in securing "stock," the mill could not start up until the first of the following week. A word of acknowledgment of their straitened circumstances was added to this, with the promise of half pay for the week of idleness to all those who were in readiness to go to work on the date given.

A week without work! Even on half pay this meant an extreme of destitution that, in God's mercy, but few in this country are called upon to realize. But there was no way out of it, and with the thought of Mr. Betteredge's promises, they were forced to be content.

In the meantime, while the retired box manufacturer and the brewer were chuckling over the misery of the help, Miss Pitcairn, with the aid of Sarah Murdock and a gray-haired clerk of her father's, was busily acquainting herself with the state of affairs in the mill. By Wednesday, after hard work, all was ready, and a message summoned the girls to the "packing room," where was spread a substantial supper. To this the half-starved workers did justice, most of them indulging the idea that they were indebted to Mr. Betteredge for it. They were, however, undeceived when Sarah Murdock told them, in her direct, business-like way, that the property had changed hands, and that Betteredge would man ufacture no more, hastening to add that there would be work the next morning for all that wished — as if they were not wild for it — and that for the first week they should receive their pay daily.

Had the audience been boys or men, such statements would have been greeted with cheers, but as all present were girls and women, a buzz of satisfaction and a general gladness of expression took the place of applause.

"Shall we take the 'alf pay that the Halderman gives us?" asked one of the girls.

"Certainly. If he wishes to present the help in the mill with two dollars a week apiece, they should be very thankful to get it," was a reply which caused general satisfaction.

"There is one person who is not here, whom the girls missed," said Miss Murdock, as the guests were departing, after having received their instructions for the next day.

"You mean Kate Thomas?"

"Yes."

"Let them have patience; I have something

in store for her that I think she will appreciate," replied Miss Pitcairn, mysteriously.

The new owner wished to see how well Miss Murdock could manage the assembled box-makers, and feared that the presence of Kate Thomas would prevent her from judging with exactness how well she succeeded. It will be seen that this course was far from being a slight, but was the rather a compliment to the restraining influence that the worthy Kate exercised over her companions.

Since first meeting that simple and devoted Christian, the young heiress had felt that Kate was a woman of more than ordinary force of character, and that she would, with her firm faith and straightforward common sense, be an invaluable aid in the work of raising the box-makers to a higher level, and she had, as was intimated, found a special field for her to work.

Bright and early on the morning of the opening the girls were on hand, took their accustomed places, and went to work at the "regular stock." At first, every thing did not run as smoothly as might have been expected in a carefully regulated mill; there were a few "waits" for stock, as new cutters had been hired; the paste gave out, because no one had remembered to order it, but all of these trifles were remedied after short delay, and, as the girls knew what to do in their several departments, a fair day's work was accomplished.

At noon, however, came a note from a customer, requesting the "Company" to "send their representative down to take an order." This meant, evidently, that they expected the salesman who had been discharged two weeks before Betteredge sold out, to come to their office with samples and prices. The young man had acted as commercial traveller, and had also taken care of the office sales, travelling only in New York city, Brooklyn, and Jersey City, and the problem that now confronted Miss Pitcairn and her assistant was the hiring of a like salesman or losing their trade.

"If I was only more familiar with the styles and prices, I should go down myself," announced Belle, determinedly.

"Why could n't I go," inquired Sarah, "and attend to that part of the work right along? I know the styles that the different customers fancy, and the prices, and have seen many of the buyers here."

"Are ladies ever commercial travellers?" asked Belle, with some hesitation.

"I do n't know, but I do know that we shall lose that order if we do not go in person and take it, and if you will give me leave, I'm going to get it," was the brave answer.

"Go, and success attend you, and remember, if you can and will do this work your salary shall be the same as that paid to a man," was Miss Pitcairn's reply.

So Miss Murdock went, returning in a couple of hours, her cheeks pink with excitement, bringing an order twice as large as any before given by that house.

"I had splendid treatment," she declared. "They acted as if they were accustomed to deal with women."

Thus it happened that, through stress of circumstances, the Van Alstyne mill had a feminine "traveller," and one who neither smoked, drank, nor squandered the firm's time in playing "poker."

Two weeks of intense application, and Miss Pitcairn, under the guidance of the old book-keeper, who was as wise as he was modest, had the business well systematized and running smoothly. Competent heads were chosen for the various departments, and were in every case made personally responsible for the work under their charge. In this way it was possible for the Governor's daughter to know just what was done, by scanning the daily reports, and yet not assume the drudgery involved in the following up of petty details. So it happened that she returned to society after an absence of two

weeks, and still gave regular hours each day to
her business. One of the first reforms that had
been instituted was a revision of the prices paid
the piece workers, so that there were few of
them who were not making, at least, seven dollars a week, and most earned more.

For two weeks Betteredge paid the girls their
half wages, and rejoiced in the firm conviction
that they were starving in their attics, and waiting for the factory to start up. At the end of
this time it occurred to him that the "good will"
which had been sold with the stock might just
as well "net him something," so he went over
to the Hebrew who had formerly desired to purchase, and prepared to offer him a bargain. To
his amazement, the latter flew into a towering
passion, and ordered him out of his office. Betteredge, however, did not go, but sat down and
demanded an explanation.

"You think I buy what you ain't got to sell?"
yelled the Hebrew, fairly hopping with wrath.

"But I can hold those customers. My selling
out was only to get rid of the lease. Why,
you fool, I did n't sell to a box man. I sold to
a party who would n't go into the box business
if there was millions in it. Come, be sensible.
I 'll go round to these customers with you, and
turn over their trade for five hundred dollars."

"*You* vas the fool," yelled the other, "to think that you could sell against that vooman drummer."

"Woman drummer?" was the wondering reply.

"Ain't that vat I said?"

"Look here, what are you driving at?" asked the caller, more and more bewildered.

"Humph! you vas the big hypocrite. You make believe you don't know that the mill vas running, and that they have a vooman drummer what sells more boxes as all of mine. She takes seven of my customers quick, already."

"The mill running!" gasped Betteredge, "and I've been paying those hussies two dollars a week to loaf! Why don't somebody kick me to death!"

"I'll do that pretty midty quick, meinself, if you don't get oudt of here," returned the other, and Betteredge, in a trance of amazement and anger, went out, followed by the maledictions of the Hebrew.

The following afternoon Mr. Crittenden, remembering the honest penny that he had intended to turn, which a pressure of business had driven for a time out of his mind, mentally canvassed the box-makers that he knew, and came to the conclusion that a well-known Hebrew, none other than Betteredge's acquaintance, was the very man for his purpose. With a cheery briskness that the prospect of money-getting always imparted to his demeanor, he stepped into the office of the Israelite, and after a greeting, said, —

"Moses, I 've got a bargain that will make your eyes shine when you hear of it."

"Humph," grunted the other.

"A full stock, carefully selected, at less than a third of the cost, and the good will at a song."

"Vat line of goods?" was the suspicious query

"Why, boxes, of course; you know the Van Alstyne mill?"

"Look here! vat's the matter with you fellers, hey? Do you think I vas an altogedder crazy fool?" interrupted Moses, his ire rising rapidly.

"Hold on; do n't get angry. This good will, worth ten thousand dollars, I will sell for a thousand, cash "——

"Ach, mein gracious! do you vant me to commidt some murders? I do n't vant to hear any more of dot Van Alstyne mill. You vas a big schwindle, you and Betteredge "——

"Has Betteredge been trying to sell it tc you?"

"Of course he has, undt I pelieve you sent him," was the wrathful response.

"The rascal! Trying to sell what is n't his. Why, I bought it of him two weeks ago," said Mr. Crittenden, with such evident sincerity that

the Hebrew was for the moment staggered, but
he rallied to inquire, —

"Does the vooman vant to sell out?"

"What woman?"

"Mein gracious! de vooman what is running
it, and spoiling mein trade."

"Pshaw! some one has been stuffing you.
The daughter of Governor Pitcairn bought it to
turn into a sanitarium or something of the sort,
and she wants to get rid of the stock. The
place has been shut up since Betteredge left,"
replied the agent, easily.

"I tinks you vas the premium liar of the
vorldt, undt I don't wand nodings more to do
mit you. Shut up? I vas oop there meinself,
one, two, dree days, undt all vas at vork. The
office vas full of voomans, undt they are making boxes by the hoondret. Your leedle trick
vas no goot. I snap my fingers at you. See?"

Like Betteredge, Mr. Crittenden departed, his
mind in a whirl. As it was late, he did not go
up to Harlem that evening, as was his first intention, to verify the statement of Moses, and
before the morrow dawned chance furnished him
all the information he needed. He happened to
be treasurer of the fashionable up-town church
to which the Governor belonged, and that very
evening was present at a pastor's reception.

Among other beautiful women, Belle shone, and, as she stood talking with his wife, the curious real estate man ventured near and said, —

: "May I ask after the Harlem scheme, Miss Pitcairn?"

"Certainly. What can I tell you about it?"

"Who has charge of the business now?"

The young heiress drew out an elegant card, upon which was printed, —

The VAN ALSTYNE MFG. CO.

PAPER BOXES.

B. V. PITCAIRN, Gen'l Mgr.

"Mr. Crittenden, you have monopolized Miss Pitcairn long enough. She has promised to sing, and we are more than impatient," interrupted the hostess, leading the young lady to the piano, and leaving the agent speechless at the dawning of the truth.

IV.

"Conlon's."

BRIEF acquaintance with Kate Thomas was enough to convince the most cursory observer that she had a mission; for even in the factory, her helpfulness was ever acknowledged, and her influence for good among the hands was constant. When her sudden discharge came, and she had gone to her humble lodgings, discouraged and weary, yet with the certainty that the trouble was but for the moment, there came a letter enclosing a bank bill and bidding her rest. Where it came from was more than the astonished recipient could guess, and had it not been for the illness of two of the paper-box makers, it is doubtful if she would soon have discovered. Word had come that two of the best workers were ill, and soon after this bad news, a second letter, this time signed by Miss Belle Pitcairn, requesting Miss Thomas to call at her earliest convenience. The place mentioned being the box factory, the girl thought nothing of it, and answering the summons, was amazed to see the young lady whom she had known as a learner, but a short time before, sitting at a desk upon which were a mass of letters, while Miss Murdock stood at her elbow, explaining and making notes upon the replies to be sent.

"Come in, please, and sit down. I will be at leisure in a moment," said she; and the visitor, greatly wondering, did as she was bidden.

"You received my letter?" said Miss Pitcairn, the pile of mail being disposed of.

"Yes."

"Are you employed anywhere?"

"No"—with a sigh.

"Ah, I am glad of that, for I want you myself. I have purchased this business of Mr. Betteredge, and shall want your help, although in a different line from what you have been accustomed to work."

"I'm sure I shall be very thankful to get any thing honest to do,—if I am competent," responded the girl, her face lighting with eagerness.

"Do you know where Mattie Vascoe and Jessie Wilson live?"

"Yes, miss, down at the 'Wedge.'"

"Very well, I wish you to go there and call on them both and learn their circumstances. It will not be necessary to tell them that I sent you, but simply allow the visit to pass as the expression of your interest in their welfare. If they need food, or medicine, supply it, and, let me add, that you have my cordial permission to read, converse, or pray with them, if the way is open. They will ask you, possibly, if you have found work, and you may say that you have, that you are engaged at the Van Alstyne mill. When you know what these two girls need, please report to me."

"The Lord has answered my prayers. I have begged Him to allow me to help the girls whom I saw suffering," said Kate, her eyes full of tears.

"Perhaps it is not business-like, but I am going to take as good care of my help as other manufacturers take of their machinery," said Miss Pitcairn, with a rare smile. "When a cutting machine or stock press is out of order, is 'ill,' the machinist is at once sent for, and the machine is strengthened and helped, until it runs smoothly and is recovered; but if a good box-maker falls ill, they let her go, and take a new hand in her place. I shall reverse the order, and, therefore, engage you as superintendent of repairs, physical and moral, among my help. When all are well, and at work in the factory, I shall expect you to be here; but when any are absent or ill, you must look them up, and help them quietly and wisely. Your salary will be, to begin with, twelve dollars a week, and Miss Murdock will now pay you a week in advance."

The new superintendent of repairs gasped with astonishment.

"Twelve dollars a month, you mean, miss," she said tremulously. "You said a week."

"That is what I mean, twelve dollars a week, and you can earn it. By the bye, I am not here much of the time, but will leave your orders in this little box. I shall expect you, in turn, to make out reports upon each case that comes under your notice, giving name and residence."

"I will do my best to serve you," said Kate, earnestly, yet there was a ring of uncertainty in her voice, for the thought struck her that with a mistress so munificent there would be new trials and probable lack of discipline among the employees. As she counted her week's pay, her mute questioning · was answered in a way most satisfactory. A burly, heavy-jawed woman entered the office, and waddling up to the low gate that served to keep the public out of the space allotted to the desks, attempted to open it. In this she was unsuccessful, for the catch, although simple, was not ostentatiously placed, and puzzled the uninitiated. When it dawned upon the caller that the gate did not open at her touch, she waxed wrathful, and gave it a violent shake.

"Whom do you wish to see?" asked Miss Murdock, stepping forward.

"I want ter see the woman boss, and not you, Sarah Murdock," was the reply.

"You mean Miss Pitcairn?"

"I do n't know wot 'er name is, and do n't care, but I hintend that she shall 'ire me ter do the scrubbing 'ere, hor I 'll know why."

"She is engaged now, and can't see you," said the assistant.

"Hingaged is she?" yelled the termagant. "Well, I 'll dishingage" ——

"Come, Mrs. Tarpy, you are making yourself a nuisance. I must request you to git," said a clear masculine voice, and the engineer of the factory stood by the side of the woman bully.

"Maybe I was speakin' loud, but I was that hanxious to get work," said the woman, suddenly meek and tractable. "Speak to the young missus, Mister Hengineer, and hask 'er ter give me a job."

"No use, she is writing letters, and do n't allow no one to disturb her, so you had better go right away. If she wants you, she will send for you," was the reply, as the man opened the door and gently pushed the wrathful caller outside.

"One of Mr. Betteredge's tricks," said Sarah. "He, no doubt, thought so formidable a person as Mrs. Tarpy would put to flight a whole factory of girls. She is the crack woman fighter of the 'Wedge.'"

"Poor creature, she looked like a hard drinker, and as if possessed by furies. I was so glad that I had only a button to press to call the engineer. Mr. Betteredge evidently is not aware that we have new means of communication between different parts of the mill," responded Belle, turning again to her writing.

During this episode, Kate Thomas had remained a silent spectator, and now left with a look of satisfaction on her expressive face. As she hurried up the street toward the car station, she gave vent to her approval by a series of emphatic nods, and said, "She'll do," "She'll do."

It is probable that no one could have been found who would better have served the purpose of missionary to the factory girls than Kate Thomas, and under her efficient and loving care, the workers, and indeed many others, began to lift up their heads, and feel that there was a certain amount of hope yet left, even for them.

In the course of her calls upon the girls, she found that at least half of them lived in New York, down town, and on the East side, and rode to their work each day over the Second Avenue "L" Road. They claimed that they could live cheaper in New York, as they boarded themselves and paid but a trifle for the tiny attics that they occupied.

As fast as the missionary's reports were handed in, Miss Pitcairn had them arranged in a record book, which showed at a glance the condition of all her help, and incidentally of a large body of women, who, like them, were working for wages in various manufactories.

It happened one evening that Kate had come to the Pitcairn mansion by special request, and there discovered that she had left her notes at her room on the East side. She, therefore, made her report verbally, and as it was necessary that certain addresses be secured that evening, the Governor's nephew, young Mr. Chick, volunteered to accompany her home and get them. This offer on the part of a youth who was in every sense of the word an exquisite, and who was not given to self-denial, nor to good works of an unfashionable nature, was a surprising circumstance; so much so, that Belle, who had been on the point of sending for a

messenger, stayed her hand and allowed the sacrifice to be consummated. Behold, then, a slight,
stylish man of twenty, with cane, eye-glass and
English habiliment, on his way toward the East
side, in company with plain, matter-of-fact Kate
Thomas. A "cross-town" car took them to the
Bowery, and left them in the thick of the jos-
tling evening crowd.

"I beg pardon, but have we far to go?" inquired the young man.

"Not very, but perhaps you would rather wait
here somewhere, and let me go and get the
addresses. It is n't very safe, part of the way,"
replied Kate.

"Not for the world! I am perfectly willing
to go wherever you can."

"I do not find it dangerous to myself to go.
about these streets, because most of the people
know that I am engaged in missionary work,
and they never trouble our kind, but with you
it is different," continued Kate.

"I presume so," assented Mr. Chick.

"When I am out evenings I have a friend
who often comes to meet me,"—said Kate shyly,
a blush mantling her cheek — "Ah, here he is.
Let me introduce you to Mr. Thomas."

"Glad to meet you, I 'm sure; you are a relative, I presume?" remarked the young man,

gazing at the new comer through his glass with mild approval.

"Not yet, but I expect to be, one of these days," replied the gentleman with a jolly laugh. "Our names are the same, but that is merely a pleasant coincidence; another coincidence is the fact that we both do missionary work in the vicinity of the 'Devil's Wedge.'"

Miss Thomas, still blushing, briefly detailed the reason for Mr. Chick's visit to the East side, and as their destination was quite near, they pushed on up the dark, ill-smelling side street, that seemed strangely silent, when contrasted with the turbulent life of the Bowery. As they left the lights behind, the Governor's nephew began to appear nervous and to glance apprehensively at the dark doorways and deep shadows that lined the street. Not so his companions, however, for they hurried along, absorbed in conversation, threading their way with an ease that betokened familiarity with the uncanny surroundings.

"Say, young feller, tell us the time," said a hoarse voice, and a heavy hand was laid on Mr. Chick's shoulder.

"Nine o'clock," answered Mr. Thomas, shortly, crowding the questioner back, and hurrying the others along, leaving the suspected foot-pad far behind.

"Please, fer the love of heaven, give me a penny! I ain't had a morsel of food for two days," came a plaintive voice from a doorway, where could be dimly seen a crouching figure.

Mr. Chick halted at once, and searching for a few cents, was about to step up and relieve this misery, when his guide seized his arm and hurried him away.

"What's wrong?" panted he, when they were a few doors off.

"It's a trick. There is a 'gang' down there, and they steal from every body. If you had stepped up to the door, they would likely hit you over the head with a club, and strip you of all you possess," explained Kate's friend.

"Horrible!" was the shuddering exclamation— then after a pause, — "Say, let's leave this precious neighborhood. I'm sure, I didn't suppose we would go through such a place. Gracious, see there!"

On the opposite side of the narrow street, a man had been walking quietly along, when as he came under the apology for a street lamp, a powerfully built negro had sprung out, and catching him by the shoulders, looked into his face with a cry of exultation that was like the roar of a wild beast. Although taken by surprise, the other made strenuous efforts to break away but without avail, until by a sudden trip, the attacking party threw him on his back and fell heavily on him. But getting a man down is not holding him there, and so the assailant found; for in falling, the smaller man drew one foot up under him, planted it against the broad chest of the negro, and straightening it out with terrific force, threw him over backwards.

At this juncture Mr. Thomas, followed by his companions, hurried across the street; one or two burly loungers appeared on the scene and drove the black away, while the prostrate man tried with difficulty to rise.

"Are you hurt?" asked Mr. Thomas, with solicitude.

"Who are you?" inquired the man, with a blood-curdling oath.

"Are you hurt?" he again inquired.

"Yes, I'm cut. That 'coon' caught me on the leg with his razor when I kicked him off — meant the blow for my face."

With deft skill the young man, used to emergencies, stripped the muscular leg, and found it bathed in blood that was welling from a cut across the knee.

"Artery?" said the man, faintly.

"Yes," was the brief reply.

There was no time for extended conversation,

and all seemed to know it. The crowd of roughs
who had collected, kept the lesser fry at a respectful distance, and allowed the amateur surgeon all
the room he wanted. Under his skilful management a tourniquet was soon formed with a silk
handkerchief and a bit of Mr. Chick's twenty-
dollar cane; then the angry jets of blood ceased
to flow, and the man's life was saved.

"Where does he live?" inquired the young
man, rising from his knees and surveying the
nard-looking faces.

"Down at the 'Wedge,'" was the response,
and Miss Thomas realized that her friend had
helped one of her neighbors.

"It is not far, then?"

"Only a few blocks. If you say so, we will
fetch a door and bring him down there."

"Very well, he ought to be moved at once."

A brief delay occurred, while the door was being brought, during which one of the crowd, who
bore on his face every mark of the depraved
thief, chased a boy who had stolen the dandy's
dainty cane-head, returned to the crowd, and
made the frightened youngster beg the gentleman's pardon and give up the booty.

When the wounded man was lifted upon the
stretcher, he said feebly to Mr. Thomas, "Wish
you 'd come on, too."

"But I ought to get home," remonstrated Mr. Chick, horrified at the idea of going deeper into this wilderness of sin.

"Do n't you be afeared, young feller," said a huge man with one eye and an Anarchist beard — "you 're safe as you 'd be in yer mother's arms; you 'll be treated right; do n't be afeared."

"Have a chaw?" said another, in a hoarse growl that he tried in vain to make alluring and expressive of friendliness.

A few minutes' walk brought them to a dark-looking building, from the lower story of which came light and sounds of revelry.

"This yer 's the place," said the spokesman; "shall we fetch him into the bar-room?"

"Yes."

So in went all hands, and the crowd that had gathered before the long bar turned with one accord and moved toward the new comers.

"Now jes stand back as fer as yer kin, gen-.tlemen," said a man whose appearance stamped him as a professional gambler. "Con is hurted bad, and don't want to be bothered. Jes tend right to yer drinking there, and do n't get in the way. After Con is comfortable, some of you might ask the big chap an' his gal an' the little red-headed feller up fer a drink. Ef it

had n't been fer them, the 'old man' would hev
bled himself ter death."

In the rear of the saloon was the bed-room
of the wounded man, and into this he was carried and laid gently on the couch. Once here,
the tourniquet needed fresh adjustment, and some
little time was consumed in making the patient
comfortable. Then Mr. Thomas turned to go.

"What's the damage," asked the patient, feebly
reaching for his pocket-book.

"That's all right, no charge," was the reply.

"But I'd rather pay you — I guess I'm able
to pay my bills — hey, boys?" This was said in
a triumphant tone that had in it the real arro-
gance of the successful rumseller, and it so
grated on the listener's feelings that it betrayed
him into a speech that was far from safe, considering the inflammable material gathered in the
room.

"It's rum money! I never touch it," he said.

A flush dyed the handsome face of the liquor-
dealer; and his deep-set eyes burned for an instant, and then softened down as he said, and
his tone was almost entreaty, —

"I've got the first five-dollar bill that ever I
earned in New York city, when I was a young
feller, and had just come from the country. I
earned it in an honest business, and have kept

it ever since, as a sort of Mascot. Will you take it?"

The sternness faded from the missionary's face, and his smile seemed to make the room all alight.

"Bless you, man," he said, heartily, "I'd take that quick enough, but for the fact that I did this little act for a kindness. I like to give a fellow-creature a lift, without getting paid for it. Your gratitude is enough. I am glad, very glad, that I happened along in time to help you, and I hope, when you are better, you will get into some honest business. Better be a hotel porter than the richest rumseller in Christendom."

"I'd like some way to show that I'm thankful," said the man, uneasily.

"Very well, then, call the others in here, and let them listen while I pray with you," said Mr. Thomas, boldly.

The man hesitated a moment and then, in a tone of dogged resolution, said, "Sam, open the door and call the boys!"

The occupants of the bar-room filed in till the apartment was full, and those for whom there was no room stood in the door-way, or back in the larger room where every word could be heard.

"Gentlemen," said the missionary, looking into the faces before him, "our friend here has had a narrow escape from death. Even now he is not entirely out of danger. I believe in doing all that I can, and then asking God to do the rest. It has been my habit to pray for those whom I try to help, sometimes in the presence of others, sometimes alone at home. I am sure that many times God has heard my prayers, and helped those who were ill and for whom I prayed. Let us pray."

A sudden silence had fallen on the group of men and youths when this strange address was made, and at its close, as the speaker knelt by the bedside, there was a rustle that seemed to portend flight, but some power held them there, half willing, half reluctant listeners.

"Our Father in Heaven, look down, we pray Thee, and bless this man who is wounded. When he was a child Thou didst know him by name; as he grew older and became a young man, and came to this great city, Thou didst many times whisper in his heart of Thy love for him, and of the grand and noble manhood he might attain by giving himself to Thee. O! Why did he not listen — why does he not now listen, and turn from this dreadful business — turn from this wicked traffic which damns men's souls?"

The sharp click of a revolver came from the bar-room, and almost with it a double click from the bed. The missionary heard both, but prayed on, —

"Our Father, he is Thy child, even now, as are all of these Thy children, although they have wandered far from Thee. Lead them back to Thy fold. Show them the sinfulness of their lives. Let the light of Thine own life shine into their hearts, and bring them into Thy peace. Lord, we pray, believing that Thou art listening to us, and that Thou wilt answer in due time, for we ask these favors, not in our own strength, but remembering that Jesus Christ died for us. Amen."

As he rose from his knees his eyes rested first on Mr. Chick, who stood white as a sheet, looking out of the door into the bar-room. Following his gaze, he saw Betteredge, his face convulsed by passion, with a revolver in his hand, and a look in his eyes that meant mischief. A glance at the bed showed the wounded man sitting up with two pistols, ready to resist any attack.

"Put up your gun, Tom, it's been done," said the owner.

Slowly and reluctantly the man turned away and went back to the bar, and one by one the rest of the men slipped out. All were quiet and respectful, and some had a look on their scarred faces that showed that the Holy Spirit was striving, even in their calloused hearts.

"You must excuse 'big Tom,'" said Conlon, — for that was the rumseller's name — "you must excuse him, for he and I agreed long since, if any parson or missionary came in here and tried to pray or sing, we would hit him with a bottle, or shoot him. Tom is awfully down on such things, and I s'pose he thought he had a right to shoot."

As they left, one of the listeners, the big man with one eye, said prophetically, —

"This place will bust now, sure. No bar-rooms have luck after they are prayed in; not that I blame you, Mister, but you mark my words, there 'll be one less saloon in the 'Wedge' six months from now, and the one that 's wiped out will be handsome John Conlon's."

"I hope so," responded the missionary.

V.

An East-Side Attic.

OBEDIENT to the wish of his fair cousin, Mr. Chick appeared at the Governor's mansion, one bright day, prepared to visit the section known as the "Wedge," where Kate Thomas had discovered the little girl, Jack, who had left the factory with Betteredge.

"Are you ready, Augustus?" asked Belle.

"Yes."

"With lavender kids?" glancing into the silk hat that was deposited carefully on the piano.

"Are they not the proper shade?" was the anxious query.

"I am afraid they look too new and 'dudish' for an expedition like ours, but perhaps it will not matter."

"But, Cousin Belle, you are not really going down to that horrible place? Do you know its real name is the 'Devil's Wedge'?"

"I doubt if it is very horrible, for the missionaries live there, and in addition to that a large number of our girls have rooms in that vicinity. If they are not hurt why should we be?" was the reply.

"But this place has a very hard name, and is infested with burglars, pick-pockets, and all kinds of desperate characters " ——

"Cousin Augustus, are you afraid?" said Belle, with a roguish look.

"Perhaps I am, for I certainly was frightened 'most out of my wits, the night I went down there with the Thomases."

"But you survived?"

"Yes," was the answer with a sigh of resignation, "but I did n't expect to, when I was there."

"O, well, it 's very different in daylight, and I must find out more about that little Jack. Did you know her grandfather was blind? Poor old man! Kate told me he formerly had a Bible printed with raised letters, and that it had been stolen, so I have purchased him another."

"I should n't wonder if he lost this one, too," said Mr. Chick, a suggestion that was ignored by his cousin.

When the start was made, the young gentleman found himself utilized as the bearer of a book as large as an unabridged dictionary, and contrary to expectation he accepted the charge very cheerfully, until he met a messenger boy, to whom, with an expressive wink, he transferred the bundle. So quietly was this done, and so deeply was Miss Pitcairn engrossed in her thoughts, that she did not notice it until, her heart smiting her at thought of her little relative working so hard, she turned to suggest that they take a car, and then discerned his action.

"Augustus Chick," she exclaimed, with true feminine change of base, "are n't you ashamed to make that mite of a boy bear your burdens?"

"It 's Scriptural — ' Bear ye one another's burdens,' — he is bearing mine," explained the young gentleman; "besides, I pay him ten cents for it."

"You ought to give him ten cents any way, he is so small."

"Very well, I will give him ten cents any way, and ten cents more for bearing the burden," was the calm reply. "Now if he does n't choose to work for his money, he can hire some other boy to carry it the rest of the way, and pay him five cents, and still be the richer."

"You are irresistible," replied his cousin, laughing.

"Thanks," murmured the youth, blushing slightly and arranging his rainbow tie with an air of satisfied vanity.

Since her promotion Miss Murdock had taken rooms at the Young Women's Christian Association, and as she was to be one of the visiting party they turned their steps in that direction. Answering the bell, appeared a rosy-cheeked girl, who showed the visitors into the waiting-room, where they had a full view of the broad halls, and the constant stream of young ladies that went in and out through the hospitable entrance.

It was Saturday afternoon, and Miss Murdock was at home and came in at once, looking fresh and pretty, and nodding brightly to several of the girls who passed the open door as she was shaking hands with Miss Pitcairn and being presented to Mr. Chick. After a little general chat the real business of the hour, the visit to the blind man, was broached. Miss Murdock was more than willing to accompany them, and even offered to bring some of the girls, a proposition which the masculine element of the party silently favored, but one that was ruled out on second thought as impracticable. In a few minutes they were ready, and erelong were rattling down Sixth Avenue in a crowded elevated train. After a time they took a "cross town" car, when they were where they could reach the right one, and Mr. Chick, much to his discomfort, was forced to stand, and that, too, with the book in his hands, for the doubly paid carrier had disappeared. Miss Murdock, in a matter-of-fact way, stood up and paid her own fare, and Mr. Chick, without knowing it, walked the length of the car and, paid it again.

Miss Pitcairn saw the young lady's action, and put it down as another instance of an innocent independence, which she greatly admired.

As a matter of course, there was a Saturday blockade, and a ride, that in less crowded streets would occupy fifteen minutes, consumed a half hour. Mr. Chick was, perhaps, the only one in the trio who was not impatient at this delay, and his content might be accounted for by the quiet flirtation in which he was indulging with a brunette, with a cast in one eye. This latter feature, however, was studiously turned away from the smiling young man, and he did not discover what would have been a sudden and awful shock to his critical taste; yet his absorption in this affair was not so great that he took no note of place and time, for when a certain corner was reached, he hooked down the bell-strap by means of the claw on the head of his cane, and with a farewell glance at the brunette, assisted his charges to alight.

They were now in a portion of the city not in the least familiar to Miss Pitcairn or her companion. Even Mr. Chick lost his reckoning, and appeared at fault, when suddenly Miss Murdock gave a joyful exclamation, and seizing a combination of bare arms, calico, and flaxen hair, introduced her with, "Here's Jack!"

The little sweeper had appeared at an opportune moment, for policemen were scarce, and in the tangled network of streets had they encountered the usual formula,—"Go straight ahead two blocks, thin turrn to the left, an' go won block more, thin ask the next person ye mate, for I don't know where it is, at ahl"— would only tend to confusion.

Jack gladly accepted the task of escorting them to her home, after a few shrewd questions regarding their errand. On the way, when there was room, she walked by the side of Miss Murdock, and Mr. Chick escorted Miss Pitcairn and the volume, one on each arm; when the way degenerated into the width of the primitive Indian trail, by reason of beer barrels and other impediments that choked the sidewalk, they walked single file, Jack leading, and Mr. Chick in the rear. Through many a narrow street they went, elbowed by pawn-brokers, junk-dealers, beggars, thieves, and shoals of children, till they were in the very heart of the foulest part of the city.

The people whom they met seemed as warped, distorted, and crooked as the streets they trod and the tenements that hemmed them in. Very rarely was a healthy face seen; here sin and disease appeared to have their strongholds.

Closely following their guide, who was familiar with every crook and turn of the devious way, they plunged into the depths of the reeking settlement, and finally reached a tumble-down lodging-house, the door of which stood wide open. Swarming up and down the stairs were dozens of children, ragged, unkempt, noisy, and like their elders, indulging in brawls, and expressing their anger or approbation by shrill yells, mingled with profanity. Never before had either of the ladies been in such a place, and had they followed their feelings instead of their guide, would have retreated; but, repressing this cowardly impulse, they struggled on, clinging to the banisters and stepping as carefully as possible.

The weary climb ended at a small attic, almost bare of furniture, the floor carpetless, the walls stained and shattered, showing the skeleton laths and yellow beams. The one window was open — not that it mattered, for, open or shut, it had but one whole pane, and could, at its best, afford but scanty protection against the weather.

In the warmest corner of the room sat a very

old man, his hair and beard snowy white, while his face, though scarred by age and penury, was calm and peaceful. With a gentleness that appeared strangely foreign to her nature, Jack stepped up to her grandfather and whispered a brief sentence. As she finished, he raised his hand and caressed her bristling hair with his long fingers, while he turned his beautiful brown eyes upon the visitors, as if he could, indeed, see and welcome them. His looks were all hospitality, and the smile that grew on his wrinkled features gave assurance that, as Jack's friends, they would be considered his.

Without knowing it, the visitors had presumed that their mission to that attic would mean a few kind words, a little money, and an adieu, after which all present duties would be finished; but somehow the question of charity did not seem the thing to consider at that time. The patriarch was so venerable and dignified that he appeared rather some kindly gentleman entertaining in his own halls, than the blind peddler who was often led about the streets by ragged little Jack.

Miss Pitcairn was the first to solve the riddle of embarrassment that had fallen upon them all, by taking the book from the hands of Mr. Chick and saying, —

"We understand from your granddaughter, sir, that you greatly miss the raised-letter Bible from which you learned to read."

"I do," was the instant and eager reply.

"I have taken the liberty of bringing you another, and beg that you will accept it."

The young lady spoke hastily, and her voice had in it a tone of entreaty that would have moved one with far less sensitive ears than the blind. As it was, the old man listened with delight not alone to the news that was in itself of great gladness to him, but as well to the sympathetic tones that were so unusual. Who can tell what vision grew in the patriarch's mind, as that voice set the finely attuned chords to vibrating? No doubt it was a beautiful picture, of a maiden, pure, fresh, and lovely, full of all gentleness, breathing kindness and love; and, in truth, was not the blind man's estimate as sure and true as that of more skilled observers?

"I thank you, my daughter," he said.

It was a simple speech, and might have seemed lacking in the grace of true thankfulness, but to Belle Pitcairn it was eloquent with feeling, for she understood the emotion too deep for words.

During his brief word of thanks, the intelligent fingers had been seeking the chapter head-

ings, and in a short time were at home. Then
ensued a strange service. In a low, clear voice,
the old man read the Sermon on the Mount,
and as he read the sad eyes roved from one to
another of his listeners, as if he spoke with
them personally, and the periods of that match-
less discourse fell on the ear, producing an impression never to be forgotten.

Even Mr. Chick was awed by the majesty of
the scene, and saw not its incongruities, while
Jack, perched upon the swaying footboard of the
attenuated bed, listened, and the lines about her
mouth had less of the hardness, and her keen
blue eyes were soft and tender.

The sermon finished, without comment, all shook
hands, and again piloted by the little girl, descended
the stairs, passed through the crowded streets, and
gained the better portion of the city, and soon
after, weary and thoughtful, reached home.

"Say, Cousin Belle, what address did the little
girl give you when you left?" asked Chick, as
they parted.

"Number 10 Midnight Street, east corner of
the 'Wedge.'"

"So I thought — it's the very place," was the
mysterious reply.

"Have you ever been in that house before?"
inquired the Governor's daughter, with interest.

"Conlon's saloon, where Miss Thomas and I spent a very disagreeable evening, occupies the lower part of the house," said the little man.

"Well, we certainly were not harmed by the proximity of that dreadful place. I 'm sorry it is so near, for I intend to see considerable of Jack and her grandfather. I wonder why it is he won't allow her to come back to the factory, and I wonder further what Mr. Betteredge has to do with the matter," replied Belle.

True to her determination, she called whenever she had leisure, and always found a cordial welcome, but with all her efforts she was not able to impress the blind man with the advisability of allowing his child to return to the mill, although she was earning but a scanty living selling papers on the street.

In spite of her desire to ease the poverty of their lot, and to place them where they could be more comfortable than in their present quarters, she found herself opposed by a strange pride that was difficult to understand.

The grandfather, although kindly, thankful, and humble, was, in matters pertaining to his or the child's family history, strangely silent, and sometimes it appeared as if this reticence was the result of some sort of terrorism exercised by a dominant evil will. Of this there was no tangible proof, and the visitor could not say but that it was a romantic fancy, and thus it happened that while the two attic dwellers received many comforts from Miss Belle, neither the plans for Jack's education, nor the idea of securing for the grandparent a place in an institution for the blind, were carried out.

During this waiting period in the fortunes of these two, another actor was added to the scene in the person of Mr. John Buckingham. It happened that he was out for a walk, and was crossing Union Square when he awoke from a fit of abstraction to find a little girl running by his side, holding up a paper, and crying, —

"Say, mister, buy my last paper?"

He was about to comply, when she was gone, and her place filled by a half-grown boy, who shook his fist at her and cursed, even as he proffered his own papers in a voice that sounded as if it emanated from a fog-horn.

"That is right, my boy, whenever you get a chance hit the girls! When you grow up maybe you will marry one of them, and then you can kick her down stairs, and throw lamps at her, and have lots of fun," remarked the Professor.

The boy looked into the smiling face a bit doubtfully, and said, —

"Paper, sir?"

Deep down into his pocket went the gentleman's hand, and among jingling coins he felt for some small change. The newsboy's eyes brightened, and he stood expectant with paper all ready, while the rival vender drew nearer and watched the transaction with longing eyes.

"I suppose if that girl does n't sell her papers she will have to go hungry — but we do n't care, do we?" continued he, still hunting for a nickel.

"No—o," said the boy, giving the child a quick, comprehensive glance.

"H'oh, he's guyin' yer, he's goin' to buy of me, anyhow," shouted she, executing a grotesque dance.

"You shut up!" called back the boy, looking about for a stone.

"Yes, shut up!" echoed the gentleman. "Girls have no business to be heard, nor to sell papers, nor to do any thing but starve. Get a stone and fling at her, or hit her with a club. If we only had a shot-gun we could shoot her, could n't we, my lad?"

The youngster hesitated a minute, kicked the ground awkwardly with his bare toes, and said, —

"Huh! you 're an old wind-bag!" and was off across the street, leaving the field to the first comer. In less time than it takes to write it, the girl, who was none other than Jack, sold her paper, and walking by the purchaser's side, was answering his questions.

"So your grandfather is blind, is he, and can read with his fingers? Now, how does it happen that he has any thing to read? Those books are expensive."

"Oh, some of our friends pervided for that," was the lofty reply. "They gave us a little surprise party. Miss Pitcairn was at the head of it. She, an' her feller, an' another girl, come an' give the book. Oh, but ain't her feller a daisy. He had a necktie that would make you dizzy, an' his teeth was gold-mounted."

"What Miss Pitcairn was this?"

"The Guv'ner's darter. One of the first famblies. They eat on gold and silver plates, with dimind spoons. They owns most all of Fifth Avenyer, an' they live there winters."

"So," thought the Professor, "our rich society belle has been visiting the poor, and giving away Bibles. But who was the strange necktie fellow? Necktie — um — necktie — all the fellows wear rainbow ties." Then turning to Jack, "Little girl, did this young man have red hair?"

"Yes, 'n' red side-lights, an' his name is Hen."

"Hen? — I see — you mean Chick."

"So 't was, Chick. I remember now. I s'pose he'll be a hen, though, when he gets a little bigger — Chick ; so 't was."

"And who was the third person, the other lady ?"

"She works in the 'Box Shop.'"

Here, then, was news, and the Professor, as he walked on and on, pondered it. He had a strong desire to see this old man in whom the beautiful Miss Pitcairn, the radiant Mr. Chick, and the unknown young lady had taken so un-accountable an interest. By way of experiment, he said, —

"I presume there is no one ill in your family ?"

He ought to have said sick, and was forced to put his question in more intelligible form.

"Gran'dad 's sick," the child returned, gravely. "He 's bilious, anyhow, but this is the biliousest turn he ever had. Ain't ben down stairs for two weeks. Say, mister, if you 'll come up an' see him, I 'll pay you if you cure him."

"No cure, no pay," laughed he, highly amused. "All right, lead the way, but I 'm not a phy-sician."

They were almost there, and a few steps farther on were threading the same paths that the former exploring party had passed over. There was a more villanous-looking crowd out now,

for it was night, and several times the athletic
Professor unceremoniously shouldered some surly
fellow out of his way, and by his determined
air, as well as by the breadth of his shoulders,
won a respect that averted trouble.

With Jack in the lead, he groped his way up
the long flights of stairs, and at last stood in
the presence of the blind. As usual, the good
face and benign manner had their effect, and
the visitor no longer wondered at Miss Pitcairn's
interest. Even to Mr. Buckingham's unprofes-
sional eyes, the old man appeared weak and near
to death, though not from disease. It was simply the going out of the lamp of life, because
the vital forces had been expended. All that
could be done was to prescribe nourishing food,
and good care, and make him as comfortable as
possible. With characteristic promptitude, the
visitor wrote a note to a friend, a missionary
who knew every in and out of that part of the
city, instructing him what to get, and directing
him to send the bills to him. Then, with a
good-by, he was gone, leaving a bright, crisp
bill in Jack's hand.

Two days after this visit, the blind man
breathed his last. His death was as peaceful
and painless as his life had been blameless, and,
although conscious to the last, he seemed not to

worry about Jack, but to be assured that she would be cared for. At the last moment he called one of the neighbors, and asked him to post a letter, which he did, returning in time to assure the sender that the errand was done.

When this great affliction came, Jack was almost desperate, and spent her time wandering about in a sort of stupor, living she could not tell how. At this particular time Miss Pitcairn was very busy, and a week fled swift-winged before she had time to go to the "Wedge." The Professor also, unconscious that his friend was out of town, and had not received his note, staid away, fully occupied with college affairs.

Thus Jack, apparently deserted by all, daily grew more pinched-looking, and cried herself to sleep every night.

The meager funeral rites were attended to by the city, and the child, more desolate than ever before in her lonely life, started out to sell a few papers to get money enough for supper.

The letter that the old blind man caused to be mailed before his death was addressed to Miss Pitcairn, the superscription written in a neighbor's sprawling hand, while the note within was by the grandfather, in raised letters produced by pin pricks through the paper. The address being far from correct, it was some days

before Belle received it, and its contents startled her. It read:

UNDER THE WASTE LEAF IN MY
   BIBLE IS A PAPER THAT WILL
   TELL WHO JACK IS -- AND THE WILL
   --- TAKE THE CHILD AWAY, OR SHE
   WILL BE

It was not finished, nor was it signed, and
Belle, alarmed at its vagueness, hurried at once
to the "Wedge," but could find neither Jack
nor her grandfather. After a deal of questioning, she learned of the latter's death, but as to
what had become of the little girl, not a soul
could tell. It is true, Mrs. Tarpy asserted, that
"a huncle of the girl 'ad lugged 'er hoff," but
as there was no one to corroborate this story,
and as the woman herself seemed not to believe
it, her listener was skeptical.

"Do you know what became of the large book
the blind man read?" inquired the young lady.

No one knew till Mrs. Tarpy remembered to
have seen the "hold man a-lightin' of 'is fire
with paper that looked as hif it might be from
that buke, an' he looked terrible 'shamed w'en
he see me a-watchin' of 'im."

As there was neither stove nor fireplace in

the room, and as the blind man was not in the habit of *seeing* people, this tale did not impress the audience deeply, while Miss Pitcairn began to think that Mrs. Tarpy might know where both the child and the book were.

In the midst of this cross-questioning, which took place in the bare attic that had once been Jack's home, and that now was awaiting another tenant, there came a brisk step on the stairs, and Professor Buckingham stood in the open door. His face lighted with pleasure when he saw the visitor, but for some reason, she colored deeply, and to hide her confusion, spoke hastily.

"Do you know where Jack is, Professor?"

"Is n't she here?"

"No, she has been gone two days. Do you know that poor old man died all alone, and Jack has gone out into the world without a friend?" Her voice broke, and the beautiful eyes were full of tears.

"But Mr. Thomas, the missionary, has been here, and has helped them through. He doubtless knows where the little girl is."

"Ah, yer honor, he was here this morning, an' said as how he'd got the letther, but he'd been away on a bit av a vacashin, an' had only jist got back," said a toothless old dame.

The gentleman looked grave. "Foor little Jack!"

he said, and then was silent for a moment, in deep thought. "I'm sorry — very sorry. I should have gone in person to Thomas' place, and then there could have been no mistake. Jack, however, can not be far off. She will, without doubt, come back here, and if she does, one of these good women will come and tell us, and earn a five-dollar bill."

At this juncture a new-comer arrived, none other than Mr. Chick, who had been down to the corner to see the intelligent policeman, and inquire if he knew any thing of the missing child. As usual, he had helped deepen the mystery to the best of his ability.

"Is it Tom Daly's Jack ye mane, the won wid the cast in his —— oho! it's a *girl*, is it? An' she named Jack! Maybe it's ould man Connor's Jack, he's about that age, but thin he's a b'y too. I have it, there's little Jack Dempsey sells papers."

"Is he a girl?"

"Bad cess to it, no. He's a bye, too, — sure that's the trouble, not one of the b'ys around here is a girl. Now if her ould man had named her Mary, or some dacent girl's name, sure I could aisy find her, but wid a b'y's name, how is a body to know but phat she's somebody else?"

With this report, Mr. Chick returned to the attic, and there met the Professor, with whom he shook hands, and then stepping in front of him, gave his whole attention to Miss Pitcairn.

When a man, five feet one inch in height, steps in front of a six-footer, the eclipse is not as total as it might be, and of this fact Mr. Chick was aware. Had he been able to add a cubit to his stature, then and there, how gladly would he have done it, for that exasperating Professor talked calmly over his head, as if no obstruction were there. The thought that his friend might make up his mind to accompany Miss Pitcairn home, and leave him to walk behind, occurred to the little man, and he turned pale with apprehension, and when the toothless old woman absorbed the young lady's attention for a moment, he said, —

"Say, Professor, I escorted my cousin here by particular request."

"All right, I comprehend," was the good-humored reply, "but do n't allow any harm to come to her, or I shall never forgive you."

"What does he mean by that, now?" thought Mr. Chick. "Does he speak as a friend, or a possible suitor? I 'd like to know, for that 's a pretty bold speech for a man to make to an escort. These professional men have a way of expressing all sorts of sentiments that may be professional, or may be something else, and there's no way of pinning them down, and finding out what they mean. It gives them a great advantage over the rest of the fellows, and first thing one knows, they have stepped in and cut out better men, by means of this privilege."

VI.

Armitage Hall.

IN the fashionable part of the gayest city in
our country are some pleasures that are far
from being follies, and of these the reading clubs
are perhaps the most conspicuous. One of these
clubs, known as the Shakespeare Circle, flourished
in the vicinity of the Pitcairn residence, whose
members, while attending select parties, enter-
tainments, and receptions, were not so absorbed
by these allurements as to be blind to more
intellectual gratifications. The purpose of culti-
vating genuine literary and æsthetic taste had
originated this society. It was exceedingly select,
being one of the few in Gotham where wealth
alone did not provide instant admission. The
members, without exception, were of good birth
and breeding, most of them wealthy, while some
were distinguished for literary or artistic work
that had attracted wide attention. Every Wednesday evening the Circle met and discussed
current literature for a while, and then, taking

up the work of the greatest poet, spent the rest of the evening upon it. At times this course of procedure was varied, and some other writer or essayist claimed attention, and by skilful rendition; subtle analysis, or sparkling wit, was the text of many a classic made to glow with new and beautiful meaning.

It was at the home of Mrs. John Armitage that the Circle met on the particular evening we have in mind. One of the most beautiful and cultured women of New York was this young Mrs. Armitage, who, possessed of rare taste, made her home a temple of art. Unlike any other in the city, in the arrangement of rooms and in decoration, it was simple, elegant, a poem throughout, and pervaded by a rare atmosphere of homelikeness that imparted a sense of security and rest. This perfection, however, was noticeable only on the inside, the exterior of the house appearing like its neighbors, a plain, substantial brown-stone, so similar to the ordinary city dwelling that a stranger would detect nothing unusual about it.

The hostess was lovely in person and in mind, admired by all who knew her, and much loved by intimate friends. On the evening in question, she had as a guest one who was most welcome to the Circle, a cousin of her husband,

a young man upon whom mammas with marriage-
able daughters were known to smile with exceptional sweetness, for he was unmarried, wealthy,
finely educated, and one of the most brilliant
financiers that Wall Street had known.

Although still young, he was the President of
a large railroad corporation, had formed powerful
syndicates that had been successful, and was
many times the millionaire. The knowledge that
he expended something like a thousand dollars a
week on his yacht, that he travelled about the
country in a special car, magnificently fitted,
that he drove the finest horses to be seen on
the Avenue, while not quite passing him into
this select Circle, certainly detracted nothing from
his charm of manner, his broad fund of general
knowledge, and his position as a relative of Mrs.
Armitage.

Strange as it may appear, Stanley Armitage
was not to all appearance spoiled by the flattery
of fortune, or of the world. He was ever well-
bred, and said the right thing at the proper time,
but whether this was sincerity, or native tact, was
not rigidly looked into.

During the "preliminaries," the gathering guests
discussed, as a rule, society events, and found
the time brief enough for the constant happen-
ings.

"Dear Mrs. Armitage, will not Miss Pitcairn be here to-night?" inquired a tall, slender lady in black, who had dropped fashionable life long enough to produce a brochure that had won her instant and lasting recognition.

"I sincerely hope so, Miss Sunderlin, for we miss her sadly when she absents herself. She is such a charming young lady," replied the hostess.

"She won't be here," announced a petite brunette, with sparkling black eyes that had played havoc with many a manly heart. "Did you not know that she had found more congenial companions?"

"Prepare for some absurdity!" said Mrs. Armitage, smiling at the young girl's roguish look.

"An absurdity, I grant, but not of my manufacture. Belle Pitcairn has gone into business!"

"Into business?"

"Yes, beloved friends! that is, she has bought a mill up in Harlem, and goes up there every day, and she told me that she should be too busy to come over here this evening. She is doing it as a charity, you know, because the help were just about starving."

"I'm sure it's very sweet of her," murmured Mrs. Armitage, but without enthusiasm, looking over at her husband's cousin, who was sitting an unobtrusive listener to this conversation. If his looked expressed any thing, it was incredulity, slightly tinctured with disapproval.

"Of course she does not go there in person, but delegates that to some one else?" interrogated Miss Sunderlin.

"She goes herself, and has a desk, and shakes hands with them, and — and — asks after their families," said the informant, concluding in the midst of a general laugh, at the sparseness of her information.

"A grave misdemeanor, surely. I can not imagine how she can so far forget herself as to inquire after the family of a person, who must necessarily be a person of no family at all," said Mr. Armitage with a smile.

"Behold what fine sarcasm he brings to his aid, to champion the cause of the absent one," returned the brunette.

"No sarcasm, I assure you, but I think society can trust the daughter of Governor Pitcairn among the Harlemites," was the reply.

The brunette bit her lips with vexation, and subsided, while Mrs. Armitage, seeing that her relative did not intend to have Miss Pitcairn discussed, by even her intimates, in a way that implied discredit, called the meeting to order, by tapping with a pencil on a tiny Japanese god, and announced the topic for discussion.

As was prophesied, Belle did not appear at the Circle that evening, and after the last guest had departed, Stanley Armitage sat down near his cousin's wife, and asked in a tone of annoyance, —

"Do you imagine, Bess, that there is any truth in this tale?"

"I'm sure, I do not know. Belle is different from the ordinary girl. That she takes an unaccountable interest in persons who are far beneath her, I have noticed with surprise; but it is in all probability only girlish romance. Why not call and see her, and ascertain for yourself what she has been about? If she has gone into business, to the exclusion of her society duties, I am sure it will not be difficult to bring her back. Indeed, I am almost certain that the people with whom she comes in contact will teach her to value those of her own station more than ever."

It would seem from the foregoing that Mr. Armitage had more than a passing interest in the fair daughter of the Governor, and had not scrupled to make it known to his cousin. She, in turn, was delighted that he should appreciate a person so gifted and lovely as Miss Pitcairn, and the Shakespeare Circle had been to her mind the very place to bring them together. A small cloud had risen, however, in this new fancy of the beautiful girl, that led her to absent herself from the meetings and to step down among plebeians. She was not by any means discouraged by the prospect, for did she not know that her cousin could marry practically whom he pleased? With a false estimate of the power of money, she was sure that none could be found who would refuse the most desirable *parti* in New York. Had the clever woman but known it, there was not the least chance that Belle would care for this man because of his wealth, or his position; but when it came to his rare tact, pleasant companionship, and fine appearance, there was opportunity for her actually to fall in love.

Quite sure that Belle would yet be her cousin's wife, Mrs. Armitage was not willing that her name should be coupled with any acts of philanthropic enthusiasm that would furnish a topic for busy tongues, and in this she felt quite sure she had the full sympathy of her relative. The manner in which he looked upon the working people, especially of the lower classes, is difficult of description. Perhaps it was as much a systematic overlooking of their existence as any thing; a feeling that they were of a different world, of little consequence, and of less

interest. When circumstances throw a person of
Armitage's stamp in with a man of lower sta·
tion than himself, and he is obliged to speak
with him, it is in a manner that chills the heart
of the poor fellow, for it is cold, calm, grave,
with no kindly courtesy, with no spark of human
sympathy. Such a man is never loved except
among his most intimate friends, where he is
usually as courteous and affable as possible, and
in unbending with rare smile and clever speech,
is often valued the more, because of the frugality with which he dispenses these favors.

Mr. Armitage was of this type except in busi·
ness, where he was keen, cool, incisive, and
many times daring, even to the verge of folly.

On the afternoon following the meeting of the
Shakespeare Circle, Mrs. Armitage, driving up
town, had stopped at the Governor's and carried
Belle off to dine at her home. The young lady
knew intuitively that this meant that Stanley
Armitage had returned from his tour of railroad
inspection, and wished to enjoy one of the quiet
dinners for which his cousin was famous, and in
the old cordial way that had made Belle a frequent guest. What cosy meals those of the past
had been, with only Mr. and Mrs. Armitage and
the millionaire cousin, with the Governor and
his wife, and Belle! How easily things moved

in this Palace Beautiful, and what a treasure of a French cook took charge of the *cuisine!*

To-day the party would be diminished by the absence of Mrs. Pitcairn, but the host promised to bring the Governor up in his carriage so that no feeling of loneliness could oppress Belle.

When the fair young guest arrived, Stanley was in the elegant smoking-room, enjoying a choice Havana. He quickly threw it away, and in response to his cousin's summons, appeared at the drawing-room a few moments later, with his own apt word of welcome and smile of pleasure.

"Delighted to see you again, Miss Pitcairn," said he, holding the white hand a moment. "I wished to call upon you yesterday, but Cousin Bessie assured me that you were away."

"I was away, and should have regretted miss-ing your call — you will venture again?" replied the young lady.

"Most assuredly, I shall look forward to it with impatience. By the bye," dropping his tone to a confidential pitch, "have you decided what blossom you would name as my 'Flower of Fate'? Let us step into the conservatory and ——."

"Alas, for a failing memory," replied Belle, mischievously. "You did not ask me to select the flower. It was some other maiden whom you have forgotten."

He drew a step nearer, and looking into the clear eyes, said:

"Granted the failing memory, but not the impeachment, that other than you was to give the flower. It was also your promise. Shall we go?"

It had been almost a promise — one obtained on such an afternoon as this, when the room had been full of friends, and it had so happened that Stanley had been quite close to her. To the ordinary observer he had on that occasion mingled courteously in the general conversation, but between whiles he had also been telling with effect a weird tale of the Fate Flower. There had been a potent charm in the fact that all the guests were within ear-shot, and he was conning a bewitching love-tale, and to her alone. Aside from her interest in the story, the audacity and consummate tact with which the remarkable man played his double part, won her admiration. His manner of seeming attention to Mrs. Van Brunt's prosy commonplaces was without flaw as a piece of acting; yet through it all, under the drooping moustache came the tale of the Fate Flower, and none knew it but these two. What a strange episode had been the dinner! Quiet, ordinary, yet the air was full of suggestion, and even at the table, with the Governor by her side, and Stanley Armitage at the other end of the board, it had seemed to Belle's fancy that the low musical voice was still telling the tale that breathed an oriental fragrance of romance and love. With so vivid a word painter, as the young railroad king, was it a wonder that Belle had many times thought over the tale that had on that afternoon so thrilled her with emotions before unknown? Was it surprising that, when the sudden summons came for him to start on the inspection-tour that he had so long been striving to consummate with other railroad mag-nates, she felt a sense of disappointment. To be sure, his departure was known to her as soon as to any, by the note that an exquisite bouquet of flowers held,—a note that even then was treasured.

The tale had been told, and only they two knew it. Now for the sequel, which was to come, when the beautiful maiden, who in this case was Miss Pitcairn, should choose the flower whose petals would make known the fate of him to whom she gave it. With the pleasure of a genuine æsthete, Stanley Armitage had watched the growth of her interest in the story. Accustomed to read faces, the almost imperceptible changes that came into the splendid eyes, the slightly quickened breath, the delicate deepening of color, all gave him supreme satisfaction. During the few leisure moments that his business trip afforded him he had reviewed the whole scene with delight, and determined as soon as he returned again to lead her thoughts to the quaint old tale, and get her to fulfill the half-promise made on that afternoon. Here, however, he was a little at fault. Had he made it plain what the choosing of this flower meant? He was not sure. The thought that Belle was dealing coquettishly with him did not enter his mind, but it did occur to him, although as an afterthought, that it might be possible for a young lady to be charmed with an ideality, and not at all favorable to its materialization. He was, however, fairly confident of victory, while Belle —ah, who shall say what a young and beautiful woman does feel in such a case?

"Shall we go?" said Stanley Armitage, looking into the depths of Belle's eyes, as if to read their secret, even before the flower should reveal it.

"Here is your cousin, perhaps she will accompany us," was the indefinite answer, as Mrs. Armitage returned to the room at that instant.

The gentleman did not apparently favor this

plan, for he adroitly addressed the lady and kept a general conversation going on, until the Fate Flower, for the time being, had dropped out of sight; he relaxed his efforts, and began to look bored.

"My dear, we missed you last evening," said Mrs. Armitage.

The young lady instinctively glanced at Stanley, and seeing that he was interested for a moment, was embarrassed, but recovering herself quickly, said, —

"Papa and I were talking business."

"Then rumor for the once tells the truth: you are a mill owner?"

"I was not aware that rumor had aught to do with my actions. Why should it be considered so strange if one uses time and money for the benefit of others, instead of spending it upon one's self?" said Belle, the more boldly, as she thought she saw a tightening up of the firm lines about the young millionaire's mouth, which meant decided censure.

"I'm sure, dear, it is very kind of you to take an interest in the working people, for of course that is your object; but it seems a waste of effort, for they never appreciate what is done for them," said Mrs. Armitage, rather sadly; but whether from sorrow for the obtuseness of the common folk, or the misdirected effort of our heroine, it would be difficult to decide.

Stanley Armitage, too courteous to say a word against an action that he entirely disapproved, at this juncture arose, and seeing the Governor and his cousin coming, went into the hall to meet them, and to open a discussion which lasted quite through the dinner, and which effectually prevented any return either to sentiment or to Harlem. It is possible that this subject went further and became of more general interest than the shrewd man of affairs had anticipated, for toward the last of it he began to assume a look of polite weariness,—an appeal not often resisted.

After dinner it appeared as if every thing was against the wooer. With his former self-confident manner he had attempted to establish himself close by the side of Miss Pitcairn, that he might in his musical monotone get her to promise that, then and there, he should have the Fate Flower. He had been for the moment provoked that she had condescended to be interested in shop-people and laborers; but when he looked at her fair face, he forgot that, and only longed to know that he was to be the happy mortal who was to carry off this prize among women. His calculations were, however, upset by the obtuseness of the Governor, who was determined to settle the question that the young man had raised, and who, his fine face aglow, was recounting varied personal experiences that would have convinced any one but an absent-minded, half-angry lover.

Once, before the Governor's carriage came, Armitage had a chance to whisper, —

"Can I call to-morrow and get my Fate Flower?" But there was no answer, and whether he was heard, he could not decide.

As he handed the lady into her carriage, he bowed to a gentleman passing, whom the Governor hailed with the invitation, —

"Ah, Professor, get in and ride up with us. I have wanted to see you for some time."

The invitation was accepted, and Mr. Buckingham, despite the look of cold hostility that the young millionaire gave him, was seated by the side of the Governor's daughter.

VII.

An Amateur Detective.

"I FEEL so guilty for neglecting that poor child, Jack, in her trouble," said Belle, her eyes full of tears, as she sat at her desk in the mill, the morning's mail untouched.

"But you did not suspect that she was in trouble, and, therefore, are not guilty; besides, she can be found," replied Mr. Chick, positively; for he was present, having taken quite a fancy to the daintily furnished office.

"Do you think so?"

"Why not? She is not likely to stray far away from the places she has always known, and a careful search of them would, without doubt, discover her more than anxious to be found," was the wise reply.

"But somebody may have stolen her."

"She is n't the kind of cherub that child-stealers fancy. I doubt if you could hire the most depraved among them to purloin such a lean little rat."

"Augustus Chick, you surprise me," said his cousin severely. "The blind man's granddaughter is a very interesting child, and one whom we are bound to help, knowing as we do that there is some good fortune in store for her, if she can only be found, and the Bible recovered."

"Don't be provoked, Cousin Belle, I will find both," said the youth meekly.

The beautiful girl looked at him in unfeigned astonishment as he continued, —

"I know something about that part of the city, and think I can tell pretty nearly where Jack will re-appear. I should be willing to bet that I could secure her within twenty-four hours."

Belle's eyes sparkled, and she gave her little cousin a look that thrilled him down to his patent-leather boots, as she replied, —

"O, if you only could find her, I should be so happy! The thought that she is wandering about the streets, with not a soul in this great city that cares whether she lives or dies, makes me wretched."

"Very well, let us consider it settled, then," said Mr. Chick in a tone of deep self-satisfaction. "I will at once return to my rooms, put on the seediest suit that I can find, even if I hire one, and spend my time in the vicinity of the 'Wedge' until I find Jack."

"You will not be in danger?" hesitated Belle.

"O, some, but if I have no money to speak of, and no jewelry, and am shabbily dressed, there will be no object in hurting me," replied he.

"Had you not better engage a detective?"

"A detective!" was the exclamation, in which was expressed infinite scorn. "No, indeed! We want Jack and the Bible; we are not seeking simply for clues."

True to his purpose, Mr. Chick at once went home and made arrangements for this new and, to him, startling adventure. With a strange readiness, considering how much his heart was bound up in such things, he was about to renounce the splendidly furnished rooms, the faultless *cuisine*, and, what was still nearer and dearer, the dainty attire, and appear as a shabby — artist, perhaps — to dine in cheap restaurants, and room at some musty lodging-house until Jack should be found. It might take a day, or a week, he pondered, but he would do it just the same.

Feeling the full force of his self-denial, and rather enjoying it, he donned the old clothes, went down to the "Wedge," and began the search for lodgings. On many a door-post was pasted a greasy slip of paper, announcing that within was to be found "bord," "boord," or "board," with prices that sometimes were stated, and at others left to be guessed.

A single, furnished room, on the second floor, with a bed of ordinary comfort, and a door with a double lock, was what he wanted. He decided to take his meals at restaurants in the neighborhood, and if he could not stand the food furnished, could ride down town ; but the first thing was the room, and in search of this, the young detective walked up and down the streets for some time before he could make up his mind which of the houses to attack. At length he decided to try the "Cosmopolitan Hotel."

On a large sign which had previously informed the public that Jacob Dimmel furnished "ales, wein, and lager," and which showed a frisky goat attempting to butt a man off a barrel, was now the legend, "Good clean lodgings 15, 20, and 25 cents per night. Separate beds for all. Time beds 10 cents each."

Opening the door, he found himself in a long room, where were a dozen or more men, some of them playing cards, others sitting tailor fashion and sewing, and still others gathered around a charcoal brazier, cooking a not unsavory smelling stew. The treasurer of this last close corporation held an enormous iron spoon, which he used to stir the pottage and rap the knuckles of the impatient ones who attempted to spear bits of meat with their jack-knives.

"Can I be accommodated with a room?" asked Mr. Chick.

"Ye can," said the proprietor, who was utilizing the counter as a bath-slab for a growling bull-pup. "Hoo much siller hae ye?"

" —," replied Mr. Chick, hesitatingly.

"Pass it oot, an' hie yersel' aroond here at 'leven the neet, hand in yer ticket, an' take yer place on the 'Jouncer.'"

Very meekly the youth produced a ten-dollar bill and passed it over the counter, while the Scotchman's eyes opened wider and wider.

"Why—why—what d'ye mean by that, mon?" he gasped. "You don't want no 'Jouncer.' You kin affoord the best bed in the hoose."

"I 'm a stranger in these parts," began the new comer, but was interrupted by the other, who said jovially, —

"Aye, I kenned it, yeer English, like the pup here, but don't be afeerd. Jack McFadden alloos nae one to trifle wi' his guests. Noo, wull ye take a fifteen, a twenty, or twenty-fie cent bed, or wull ye save yeer siller an' go in on the 'Jouncer'?"

"Can I look around and see which I prefer?"

"O, aye, to be sure. Here, O'Toole, show the lad the bed-rooms. He's but joost come ower, an' he hasna' got civilized yet."

At the summons, a short, stout Irishman left his chance at pot-luck, and advanced to the counter, a jolly smile illumining his broad face.

"Arrah! thin, an' it's ahl right to talk about bein' civilized, but don't I wish I was uncivilized again. Phat's yer name, me bye?"

"Chick," replied the victim, because he could think of no other.

"Troth, it fits ye, me little game-cock, wid yer rid hid an' foine clothes. Come along, me bantam, an' see the 'Cowsmopolitan Hotel,'—rooms at any price; patronized by His Royal Highness, the Prince Imparial, who always takes his resht on the 'Jouncer,' bad cess to him!"

Following his voluble guide, Mr. Chick was soon shown some of the rooms in the hotel. Some were nothing more than tiny closets, made of pine boards, in each of which was a broad shelf in lieu of bed, and two nails driven in the wall for a wardrobe; these were the twenty-five cent rooms. The fifteen and twenty cent apartments were bunks placed one above the other, against the walls, and were high or low-priced, according to location.

"Where is the 'Jouncer'?" asked the some-what bewildered dandy.

"That is n't put up until late in the avening, as we nade ahl the flure space to undress in. Afther the millionaires are in their boonks, thin the 'Jouncer' is put up, and the tin-cent rabble have a chance to slápe until six in the marning, thin they are 'jounced,' an' med to get out of the way for dacint paple."

In response to further inquiries, O'Toole explained minutely the working of the great ten-cent receptacle. It seems that McFadden, the thrifty proprietor of the Cosmopolitan, had formerly been in the habit of letting the "ten-cent rabble" come in at the price named, and sleep on the floor, provided they got out of the way of the regular "bunkers" and "roomers" in the morning. One and all had promised this, time and again, but the spirit in the evening often promises what the flesh is too weak to perform in the morning, and thus it happened that the sleepy occupants of the floor could not be wakened, and the lodgers in the bunks, indignant at being obliged to wade through the morass of humanity, threatened to leave. At this critical point, McFadden showed his genius by inventing the "Jouncer." It was simply two stout cables stretched horizontally across the room, and drawn tight over a wooden drum. Over these cables were laid the mattresses, which were strapped to slats, and upon the mattresses slept the impecunious "ten-centers." At six in the morning, the ropes were slacked a trifle, and the line of sleepers thoroughly jarred into life. At five minutes after six the drum was suddenly released, and the elongated bed dropped to the floor, with what might be justly described, a "sickening thud."

The invention had been a complete success from the first, and the lodgers, proud of the arrangement, earnestly urged McFadden to secure letters-patent on it, asserting that if he did not, the leading hotels of the country would steal it, "first thing he knowed." The old Scotchman seriously contemplated the securing at least of a caveat, until he learned the price to be paid for such protection, after which his enthusiasm waned, and he was willing to take his chances.

Mr. Chick secured a closet, with a window facing the street, directly opposite the blind man's house, and then sallied out for supper. The prices which ruled in lodgings were paralleled in the few smoky-looking restaurants, and unable to settle on any of them as places where he could find any thing eatable, he was about to take a weary ride down town when he noticed a newsboy coming out of an alley with a piece of pie that looked very respectable. Now Mr. Chick had the true American fondness for pie, and felt at once that could he duplicate the section that he saw being rapidly demolished, it would make a satisfying meal.

"Er — say, my friend, where did you purchase your lunch?" he politely asked, wondering at the ludicrous expression of amazement that came over the boy's face as he spoke.

"Wuff?" inquired the youngster, speaking through a couple of inches of half-masticated pastry, and producing a muffled tone that gave one the feeling that his vocal organs were lined with flannel.

"Where did you get it?"

"Wuff?"

"The pie, I want some."

With a violent effort the youngster gulped the mass, and turned his attention to his questioner. In this he was whole-souled and conscientious, and so deep-seated was his principle of thoroughness that he even walked twice around the waiting youth, before replying. Finally he said, —

"Broke?"

He meant to inquire, with delicate tact, if the other was out of money, but Chick, with quick, though false apprehension of this slang, imagined him to refer to the state of his stomach, so he said "Yes."

Without more ado the little ragamuffin caught him by the coat-sleeve and dragged him up the alley. A few steps, and a door was reached, opened, and the young man found himself in a dining-room, the like of which he had never before seen. About thirty feet long and seven feet wide, it yet contained tables, chairs, kitchen, store-room, waiters, and fully thirty guests. To accommodate all of these essentials the most rigid economy in space was necessary, and was thus .secured : the tables were narrow shelves nailed up against the walls, a narrower shelf above holding the pepper, salt, and mustard. The chairs were three-legged stools, the kitchen was parted off from one end by a counter piled high with pies, and the guests were all boys. From cards on the wall Chick learned that baked beans and brown bread were three cents, that pie was three cents a cut, that coffee was two cents a cup, and that cider was five cents a glass, but before he had time to put in an order for any of these dainties, his guide called out to the man behind the counter, —

"Say, this yere *bloke* is dead broke, an' he wants some pie, dy'ye hear me squeal?"

"Wot kind?" asked the proprietor, raising his knife.

"Take mince, then yer know what yer gettin' —a little of ev'rythin'," suggested the lad.

But Chick felt most at home on lemon, and this he took regardless of the other's insinuation that he was so "toney" that next thing he would be "callin' fur quail on trust."

When he had finished his pie, which was good, excepting the crust, and that, in accordance with the free-and-easy etiquette of the place, he was told to throw under the table, he essayed another piece, but to his amazement was indignantly refused by the proprietor, —

"Sure, an' it's a shame that an able-bodied feller like yerself should be thryin' to live off a little bye loike him. Why do n't ye pay for yer own pie? Is n't it as aisy fur you to errn a price av a cut as fur him?"

"Really," said the novice, greatly surprised, "I am perfectly willing to pay."

"Ah, yes, widout doubt, an' and there's more like yer, mighty willin', but they niver does pay."

Here the offender drew out a handful of small change, and was about to prove that he was speaking the truth, when at once the little Arabs about him, who had been interested spectators, burst into a roar of rage, above which could be heard the stentorian voice of the pie-man, —

"Is that the kind av man ye are? Gettin' a babe in arrums to fade ye, whin yeer pockets are full! I wouldn't blame the byes if they leathered ye!"

It was the too evident intention of the law-less horde to wreak substantial vengeance on one who they thought had violated the com-mon code of honor. Some of them grasped the three-legged stools, and others caught up the thick white coffee-cups and prepared for action. These latter were, however, sternly rebuked by the proprietor, who, taking up a pint dipper of hot coffee, remarked: "The bye what trows dishes will resave the full av this!"

Poor Mr. Chick stood helpless. He did not dream that he had entered the place as the guest of the little pie-eater, or that the latter had supposed him to be penniless and hungry, and out of sheer good-heartedness had volun-teered to supply his wants, perhaps at the ex-pense of his own breakfast on the morrow. So he stood, trying in an uncertain way to explain, his voice drowned by the yells of the boys, who were edging toward him, with fight in their eyes. Truth to tell, he was greatly startled, but did not outwardly betray signs of panic, and his cool bearing, by delaying the attack, was the means of saving him from severe punishment.

"Hello, hello, byes, phat is this?" called out a rich voice, as O'Toole entered the room. "Sure, it looks loike a Donnybrook fair. Phat is it, just a bit av a row among yerselves for the love of it?"

"We're goin' ter punch the stuffin' outer that red-head cove," exclaimed one of the boys, raising his stool.

"Indade, thin, ye'er not, for he's a friend av me own, just landed to-day from the ould coun thry!"

"What did he try to beat Nick out of a piece of pie for, then?" was the universa. query.

"O, he was only funning. Sure, in the ship he come over in, he was full av his pranks, an' he had thim ahl crazy—phat wid puttin' soft soap in the soup, and shoe-blackin' in the captain's bid, an' grasin' the masht so that the sailors could n't climb up at ahl. He's one av the funniest min that iver ye saw, an' he fooled the whole av yez complately."

The crowd were uncertain, and, once in doubt, a mob is no longer a power. The stools were lowered, the belligerent attitudes dropped, and all that was thought of, was, that as long as they were fooled, it was somebody's duty to treat, and O'Toole, seeing the opportunity, shouted, —

"The little bantam from the ould counthry stands thrate to pie!"

Then followed a scene that makes the veriest beggar of description, for in a solid phalanx they rushed upon the astounded pie-man, one and all, and helped themselves. The kind of pastry that they took did not matter, and where the chance offered, two and three pieces were snatched. In the midst of the melee, O'Toole took the cause of the disturbance by the arm, and quietly led him out of the open door, and a minute later they were within the protection of the Cosmopolitan.

"Who pays for the pie, though?" inquired Mr. Chick, in dismay.

"No one," was the calm reply.

That same evening, as the young man ventured to walk by the tenement-house where Jack had formerly lived, he saw the little newsboy drawing pictures on the outside of a brilliantly lighted saloon window. As Mr. Chick passed, he looked up, recognized him, smiled broadly, and said, —

"Huffo."

His mouth was full of pie, and the crayon

with which he was pursuing his art studies was a piece of pie crust.

Let us now for a moment see what had befallen desolate little Jack, whom we left on the street with a few papers as the only means of supplying herself with supper. After a long and persistent struggle she succeeded in obtaining five cents, with which she purchased a plate of beans, and with more courage than for some days resolved to return to the tenement-house, collect the few treasures that were hers by inheritance, and start out in the world to seek her fortune.

To what part of the city or country she should direct her steps, she had not the faintest idea; but the feeling possessed her that few places could be worse, and that some might be better than this in the "Wedge." Yet the conclusion was not an easy one for the child to reach. Vile though the quarter was, she called it home, for there she had spent the few and evil years of her life, and about it clustered all the love that her poor heart had known — the priceless affection of her grandfather. Had he lived, she would never have dreamed of going elsewhere, but now why should she tarry?

Slowly she mounted the stairs for the last time, and entered the little attic with bowed

head and eyes filled with tears. Every step
brought pain to her heart; the sight of the meager furniture and the blotched and scarred walls
almost broke her down.

"So you've coom back, 'ave yer?" said a
harsh voice, and for the first time Jack was
aware that Mrs. Tarpy was in the room, and
not only that, but her apron was full of the
few treasures that her grandfather possessed.

"What are you doing with those things?"
demanded the child, her voice choked with
wrath.

"What ham I doing is hit? I'm jest taking
account of stock, to see hif there is the price
of a drink 'ere; I doubt hit, but hintend to
find out to wonst."

"Indeed you won't do any thing of the kind.
They are mine, and you shall not sell them!"
screamed Jack, flying at the harpy, tooth and
nail, to rescue the sacred relics. She had, however, to deal with one who could hold her own
in any ordinary fray, and before she realized
what had happened, she was lying in a heap on
the floor, her ears ringing with a vicious boxing,
and her head dizzy with a shaking that had
made her teeth chatter like castanets. Mrs.
Tarpy had meanwhile disappeared, and only the
thump, thump, thump of her heavy boots, and

ner loud oaths at the children who were in her way, proved that she was in the vicinity. The thought flashing into Jack's mind, that the woman had the precious Bible, — Miss Pitcairn's gift, — stirred her to new activity, and she sprang to her feet and hurried down the stairs. A familiarity with the ways of Midnight Street led the child to suspect that the thief would seek the nearest pawnshop. In this she was right, for some distance away she descried her hurrying along, shoving the idlers right and left. Half-crying, half-desperate, Jack followed. The path that the brawny woman made closed up again, and the pursuer had to make her way by dodging, squeezing, and hurrying to the very best of her ability; yet, so well did she improve the time, that when the former, with a push, threw open the pawn-shop door, the latter was able to slip in before it was closed. So intent was Jack upon the movements of her enemy, that she did not notice a slight, plainly dressed young man, with very red hair, and an air of suppressed excitement, who hurried up and crowded in just behind her. The last comer was Mr. Chick, the new lodger at the Cosmopolitan Hotel, and the cause of his opportune appearance was this: Contrary to general usage he had, after supper, retired to his room to watch the house opposite, and dutifully seating himself on the foot of the bed, was thinking what a fool he had made of himself in volun- teering to do such unsatisfactory work; when whom should he see but stout Mrs. Tarpy hurry- ing by on the opposite side, as if her life de- pended on her haste. The watcher was con- templating her exertions with calm amusement when Jack appeared on the scene, frantic with excitement and anger, and in hot pursuit of the woman. In an instant the watcher had seized his hat and, hastening through the " Jouncer-room," sprung out of the door and joined the chase Many of the lodgers followed him as far as the sidewalk, under the impression that there was a fight, but seeing none, returned disgusted to their various occupations.

Mr. Chick sighted Jack the instant he was out of doors, and afraid of losing her, took the middle of the street, and as we have said, arrived at the pawn-shop door in time to enter close behind her, in company with a red-nosed man, who held a battered cage in which perched a dilapidated parrot.

The shop was a dark, ill-smelling place, the counters piled high with second-hand clothing, the shelves packed with ticketed bundles, the one window choked with a confusion of smaller articles that lay bedded in the dust of years. There were several people awaiting their turn at haggling with the spectacled Hebrew who owned the place, and in spite of her aggressive manner, Mrs. Tarpy had to bide her time. Mr. Chick was about to speak to Jack, but the latter, without seeing him, concealed herself behind a pile of clothing, and fixed her eyes on her enemy, while the latter, tired of holding the heavy volume in her apron, and apparently feeling no apprehension, laid the book on the dusty show-case for an instant.

"Stolen propputty!" said the parrot, with a suddenness that made every one jump, and an aptness that aroused Mrs. Tarpy's fear and anger.

"Take the dirty thing away, or I'll mash 'im!" she said, taking up the book again.

"Ah, there, my sweet-heart!" remarked the bird from under his owner's coat, and looking so dilapidatedly waggish, that even the "Uncle" smiled.

Quiet restored, the woman again laid down the Bible and began to sort the smaller articles in her apron. Jack, whose heart beat high the first time she saw the hateful grip released, and had almost stopped beating when the parrot interfered, again began to hope, and stole nearer to the counter. Chick saw what she was after, and determined to aid her all in his power, stepped around' to the further side, and dropped his own fine silk handkerchief on the floor at the woman's feet, saying a minute later, —

"Did you drop something?"

Mrs. Tarpy looked down, and very naturally said, "Yes," and stooping to pick it up, lost sight of the Bible, and afforded Jack the coveted chance. The manner in which she improved it was surprising, and perhaps astonished the young man as much as any one; for, as Mrs. Tarpy stooped, she darted forward, and with her whole strength gave her a vigorous push. With a wild clutch in the air the heavy woman plunged forward, striking Chick in the stomach, and knocking him out of harm's way, hitting the red-nosed man, and bringing him to the floor, parrot and all. In the brief time that Mrs. Tarpy occupied in cursing and struggling to her feet, and while the parrot was yelling, "Fire! murder! thieves!" and showering epithets that showed his bringing up, Jack had secured the Bible and slipped out of the shop. The woman rose in time to see her, and her wrath knew no bounds, — whatever happened, she intended to catch the child, and if her eyes said any thing, they said that she would kill her,

But Jack had no intention of being caught, and when Mrs. Tarpy and Mr. Chick hurried out upon the street she had good start and was making the best of it. In ordinary cases the cry of "Stop, thief!" would have brought a policeman, and Jack would have been stopped; but her pursuer had no desire to attract the attention of the law, so she simply hurried on, and Mr. Chick, taking the opposite side of the street, hurried on too. As they approached the corner where stood the intelligent officer with whom he had conversed on former occasions, the young man slipped a dollar into his non-reluctant hand, and asked him to stop the woman a moment, as she was about to abuse the child. At that instant Mrs. Tarpy arrived, panting somewhat, but determined.

"Stop a momint, missus," said the son of Erin, extending his club impressively. "Don't you go no further, or I'll hand you over to the 'Society for the Prevention av Accumulation av Childthren.' Do ye mind that, now?"

"Don't delay me, mister hofficer. It's a little brat 'as stole me Bible," panted Mrs. Tarpy.

"Your Bible! tut! tut! phat 'ud the loikes av you do wid a Bible? That for a brazen lie to me face. Go home, woman — move on, now! move, or I'll put the twisters on ye an'

pull ye in for contimpt av coort. A Bible!
Howly mither! Next thing ye'll be accusing
somebody av staling a church! Move on, I
say, — Phat, to me face? Come along, thin,
come — Oho, ye will go paceable, thin, will ye,
an' stay at home where ye belong? Go, thin."

She went, stopping at the pawn-shop to ease her
mind, and push a pile of clothing over on the
alarmed Hebrew, and then continuing her journey
with black looks and muttered imprecations.

Meanwhile Mr. Chick kept track of Jack in
spite of her efforts to dodge him. Several
times he essayed to speak with her, but she
darted off and eluded him, and he began to
fear she would succeed in escaping him altogether, when all out of breath she stopped in a
dark doorway and sobbed out, —

"Say, mister, what yer follerin' me fur? I
ain't done nothin'."

"Why, don't you know me, Jack?" exclaimed
the other, in great surprise. "I presumed you
recognized me from the first."

"Jolly!" said she, "if it ain't Mr. Hen!
Wish 't I knowed it was you afore, then I would n't
a hurried so. Say," with a little sob, "say, did
you know that grandad wuz dead?"

"Yes," said he, his voice falling into a tender,
comforting tone. "We all know it now, and are

awfully sorry. But he was such a good old man, that I think the angels took him right straight up to heaven. I do n't suppose he is blind now, but can see as well as any of us, and he must be very, very happy."

"I s'pose so, but it 's rough on me."

"Perhaps,—that is, if we love the Lord and do what is right, we shall see him sometime."

The young man spoke with difficulty, for this was new work for him.

"I wish 't I could. He was a boss old man; never cussed, nor swore, nor drank, nor nothing, jest sold pencils and prayed for me."

"Miss Pitcairn wanted me to bring you up to her house, when I found you," said Mr. Chick, awkwardly.

"What! on Fifth Avenyer?" exclaimed Jack.

"Yes."

"When does she want me to come?"

"Right away," was the reply.

"I guess I wo n't go to-night. I 'll see yer to-morrow," was the child's reply.

"But where are you going to sleep? you wo n't go back to the attic?"

"No," said Jack, with a little shiver, "I sha' n't go back there, cause if I did, the old woman would kill me sure, but I kin find some hole to crawl inter"

"Now, see here," said Mr. Chick, in his most persuasive tones, "my cousin will be awfully put out with me, if I lose sight of you. Now I'll tell you what to do, — you go to some nice, respectable place, and get a room, and I'll give you the money to pay for it, and then you can see Miss Pitcairn in the morning, and I shall know where to tell her to go to see you."

Jack was too tired to discuss further, so she accepted fifty cents, but absolutely refused more, and began to look for the right place to spend the night.

Many houses displayed cards variously inscribed, "Furnished Rooms to Let," and erelong they found one that looked respectable, yet was not too stylish, and taking the Bible, Jack mounted the steps, refusing to have her companion appear in the bargain for a room.

Ever obedient to feminine caprice, he retired to the shadow of a lamp-post, and waited, — but before she rang the bell, Jack beckoned him nearer, and whispered, with a sob in her throat, —

"Say, you've been awful good to me."

"I'm glad of the chance," said Mr. Chick, honestly, kissing his hand to her, and again retiring, while she mustered courage to ring the bell. It was, not answered at once, and she turned about and looked anxiously at her friend, wondering what —

"Well, what is it?"

The door had been opened by a brisk looking woman, and Jack, who had for the moment forgotten that she had rung, and stood leaning her whole weight wearily against it, almost fell into the hall.

"Speak up! what do you want?" exclaimed the woman, eyeing the child impatiently, and tolerating her only because of the big book she bore, which roused her curiosity.

"Does Mrs. Smith live here?" faltered the child.

"That's my name. What do you want?"

Jack almost fainted, for she had no idea her hap-hazard name would so soon find an owner Something must be done at once, for the woman was growing more impatient, so she said, —

"Can I"——

"Come inside, I can't stand in this draught all night and catch my death of cold."

Jack stepped inside, and the door was closed.

Mr. Chick, secure in feeling that he had left her safely housed until morning, made careful note of the street and number, and hurried off to his lodgings, — not at the Cosmopolitan Hotel, but at the Hoffman, — where he had a bath and a supper, and was soon dreaming of the exciting scenes through which he had passed.

VIII.

Two Heiresses.

WHEN Miss Pitcairn learned that Jack had been found and cared for, and that the Bible containing the paper that was to be of such use to her was also secured, to say that she was delighted would but feebly describe her emotions. Her open praise of Mr. Chick almost turned that young gentleman's head, filling it with rapturous imaginings that were, at least, a trifle premature.

The next thing was to have the waste leaf raised, and its secret revealed. That this might be the more speedily accomplished, the carriage was despatched at an hour which made the coachman deeply indignant, and after due delay, the little girl and the big book were before the brown stone front, and Belle in her enthusiasm ran down the steps, deeply shocking the footman, to welcome both.

It happened that the Governor was at home that day, suffering from an attack of something

that greatly resembled gout, but which he called
rheumatism, with a peculiar aggressiveness that
admitted of no suggestion that it was any thing
else. It was but natural that Belle should hurry
her prizes into his study, and expect him to
admire, before he knew what it was all about.
It looked very much as if his petted daughter
had been taken in by some remarkable specimen
of the genus agent. He glanced first at the
great book and then at the small girl, and a
look, half of vexation, half of amusement, passed
over his face; yet almost any thing that his beautiful daughter did was right in the Governor's
eyes, so he laid aside the morning paper, and
replying to Belle's introductory remark, said, —

"Open the book? Why, yes, my dear, but —
is it very difficult?"

"O, no, that's not it, but there is a document within the waste leaf that is very valuable,
and — and it frightened me so, I wanted you to
open it."

"Some new idea in a prize package that the
girl has been wheedled into buying. Wonder
what she paid, and why people do n't hire bet-
ter-dressed messengers," thought he, with a
twinkle in his eye, asserting his love of a joke.
Without another word he took the book, and
under his daughter's direction turned to the back

cover, and found the waste leaf pasted down. In so bulky a volume as this Bible, with the raised letters, a circumstance like this was not at all noticeable, as each leaf, and the cover as well, of necessity looked thick and bulging. A pen knife slipped under the pasted leaf easily released it, and within were revealed a letter and a sheet of paper, yellow with age, that looked like some sort of a deed or will.

With his first show of real interest, Mr. Pitcairn asked, —

"Whose is this book?"

"The young lady gave it to grandad," replied Jack, who had been keenly watching every movement.

"Who put these papers in here?"

"Me and grandad. When he took sick he was afraid 'Big Tom' would get holt of them an' tear them up, or burn them, so I got some paste, and we just stuck them in there."

"Do you know what is in these papers?" inquired the Governor, still holding them unopened in his hand.

"Yes, sir, the letter tells who I am, and the yeller paper is the will that tells about my propputty," was the prompt reply.

"And your name is" ——

"Lucy Betteredge Jackman," said the waif, with

the tone of a child who had learned a lesson through the most painstaking drilling.

"This is most extraordinary," exclaimed the Governor, hastily running over the papers and again turning to the group that were now reinforced by Mrs. Pitcairn and Mr. Chick. "Daughter," continued he, "tell me in detail all you know about this singular affair."

So Belle, her cheeks red with excitement, her eyes alight with the romance of the affair, rehearsed rapidly all she knew of Jack from the moment she first met her in the box factory. Then Mr. Chick indorsed what she had said, and lastly Jack herself told all that she could remember of the early years of her life, which by the way, was but little.

The letter written by the blind man, which was a marvel of neatness, gave the names of witnesses who could prove Jack to be Lucy Jackman, daughter of Frank E. Jackman and Matilda Betteredge. The will gave the name of the mother as owning the property, but during her lifetime it was to be held in trust by her brother, Thomas Betteredge.

"Who is this Thomas Betteredge?" asked the Governor.

"He is 'Big Tom' what tends bar down in Conlon's. Folks say he really owns the place,

but he pertends he do n't. 'Big Tom' was hang-
ing round all the time when grandad was sick,
and he hunted all through the room, makin'
believe he was lookin' fur to see if the mice
was injuring the house. An' then I heard him
tell grandad if he said a word to a soul about
something or nuther, that the kid should n't live
to enjoy it."

"This piece of property is described as a
building on the corner of Midnight and Bruges
Streets, — it must be part of the 'Wedge,'" said
Mr. Pitcairn.

"Why, papa, how did you know that?" exclaimed Belle, greatly surprised. "I'm sure none
of us have mentioned that name."

"Very true," was the reply, "but we have
one among us who owns a second corner of this
historic 'Wedge.'"

Belle looked puzzled and asked, "Is it mamma?"

"No, dear, it is your own innocent self. The
storage house, at what might be termed the
apex of the 'Wedge,' is yours, with the rest of
Grandfather Van Alstyne's real estate. It lies at
the corner of Bruges and Van Alstyne streets,
and was occupied by Grandfather Van Alstyne
years ago, as a warehouse for silks and other
goods from the China trade."

"I remember the building," said Belle slowly

and soberly, "and I think I am sorry that it belongs to me. It seems dreadful to own property in that neighborhood. Since I have been down there, the sights and sounds have fairly haunted me, they are so full of sin and wretchedness."

The mother's heart was stirred by this outburst, and the graceful, gentle woman glided over and slipped an arm about her daughter's waist, saying, —

"You must not go there again, darling, and it need not trouble you that father's old warehouse still remains in the family. Since it was built the character of the neighborhood has entirely changed. It may change again, and for the better."

Jack, who had been watching this little scene between mother and daughter, said, with a sob in her throat, —

"When I get my propputty that rum-shop has just got to 'git.' It 's them places that spiles a neighborhood."

"There 's a reformer for you!" laughed the Governor. "When she is grown, things will have to move in straight paths."

After a serious talk between the members of the Pitcairn household, it was decided to keep Jack with them for a few weeks, at least, until it was possible to learn just where she belonged, and her inheritance could be secured to her. This course necessitated a complete outfit in clothing, a room of her own, and an initiation into the mysteries of civilized life. As this latter was a work of some little time, it was found advisable to secure for her a governess, and almost before Jack knew it, she was transformed into a very proper little girl named Lucy, who had regular studies each day, and was no longer allowed to run down the streets bare-footed and with tangled hair, calling the morning papers.

In the meantime the Governor put the matter of righting the little waif into the hands of the legal firm of which he was a member, and the work of getting witnesses and preparing for the Court of Probate went rapidly on. As this is but a side issue in our story, we may as well state that there was no trouble in proving that the property belonged to the child, and that she had been defrauded of rentals for a long time back. The sudden absence of 'Big Tom' prevented any thing being done towards the recovery of this money, and Conlon's lease having run out, the place was shut up until a desirable tenant could be secured. The court appointed Miss Belle Pitcairn guardian of the child Lucy Jackman, according to her desire, and the work of her education went on slowly, but surely.

It happened, soon after this, that the Professor was at the home of the Governor to pay a "party call," and as was natural the talk drifted from the news of the day to the part of the city which had been of such deep interest to them all — the "Wedge."

"I see you have let the Conlon saloon to an old friend of mine," said he.

"Yes, the agent came to me a week ago with Mr. Thomas, and I had papa look him up, and found that he was just the man for the place."

"I have known him for many years," continued the Professor, warmly, and a more conscientious man does not live. He has laid aside money-getting, — and his prospects were brilliant, — to go among the poorer people as missionary. By the way, is he related to Miss Kate Thomas, whom I met here one evening? She also was a missionary, I think?"

"At present they are not related, but expect to be this week," was the smiling reply.

"Indeed! of the same name, the same faith, and the same purpose in life, they certainly should be happy."

"I am sure they will be, and am so thankful that Kate can still continue her work, for she has grown invaluable to me," replied Belle.

Neither the Professor nor the world at large

were aware that the rent for the rooms at
Conlon's, hereafter to be known as the "Faith
Mission," was regularly sent by Bellé to the
new Mrs. Thomas, and by her given to the
agent who managed the property for the blind
man's granddaughter. The responsibility that
she felt as an owner of property in so wretched
a place as the "Wedge," and now the additional
feeling that she was answerable, in part, for the
good management of her ward's place, had led
her to do so much towards sweetening the atmosphere. She felt that good would be done by
the Mission, with its evening songs and its
work among those who could be induced to
come in there; but she wanted some wider and
more sweeping change than this, and just how
it was to be accomplished, or, indeed, what its
outward manifestation would be, she had no idea
as yet. How many times she had encouraged
conversation with "workers," missionaries, and
reformers, hoping that some practical plan would
be suggested that would make the way plain,
but it came not. Her father, engrossed in business, was ever willing to put his hand deep
down in his pocket for charitable or religious
projects, and was not at all averse to her spending
money in the same way; but even that did not
suit her. She wanted her work to go further

than to just feed and clothe the girls in her mill; she wanted to reach the heart, the soul, and to awaken in them a desire to be doing for others.

It often happens that woman, while she may be modest and ladylike in every thing, appreciates the fact that her word is law with many of the sterner sex, that she can mould their actions and cause them to do well or ill as she wishes. If she offers a glass of wine in dainty banter, few enjoy refusing it, — if, on the other hand, she is opposed to its use, her admirers are at once carefully abstinent. Belle knew, if she so desired, an association of young people could be formed in their rich city church, that would put missionaries at work in this quarter, — that would send old clothes down to the half-clad children, and that would do good. She knew that Mr. Chick would be a leader in this for her sake, that there were other young men who would come in if only the ladies took the initiative; but that did not satisfy her. It should be a work for its own sake, not for the sake of some lady friend, and she also felt that a way should be devised by which these people could help themselves.

"Is the missionary spirit still striving?" inquired the Professor, as Belle awakened from an instant's reverie to find him smiling at her rapt look.

"If I say yes, you will imagine that you are a mind-reader, which would be a calamity," replied she, brightly; "but I will acknowledge this,—my brief acquaintance with the miserable condition of the people at the 'Wedge' makes me long to help them. Something should be done,—must be done, and the question that I am trying to settle is, what can *I* do? My mill, as yet, only touches a few of the residents there."

"An honest ambition, and one in which the Lord will show the way," replied he, heartily, somewhat to her surprise, for he was naturally reticent on religious matters.

"Thank you," she replied, "you are the only one of my society friends who, as yet, *believe* in my plans. Of course they say it is 'sweet of me,' and all that, but they do n't say, 'Your purpose is honest, God bless you in it.'"

IX.

"A Freeze Out."

SHUT in a tiny mahogany closet, with the telephone, Stanley Armitage was conversing with a friend who was a well-known West-side manufacturer.

"Do you accept my offer?" he called.

"Say it again, somebody cut us off just when you reached the interesting part," came in a muffled voice from the further side of the city.

"My proposition is this: I will let you have the money you asked for, provided you let me have the control of the votes of a majority of your stock on a scheme for a combination."

"But are n't paper boxes a trifle out of your line?"

"Possibly, but I have a side issue to bring about, by means of this combination, that will be of advantage to me, and incidentally will help your business. I can't elaborate my plans by telephone, but if you can arrange to dine with me, this evening at the Hoffman, I shall be glad to give you all of the details."

"All right, good-by," came over the wire, and the railroad king, with a look of shrewd satisfaction on his handsome face, went back into his office, and was soon deep in the intricate problems of his regular business.

That evening, true to the appointment, the gentleman came, and seated before a sumptuous repast, was in a position to receive very favorably any proposition that his wealthy host might bring forward. Two hours at the table sufficed to dispose of the various courses, and further to arrange a plan whereby Stanley Armitage became a stockholder in the Eagle Box Manufacturing Company, and so placed that, with his guest's assistance, he could control a large majority of the votes cast by the holders of stock.

When this arrangement was consummated and the gentleman had been made a director in the company, he began at once with his own peculiar energy to make his presence felt. In the first place he took time to learn the line of goods manufactured, the profits at the present market prices, and the amount of goods that the market would stand. When he had mastered these necessary details, and had a list of the competitors in the business, he brought out his first address on the subject of a combination, or as it is often called a "trust." It was at a regular meeting of the board of directors that he defined his wishes, which by this time had become the law of the corporation ; he said, —

"The business done by this firm should, at fair prices, net us one hundred thousand dollars a year, instead of thirty or forty. The trouble is, all of the box manufacturers are cutting prices, and in doing that are cutting each others' throats. It is time it was stopped, and the only thing that will avail to stop it is an iron-clad combination of the reputable firms, and the 'freezing out' of the rest. Now, let our Secretary notify the list of box manufacturers that I have handed him, to consider this question and to attend a meeting here, say, — next Monday. Let each send a representative, with full power to act. You may add that I will address the meeting."

The plan was received with enthusiasm, and the circulars went out, — the only mill of .importance that was ignored in this general conference being the Van Alstyne Manufacturing Company, in Harlem.

Perhaps it was fortunate that the Secretary of the company knew so little of the private affairs of Mr. Armitage, else he surely would have suspected there were personal interests at stake,

when he received so positive an order to pass
that house by.

"But, I understand they are a growing firm,
and doing a large business, with plenty of capital back of them," he had ventured timidly.

"I intend to force them out of the business!"
was the short reply, and the Secretary wisely
forbore to question further. In a word, that
was the cause of the gentleman's sudden interest
in box manufacture. He disapproved of Belle's
course in owning and running a factory, even if
it did good, yet was too proud to say a word
to her against her pet project. He, therefore,
intended to employ a method not uncommon,
that of forming a strong combination and of "freez
ing out" those who are unwelcome. He was
confident that the Van Alstyne mill would not
be run at a loss, and even if it were, for a time,
and Miss Pitcairn lost fifty or a hundred thousand dollars, he could make it all right with her
when she had given it up and surrendered herself entirely to him. Even in the midst of his
planning to wreck her business and dash her
hopes, he gave indulgence to love dreams; the
resistance that he met with, of late, tending in
no way to diminish his passion.

When the day appointed came, and with it a
goodly gathering of those interested, Mr. Armi-

tage appeared at his best, and laid down a line of procedure, that, after considerable discussion, was unanimously adopted.

Thus it was that a "trust" as strong as any in the country was formed, and the Van Alstyne mill left out in the cold. A well-known feature of such combinations is the crushing of competition, by means fair or foul, and in this case to the Hebrew Moses was delegated the task of driving the Van Alstyne Manufacturing Company out of the market.

"Would it not be more in accordance with commercial courtesy, to offer first to purchase their place, thus giving them a chance to get out without loss?" inquired one of those present, when this matter was up for discussion.

"Perhaps so, but this factory is operated on a different plan from ours. It is controlled by the help, and for the help, and, if it is not made a signal failure, it will, in my judgment, bring about a dissatisfaction among our employes, that will cost us many thousands of dollars. This new doctrine, that capital must take a back seat, and allow labor to come to the front and enjoy all the fruits of enterprise and thrift, is a dangerous menace to our interests, and I am in favor of stamping out this new heresy so harshly that it shall be a lasting lesson."

To this statement of the case, there was no reply, and the Van Alstyne Company was doomed, as far as the combination was concerned. Moses, his face aglow with anticipation at the thought of "getting even with the vooman box-maker," went back to his factory and instructed his salesman to offer goods to all of the Van Alstyne customers at five per cent. below the prices then ruling, and to continue this "cutting," no matter how low prices dropped. In the mean time the other mills kept up their regular lines of goods, and Moses shared in their profits through his stock in the trust, even if his own mill kept on at a loss.

The first intimation that Miss Pitcairn had that the new combination was in any manner to injure her business, was in the gradual diminution of orders. Night after night Miss Murdock came back to the office with smaller orders, and sometimes with none at all, and with the constant complaint that somebody was underselling them. Of course this necessitated a "drop in price" to get the work, — an expedient that availed for a short time, but was met by the hidden enemy, who quoted a still lower price, and thus was able to secure the contracts.

One morning, during this time of trouble, Miss Pitcairn was opening the morning mail,

a small one compared with what it had been,
when looking out of the window she saw a
young man sauntering leisurely by, eyeing the
factory with a keenness that ill comported with
his lazy air. In a misty way it came to her
that she had seen this man a number of times
during the past week, and always in that vicinity.
As he passed the door of the shipping-room, he
paused to exchange a jovial word with the ex-
pressman, and to give him a cigar, while with a
swift, comprehensive glance he read the address of a
huge crate of boxes. Then he passed on lazily till
some distance up the street, when in fancied security he drew out a note-book and wrote the name
and address that he had read on the crate.

"One of my best customers," remarked a
pleasant voice at his elbow, and turning quickly,
the spy saw Miss Pitcairn.

"I — I beg your pardon," he stammered, a
look of shame coming into his face.

"May I ask you to come into my office for
a few moments' conversation?" asked the young
lady, still pleasantly.

"I'm in somewhat of a hurry"——

"Let us not misunderstand each other. I
recognize your profession, and wish to talk with
you on business. Of course I comprehend that
you are not here through any feeling of malice

on your part, but simply because you are well paid to be here. Now it is possible that you are ambitious to earn more."

"You have said enough," said the detective, his self-possession returning, and a smile breaking over his face. "I will gladly hear your proposition in your office."

Returning to the factory, the lady ushered her caller in, now perfectly at his case, and feeling that he was in a fair way to make some money. When seated, Miss Pitcairn took out a check book, and said with a sweet smile, —

"I do not expect you to serve me in any way, even to talk, without pay, and I will now draw you a check for one hundred dollars, — your name, please?"

The young man hesitated, glanced around the room, and then, emboldened by the fact that there were no witnesses, told the truth, when he said, "Arthur E. Williams."

"Now," said Miss Pitcairn, "it is necessary that I know exactly how matters stand, that I may circumvent my enemies. By whom are you employed?"

"By Moses Cohen & Co., for the Box Trust," was the bold reply.

"What are your duties with reference to my mill?"

"To secure the names of all customers who call, to get the addresses on all packages, and to disaffect your help as much as possible."

"How long have you been doing this?"

"About three weeks."

"How far along are you now?" was the next question, after a pause.

"The names of all your customers are secured, with one or two exceptions. My next job will be to tackle the help, and I was planning to begin at that, next Monday."

"One thing in your replies makes me a trifle suspicious of your sincerity. You are very frank and very explicit. Why is it?" asked Belle pointedly.

The young man flushed, and then answered, —

"I have two reasons: The first is, you have given me quite a substantial retainer, and I hope for more; the second is, there are no witnesses, and you would find it difficult to prove any thing against me."

"One thing more, I wish to ascertain," said Miss Pitcairn. "How much are you paid for this system of spying?"

"Two hundred dollars a month," said the young fellow, with a look of annoyance at the word so obnoxious to detectives.

While the last question was being answered,

Miss Pitcairn had pushed an electric button, and in obedience to the signal the burly engineer came in and stood quietly, waiting as if to ask a question. Without noticing him, Miss Pitcairn rose, stepped to a curtain that hung but a few feet away, and drawing it aside disclosed her stenographer, who was quietly gathering up a half dozen sheets of paper.

"You have this gentleman's statement in full, Clara?" she inquired, with dignity.

"Yes, Miss."

"Read it over, please; perhaps —— "

"I shall not allow the lady to retain those papers," said the young man, determinedly stepping toward the amanuensis.

"You can't say 'shall' or 'will' in this 'ere office," said the engineer, coming forward.

"I am an officer of the law. Stand aside!" roared the other.

The big engineer, without another word, picked the refractory detective up in his arms, carried him to the door, and gently dropped him on the sidewalk, where he stood for a moment, almost bursting with rage, and then, realizing the completeness of his defeat, hurried off out of sight.

The next day a circular, headed "The Box Conspiracy," and containing a verbatim report of the interview, was sent to all of the former custom-

ers, and to their credit be it said, many began
again to buy of the Van Alstyne Manufacturing
Company. The good turn that things had taken
was but temporary, for the trust, in secret
session, reprimanded Moses Cohen for divulging
its secrets, and elected another mill to carry on
the warfare with the Harlem company, and to
do it "decently and discreetly." The result was
as before, that orders were hard to get and that
there was but little profit in manufacturing the
staple goods.

About this time Miss Pitcairn, determination
stamped on every feature, called on a box-making house, — the very one, it happened, that
Armitage had secured control of, — and requested
an interview with the manager. She was ushered
into a handsome office, where sat a benevolent-
looking gentleman of some fifty years of age, the
same who had dined with the railroad king when
the details of the combination were formed.

"Happy to see you, Miss. Pray, be seated.
How can we serve you to-day?"

"I called to see if some arrangement could
be made that would allow me to manufacture
goods at a small profit, instead of a constant
loss," said she, coming directly to the point.

"But I do not understand. What has our firm to
do with this?" he replied, with apparent surprise.

"Have you not the ear of the trust, so that my business could be let alone, in case I agree not to cut prices?"

The indulgent smile that greeted this speech was calculated to make the caller feel exceedingly small, but it did not succeed, and after a pause he said, —

"The newspapers have a great deal to say about trusts, and I believe they have given the public to understand that there is a box-trust. Now, it may be so; but if it is, I should be glad to know it, and join it myself. There is need enough of it, for there is no money in the business at present."

"Do you deny that there is such a combination?" asked Miss Pitcairn.

"Not at all; not at all. There may be two or three of them; but, you see, our line differs a little from the rest, for we cater to trade that want goods of special kinds, that have originated with us. Wish we could help you, but really I am inclined to think that it is the hard times that are troubling you, more than any real or imaginary trust. Really, my young friend, if you will pardon my saying it, I doubt if you have the peculiar traits that are so necessary in the successful manufacturer."

"You refer to the faculty for spying on other

firms?" asked Belle, so innocently and pleasantly that the man did not know he was hit till after she was gone, when the shot began to rankle, and he was angry and ashamed by turns.

X.

Simple Addition.

THE narrative of Mr. Chick's adventures at the "Wedge," and more especially at the Cosmopolitan Hotel, had proved quite a treat to his friends, and had resulted in calls from various club-men, who became acquainted with McFadden, and were tendered the hospitality of his hostelry, with hearty good-will. As a rule, these youths saw nothing of especial interest, and having once been in the place were content and thereafter remained away. Of the visitors who were led to an acquaintance with the thrifty Scotchman through Mr. Chick's introduction, Professor Buckingham was, perhaps, the most distinguished.

From the time of his first visit, both McFadden and O'Toole had taken a strong liking to him, always inviting him into the "private office," a basement where stood a small furnace and engine, and where, when the weather was chilly, the friends of the proprietor gathered to talk politics and socialism. In point of fact, it was here that a brotherhood, of which McFadden, unknown to the world, was president, had its inception, and here secret conclaves had been held until, the membership increasing, a larger apartment was found necessary. It is possible that the wily Scot hoped to convert the talented young scholar to his own peculiar views, and gain a recruit, whose strength should be as a thousand, when he let him into this sanctum.

However this may be, the Professor was treated with the warmest cordiality, and his views listened to with respect, if not always accepted as correct.

Almost the first difference of opinion that came up between Mr. Buckingham and the habitues of the Cosmopolitan, was the temperance question. It was introduced by O'Toole, who, his jolly red face beaming with hospitality, passed a flat bottle over to the distinguished guest, saying,—

"Take a drop o' comfort, Priffesser!"

"Thanks! I am too much of a chemist to poison myself!" was the smiling reply.

"Pizen!" exclaimed the Irishman, with a quick flash of temper. "An' do you ye think that we are such blackguards here, that we would pit pizen in yer drink?"

"O, no; not that! I referred only to the poison that all whiskey contains."

"O ho! I see; but I'll fix that all straight
for ye. Sure it's McFad, up-sthairs, has a fine
lot av ould poort wine, just phwat ye want, an'
if ye'll wait a bit, I'll fetch ye down a pull
av it."

Quick-motioned and full of the new idea, and
moreover possessed by an uneasy hospitality, the
speaker darted up the stairs, and soon returned,
not with the wine, but with McFadden, who,
with Scotch · carefulness, wished to see that it
really was for the guest before the cork was
drawn. Doubtless his natural frugality was in
this case, in a measure, supplemented by a knowledge of the weakness of his co-worker.

"O'Toole tals me that ye were wishin' fur a
drop o' poort," said the latter, cordially. "Noo
here's a wine that is a pure juice o' the grape,
an' lively enough to put life into a graven
eemage. I oopen it wi' pleasure."

The Professor was a man of discrimination,
and while the Scotchman spoke, was rapidly re-
volving a course of action. He was, to begin
with, aware that the laboring men make but little
distinction between different kinds of alcoholic
drinks; that they believed the fine wines are
imbibed for precisely the same reasons as are
the stronger liquors, — the object in each case
being a "cheering of the heart," — an artificial

exaltation; in other words, a certain degree of intoxication. Although a Christian, he had never experienced scruples at dinner parties in drinking a glass of wine, for he had been educated to believe it to be a generous and goodly custom. Many times had he been approached by those who were deemed fanatics on the temperance question, and bored by appeals that seemed ridiculous; but now there suddenly flashed across him a new phase of this question, and as he would not evade an issue when fairly presented, he faced this, and acknowledged that he had been blind to a patent fact. The thought that produced such instant conviction was, that alcohol was alcohol, whatever it might be named, and wherever served, and that drinking was drinking, whether among the *élite* of the wealthiest city in the Union, or among the coal handlers and stevedores of the same city's water settlements.

With singular force came to mind the remembrance of the look on Miss Pitcairn's face when a brilliant, young society man, who had taken too much champagne, was being hurried out of sight. Her look had said: "That man is intoxicated, disgraced; the only one, perhaps, in all this company who has overstepped the bounds of moderation, and yet,"—here her glance had wandered up and down the long table, where gathered the wit, beauty, and genius of a half dozen cities, with a look that he could not at the time fathom. Like a flash it came to him now that she was wondering if the sin were not the same, whether or not the consequences were then apparent? Had not her woman's intuition recognized what many wise men, many mighty men, have failed to perceive — that the dallying with temptation was wrong? After all, was it not plain that when there was no tampering with questionable things, there would be an end to sinning? Was it not the part of wisdom to let alone the thing which had been a constant source of misery to others?

It was an eloquent sermon that the remembrance of the young lady's beautiful face, full of surprise, pity, and sudden awakening, was now preaching to the Professor.

The decision that these thoughts led to was, "Touch not, taste not, handle not," and of all the unpopular principles that he had in the past deliberately scorned, this was to him the most unpleasant. Yet he at once accepted the situation, and replying to McFadden's invitation to taste of the wine, said positively, but without the regulation horror in his voice, —

"I have decided never to drink intoxicating liquor again."

"Eh, mon, dear! but why did ye saund for it, else?" inquired the host, with profound amazement.

"Your friend thought my refusal of the whiskey meant a call for a different liquor; he was wrong. I believe you will agree with me in saying that enough misery has already been brought about by alcohol to warrant its being forever boycotted."

"That's true enough, an' so it is," said O'Toole, wiping his lips and restoring his own private bottle to his pocket. "It's phwat I'd like to do; but the bye that tries to byecott whiskey down here is just the bye that's goin' to be cott by it himself."

After this speech he sat back in silence and waited for the Scotchman's ideas upon a subject in which he certainly should be deeply interested, as a prominent part of his business was the dispensing of liquors to the "roomers," the "bunkers," and the occupants of the "Jouncer." In addition to these regular customers, he also had a goodly trade from the outside, where his wide acquaintance and advanced ideas had made him a man of considerable prominence.

"Meaning nae eensult, ye are what I suld ca' a fanatic!" said he, with a solemnly aggressive look through a pair of immense iron-bowed spectacles, which he had assumed the instant there was an indication that a discussion was coming.

If one assaulted McFadden's jealously-defended theories when he was without his spectacles, he could not protect himself, but would hunt industriously and silently for this intellectual armor, and once found, would turn the tables with a vigor that almost invariably won the battle.

The Professor was not aware that the Scotchman was making ready for a word-battle, and was therefore totally unprepared for an outburst; but O'Toole, who had been in many a debate with this doughty champion, was highly gratified to see a man as "well learned" as their guest about to be worsted.

"I hae verra little scempathy wi' them as canna' controol their appetites, and I dinna believe the cock-an'-bull tales aboot liquor ruining men as the fanatics claim."

"Fanatics," thought the other, "that is what I used to call the temperance advocates, with perhaps a mitigation of the accent, and now I am called one." Then aloud, "Well, if it is fanaticism to see things as they are, and not to be afraid to say so, why, I am a fanatic."

"Thrue for you," said the Irishman.

"The truth o' it is," remarked McFadden,

"there is a band o' persons and lecturers wha' are doon on drink, because they see the profits in the business, which they canna share on account o' public sentiment, ye ken, and they joost lee and lee aboot it. I ca' to mind a case wheer a young mon lay a-deein', and the doctor giv him poort wine and keppit him alive for weeks, and when he finally deed the meenester claimed that the wine killed him, but every ain o' any sense kenned that he deed o' toobucles on the lungs."

"Two buckles on the lungs? How many buckles should a man have on his lungs?" inquired O'Toole, interestedly, and with tipsy gravity.

"Only one, I suppose," said the fireman, who had joined the group.

"I suppose so," echoed the other in a tone of doubtful assent.

"Have you ever known any one die of hard drinking?" asked Mr. Buckingham.

"I hav knoon those that never tasted it to dee sooner than those that spent all their days in carousin'," was the evasion.

"Let us stick to the point in question," said the other courteously, "which is, Have you known one man who came to his death through drink:"

It was McFadden's special privilege to continually request his opponent to stick to the point, and for the other side to get ahead of him in this, and request him to desist from wandering, was an unexpected set back, and for the moment confused him.

"I preesume that auld John Duncan drank himself to deeth," he admitted.

"So he did. I was n't thinkin' av him, sure I was rememberin' young Bob Jacobs," said O'Toole.

"And I was thinkin' o' Terrance Cotter and his wife, and it 's a queer thing, but every one of his five boys went just as the old folks went," said the fireman.

"Nine persons in all," said the Professor, sententiously.

"Eh, and what o' that? Look at yeer railroad and steamboat accidents, and yeer boiler explosions. Noo that I ca' it to mind, there was ain but last week that killed the same number — nine, and right in this deestrict, too. Wud ye banish all o' the boilers?"

"Thrue for you," said his friend, approvingly, "an' that accidence goes to prove just phwat McFadden is saying, for the only man in the place that had a bit o' liquor in him, was the engineer, and he was n't killed."

"How did that happen?"

"He just wint acrosth the strate to get a sup o' something to wet his whistle, he havin' been on a bit of a spree the day before, and he staid longer than he thought, and the boilers was old, so whin the staim run up, sure they jist bust."

"And nine more were killed by rum!" interposed the Professor, with energy.

The announcement caused a sudden silence, broken at length by the fireman, who said, —

"That's so. If the engineer had attended to his boiler, instead of being drunk, he would have kept the steam down, and not been across the street in a rum-hole. It was the fault of rum, and I believe in putting blame just where it belongs."

"Eighteen persons thought of in so short a time, who came to their death directly through the use of liquor," said the new temperance advocate, impressively.

"I dinna like the way that this conversation is teending," said McFadden. "This is a subject that has poozzled the minds o' many wise men. Theer's nae use o' being dogmatic on it, — we differ, an' that's the eend o' it."

This sudden and unaccountable backing down, astonished O'Toole, who said, —

'Gracious man, why don't ye stick to your

side? Sure the man that's had the wide experience av yourself should never own bate. Why,
Priffiser, dear, ye don't know phwat a harrd man
to convince McFadden is. Sure he niver will
own bate. Even whin his own son had the
'Snakes,' and jumped in front av a train, an'
was kilt, sure, he wouldn't own that it was the
liquor that done it."

With a face convulsed with agony, the old
Scotchman threw the wine bottle into a corner,
and rushed up stairs, while the other, partly
sobered by the sight of his friend's anguish,
broke into a true Irish wail of sympathy.

As for the fireman, he turned to his fire with
a stolid face, but by his nervous movements
testified to an emotion that one would at first
think him incapable of experiencing.

XI.

Fashionable Effort.

AMONG the members of the up-town church to which the Governor's family belonged, was Mrs. Crittenden, a lady well known as a worker in many good causes, and one who contributed to the support of several missions in the less respectable parts of the city. She was the teacher of a large class of young misses, daughters of wealth, and was by them greatly admired.

One afternoon, when Belle was in the midst of a reverie, in which her newly discovered property at the East Side had a prominent place, this lady was announced. Bustling in, she kissed her warmly and said, —

"Do you know, my dear, I have been thinking of you all day long?"

"What can I have done to deserve such a compliment?" asked Belle.

"You've done a great deal," replied the lady, fanning herself, and glancing at the pier-glass opposite, to see if her attire was becoming

"Your earnestness among the young people has been a blessing to them. To be as devoted as you are is ever a power among the gay and thoughtless. The girls in my class have, I am sure, been influenced by the efforts that you are making at the "Faith Mission," and are eager to join the movement. They have, therefore, been planning to give some of the children connected with the Mission an entertainment. Is it not sweet of them?"

"It is, indeed," was Miss Pitcairn's earnest reply. "There is nothing, I believe, that will do so much good to our society girls as to come directly in contact with the poverty of the city, and show those whom they help that it is for the Master's sake."

"How true that is," said Mrs. Crittenden, the quick tears springing to her eyes. "Our girls are threatened with hopeless frivolity. As children of wealth and fashion they are petted, flattered, and taught to think only of themselves. The suffering that sin has brought into the world is carefully kept from them, and they have no idea that they can be helpers, for they do not know what the needs are. The fields are white to harvest, but society has built such high fences that our girls can not even catch a glimpse of the ripening grain."

Belle was deeply stirred by this earnestness, and her heart warmed into full sympathy with this "woman of the world," whom she felt she had, in the past, misjudged.

"Why can not you be with us at the little gathering?" said Mrs. Crittenden, cordially. "All of my class will be there. The dear girls are very enthusiastic about the affair, and would be so pleased to see you! Are you engaged for to-morrow evening?"

"Does it come as soon as that?" asked Belle, doubtfully.

"Yes, I thought, now that the fall weather had fairly begun, it would be well to see these children and give them warmer clothing and a good start for the winter. Prevention is so much better than cure. Of course we might have waited for the New Year, but all through the bitterly cold months these unfortunates would be suffering and waiting for us to move. You will come. We can not get along without you."

"Very well, I will gladly be there," said Belle. "Is it at your house that the entertainment is to be given?"

"No,—you know Egbert is so fussy about the people we entertain, that, without broaching the matter to him, I engaged a large apartment on Madison Avenue, and shall have the children brought there. Here is the address. They will get there at six o'clock, and stay until eight. I have been to Mrs. Thomas, and made all arrangements, and I truly believe it will be a day long remembered in the lives of these little ones."

The following afternoon, Belle was passing her father's office, and stepped in a moment for the warm welcome she always received, no matter how high his desk was piled with documents. For once she found him disengaged and about to go home, and as the clock chimed the hour of five, he shut his desk, saying, —

"No more work to-day, daughter. What is the programme for this evening?"

She told him of Mrs. Crittenden's enterprise, and her promise to attend, speaking earnestly of the kindness of heart shown by the lady, and of the good effect likely to follow such effor', both to the little arabs, and also to the wealthy young misses. Through the whole recital the Governor's eyes were brimming with mirthfulness, while his face was as sober as if he sat on the supreme bench.

"Am I not included in the invitation?" he inquired.

"O, papa, will you come? It would please Mrs. Crittenden, and I should enjoy it so much more. Mamma is away, so that it need n't interfere with dinner."

The idea seemed to please the Governor, for he dispatched a note to his home, and then after further inquiry into the nature of the plan, put on a light fall overcoat, and escorted his daughter to the street. A quiet dinner at Delmonico's followed, and then humoring his companion, he dismissed the carriage that he had summoned, and boarded a horse-car instead. When seated and cognizant of their surroundings, they were astonished to see that instead of the quota of fashionably-attired business men, that they might expect to encounter at this hour, there were only children, and such children! Little tots of both sexes dressed in every variety of costume, — some with shoes, and some without; some with hats, and others hatless; some clean, some semi-clean, and others positively dirty. All of them threadbare, patched, or ragged, but bubbling over with life and fun, — their bright eyes sparkling with anticipation; their shrill voices mingling in an incessant chatter that had in it an undertone of unalloyed delight. They were in the care of a plainly-dressed, sweet-faced lady, who seemed to have their fullest confidence and love, for whatever happened they mentioned it to her, and whoever said any thing funny, looked to her for an answering smile.

"A poor children's picnic," said the Governor, looking kindly down on the little ones.

"Papa, these are Mrs. Crittenden's children," said Belle, "and this is Mrs. Thomas."

The Governor at once recognized the missionary, now a bride, and a very busy one, and inquired the cause of the general rejoicing, and the destination of the little ones. Mrs. Thomas answered, —

That a wealthy and benevolent lady had sent word down to the Mission that she wanted forty of the most forlorn of the children in that part of the city collected and brought down to a given address, on such a date, that the girls in her class might come face to face with real want, and have the gratification and blessing of being able to relieve it; the lady had added that Miss Pitcairn favored the plan.

"Was it not quite a task to marshal this company?" was the inquiry.

"Yes, sir, it was. I spent all day yesterday among the families, getting the consent of the parents, and assuring myself that the children knew when they were to start, and where they were to meet me. Getting them together to-day and on the cars without accident has tired me out, but the little ones enjoy it," replied Kate, stooping and recovering a shoe that had dropped from a foot that was several inches from the floor, and slipping it on, — an easy thing to do by the way, for it was by no means a tight fit.

"Will not this movement on the part of the young girls, to do something practical for the poorer people, be of great benefit to them?" asked Belle.

"I sincerely hope so," was the earnest reply, "but I have seen so many experiments of this kind, and the good results are so small, that I fear I am skeptical. In this case, I confess I hope for something different from the usual patronizing effort, — but one can never tell what the day is to bring forth."

"I wish you could give us an idea of the usual process and its faults," said the Governor; but there was not time then, for they had reached the number given on the address-card, and the children were already moving toward the end of the car, each striving to be first in getting off, while the missionary, like a genuine shepherdess, was directing them, with a keen eye for the weaker ones, and words of admonition for those who acted with any attempt at rudeness.

"There, there, Johnnie, do n't be pushing Gracie Denny; she is such a little girl, and you so large a boy," she continued.

"She pushed me first," Johnnie replied, shame-facedly.

"I 'd div him a slap in e' mouf," Gracie declared valiantly, assured of the support of her teacher, and amazed that this measure should be at once deprecated.

"Say, teacher, that girl with the 'cock eye' is callin' me names," a young Hebrew called suddenly, stopping the whole procession for instant adjustment.

"O, I never! I just called him 'Sheeny,' and he is a Sheeny, so now!"

"Hush, here we are! Now, boys, take off your caps, and behave like gentlemen."

Belle puzzled over the statement that the Jew boy was a "Sheeny," until enlightened by a traveled friend, at a later date, who informed her that it was a name for the Hebrews, originating, no one knew where, as a term of reproach, which, although in itself meaningless, was deemed an insult by an Israelite.

During the evening she added several words to her vocabulary, that she had never encountered before, and had she been the happy possessor of the popular "common-place book," might have noted phrases, and even incidents, that would have greatly adorned it.

On entering the house, Miss Pitcairn was greeted by Mrs. Crittenden, who was flushed with gratification as she saw the noble form of the Governor towering amid the rabble of small folks. As usual, he was benignly courteous, and watched the proceedings with interest. As a matter of course, the young girls of Mrs. Crittenden's class, varying in age from fourteen to sixteen, knew Belle, thought her "perfectly lovely," and at once gathered around her to chatter, and make mental notes of her suit, for home discussion with some fashionable dressmaker. Aside from the rest, stood a bright-looking young man, drinking in every detail of the affair, and taking occasional notes.

"That is a reporter. Isn't he lovely? He has just graduated from college, and is wealthy, but instead of doing nothing as most young men would, he works awfully hard for his paper. I do adore literary gentlemen," whispered a precocious miss.

"Is he going to report this gathering?" said another.

"Yes, isn't it splendid? Mrs. Crittenden invited him to be present. I'm so glad I wore my new satin, and I do hope when he describes my dress that he will give the shade, for it's the very latest thing in Paris," replied the first speaker.

"Why, he won't describe our dress as if it were a real society reception?" gasped a miss, who, reluctantly obedient to home commands, was attired with some semblance of plainness. Then with tears in her eyes, she turned to her teacher, with the indignant wail,—

"O, Mrs. Crittenden, 'Min' says that horrid reporter is going to describe our dress, and mamma made me wear this old one on account of the feelings of the children; I shall be forever disgraced."

"Never fear, darling. He will only make a general mention of the tasteful attire of my girls, with the names of the class, and a word about their social position. The report will be submitted to me for revision, so we need not be in the least alarmed," was the comforting assurance, accompanied by a loving caress, a grateful touch, replete with elegance, and full of suggestion to a close observer of careful mirror practice.

Mrs. Thomas, who had by this time learned the location of the apartment destined to be occupied by the children,—it was the large front parlor,—ushering them into it, now stood looking about her in dismay and vexation.

A description of the furnishings of the room will take but little time, and afford a key to her embarrassment. To begin with, the walls were hung with the richest of tapestry, and the ceiling beautifully frescoed. From an elaborate centre piece hung a massive chandelier. At the large windows were rich lambrequins and lace curtains, the latter being pinned up out of reach. Around the room, extending from the floor to a height of five feet, ran a border of white cotton cloth, — a species of apron to protect the costly tapestry. An iron screen, held in place by screws, blocked the fireplace. The crowning glory of this decoration was the seating accommodations of the room, which consisted of white cloth spread upon the carpetless floor close against the walls, and here it was that the dulcet tones of the head of this worthy enterprise bade Mrs. Thomas seat her wondering charges.

If ever smothered rebellion lurked in any one's eyes, it did in Kate's, — but after a pause, ostensibly to look the children over, she issued her orders, and the little ones were soon transferred into "wall flowers," with very straight backs, and equally straight legs, the latter members, in some cases, extending outwards a surprising distance, and presenting a diversity and poverty of foot gear and limb apparel that many of the sensitive would gladly have hidden.

There was no escape from the ordeal, and there they sat in rectangular misery, wondering what next would be required of them.

The young ladies to whom they owed this good time, grouped themselves on the side of the room next to the entrance, and with the teacher surveyed their *protegés* with graceful compassion.

A solemn silence prevailed, that was only intensified by the uneasy motions of some little one who, ready to cry from a sense of scrutiny, and conscious for the first time that her little knees were black with dirt, tried vainly to make a brief dress reach as far as when she stood up. Two only of all the sitters appeared cheerful, — two boys, — each of whom had a stone-bruise on the toe, and striking up a friendly comparison, had forgotten the existence of the rest of the world.

It will be remembered that it was early fall, and the cool winds that are so delightful in the heat of summer, at this period of the year make it peculiarly chilly, and a fire is as great a comfort as when the thermometer is at zero. The fir place being blocked up, for reasons best known to the management, the chill had for several

days been creeping into the apartment, until now
it was actually cold. Mrs. Crittenden felt it, and
assumed a lovely shoulder wrap, and one after
another, her flock slipped out, and reappeared
with something pretty and warm to protect them
from the inclemency of the room.

"Do you suppose those children feel the chill?"
asked one of the girls.

"No, indeed," replied another, "they are used
to rooms without a fire. If the fireplace were
opened and a fire built, they would be positively
uncomfortable. Mrs. Crittenden said so, and
then at least one of them would surely fall in
and be burned."

"I have seated the children in this manner,
that my young ladies might see them as they
are, at rest, needy and helpless, and that their
hearts mights be stirred with pity," said Mrs.
Crittenden, in a low tone to the missionary.

The latter made no reply, but glanced at the
their faces as if to read the amount of compassion there written. Ere she had finished her
scrutiny, at a sign from the hostess, a waiter
came in rapidly, and deftly distributed napkins
and plates among the children, and as quickly
left the room. Returning, before they had a
chance to solve the problem as to the use of
the former articles, he gave out heaping saucers

of ice cream, and then passed baskets full of the richest cake.

Kate Thomas, curbing her desire to "wash her hands of the whole affair," went among the youngsters, spreading the napkins over bare knees, and encouraging the startled little ones to venture a spoonful of the delicious cream. To a few of them it was not a novelty, but the majority were as much amazed at its unqualified coldness, as if they had come from the heart of Africa. The cake they liked, but the ice cream, that is, before it melted, was not a success. Still they ate it in gingerly bits, with blue lips and faces that were very expressive.

The first round of cream being exhausted, a second was served, but this time the children were not to be awed into eating any thing more so frigid, — with two exceptions they let it alone. These two, unobserved, made theirs up into snow-balls and laid them in their hats to hit somebody with when the agony was over. This laudable design, however, was thwarted by Mrs. Crittenden, who lengthened the rest of the pro-gramme to such an extent, that all that re-mained of the missiles were two pink pools, which were emptied out on the floor cloth so slyly that none had opportunity to hinder.

After supper, Mrs. Crittenden, with a con-

cluding speech, presented to each little girl a
hood, a pair of mittens, and a pair of stockings.
The boys received the same, with the exception
of the first named article, which in their case
was a woolen cap; then, after a vain attempt
to extort a song from their guests, the sufferers
were allowed to depart.

The Governor and his daughter had almost
reached home ere reference was made to the
unique entertainment; then he said, jestingly, —

"How very happy those children were! Did
you take note of it? What a grand, good time
they must have had!"

"You are making fun, now, papa, but I am
glad I was there, for I have learned something,"
said Belle, with an unusual earnestness in her
voice.

"Ah, and what may it be?" was the query.

"That the idea of doing good to people by
sending for them to come to us, is a failure;
we must go to them. None of Mrs. Crittenden's girls would go to the homes of any of
these children. They would be afraid to do it,
— afraid of catching some disease, or of meeting desperadoes. I am dreadfully disappointed.
The little ones looked so blue, and cold, and
frightened. And poor Kate saw the ridiculous
part of the whole affair from the beginning, and

yet kept her temper, — she is a marvel of patience."

"I am surprised that you have come to such a conclusion," said the Governor, teasingly, "for I had just formulated a plan for a syndicate that should control the importation of pagans, that their condition might be ameliorated without trouble or risk to our missionaries, — our advertisement would read, — ' Heathen imported for Conversion — Special rates on car-load lots.' "

XII.

"Standing Room Only."

"DO I go to church? No, Miss, I do n't, and it ain't no use ter ask me to go, either."

"Why?"

"Well, because it's jest the rich an' 'risto-cratic that goes, and they do n't want poor folks there. O, *you* may be all right, but I tell yer where there is so much smoke, there is some fire, and most of the common folks feels as I do."

The speaker was one of the dwellers at the "Devil's Wedge," and the person whom he addressed was Mrs. Kate Thomas. Again and again had she met this strange antipathy that the masses are coming to feel toward churches, and it troubled her exceedingly. To be sure, she argued, it came from a misconception of the actual state of affairs; but that lightened her burden only a trifle, when she further reflected that the means for enlightening these blinded ones were painfully meager.

In her next week's report Mrs. Thomas faithfully portrayed her trouble, and in her eagerness to have the Gospel preached to the people in her district, was ready for almost any personal sacrifice. Her suggestions were always carefully considered by her fair patroness, and this time an interested conversation ensued.

"Suppose a chapel be built down there?" Belle said, after a few moments' thought.

"Chapels do not reach the masses. Now, at the 'Mission,' which is a sort of chapel, we do not have the congregations that such a neighborhood should turn out," replied Mrs. Thomas.

"True, there are thousands about there, and yet a preaching service attracts but a few score, and many of these are our own girls from the factory, who come to see you."

"I have thought, sometimes, that street-preaching might be what we need down there, but there isn't a convenient place near the 'Wedge,'" continued Kate.

From her desk Miss Pitcairn drew out a small blue-print map, on which were discernible the names, Van Alstyne, Bruges, and Midnight Streets.

"Some time since," she said, "I had a civil

engineer make me a plan of the 'Wedge,' that I might know just what property surrounded my own. Here it is: You see the 'Wedge' proper is enclosed by three streets, and has the following buildings on it: On Midnight Street are the Betteredge House, where Conlon's saloon was, a brick tenement house, and a second tenement house, with a 'beer garden' in its ground floor. On Bruges Street is Dittenhoffer's brewery, and on Van Alstyne Street is a German and Irish boarding house. At the junction of these last two streets is the old warehouse, the apex of the 'Wedge,' which I intend to turn into a model lodging house for our girls at the factory, when I can get time to do it. Doubtless you recognize all of these places?"

"Indeed, I do; but what is that spot on the map between the boarding house and the warehouse, marked 'Tramps' Retreat'?" replied Kate.

"That is an open lot that is a part of the warehouse property. I believe it is now used as a storage yard for old iron. My civil engineer was inclined to be facetious, and named that as you see because the old boilers, of which the yard is full, afford a refuge for the tramps and others too poor to seek better lodgings."

"If only *that* was empty and open, it would

be a grand, good place for Gospel meetings," said Kate, with a sigh, as she rose to go.

Her answer set the owner of this queer property to thinking, and as a result of her cogitations, the next day saw the fashionable Miss Pitcairn down at the "Wedge," knocking at the office of the junk-man to whom the yard was let. To his great wonder, she wished to look into the enclosure, and required his aid as a guide. What he thought might be her object in stepping daintily over the loose scrap, peeping into the huge boilers, in some of which still slumbered lazy vagabonds, or in asking him to pace its length and breadth, he did not divulge, but did all in a half-amazed way, that bespoke an utter surprise, if nothing more. His wonder changed to wrath when, two weeks later, the ubiquitous Mr. Crittenden warned him to seek other storage room, as the yard was to be used for another purpose.

It took a long time for the heavy drays to clear the ground, and when all was out it was indeed a desolate place. A little filling-in, however, with considerable rolling of the hard gravel covering, made it appear much better, and gave ample space for a large gathering.

As soon as the ground was ready, it was utilized; indeed, work was not quite finished

when the Sabbath came round, and with it the
first service, conducted by Mr. Thomas, the
worthy husband of the faithful "Superintendent
of Repairs."

He had brought out a diminutive desk, and
with his wife at the cabinet organ, began to
sing, in a clear, sweet tenor, "There Were
Ninety and Nine." At the same instant the
great double gates were flung wide open, and a
placard, announcing a "FREE GOSPEL MEETING,"
was hung out.

Before the song began there had been a clamor
of voices from the streets and from the crowded
tenements, but on the instant it was hushed,
and people began to converge toward the place.
From all directions they came, singly and in
twos and threes; some laughing and joking, others serious; most of the men smoking, and
some of the women with babes in their arms.

When the song was ended, a rough voice
from the crowd called out, —

"Hy, mon, that was gude! Gie us another."

So another was sung, and then another, and
people kept crowding in, till from the brewery
to the fence, and from the tenement house to
the storage house, there was a solid mass of
men, women, and children. As Mr. Thomas
looked over the strange congregation he could

not but reflect on the great responsibility that had been so suddenly thrust upon him. Here was the field. O, how white to harvest, and the laborers so few!

From the song the ready missionary started off into a chatty, everyday talk, that at first claimed their attention from its novelty and brightness, and then appealed to their judgment as a fair and honest arraignment of wrong-doing and oppression, and finally, by its growing eloquence and power, held them in spite of themselves. A natural orator, the speaker knew the pulse of his audience, and if they began to be weary he interwove a telling anecdote, or a song, and ere they were aware, an hour had passed, and the service was ended.

As the preacher closed his book and pronounced the benediction, an old Briton, waving his hat in the air, attempted to call for three cheers, but was anticipated by Mr. Thomas, who requested the audience to come forward and shake hands, if they approved of the service.

At this invitation most of the crowd looked foolish, and edged off, and finally, sure that there was to be no more speaking or singing, departed, but many staid and clasped the missionary's hand.

"It's wot we need, right here," said a man,

earnestly. "We can't go to meetin', 'cause we look so rough, but here, who looks at yer? They ain't a purson in all these yer tenniments, but what had jist as lief come out here as not."

"Very well, come next Sunday, at the same hour," replied Mr. Thomas, "and invite your friends."

"We'll do it, an' never fear. We don't care what yer preaches, as long as yer believe it. I go in strong on singing, I do, and that's wot fetched me here, but I'm comin' right straight along now, so you kin jist leave a space fur me an' my woman, right in front of the pulpit," affirmed a dilapidated-looking man with emphasis.

Among the more timid who had remained at the invitation were three, who were willing to discuss the subject of their own salvation, and who gladly accompanied the missionary round to the Faith Mission and, kneeling in prayer, implored forgiveness for sin.

The interest shown in the new movement was so great that Belle decided to assume all risks, and keep the "Common" open, and to give it at least a year's trial.

But in a neighborhood where wickedness had so strong a hold, it was not to be expected that there would be no opposition to the preaching of the Gospel, and the first attempt at a stampede occurred in the midst of the service on the following Sabbath, when some one in the crowd cried "Mad-dog!" and began chasing a poor little cur, and shouting till all became so frightened that a rush was made for the gates, and the preacher left almost alone.

After it was all over, and the dog was found not to be mad, and the congregation, such of them as had returned, was thoroughly reassured, the singing and the sermon went on, but with the effect greatly marred.

Mr. Thomas suspected that this was only a hoax, with the idea of troubling him, and so it turned out. That he was not alone in this idea, was proved by what was said by McFadden, the genial proprietor of the "Cosmopolitan Hotel." He had been a most attentive listener, and had, in a sort of patronizing way, looked over the assemblage to see who were there, and what effect the words of the preacher had on the hearers. His words on the subject were, —

"That mad-doorg scare was joost a trick o' the Deil, pit in motion by his representatceve, — 'Big Tom' Betteredge."

"But I thought he had long ago fled to parts unknown," said the missionary.

"Na, he did na' gang verra far. Ootside of New York he would be forlorn enough. He is aroond, ye need hae na dout, an' he'll show himsel again before election, ye mark my word," was the sturdy reply.

At the next service the gate man had orders to keep all dogs out, and at once to report acts of rowdyism to a little man in plain clothes, who quietly stood near the speaker's stand. When the singing commenced people began to gather as usual, but almost all, after a look into the yard, turned about and hurried away, as if for dear life. The missionary and his assistants saw that something was wrong, and looked anxiously about to discern the cause. It was not at first apparent, for with the exception of a few quiet men and women listening to the singing, the yard was mostly empty. At this juncture, Professor Buckingham appeared at the gate, and looked in, just as had the rest of the crowd before him, only, instead of retreating, he strode up to a man who stood looking that way, and said, —

"Come with me."

The man gazed stupidly into the stern eyes for a moment, and then, without a word, shambled out of the enclosure and up the street after the gentleman. Leading him round to Bruges Street he called a police ambulance, and had him taken away; then, after stepping into a drug-store for fumigating salts, he returned to the meeting. Now that the incubus had been removed the people flocked in, and were nearly as many in numbers as on the previous Sabbath.

"What was the trouble?" inquired Mr. Thomas, when he had opportunity to speak to the Pro·fessor alone.

"A trick of the enemy," was the reply. "As I was coming down this way I saw a man at the corner of Bruges Street, who warned me that a person badly broken out with small-pox was standing just at the entrance of the Common, and that I had best go by on the other side. In the same way he told every body else, and most people came as far as the gate, and see·ing the sick man were frightened away."

"Had he really that disease?" asked the other.

"Yes, and was ·so stupid that I doubt if he knew where he was. Probably he was left there to get the place in bad odor among the people of the 'Wedge.'"

"Eh, Meester Tummas," said McFadden, did I nae' tal ye that Big Tom was at the bottom o' this? It's the veera trick he played on oold Simpkins, wha rin a rival bar next door to him. It's a —— Eh! sirs, but how's the Professor? O'Toole, come and get a grup o' an honest mon's hand."

The little Irishman did as he was bid, with alacrity, while the gentleman said, —

"I'm glad that you are both interested in these meetings, and shall count upon you to help my friend, Mr. Thomas, to the best of your ability."

"Sure you ain't the only frind he has, Priffesser, dear," replied O'Toole. "Me and McFadden has been wid him from the starrt, and sure we will kape ahl blackguards from him, if we have ter make detectives av ourselves."

"I'm glad to hear you say that, for I fear that there are those who intend to break up these meetings if possible. McFadden, you know the men in this neighborhood, and I want you to give it out that these meetings are to be kept up right along, and that you, as the proprietor of the Cosmopolitan Hotel, approve of them. If you wish to add the weight of any official position that you may hold to such a statement, why I should be more than obliged."

McFadden looked uneasy at the words "official position," while the Irishman pulled the Professor's coat, and whispered imploringly, —

"Aisy, Priffesser, dear, sure ye niver can tell who may be listening."

With this shot at McFadden's socialistic power, which had been admitted in a previous interview, the Professor had gone away, and the few who lingered after the meeting slowly dispersed, most of them wondering what would be the next move of the combating faction.

In spite of the opposition that had at once manifested itself to this out-of-door preaching, there were a number of conversions at each meeting. The seekers after salvation were among the best, and also among the worst, of those living in that vicinity, — and all needed the most careful watching, lest the home influences choke the Word so gladly received. Mr. and Mrs. Thomas were doing what was in their power, but could not attend to all that was demanded of them. They needed assistants, — whole-souled, hard-working young men and women, in whom they could place implicit confidence, and who would be in harmony with their plans. He dreaded to send outside for some one whom he did not know, for the chances were that he would not have the same ideas about managing affairs. Finally he took his wife's advice, and stepping out of the beaten track, chose four young men from the neighborhood as "helpers."

These young men had all of them professed to be the Lord's, and were living consistent Christian lives. One was a grocer's clerk, another a teamster, a third a horse-car driver, and the

last a stevedore. In calling them to his help
he laid out certain lines of work for each, and
required regular reports of what was done. For
example: the grocer's clerk and the car driver
had rare tact in leading evening meetings, —
could start almost any common tune, and were
full of the love of Christ. To them fell most
of the extra work in this line, which allowed
Mr. Thomas to be absent many times among
the sick or needy, or to be in the audience
speaking a quiet word to some inquiring soul.
The teamster and stevedore were hearty, jolly
men, who were well suited to make calls in the
roughest portions of the settlement, and by their
every-day geniality and shrewd common-sense, as
well as by their size, to command respect.

After a time almost all of the evening calling fell upon them, and although weary with
the day's work, they seemed to find rest and
happiness in spending holidays and Sundays in
labor for souls. And the way that these men
grew in grace was wonderful. It seemed as if
they came in from the fray full of zeal and
of the Holy Ghost, with testimonies and exhortations that melted the whole audience to tears,
or filled them with holy exultation that the
armies of the Lord of Hosts were marching to
such victories.

From the Mission gatherings, it was found advisable to let these workers into the larger meetings on the Common, and erelong there was one continuous afternoon service there. Wonderfully did these four men work together under their wise leader, and when the next ruse of the enemy was tried, it had little effect.

It happened on this wise. Thus far at all of the out-of-door meetings there had been a rough, though not a riotous element. Men had come there under the influence of liquor, and had interrupted the speakers, but were at once hushed by the by-standers. On one Sunday, however, when Mr. Thomas stepped behind the desk, he found gathered in front of him a company of men quite different from those usually there, — a gathering of roughs from far and near. Well acquainted with the city, he saw at least fifty of the hardest characters, as far as rioting and hard-drinking went, that the whole East Side could furnish. They were not pick-pockets, thieves, or murderers, but were of that class semi-respectable, oftentimes, that in large cities is so frequently controlled by the rum-power. That the saloon-keeper was behind this could not be doubted, and from the murmur of many voices, came once or twice the name of "Big Tom," in a manner that showed him to have a hand in its planning.

When the regular audience had found what
sort of men occupied the places just in front
of the speaker's stand, most of them withdrew,
and indeed this action on their part seemed to
be facilitated by the gate man, who whispered
something to many of them that caused them
to nod their heads wisely and withdraw. When
most were out, the gates were suddenly closed,
and from the side entrance of the Storage
House came a file of policemen, who marched
solidly down to the rear of the ground, and
took their position between the rowdies and the
gate. The meeting then began. There were the
usual singing and prayer, while not a motion
was made to disturb or interrupt. At the close
of the invocation, Mr. Thomas said, —

"Boys, I am told that you have been hired
to come here and break up this meeting, — and
my friends, to see that it is not done, have
sent down these blue-coats. Of course, if you
were to raise a disturbance, they would be
forced to do their duty, because it is a serious
offense to disturb public worship; it is something
that even the police themselves do not dare
attempt.

"You have been sent here by the saloon
men, who seem to think that I, with my preaching, am doing them harm. Is that it?"

There was no answer.

"To prove that I have not done harm, but rather good, I am going to send these police away, and call out a few men who know what I have done. Now if I do this, will you be square and give me a hearing?"

"Aye," said a rough voice. "We'll do that, anyhow."

So the police, at a signal, disappeared the way they came, and the gates were opened, but no one allowed to enter. Then from among the wretches that had been saved from the curse of rum and sin, right in that part of the city, came testimony after testimony. With rare tact had this general marshalled his forces, and he swept all before him. Many of the neat looking men and modest-appearing girls had been known to these roughs when they were down in the lowest depths, and their witnessing for Christ was listened to with profound interest. At the close of the service, a hard-looking man, who appeared to be leader, said gruffly, —

"Parson, I don't take a bit of stock in yer cant, but I believe yer helping thim as is down, and whether yer hate rum or love it, ain't nobody's business. You'll never be bothered by any of us agin."

Immediately following this service there was

the usual "after-meeting," at the rooms of the
Faith Mission, which was fairly attended, although
none of the "roughs" were present.

Of those who seemed deeply affected by the
appeals of the earnest preacher was one who
at once attracted the attention of kindly Mrs.
Thomas. He was a slight, weak-eyed, dissipated-
looking youth, of twenty or thereabouts, arrayed
in a suit of yacht cloth that once had been
especially natty, and now frayed and soiled,
looked correspondingly dilapidated.

"Yes 'm, I sometimes, in fact always, wish to
be a Christian; but there's one thing in my
life, one experience as I might say, that I can't
get over, and it stops me."

"But what is it?" inquired Kate, kindly.

"I'm not sure as I ought to tell."

"Well, then, let it go. Turn your back on
the past and begin afresh."

"It seems as if I ought to tell this, too,"
continued the youth, "for it continually stumbles
me, and perhaps if I had it explained by some
one who, as you might say, had more experience as me, it might be all right."

"My lad, there are hosts of things to stumble
every one that tries to serve the Master. If
you can't forget this in remembering the great
love that Christ bears you, why, you had better

tell it. Here is a lady who is a true Christian, and who is able to explain any difficulties you may have. Miss Pitcairn, this young man wishes to lead a better life, but has something troubling his mind; will you speak with him?"

Belle, eager to be of service, at once sat down by the side of the penitent, and asked him his difficulty. In reply, he said, —

"Pr'aps I'd better, as you might say, tell my story."

"Very well."

"I was, as you might say, a Christian, until I went to work for a man whom everybody respects, and whom I, as you might say, just worshiped. He was a perfessional man, and a outward Christian, and I took him as my pattern." The speaker stopped, and sighed deeply, and looked at the fair listener with a countenance full of woe.

"Yes," said she, encouragingly.

"Well, things went on, and little by little I found that I was, as you might say, deceived. My master had terrible temper fits, and used to hit me with any thing that came handy. As his valet, of course I was continually with him, and I suffered his abuse more and more. At last one day, after thinking the matter over, and, as you might say, praying over it, I determined

to speak with him about it, both of us bein'
Christians, you know,—so says I, 'Professor Buckingham '——"

"Excuse me," said Miss Pitcairn, a trifle hurriedly. "Mr. Thomas is waiting to speak with
you. I shall be pleased to hear of your welfare,
and trust that you will not allow the inconsistencies of any other person to cheat you out of
your heritage, which is a full pardon of your
own sin."

With that she hurried off, and the penitent
watched her, with a self-satisfied smirk, that the
good missionary observed and pondered over,
even while praying with him, and receiving
broken assurances of "a happiness such as he
had never, as you might say, experienced before."

XIII.

The Old Warehouse.

"IS Miss Pitcairn at home?" inquired a spruce-appearing young man, who was standing in the vestibule of the Governor's mansion.

"I will ascertain, sir," was the reply, as the dignified man-servant stalked away, bearing on a silver salver a card that announced the caller as James Jones, architect.

"The lady will be down directly. Please be seated, sir. She wished me to say that she was detained at her office in Harlem, else she would be ready to see you at this moment, sir," was the report with which the august messenger returned.

The architect seated himself, and drawing out a voluminous pocket-book, took therefrom several plans on tracing-paper, and spread them out upon the elegant sofa. He then utilized dainty books and costly bric-a-brac for paper-weights, and by the time the young lady appeared on the scene, was so deep in a maze of lines and figures, that at first it was difficult to waken him from his study.

"Are these the drawings for the alterations in the storehouse?" inquired the lady for the second time, with an amused smile on her face.

"I beg pardon; yes, here are the various floors, and if you will permit it I should like to make a brief report on the condition of the property, that will have a material bearing upon your plans," said the young man, suddenly wakening to a realization of the fact that he was expected to make reply.

"Go on, please."

"The house as a whole is very strongly built, and its foundations are excellent. On the western side there is a place that will need rebuilding, which can be easily done. The apartments are unusually high-studded, and the walls as they now are would safely and easily bear the weight of two additional stories, and that, too, after the extra windows have been made," said the architect, in a brisk, business-like tone.

"Thank you. Now please give me an idea of these plans," said Miss Pitcairn.

Obedient to this request, the other, beginning with the ground floor, explained plan after plan, until the two in imagination had climbed to the top of the old warehouse, and even two

stories higher. When the Governor's daughter
did not understand any term used, or any of
the pencilled markings, she asked for detailed
explanation; nor did she leave the subject until
it was perfectly clear. The result of this thoroughness was that when the young architect
took his departure, she knew the meaning of
every line on his charts, and felt competent
either to approve or to criticise.

The general plans secured, she called a committee meeting of four, consisting of the Governor, Mrs. Pitcairn, Miss Murdock, and herself.
This was subsequently enlarged by the addition
of Professor Buckingham, by invitation of Governor Pitcairn, and Wednesday of the week following set as visitors' day.

Until then she spent what time she could
spare from the Harlem mill in viewing various
Young Ladies' Homes, Working Girls' Asylums,
and other similar institutions, and taking especial
pains to learn all she could about the disposal
of rooms, the arrangement of stairways, the
lighting, heating, and various other economic
features that would come up in the plan that
she had under consideration.

So interested had she become that she found
it exceedingly tedious waiting for her guests to
appear and join her in examining her new prop-

erty, and in a sudden spasm of impatience set off alone to visit it.

The beholding of a place on paper is altogether different from seeing it as it is in real life, and it was as much as any thing a desire to familiarize herself with the place before dis cussing it, that led the lady to set about this dubious undertaking. Arriving at the warehouse, she found the old watchman standing on the steps.

"Good afternoon, sir. Your name must be Jefferson," she said pleasantly.

"That is my name, Miss," he replied, with a surprised expression.

"My father told me of you," she continued. "I am the granddaughter of the late Mr. Van Alstyne."

"O, yes, Miss; glad to see you," said the old man, cap in hand, and a look of awe on his face. "You must be Governor Pitcairn's daughter. Glad to see you, Miss."

"Is the warehouse full of goods?" inquired Belle.

"No, Madam; two of the floors is, but one is empty. Mebbe you would like to step in and see the place that your grandfather built?"

"Yes, indeed. It was only the other day that I learned its history, and since then it has greatly interested me," replied the lady.

With no little ceremony, the old watchman unlocked the heavy front door, and ushered his charge into the building. A quietness that was almost oppressive fell upon her like a mantle, the instant the thick walls shut away the noise of the street. There was about the structure an air of ancient solidity that would have been reassuring, had it not been mixed with the traditions of a ghostly past, and Belle hurried as she walked down the long apartment that made up the main room, passing between huge bales of merchandise that reached from floor to ceiling, and that remained undisturbed for a year at a time.

"There isn't much to be seen, Miss, but great rooms filled with goods that are done up so securely that one can't even guess at the contents. In your grandfather's day this was a busy house. The teams were going and coming all day long, loading and unloading, and a big gang of lumpers and loaders were employed, but now the people who hire this house don't send a team here once a week."

Jefferson spoke in a tone that told of loneliness and disgust, and Belle listened indifferently, for she was, with all diligence, studying the general structure of the building. From the ground floor they ascended to the attic, and as it was empty, had an excellent chance to realize what an immense floor-space it contained. Indeed, to see it distinctly, the old man was obliged to throw open the iron-bound shutters and let in the light of day, as the lantern that he carried was insufficient to illumine so large an apartment.

On their return to the lower regions, thawed by her kindness, Jefferson led the way to a small room walled in by ponderous packages, and pushing open the door, said, —

"This is the old office of Van Alstyne & Co., and many a time have I seen your grandfather sitting in that leather-covered chair, writing letters to some foreign port that had such a long name that the envelope hardly had room to hold it."

Belle looked about the room with gratified interest. It was old-fashionedly elegant, was finished in oak, had a massive desk, in which were still a few pigeon-holed papers, and bore all the marks of an elegant antique, while on the wall hung the portrait of the ship-owner's father, — a fine, sturdy gentleman, of unmistakable Knickerbocker stock. The place looked as if it were simply left one night, and expected its owner in the morning, as of yore, to draw up at the desk, open the morning mail, and say, "Now to business!"

One thing in particular attracted the visitor: in the front of the desk, on a level with the eyes of one sitting before it, was a small mirror, such as organists have to view a choir, only this was cut into the polished wood in such a way as at first not to be noticeable; below this mirror lay a dainty ivory paper-cutter, of exquisite design. Belle took it up and examined it closely.

"I suppose you may have that, if you wish, Miss," said Jefferson; but the young lady concluded not to take it from the place it fitted so well.

The old man accompanied her to the door and was about to say good-by, when a sudden crash on the floor above startled him, and caused him to hurry off in the direction of the sound. Half way up the stairs he bethought himself that this was not very polite, and turning about, saw Belle already on the sidewalk; so he went on. Discovering that the noise was occasioned by the fall of an empty packing-case, he descended the stairs and left the building, locking the door after him. A moment later came a knocking with a dainty parasol handle from the inside, and the sound of a voice calling to him for release. The appeal, however, was vain, for the old man heard nothing, but moved stol-

idly away, supposing that the Governor's daughter was well on her way home.

The manner in which Belle had been so suddenly incarcerated was very simple. When she
had reached the sidewalk, a sudden impulse to
possess the ivory paper-cutter, as a souvenir of
the visit, came over her, and she retraced her
steps to the little office. Once there, she knew
where the lamp, that the watchman sometimes
used, hung, and also where matches were kept,
as both had been pointed out by Jefferson.
She, therefore, struck a match, and securing the
article was about to leave, when a yellow note
on the floor attracted her attention.

She found it to be an ancient, high-flown love-
letter from her Grandfather Van Alstyne to
Miss Mary Smythfield, which was her grand-
mother's maiden name. With deep interest and
amusement she was deciphering the singular hand,
when Jefferson came quietly down, and going
out, shut and locked the door before she could
make herself heard.

Of considerable native courage, Belle hurried at
once to the door and rapped, then to the window and attempted to open the shutters, which
on this floor were of iron, but in this was disappointed. Neither window nor shutter could
she stir, and finally out of breath and beginning

to be a little frightened, she sat down to rest and think.

Thus far the situation had seemed more ridic·ulous than dangerous, but it flashed across her that Jefferson's remark, that the teams only came once a week, might mean that she must be a prisoner for that time. She well knew his position to be a sinecure, — that he came in when he pleased, and had no one to disturb him, except when a van full of goods was to be taken out or moved in. With fresh energy, at this thought, she tried doors and windows, knocking and calling, and at last, in tears, re-treated to the little office and sank into the leather-covered chair to wait and pray for deliverance.

Night fell, and Belle still cowered in the chair, with ears acutely listening to every sound, and lips often forming a prayer for help. The lamp burned brightly, and had enough oil in it to keep its light up until morning. When the first fright was over, the brave girl had taken the drawings that the architect had given her, and going over them carefully, with a stern self-re-pression that was heroic, had become interested in her plans. In imagination, she even furnished the various rooms that she had in mind, and made additions that might not have occurred to her at her home.

In the midst of her planning and figuring, she became aware of soft but heavy footsteps approaching the office, and was, at first, about to spring up gladly and welcome the old watchman, when a second thought restrained her, and to all appearance she went on figuring and writing, while in reality her eyes were fixed on the tiny mirror in the front of the desk. The steps stopped before the office door, and slowly, carefully it was swung open till there was room for a fierce, wild face to thrust itself in and stare long at the elegantly attired lady. Then the head was withdrawn, and another no less unkempt and evil took its place, and with savage surprise gratified itself with a similar searching look. Then there was a whispered consultation, and again both of the intruders looked their fill, while Belle, praying for strength not to tremble, added again and again a brief column of figures, glancing continually in the glass.

At length the two withdrew as softly as they had come, and when they were fairly away Belle rose and, slipping over to the door, found that it could be bolted, although to a determined man the fastening might offer no serious hindrance. Then she went back to her chair and quietly fainted. When she recovered her senses, a breath of fresh air was blowing on her face, which she found came from the one window that proved to have a broken pane. Leaning forward, she was trying to reach through it and unfasten the shutter, when, close by her, but on the outside of the building, she heard a voice that made her heart leap with joy.

"Professor!" she called. "Professor!"

"Hark! did not some one call me?" said the voice.

"No, it's your imagination," said another.

"Professor Buckingham!" came the frantic appeal.

"Yes."

"It is I, Belle Pitcairn. Jefferson has locked me into the warehouse."

Now the voice of Mr. Buckingham was close to the shutter, as he said, —

"All right, keep up your courage, and we will have you out of there in a few moments."

"But don't leave me, or I shall go crazy," sobbed Belle; "there are burglars or tramps in the building. I saw two of them, and they are still walking round above."

There was an exclamation of dismay, and then, under the edge of the shutter, came the ferrule of a cane, which was pried in until there was room for the firm hand. A strong pull, and the shutter burst from its fastenings, clanged back, leaving the window free, and showing the pale, tear-stained face of the Governor's daughter. With no more ceremony than he had shown to the shutter, the young man smashed the window and sprang into the room, then turned and sent his companion for Jefferson. A moment later, attracted by the sound of breaking glass, an officer arrived and was about to arrest him for breaking and entering. A dignified explanation of the true state of affairs finally convinced him that this would be a grand mistake, and instead, he "rapped for assistance" to secure the two tramps who were still on the floor above.

At length Jefferson came, the door was unlocked, a carriage secured, and the fair prisoner driven home, which she reached just as an anxious search was about to be made for her.

In the gratitude that followed so timely a rescue it was natural that the Professor should have been seized upon by the Governor, and made to stay the rest of the evening, while Belle narrated the whole of her adventure. The thanks that the gentleman received from the family were full of honest feeling, and yet what was the embarrassment that lurked in Belle's tones as she spoke to the happy guest? Was there not a tinge of disappointment in her cordiality? The keen-witted Professor imagined he felt something of the kind and then dismissed the thought as unworthy.

After he had gone Belle stood for a moment in the heavily draped window, looking out at the brightly lighted avenue, and said with a sigh to herself, "O, why can not one so grand in appearance and so capable be free from ignoble 'temper fits'?"

XIV.

Treasurer Crittenden's Property.

ONE of the prolific sources of evil in the vicinity of the "Wedge" was the great brewery that faced Bruges Street, about which, at stated hours each day, could be seen bloated individuals, passing in and out with orders for beer in the keg for families that stood more in need of flour. In the evening, when the great wagons drove up, and the empty kegs were unloaded by the half-drunken drivers and helpers, there were oaths that could be heard several blocks away, — bursts of hoarse laughter, and often a brawling, noisy fight.

The nearness of this drunkard mill to the Mission made it a nuisance. Yet the experience already gained in the temperance work taught the management that any attempt to oust the rum-faction in that vicinity would be met by the most determined opposition. The unscrupulous methods of the liquor dealers, as evinced

by the movements that "Big Tom" Betteredge
had inaugurated, made some of the more timid
afraid to denounce this particular evil; but the
knowledge that one's cause is just is a great
incentive, and it was this in part that nerved
Miss Pitcairn to call at the brewery office, and
see what manner of persons were in charge
of it.

As she passed down Bruges Street to the
main entrance, she found the sidewalk choked
with kegs and barrels, and the street blocked
by great wagons. On the barrels sat loungers,
who, for a drink of beer, helped load the
drays, or rolled the empty casks into the cellars.
The atmosphere of the place was laden with
fumes of steaming malt, and the whole building
seemed beaded with a dank, unwholesome perspiration.

Climbing the stone steps that led to the
office, with beating heart she opened the door
into a neatly . furnished room, where sat a young
man busily engaged in writing. As the lady
entered, he looked somewhat surprised, and rising, said politely, —

"Can I serve you in any way, Miss?"

"Are you the proprietor of the brewery?"
she inquired.

"No, Miss, the proprietor is out in the

'vat-room,' I think. Please be seated, and I will call him."

Accepting the proffered chair, she seated herself and waited, although what she should say, or what manner of man the owner might be, she could not conjecture.

Presently the clerk returned, and behind him came a man, very fat, very German, and very beery.

"This is the lady, Mr. Dittenhoffer," said the young man, and the fat brewer bowed as much as he could, considering his shape.

"I am interested in mission and temperance work in this vicinity," began Belle, ——

"Yah, and you wish a leedle money, ain't it? Shames, give dot lady dwenty-five cents," interrupted the German.

"You are mistaken. We could not accept your money," said Belle, her eyes resting with lofty pity on the brewer. "But we wished to ask a favor of you."

"I guess you vos meestakened. It tooks all my dime to do favors for mineself," hastily replied the other.

"Would it not be possible to have your teamsters more orderly when they return at night? On Wednesday nights, especially, they shout and swear until they almost break up our meetings. I am sure you can not wish us to be troubled by such language."

The brewer opened his little eyes as widely as possible, in great amazement, saying, —

"Vell, if dey do n't like dot schwear, why do n't dey clear oudt? Dere vos plendty places vhere they do n't need hear it already. Why do n't dey have deir Mission in Brooklyn, or Shersey City, or Hoboken, and let the peobles go oudt dere for church? Mein cracious, we can't stop peesness for brayer meedtings."

"Our people get but small pay, and must save every penny, and can not afford to go out of town," was the reply.

"Vell, den dey moost listen to doze schwear. I can't stop the men ven I schwear meself already."

"Can you not hire sober drivers?"

"A sober man drive a beer wagon? Ach, you vas dalk like a shilds! Come, I vas in a rush. Ish dere any thing else you vould like to say."

"Yes, sir, who owns the place?"

"Dot vos for you to find oudt, mine friendt," was the reply, as the brewer, without other farewell, waddled off.

The young clerk, however, was not so uncommunicative, and informed her that Mr. Crittenden, treasurer in an up-town church, owned the building, — a statement which brought a blush of surprise and shame to Belle's fair cheek.

"Possibly you know the gentleman," said the clerk, who had been keenly watching the lady's face.

"I regret to say, he is treasurer of the church of which I am a member, but I had no idea that he was in any way connected with the liquor business," was Belle's reply.

"Well, I hear a great deal of temperance talk at home, — for my mother is a dear old lady of the strict Puritan stamp; but I must say, it does not sink very deep in my heart. I don't see but people from most of the churches do as much directly or indirectly to keep the brewers going as do the harder portions of the community. Why, you would be surprised to know whom we have for customers here. These high-toned people are the profitable customers, too, for we can charge them an extra price for the regular goods," was the young man's statement, with a look that told how he enjoyed showing up the failings of the "church people."

"I think we, who have been better taught, should feel that it involves a terrible responsibility, when we allow ourselves to become the servants of the liquor-power. Mr. Dittenhoffer is not wholly to blame for his ideas, as doubtless he was educated to consider beer as necessary as water; but with your knowledge of the evils connected with its use, it is amazing that you should choose such a business. You quote the wrong doing of Christians and well-taught people, and in so doing are you not condemning yourself?"

The young man flushed at this direct appeal, but it was made in so ladylike a manner, and with so much of Christian charity in accent and look, that he could not get angry, but returned her good afternoon politely, and turned to his books with a new set of thoughts teeming in his brain.

Shocked that the brewery should be owned by one whom she had never admired, but had supposed to be too conscientious to enjoy the fruits of liquor-making, Belle went home somewhat undecided as to her future course of action. Mrs. Crittenden, she was sure, was full of good works in a certain way, and if she could bring her influence to bear on her husband, it was quite possible that the German might be ejected, and some tenant secured who would not be a continual damage to the neighborhood.

With this thought in her mind Belle called upon Mrs. Crittenden, and was as usual overwhelmed by questions as to the progress of the work in the East Side, and the number of hands in the box-shop, and this, and that, and finally, was there any thing she could do to help along?

Just there Belle stopped her, and describing the brewery trouble, said that she wanted help in having something done to abate the evil, especially as she was having the old warehouse, which was next door, remodelled for a girls' lodging house.

"I find that Mr. Crittenden owns the brewery," said Belle, candidly, "and although possibly he does not know it, the business there carried on is a source of great damage to our missionary work."

"Why, my dear, you are surely mistaken," exclaimed Mrs. Crittenden, lifting her hands in dismay. "I am sure Egbert would not countenance any thing of the kind; indeed, he is known as a strong temperance advocate. Do you not recall the concert we had recently at the church, when he pictured so vividly the curse that beer had proved in the old country, and warned the young people to shun it?"

Her caller remembered the circumstances, and said so with quiet grace, while Mrs. Crittenden, on the spur of the moment, summoned her hus-

band, who had just returned from the day's
business down town, and after the usual greetings, broached the subject of interest by saying, —

"Egbert, are you the owner of any property
on Bruges Street?"

Mr. Crittenden was evidently not prepared for
a question of this sort, for his florid face took
on a deeper red, and his eyes shifted uneasily
from one to the other as he replied, —

"Bruges Street? Re — really, my dear, you
will have to ask Jacob about what we have
now. My real estate ventures are large, you
know."

"Yes, but on Bruges Street there is a brewery
hired by a man named Dittenhoffer, who says he
has it directly from you," continued his wife.

"You are right; I remember now. The building came to me in an exchange, and has always
been used as a brewery since the time of the
elder Van Alstyne," with a bow toward Belle.
"I guess there is but little business done in it
now. The German who leases it, I am told,
brews for a few private families chiefly."

The smooth way in which the question was
being discussed — making it appear of no consequence — was not lost upon the caller, who
said, —

"Mr. Crittenden, you are surely misinformed in this matter, as I called at the place this morning, and know that it is running to the extent of its capacity; indeed, the clerk so informed me. If you only knew the harm that this business is doing, I am sure you would at once let the building to some more reputable tenant."

"Why can't you send this German flying, as it is?" said his wife.

"Softly! softly!" said the other. "We must look at things as they are, not as we would like to have them. This man was a tenant before the place became mine, and I am but holding the property until I can find a suitable customer, when I shall sell it out, and be very glad to do so."

"But why not keep the property, and by leasing it for some business that is respectable, do what seems a plain duty?" said Belle, with spirit.

"Yes, Egbert, I'm sure your position demands it," chimed in his wife.

Mr. Crittenden looked excessively annoyed, as it was plain that he had not expected to have it known to members of his church, or even to his wife, that he possessed such unsavory property; but none the less was he unwilling to lose money by sacrificing it.

"Business is business, and I fear I could not make it clear to you ladies that we are often-times obliged to come in contact with various forms of vice in our great cities, without being able to relieve them," he said, confusedly.

"But we are perfectly willing to talk busi ness," said Belle. "I am an owner of rea. estate adjoining yours, and mine is injured by the boisterous behavior of the drivers of your tenant. Now it is possible to get redress for such things, as you well know, by complaining of them as nuisances; but I do not wish to have that done, as I propose a better way, and one that is more to your advantage."

"I am all attention," said the treasurer, meekly.

"Suppose you do with your property what I am doing with mine, — repair it throughout, and make it fit for a respectable tenant."

"Yes."

"When that is done, I will guarantee you a tenant, — a manufacturer, — who will bring good people into the neighborhood, and will raise the value of real estate twenty per cent."

Belle spoke with animation, as she was deeply interested in the practical side of her problem; and at the mention of a twenty per cent. in-crease of valuation, the eyes of the owner glit-tered suggestively, while he said, suavely, —

"I am sure, nothing would please me better than to have the opportunity to do something of the kind, for its moral effect alone. I will look the matter up to-morrow, and see what such a move will cost; and in the meantime, let me entreat you to give yourself no uneasiness, for, to tell the truth, I have long been considering how I could best remove this incubus."

Belle, assured that her mission was accomplished, and that the brewery would shortly give place to a respectable industry, refused an invitation to stop to dinner, and hurried home. As she took leave, Mr. Crittenden said something about there being a possibility of an unexpired lease that might make it difficult at once to remove the German; but Belle was so full of joy that her errand had been successful, that she scarcely heard it.

The next day, true to his word, the real-estate dealer did look into the matter, but in an original way of his own, that will bear description.

"Is Dittenhoffer in?" he said, briskly, to the clerk.

"Yes, sir. Take a seat; I will call him."

Instead of seating himself the other stood tapping his foot impatiently on the carpeted floor, as if waiting was something to which he was not accustomed.

"Ah, good day, Dittenhoffer. I just dropped in to tell you that after your lease expires, which it does in three months, I believe I shall want these premises for another business," said he, almost before the ponderous German was within earshot.

"Oder business! Mein cracious! what oder business?"

"Manufacturing."

"Manufacturing? Vot's de matter mit me? I bays mine rendt alvays, aind't it? I manufactures, don't I? Say, I guess dot Governor Pitcairn's daughter vos trying to buy you oop. Don't you know she will fail britty soon, if the 'Box Troost' keeps shpoiling her peesiness?"

"This party offers more rent than you pay," said the treasurer, but with an uncertainty in his voice that told that the shot went home, and that he doubted Belle's ability to pull through without loss.

"Vell, you didn't write down an agreement mit her?"

"No."

"Ah, dot vash all right. I vill bay more already. How much you vant?"

"One thousand dollars more," replied Crittenden, a covetous glow suffusing his face.

"Ein tousend? Great himmel! you vas ruined me. Take eight hunerd. No? Take nine hunerd. No? Vell, Shames, wridt oudt a new lease at dot most ungodly. brices, and pring it here to be sign."

Wiping the perspiration from his brow, Mr. Crittenden took his departure after the business had been transacted, and started for his office, guilty, but full of a sneaking triumph, that he had, by a stroke of genius, secured to himself another thousand a year, and that without at all compromising his position, for, like the shrewd man he was, he had dated the lease back several weeks prior to Miss Belle's visit.

When, therefore, full of -her new plans for the removal of the brewery, she called upon the treasurer, he met her with a face full of sorrow, and told her that he found he had signed a lease some time previous, granting to Dittenhoffer use of the brewery for quite a term of years, for which he was very sorry.

"You remember, I warned you the other day, when you were here, that I feared this might be the case," said he, as the disappointed lady was leaving.

"But, Egbert, would it not be better for you,

in some way, to break this lease, and allow the manufacturer of whom Miss Pitcairn spoke to have the property?" inquired his wife, when he described the scene to her.

"That manufacturer is Miss Pitcairn herself, I think; and if reports are true, another six months will knock her business venture in the head," responded the astute treasurer, with a wily smile.

XV.

Big Tom's Revenge.

BETTEREDGE, although rough in speech and manner, as were most of his associates, was not bred to such uncouthness. Once he was called "Gentleman Tom," but when the name ceased to fit him it was dropped, his present *sobriquet* taking its place. He always had plenty of money, and when he kept the saloon in partnership with Conlon, and collected the rents that were due his niece, was said to be worth several hundred thousand dollars. Certain it was, that he squandered money right and left, — that he gambled- recklessly, and bet heavily, but whether, in the long run, he lost or won, no one of his intimates could discover.

After the judgment regarding the corner house had been rendered against him, he took himself away, and remained hidden for a time, — but wearying of this, sent a lawyer to settle the affair, after which he appeared again in the vicinity of the "Wedge." That he was changed, his friends at once saw, for his manner was quick and irritable, and there was in his eyes an insane glint, that told of hate so plainly that the children in the street sped out of his way in all haste. Aside from this, he was drinking more heavily than even the most reckless of his companions approved.

The only person who appeared really to care for Betteredge was an old domestic named Meg, who had been his nurse from infancy, and who lived alone for "her Tom," and would at any time have sacrificed her life to save his. When she had joined him, after his return to the city, he had allowed her to hire a small flat which he called home, and where sometimes he ate and slept.

One night when Betteredge returned from a drinking haunt, and sat in the comfortably furnished sitting-room, there came a strange look on his pale, drawn face.

"Ye' er like to hae an uncanny neet?" ventured Meg at last, as she stood regarding him with a sad, wistful expression, — her hands large and bony as a man's, clasping and unclasping with nervous anticipation, — her bright eyes full of motherly sympathy and love. The look on his face was not a new one to her, for since the drink demon had so strong a hold on the man, he was often afflicted with morbid fears and fancies that, for the time, were much like a touch of madness.

He made no answer to her remark, but drew his chair closer to the fire, his features working nervously, as if oppressed with mortal fear.

"What time is it?" he asked at length, his voice thick and hardly audible.

"It lacks aboot a quarter o' ten."

With sudden energy he roused and said harshly, — "Put out the light!" in a tone that made the woman shiver, yet he followed her from room to room like a nervous girl, peering into closets and behind doors, with a timidity that would have been ludicrous, had it not been so painfully real. When the rounds were made, he locked himself into his own room, and the house was still. Meg, in stocking feet, brought a pillow, and stretched herself on the mat before his door.

After an hour of oppressive silence the faithful woman heard a movement in the room, and a faint light shone out into the hall. The fear was still on him, she knew by the sound of searching that came from wardrobe, closet, — from any place where ingenious fright could hide uncanny shape.

The light was soon extinguished, and quiet

again reigned, but soon there broke upon the
stillness a groan, while Meg, with beating heart
and tearful eyes, listened eagerly, echoing each
stifled sigh. She could picture her master
crouching in his chair, haunted by dreadful
fancies.

As she waited, there came an imploring call, —
"Meg! Meg!"

It was like the wail of a lost spirit, and so
unlike "Big Tom's" voice, that the old woman
paused for a moment in doubt. Then the door
was shaken with violence.

"Ye hae locked yeersel' in; turrn the key!"
called Meg from the outside. With trembling
haste the door was unfastened, and she walked
in, lighted a lamp, and, without glancing at the
blanched face, said, —

"We'll go to the settin'-room, an' stay by
the fire."

Without a word Betteredge followed her.

"I thought I could throw it off, Meg, but
it conquered!" he said pitifully.

"Ye'll be all rect, come mornin'," she answered soothingly; "ye've overwarked yeersel'."

"I have been overdoing of late," he said,
catching at the idea. "I must have more
rest."

They sat for some time in silence, the man

casting nervous glances around the room, the woman with her kind, sensible eyes fixed on his face.

"Tell me about my mother, Meg," he said, finally. "I think I should have been more of a human being, and less of a devil, if she had lived."

"Ye hae missed a mither's luve, puir laddie, but 't was na her blame. I kenned her weel, fra' the time she were a wee lassie till her marriage."

"Was she beautiful?" asked her listener.

"Aye, she were so ca'ad. She was as blithe as a bird. I hae seen her oft come flyin' over the moor bare-heided, wi' hands fu' o' posies, happy as the finest leddy i' the land." The old woman stopped and seemed lost in thought, while the man waited for her to go on.

"Your feyther," she continued, "met her of a day oot in the fields, an' before long they were weel acquaint. She was pleased wi' his fine manners an' boughten claiths, an' before it could be stopped, they were married. They made a bonny pair; he tall and canny, an' she rosy and fair, but his folk cared little for her beauty, they made her life a weariness, till she begged him to let her return hame to her feyther. But he would na' hear o' eet, an' her hairt was breekin'. It was then that you first saw the light. For a time yeer feyther seemed more kind, but his folk soon alienated him agen, an' whenever he spoke to the wife, it was hard an' crool words. So when you were sax months ould, she fled fra' him an' his kin, hidin' hersel' in a little country toon some twenty miles awa'."

"Did she have any money?" asked Better-edge, although he had heard the story many times .and knew every point.

"Not a copper o' his money," replied Meg, with spirit. "What little she had she earned by hard wark. She was resigned as lang as she had her bairn wi' her, but there came a day when she returned fra' wark an' foun' him not. She learned fra' the woman who keppet the hoose, that some o' yeer feyther's folk had tain ye awa'. So she traveled the twenty mile on foot, an' plead wi' them to gie her back her boy, but they only laughed an' said that she were daft."

"What became of her then?"

"Weel, she warked in various places, growin' thin an' losin' her beauty, till her ain folk would scarce ken her. At last word came that she was deed. Soon after this yeer feyther came to America an' started in business, an' I heard na more o' yeer folk till I came to wark for ye after yeer feyther's death."

The words of the old servant soothed her listener like an opiate. The trembling had almost ceased, and the quick, apprehensive glances toward the corners of the room were growing less frequent.

"It's twa' o'clock," said Meg; "yeer bad turrn is over. I maun as weel leave ye noo."

"No, Meg, stay here!" he entreated. "It will return if I am left alone. Stay until daylight. Don't leave me for an instant!"

His terror was so real that Meg yielded, and hour after hour kept her vigil. Sometimes Betteredge dozed a little, but waked with a start and shiver as soon as his eyes fairly closed, and Meg, patient, with an unceasing calmness, quieting her "lad" as a mother would a child.

At last morning broke. One after another the shadows fled from the poisoned brain, and the "spell" was over. The feverish night, however, had left its mark upon the sufferer. The domineering man seemed crushed; a mute, beseeching weariness was shown in his every motion. Meg insisted upon his taking complete rest, and for once she found a willing listener, and retiring to the chamber from which he had so recently been driven, he threw himself upon the bed and was soon in a deep sleep.

As for Meg, she went about her household duties, the night seeming to have made no impression of fatigue upon her. She budged around from one task to another, the thought of the strange delirium ever before her; yet she could not understand it. "Big Tom" was no coward, she was well assured, and the only reason she could give for his increasingly frequent tremons was his drinking habits, and to this cause she was loth to lay them.

The next day Betteredge attended a meeting of the Liquor Dealers' Federation, of which he was a member, and spoke of his investments in certain rum-shops in the city, and of the duties of the association in protecting their interests. To hear him in conversation and in debate, always clear-headed and master of the situation, one would not believe that he was the same man who, but a few short hours before, was crouching in abject fear of he knew not what.

Yet he continued to drink, even though he knew that while he persisted there was no hope of deliverance from these brief fits of madness. And as he drank, the hate he bore the missionary, and his wife, and all of their helpers, grew and increased, until it was his dominant passion. As he pondered the chances for revenge, he haunted the streets in the vicinity of the Mission, glared angrily at the workmen who were repairing and enlarging the warehouse, and longed for his chance to come. At last it did come, and in this wise:—

Night had fallen upon the city. From the ocean, sweeping across Brooklyn Heights, singing in the taut cables of the great bridge, came the strong, moist wind that betokened a long storm. Up and down the East River the steamers, barges, and sailing vessels were pulling uneasily at their moorings, while the busy ferryboats struggled through the short, angry, chop sea, that drove them from their course, and kept them whistling, ringing, and backing, for fear that they would either crash into the well-fenced landings, or, losing headway, be swept by current, tide or wind among the moored craft at the merchant slips.

As far away as Midnight Street the various river noises could be heard, and mingling with the whistling of the wind, the slamming of loosened shutters, and creaking of rusty sign-hinges, it seemed as if it were raining uncanny sounds.

As the city clock struck ten, there might

have been seen emerging from a saloon nearly opposite the Faith Mission, two men who halted in the lee of a doorway to look for a moment at the bright lights across the way.

"Our lights used to burn there, Con.," growled one, a huge fellow, his features concealed by a slouch hat and high coat collar.

"I know it," was the reply, with a deep curse.

"Now they have all sorts of pious foolery going on, and the people that run it were appointed as the kid's guardian, so they kin do as they please, and no one to hinder," continued the first speaker.

"It's a shame," was the angry comment; "ever since that confounded coon jumped on me and cut me with his razor, there has been no more luck for me. It's been lose, lose, lose, stiddy ever since."

"The coon didn't turn your luck, it was that pious Thomas, that prayed in the bar-room. I knowed it would bring trouble, and you had better let me popped him. I didn't intend to kill, only just put a pill in his shoulder that would give him something to think about, instead of praying curses down upon us; but you played the baby, and wouldn't have him hurt, and now where are we?"

Conlon did not answer for a full minute, but

hung his head, and seemed deep in meditation, while his companion took out a short black pipe and proceeded to light it, glancing from time to time, with contemptuous expression, at his companion. Finally the ex-rum-seller said, —

"Betteredge, if I died I could n't help it, but that prayer has hung by me ever since. Many 's the time I 've found myself repeating of it when I was alone, and cursed aloud to stop it. I wish that missionary had left me to take my chances and never showed his face to me. Just as I was getting a good start and money ahead, and the boys were filling into the saloon, — he comes along and spiles the whole thing. Then comes the summons to get out of the corner, the best on the street, and though we offered twice the old rent, it warn't even looked at. Luck! it 's the meanest streak that ever a man had, and I 'd like to spill some of it on to these missionary folks."

"Wal, let 's do it. Let 's ketch that feller, Thomas, and punch his head, and tell him if he do n't get outer this neighborhood that we 'll kill him," was the savage response.

"No use! No use at all! You do n't know that breed of people. They ain't no reason in them. Do up one of them, and two come to take his place. You try to lick 'em, and they

just flop down and pray, and it takes the grit
right outern any one. All we can do is to look
up another stand, and take our chances again of
being driven out." The man spoke with conviction, and his companion's smouldering wrath
broke into open flame.

"You —— baby," he growled. "You have n't
got grit enough to be any thing but a whining
missionary yourself. Better go in and join them.
They would be mighty glad of a convert like
you."

The smaller man, with a gleam of fierce
anger in his eyes, turned like a cat and leaped
at the other's throat, clutching it with fingers of
iron, and rendering the giant weak as a child,
by a sudden and vicious choking, when he released him and said, —

"I 've got grit enough to settle you at any
time, and don't you forget it. If I do jine
the missionary, it will be my lookout, although
I 'm fur enough from it."

Very meekly the big man accepted the rough
lesson, knowing that, in spite of his large frame
and great strength, he was no match for Conlon.

"You need not be so savage, old man," he
said, as soon as he could speak. "I was only
joking, except in my wish to smash the mis-

sionary's head. You and I do n't need to fight; we have allus been friends."

But Conlon, out of sorts with himself and the whole world, and hating for the moment even his best friend, gave an incoherent growl, and strode away into the darkness. "Big Tom" looked after him with an expression of regret, and then turned again toward the Mission with fresh wrath because it had been the means of separating him from his former partner and friend.

"I 'd like to blow your whole ranch into smithereens," he muttered, glaring at the peaceful light that streamed from the bright, clean windows. The more he pondered over the change a few short months had wrought, the more savage he became, until finally in a sudden burst of rage he snatched up a half-brick that lay in the gutter, and hurling it through the window, turned and fled.

Two hours later he again visited the place, and found the window patched with brown paper, the light still burning, and the missionary talking with a poor, half-drunken sailor, who, drugged and robbed, had wandered in there for shelter.

After a careful survey of the room, from the outside, "Big Tom" skulked off around the

corner, up Bruges Street toward the brewery.
He knew the ground pretty well, and had in
his less wrathful cogitation evolved a plan that
he thought would be successful in at least putting a check on the aggressive Christian work
of the Mission.

Between the rear of the Mission building and
the side of the brewery, ran a narrow alley
that had been roofed over and let to a man
who sold wood in small bundles, and coal by
the basket. This place was piled high with
packages of kindling, and was in the condition
that "Big Tom" desired to carry out his plan.

Cautiously he tried the door that he had so often
entered to collect rent from the humble tenant.
None knew better than he how it was fastened,
and he had no difficulty in forcing it open,
although it made no little noise, which, however,
blended with the many noises of the windy
night, and brought him in no danger of detec-
tion. After effecting an entrance he disappeared
within for a few moments, and when he reappeared, it was only to shut the door hastily, to
pull his slouch hat further over his eyes, and
keeping close in the shadow of the brewery, to
hurry off until the great city and the night
had swallowed him up.

Five minutes after the revengeful rum-seller

had disappeared, there came a slight muffled report that sounded to those who heard it like
the slamming of some extra, heavy door, and
then all was quiet. The officer whose duty
it was to patrol Biuges Street had stepped
into a convenient saloon, and with a mug of
beer before him, sat listening to the patter of
the big drops of rain that were now beginning
to fall in earnest. He was "solid" with the
beer men in that vicinity, and so felt very secure, and was fully as well content to draw his
pay for this sort of work as for tramping up
and down in the cold, swinging his club, and
keeping his eye out for possible wrong-doers.

Following the report in the kindling-shop,
there had been a sound of falling wood, and
later, the crackling of flames, — sounds that had
"Big Tom" heard, would have assured him that
his plan of vengeance was in a fair way to be
successful.

XVI.

An Evening at the Battery.

CONLON, almost as angry as "Big Tom," but without his intention for securing revenge by the commission of crime, had separated from him, disgusted with him and with the world in general. He felt as if there was no place in which he could pursue his business unmolested by missionaries and his conscience; for the words of Thomas' prayer rose still fresh in his memory, nor could he shake off the impression they had produced. While in this state of mind he had looked at several saloons with a view to buying, but none suited, and at last the real-estate agent, out of all patience, declared he could spend no more time on so unprofitable a customer, and that he might thereafter look up his own chances.

Determined at length to take any place that offered, he began to read the advertisements in the daily papers, with but little relish, however, until the need of a "strong, active man, well acquainted with box machinery," caught his eye. Naturally ingenious, and a machinist by trade, the old longing came over him to be among the whirling wheels again, and he decided to apply for the place. It was in Harlem, he found, but that made no difference to him, and in the course of an hour he stood in the office of the Van Alstyne Manufacturing Co., answering the questions of the foreman of the machine-room, with a half-defiant air that was in no way helpful to him.

"Your name is ——," began the foreman, and waited for the other to finish, but Conlon indifferently waited also, with an expression on his face that said plainly: "If you wish to know, ask."

"What is your name?" said the questioner, sharply.

"John Conlon."

"Where are you now employed?"

"Nowhere."

"What were you doing when you quit work?" said the foreman, a trifle impatiently.

"Running one of the toughest bar-rooms in New York," was the cool answer.

"If that is where you learned your trade as a machinist, we do not want you," said the foreman.

"Hold on a bit, young man. I never said that was where I learned my trade, and while I know you won't hire me 'cause I ain't humble enough, I want you to understand that when I say I understand machine-work, it's true. Jest you go down to Liebert's Machine Shop, and ask who was the only person that drew two men's pay for two years, and they'll tell you it was John Conlon. Understand machinery? Why, I could build all you've got here out of raw material while you were smoothing a casting."

During this conversation Miss Pitcairn had been listening with interest, and she now came forward, saying decisively,—

"Mr. Smith, you had better engage this man, I think, as our machinery must have the best of care. It need not weigh against him that he owned a saloon, for he has given it up, and turning to a better business is to his credit."

"I had to vacate because my lease expired," explained Conlon, sturdily, but with a softened look at the fair woman who had taken his part, even though he did not care a whit for the position.

The next day he took his place, and seemed at once consumed by a feverish activity. The slow ways that the ordinary workmen indulged

in, made him frantic with impatience, and his
contempt for danger and weariness soon gave
him a place as leader, ˜ especially among the
younger men.

The foreman watched the growing popularity
of the new machinist with much distrust, and
kept Miss Pitcairn well informed regarding his
movements; but while she disapproved much
that he did, it seemed best not to scan his
actions too carefully, until the strength of his
recklessness should wear itself out.

It was not alone in work that he was feverish
and impatient, for his bad habits seemed to keep
pace with his industry, and while he was never
unfit for duty, nor in any way offensive during
working hours, yet it was known that he was
drinking more than ever before, and chewed a
plug of tobacco a day. In speech, the old, quiet
way had long since departed, and he had grown
loud-voiced and profane.

His former friends avoided him to an extent,
when they discovered how he had altered; for,
evil though they were, there was a semblance
of sanity in their ill-doing, while Conlon seemed
to be insane on every thing. The truth was,
the man had been deeply stirred by the missionary's appeal, and, do what he would, could
not shake off the effect of his words. He did

try, — every oath, every carousal, each reckless deed, each day of frantic work, was an appeal to forgetfulness; and yet, when he retired late at night, or often early in the morning, the words of the prayer were with him, and the Spirit of God was striving with the hardness of the awakened heart.

His skill and strength, even if he did drink and was profane, procured him advancement among a class of men who were opposed to doing more than they could help in the way of work. When he hurt his back by over-lifting, instead of discharging him to make room for a better man, he was made assistant engineer, and within a month, the burly engineer accepting a position in the West, he had full charge of the great engine, and the care of all the machinery in the mill.

One evening, as he was passing the "Wedge," he noticed the usual crowd in the "open lot," saw a preacher in the little wooden pulpit, and out of sheer curiosity he drew near and listened, with a look of angry scorn in his eyes. Once or twice he started to go away, with a touch of his old impatience of movement, but for some reason remained.

When at length he did leave the Common, it was not to spend the night in carousing as he had

planned, but to wander off away from his companions to a part of the city that they never
frequented. Fiercer than ever burned the fever
in his veins, more acute was the pain of the
unrest in his heart, and half-delirious, he strode
along till he reached Broadway, when he turned
and hurried up-town. Here and there the
bright lights of the liquor palaces called him
in, but he was not in the mood for drinking,
and did no more than cast an occasional glance
at their alluring splendor. Where Broadway and
Sixth Avenue cross each other, he halted and
leaned against the stair-case that runs up to
the elevated railroad. As he stood vaguely
watching the uninterrupted stream of passengers,
ascending and descending, he caught a bit of
conversation that came into his heart like a
sudden blessing. Two gentlemen were coming
down the stairs, hearty, jolly, and loud-voiced.
Said one, —

"Helping some one else is the secret of
happiness."

"I believe you," said his friend.

Conlon started forward to hear more, but they
carried that topic no further, and he was disappointed. Yet, had he not heard the whole
story? Helping others? What was there difficult about that? He determined at least to

give the idea a trial, and see if it would ease the pain in his troublesome heart.

He had not long to wait for an opportunity to be of use to one who surely stood in need of assistance; for toward him, struggling slowly through the crowd, came a little girl, bare-headed, bare-footed, crying softly to herself, and carrying a heavy basket.

"Here, sis, let me help you carry it,'" said Conlon, kindly.

"You git away, or I'll holler," was the sus-picious response.

"Don't let him touch it, sissy, he means to steal it," cautioned a fat woman, stopping to bestow a look of horror on the astounded man.

"Have him arrested. Somebody call a police-man. It's a shame that these great, strong men should try to rob children," exclaimed an ex-citable old man, in a voice that attracted sev-eral loungers.

Seeing that a crowd was forming, and that every soul in it would testify against him, Con-lon, elbowing his way out, started down Sixth Avenue, the fat woman and the old man follow-ing him a little way, accompanied by a part of the crowd, all breathing vengeance.

After this repulse, more bitter than ever, he continued his half-desperate walk, crossing into

Broadway again, and this time going down town. The happiness that he had, for the moment, hoped to find in assisting another had not come, and too proud to try again, he moved on with his head down, his lips tightly closed, and his mind in a ferment of conflicting emotions. At length, after a walk that wearied even his toughened muscles, he found himself down at the Battery, facing the waters of the harbor. Certainly he could go no farther in that direction, and throwing himself upon a settee, he looked across at the twinkling lights of Staten Island.

Just in front of him rose the dark mass of the Bartholdi statue, its brilliant torch all aglow, —a little farther off shone bright and clear the light on Governor's Island, while far away in the Narrows, the fire and sparks from a puffing tug showed the noble outlines of a great ship slowly swinging into port. Close at hand, passing and repassing, were schooners, lighters, tugs, and an occasional ferry-boat of the "Annex," that sent great waves splashing against the sea-wall at his feet.

Even in the contemplation of this beautiful scene there was no enjoyment to him, nor did the cool breeze from the water abate the fever that raged within. At length he stepped to a convenient lamp, and drawing a worn piece of paper from his pocket, unfolded it and read, — "He is Thy child. Bring him into Thy peace." Again and again he conned it over, and finally went back to the bench, and kneeling on the ground, prayed, —

"O God, for Christ's sake forgive my sins." That was all he could say, but it was enough, for he asked it, believing that it could and would be done. The struggle was over. The stubborn heart that had been so long in rebellion, although knowing the way of life, was broken, — and a full surrender was made. And O! the instant, abundant peace that came as a balm into the sin-torn heart, soothing, healing, sanctifying. How it cooled the brain, and calmed the throbbing pulse! How, as with a cleansing flood, it swept away the poison of sin and left the whole man free and sweet and clean!

"Are you ill, sir?" said a hesitating voice, as a light hand touched him on the shoulder.

Conlon rose, his face full of joy, and confronted the speaker, who was slight and girlish in figure, but whose face and head were so muffled in a shawl as to make it impossible to tell whether she was young or old.

"No, Miss, I 'm all right," began Conlon, but at the sound of his voice the woman uttered a smothered exclamation that was full of horror and pain, and turning, fled swiftly away.

"I guess she must know me as I was. It'll take a long time to live down my record, but with God's help I'll try it," said he sadly, yet with a heart full of the strange, sweet peace that comes from sin forgiven.

"Come, come, this is no place to loaf," said a harsh voice of an officer, who had come up unobserved.

Conlon turned with such a happy, peaceful look, that the policeman was puzzled, and said, hesitatingly, —

"I thought you were asleep; what are you doing down here at this time of night?"

"Well," said Conlon, simply, "I came down here a wretched rum-seller, and found the Lord Jesus."

"Bless ye, my brother!" exclaimed the officer, seizing his hand. "You've found the best friend ever a man had. Get a good grip on Him, and don't let Him go, for He is able to keep ye, even here in this wicked city of York."

The happy man walked with the sympathetic officer to the end of his beat, which was the foot of the Battery station of the Elevated, and with a warm hand-shake they parted; the one to take the train up-town, the other to spend

the night in pacing the grounds of the little
waterside park.

Conlon was not a man to hide his light under
a bushel, and it was but natural, although a great
surprise to his mates when he appeared at the
next meeting on the Gospel Common, and told
just how he had found the Saviour. When first
he began to speak, his friends, and even the
missionary, had believed that there was to be
some reckless harangue that would inaugurate
disorder, but his earnest bearing and words soon
undeceived them, while his simple faith and
happiness brought tears to many eyes.

At the factory the next morning the men
made excuses to run into the fire-room or the
engine-room many times, just to get a look at
the new convert, but the fact that he was still
as muscular as of yore kept them from troubling
him with scornful questions, for they did not
feel at all sure that he was not as ready to
defend his new faith by a "shoulder blow," as
he had been to stand up for his various errors
in times past.

For several days all went well. Conlon attended to his work as faithfully as ever, but in
a quiet peaceful way that amazed the lookers
on. Instinctively the convert felt that for the
present the most powerful sermon he could

preach to the boys, would be a silent one, — a
sermon full of deeds, rather than words. So he
worked on, and neither chewed, drank, nor
swore. A state of affairs, however, when he
was to have no outside temptation brought to
bear upon him, that could not long continue.

The turbulent element, and it existed even in
the Harlem mill, soon found that he was not
subject to the old-time temper fits; and once
assured of this, the fear that he might resent
any interference with his new belief by a resort
to violence left their minds, and they began to
throw little temptations in his way. Nothing
was easier or apparently more natural than to
tell one another in his hearing of the frolics
that they were enjoying, — doing their best to
lay special stress on the parts that they knew
appealed to his weakest points, and doing all
this when the foreman's back was turned. Very
closely was he watched as these tales were
told, and it was with wicked glee that several
noted the fact that he had, on one or two occasions, turned pale and shut his lips with an
expression that denoted pain.

"He can't hold out much longer," said one
of his tormentors. "I know by his looks that
he is just burning up for need of a good drink,
and a chaw of terbacker would be ez sweet ez

honey to him. I bet five dollars I can fetch him within the week!"

The wager was accepted, and the man made his preparations to carry out his plan. He chose the time when Conlon was "working" the engine, just before starting up. As it was situated some little distance from the boiler, there was considerable "condensation" formed, much of which by awkward piping was run through the cylinder. This made it incumbent on the engineer to work it out carefully before the great machine was fully under way, lest, a sufficient amount of water getting between the piston-head and the cylinder-head, the latter be blown out.

Conlon knew the danger of this well enough, and had always been especially careful, allowing nothing to interrupt him when starting up. He was in the midst of this work when the tempter came up behind him, and thrust a plug of tobacco which had been soaked in whiskey in his face, almost resting it on his lips, as he said,—

"Have a chaw of a new kind, old boy; it's the best I ever struck. Bite off a crumb."

The smell of the weed, of which he had been so passionately fond, coupled with the fumes of the liquor, almost unnerved Conlon; but with real grit, and an agonized prayer for help, he

shut his teeth hard together and kept at his
work. How gladly would he have given ten
years of his life for one "chew" of the weed!
But he had heartily prayed for help, and help
came, as it always has, and always will, and
even with the plug held close against his lips,
and its tempting fumes in his nostrils, he received strength to hold out. Then the hand
was removed, and the man stepped round so
that he almost faced Conlon, saying, —

"Won't you try it, old fellow?"

"No," was the steady reply.

"Do you want me tell you *why* you won't
take it?" continued his tormentor, assuming a
most insulting attitude, and raising his voice so
that the men who had gathered from the fire-
room could hear every word.

There was no reply.

"I'll tell you why. You are a coward; you
don't dare take a chaw of terbacker for fear
Miss' Pitcairn will smell it in yer breath. She
talks about us fellows being the slaves of rum,
an' terbacker, an' the like, but I say you are
her slave, and the more fool are you."

Conlon had by this time got his engine running, so that there was no longer need of working it, and he stood up straight and looked
over the crowd that had gathered.

"Boys," said he, "Joe calls me a coward, — a slave Have any of you ever known me to take a dare, or to be in any way afraid of any· thing ?"

"No."

"Well, now, I will tell you of one thing that I am afraid of. Joe is right. I am afraid of taking a chaw of terbacker. I am afraid of doing any thing that will lead me back to the old life. I am happy now, boys, and I used to be wretched. I believe my sins, and the Lord only knows how black they were, have been forgiven. The blood of Jesus Christ has cleansed me from sin, and now I am his servant. O, boys," — the speaker's voice broke, and there was an answering sob in at least one brawny throat. "Why can't we all stop killing ourselves and doing wrong, and turn round and do what is right ? I 've tried both ways, and I declare to you that I never knew what happiness was until this week. I 've dipped into all sorts of sin, God forgive me, and tried every thing that is called fun, and to-day, if I had all of Vanderbilt's money offered me to go again into the old life, I would say no. Boys, do n't shut yer hearts to such a chance for happiness as this, without trying it. Jesus Christ died to save is all. He knows that we

are sick of ourselves, that even when in drink
and trying our best to have a good time, we
are not satisfied. O, boys, let Him have a
chance."

The crowd dispersed slowly, and Joe, after a
hard struggle with himself, came up and said
huskily, —

"Con, I'm just in need of what you describe. I didn't honestly think it could be
found in this world. I know you well enough,
old man, to be sure that you wouldn't have
any make-believe about this, and although I'm
an ignorant feller about pious things, I'm
willing to learn about them if you'll teach me,
and I shouldn't wonder if some of the rest of
the gang would come in on the same deal if it
pans out well."

There was no mistaking the earnestness of
the speaker, and Conlon thanked the Lord that
the worst one among his tormentors had been
vanquished and brought to the foot of the
cross. With more than brotherly love he welcomed him, and though but a novice himself,
was able to point him to the Saviour, and ere
long Joe Sayles was rejoicing in hope, and
eager to tell the glad news of salvation.

News of the movement among the men in
her factory was soon brought to Miss Pitcairn.

and although they were but few in number, as compared with the girls, she felt that her prayers were answered by their conversion, and that even if the Van Alstyne Manufacturing Co. proved a financial failure, the saving of souls like Conlon's and Sayles', was positive success.

XVII.

A Neglected Corner.

WHILE unhappy Tom Betteredge was planning to burn the "Corner house" and
break up the Mission, his niece Lucy was pro-
jecting a scheme that should help build it up.
Naturally a precocious child, her life at the
Governor's developed her powers very rapidly, and
she drank in knowledge as a sponge absorbs
water, — indeed, so fast did she learn, that her
governess was afraid that she would overdo and
injure herself, which fear might have been rea-
sonable were it not apparent that the little girl
was thriving physically as well as intellectually.
When first she had appeared at her present
home she was thin and pinched, to a degree
that it made one's heart ache to look at her,
— but within three months she had gained flesh,
color, and shape, and was now quite pretty
Her manners, too, were wonderfully improved;
she could enter a room gracefully, and was as
much at home at a dinner of several courses

as she had formerly been when she had dined on a crust. Very proud was she of the fact that she had improved since she came under the tuition of her governess, and was so punctilious about what minor points of etiquette she knew, her actions filled the genial master of the house with constant food for mirth.

The ruling passion of this queer bit of humanity was to be exactly like Miss Belle, and child-like, her impatience to reach this climax at once, was always manifest.

Of the many callers at the home of her guardian, she saw but few; as yet those who did notice the child thought her a relative, — greatly to her delight. Even Stanley Armitage, on the occasion of one of his calls, had met her in the hall and stopped with his fascinating smile to win her friendship. In this, however, he was unsuccessful, for the child suddenly grew very dignified and backed off, her large eyes full of reserve.

"Don't you like Mr. Armitage, Lucy?" inquired Belle, afterward recalling the scene.

"I don't think I do. He is so sure. It isn't a proper thing for a gentleman to be so sure that young ladies will like him," was the wise response.

This dignity on the part of the child was a

source of much enjoyment to the Governor, but sometimes led the little one into acts she had better have put off until her years equalled her aspirations.

Aside from Belle the usual sharer of her confidences was Mr. Chick, who, as a relative, was often present and always welcome at the gubernatorial mansion. It was to this good-humored little man that Lucy developed a plan that she had for mission work, that should rival Miss Pitcairn's. The objective point was the "Wedge," and the class of persons with whom she meant to labor, were some whom she believed had been sadly neglected.

She had broached her plan in this manner. Mr. Chick had been relating for the hundredth time his adventure in "Pie Alley," and the child had been listening eagerly, calling the various newsboys by name, and explaining how many times she had been to the same place for food, when she suddenly broke in with the astounding proposition, —

"Say, Mr. Hen, I beg pardon, I mean Mr. Chick, why can't you and I start a mission among the newsboys?"

"O, but they would n't come into any mission. Mr. Thomas has tried it, and they just would n't," said he, in dismay.

"They would come for me," replied Lucy, stoutly. "Don't you s'pose if I told Teddy Timmins to go any where he would go? Ain't I give him — I mean *haven't* I give him — I mean haven't I *given* him — cold beans when he was starving? And there's Bobby Ames, and Franz Dinkelspeil and his sister, and lots more that I know better than I do you, — come? I guess they would be absolutely enchanted to come."

"Well, what can we do when we get them into a mission?" was the dubious query.

"In the first place we will give them a good nice 'spread.' Plenty of oyster stew, and pie, and milk, — I guess ——"

"Where is the money coming from for this feast?" asked Mr. Chick.

"From our pocket-books. What we own is only held in trust to be used for the good of others. We are only stewarts," was the pious reply.

"O, I didn't know but that we were Vanderbilts," said her companion.

"No, we are only stewarts, the minister said so last Sunday, and it is our privilege to assist in this — in this ——"

"Infelicitous pandemonium," supplied Mr. Chick.

"Is that what it is?" asked Lucy, suspiciously.

"That's what I should name it."

"All right, to assist in this — infelicitous pandemonium," continued the little girl. "Now I
have got twenty dollars saved up, and you ought
to have some money, so do n't you see we could
get Mrs. Thomas to let us have the front room
right over the Mission? It is empty now, and
we could borrow some tables and chairs from
down stairs, and have things fine for the boys."

"How are you going to invite them?"

"I guess the best way would be to call Teddy
Timmins up here, and get him to tell the rest, —
or stop, I 'll write a note to each of them."

Thus it happened that Mr. Chick was in-
veigled into a plan that was, to his mind, of
doubtful propriety; and yet as he had given his
word not to tell of it to any one, it was impossible for him to get help, either from Belle
or her parents. He had argued with Lucy as
to the advisability of admitting Miss Pitcairn to
this plan, but on this point the child was firm.

"No, indeed," she said, "she feels perfectly
capable of persecuting her religious endeavors,
and so do I. When I am really successful I
will march up before the Governor and the rest,
with a lot of poor little boys and girls, and say,
'Here am I, and the children that thou hast
given me.'"

Such argument was more than Mr. Chick could

stand, so he submitted with what grace he could muster. At the command of this precocious juvenile, he enticed Teddy Timmins up to the back gate, where he recognized Lucy in great amaze, and heard the story of her new home. When he knew that she was to furnish him and his companions with a "pie spread," his delight manifested itself in a sudden hand-spring that the little girl watched with great complacency. He promised to come the next day and get the notes that had been more than the young missionary could get ready at such short notice, even with Mr. Chick's help.

One part of this strange project that did not displease Mr. Chick, was the manner in which Mrs. Thomas received the news. He had a profound respect for the opinions of this lady, who was doing such a good work among the people at the "Wedge," and he knew her to be thoroughly practical in all that she did or said. Her approval of Lucy's idea was emphatic, and as she promised to be near by to see that every thing was ready, as well as to engage a cook to make the oyster stew, he felt there was a chance for the supper to be a success. The lady's eyes twinkled, as she had been told that it was Lucy's own idea, and that she was so particular that Miss Pitcairn should not be told of it.

"I am not sure that I blame her," she exclaimed. "No one asks her advice about the management of affairs down here, and the little one feels that having lived here she knows some of the needs of the place. Perhaps she can teach the rest of us a lesson. Let her go ahead. I would say God bless the effort of a child, just as soon as I would of a grown person."

The preparations went on, the day came round, and, obedient to request, Mrs. Thomas called at the Governor's and received permission to take Lucy to a meeting.

At first it was not deemed advisable by Mrs. Pitcairn, — Belle being away for the evening; but she was so eager to go, and the missionary pleaded so earnestly, that consent was finally obtained.

The ride to the "Wedge" was without event, and on their arrival they found a motley crowd of boys and girls about the door, who drew back abashed as the nicely dressed child, accompanied by the missionary, appeared among them. But she did not give them time to be frightened, for she said, cheerily, —

"Hullo, Teddy, — hullo, Sally, — why, here's Jimmy Cluts. Throw away that stub, you silly boy, — hullo, Franz, how is the paper trade?

Remember when I gave you some to start with ? "

This off-hand and eminently natural way of greeting her former companions was what was needed to make them at ease, and was responded to by a chorus of hullos and reminiscent sentences that came in a perfect jumble of words and phrases.

Admission to the room was secured by invitation notes instead of tickets, yet this rule was by no means arbitrary, for there were many wistful faces outside the door that were familiar to Lucy, and all were admitted until there was room for no more. Once seated before the steaming stews, how the little fists carried great spoonfuls to the ready mouths ! When before had any of these youngsters enjoyed a feast like this ?—a genuine oyster stew with crackers by the half-bushel.

After the keen edge of their appetite was taken off, came a piece of pie for each, and a glass of milk. What a royal good time the little people had, and how the look of contentment that should always accompany the hearty meal of childhood, spread over the sharp, restless faces !

Lucy sat down and ate with the rest, and more than one by stealthy sidewise look saw how she crumbled her crackers into the stew, noticed that she did not gulp or smack, and in a half-awkward manner imitated her. When it came to the pie, however, she was the only one who found use for a fork. The rest were perfectly satisfied with the ancient way in vogue before forks were made.

During the meal there were a few accidents, some slopping, and an embryo fight between two boys who had a little falling out; but the fat cook wiped up the little pools of stew that stood on the table, and Mrs. Thomas in her smiling way settled the dispute before the boys actually came to blows.

After all had been satisfied and the dishes were removed, they had a sing. The tunes were not all of a religious character, although " Hold the Fort " went well, and " America " was known to a few. Then Mrs. Thomas read them a story that was at once simple and interesting, and Mr. Chick recited a funny poem that made them all laugh. The next thing on the programme was something that neither Mrs. Thomas nor Mr. Chick was at all sure would be wise. It was nothing more or less than Lucy's speech.

" Boys and girls," she began, " you all know me, do n't you ? "

"Yes," came in a chorus, sudden and startling.

"An' you all remember how I used to be hungry, and barefoot, and ragged?"

"Yes," came again with extra vim, accompanied by a few "you bet we do's."

"An' how I used to sell papers sometimes, even if the big boys did lick me, an' how Mrs. Tarpy used to cuff me when I went by her door?"

"Say, I hit old Tarpy in the jaw with a rotten tummatus," called out a black-eyed urchin, and in an instant the whole alert crowd was in a roar of laughter.

Lucy stood perfectly quiet until the room was still, and then said, —

"Any of you boys mustn't talk while I am speaking. It isn't polite.

"Now, as I was saying, I was just the same as the rest of you, when Miss Pitcairn found out that this house belonged to me, and that my folks had left me some money. So I had to go away to learn about things that I didn't know; but I haven't forgotten you boys and girls, and I don't want you to forget me. Next Sunday I am coming down here with some books, and want you all to meet me in this room at three o'clock. Will you come?"

"Yes," came in full chorus.

"Thank you, that's all," said Lucy, stepping down from the chair on which she had been standing, and slipping up 'to the side of Mrs. Thomas with her first appearance of shyness.

There was a tendency among the little Arabs to stand around and stare at their former play-mate, and some of the girls were greatly exercised about the texture of her dress, and the beauty of a little breast-pin she wore ; but the kindly cook, seeing that all was over, began to pilot them to the door, and soon all were outside.

"Was every thing *recherché*?" inquired Lucy quickly, when the last guest had disappeared.

"Extremely," replied Mr. Chick, venturing a wink at Mrs. Thomas, whose eyes were dancing with fun. "I do not see how any thing could be more so."

"I'm so glad ; such a work revolves great responsibilities, but I guess we shall be able to do them good," said Lucy.

"Dear heart, I guess so, too," said the missionary, kissing her good-night, and consigning her to the care of ubiquitous Mr. Chick.

The next day after her lessons were ended, Lucy sought out Miss Pitcairn, and hung round with wistful expression, until the young lady noticing it, said, —

"Lucy, dear, if you were n't such a big girl, I should ask you to come and sit on my knee, and tell me what you have been doing."

"I suppose it would be devisable to acquaint you with my new enterprise," said the child carefully, choosing the largest words in her vocabulary.

Mrs. Pitcairn, sitting in the recessed window of the next room, heard the reply, and in her low, sweet voice, said, —

"Come in here, dears, and let me also know what the new enterprise is."

So they went in, and Lucy took her place on the broad arm of the easy chair, a place of honor which she never assumed, except when expressly invited to do so, and Belle sat down on an ottoman at her mother's feet. Then the child with great fervor told the whole of the tale of the supper for the newsboys and girls of the East Side, not neglecting her speech, nor one iota of the scenes that would be of interest. As she finished, Mrs. Pitcairn placed her beautiful hand over the childish fingers with a very loving touch, saying, —

"I am so glad that our little Lucy is not growing up selfish. Do what you can, dear, for these children, and remember that the wisest of us can not accomplish any thing without help from above. Do not forget to pray for them, as if they were your own brothers and sisters."

As for Belle, she kissed the little missionary, and gave her a hearty embrace, accompanied by a look that spoke volumes of praise for the genuine, unselfish effort.

An hour later Belle, in the little hexagonal room that commanded so fine a view of the avenue, was sitting, and watching, and thinking. Of late her pondering had been chiefly upon the welfare of her many *protegées*; yet with all her thought she resolutely put aside all worry; nay, she determined to be happy whether or no her plans were successful. That was why she was sitting doing nothing, when she felt that letters should be written, and the work of a month done in a day. At first for one so enthusiastic, and possessed of· so much executive ability, this self-repression had been irksome; but· she had happily hit upon the expedient of planning ahead each day's work, and so systematizing it that it would move smoothly and allow time for recreation, and even for quiet, restful meditation.

As she pondered, her eye caught a tiny dog that, down in the street among the stately horses, was barking, and jumping, and having a glorious time. He was evidently a cur of low

degree, who playing the truant from some humble back yard, determined to frolic with the
best in the city. From his neck dangled a rope,
its frayed end covered with mud, constantly
getting under his feet, and tripping him up.
As the carriages rolled past more than one
dignified coachman cut at him with his whip,
sometimes eliciting a yelp from the happy cur,
but more often missing him altogether. Even
when hit the pain was soon forgotten, and he
was as ready as ever to bark at the next carriage, or to attempt the reckless feat of seizing
the flashing wheel spokes. This last seemed
such exciting fun that he could not desist from
it, and many a narrow escape did he have as
he thrust his snub nose so close to the whirling
wheels.

Among the carriages were many light vehicles
drawn by pretty pairs, hitched tandem or abreast,
belonging to the bachelor class. Professor Buckingham's was numbered among them, and his
athletic figure, erect as if on dress parade, drew
many an admiring look. There was another,
however, on whom many looked with greater
admiration, not because he was any finer looking, perhaps, but because of his great wealth,
and that was Stanley Armitage. Mounted on a
powerful black horse, of whom in spite of re-

bellious eye and fretful step he was absolute
master, he made a fine appearance, and who
shall say he was not aware of it?

The Professor was not self-conscious on this
particular afternoon, for he was mentally conversing with one who had of late been occupy-
ing a considerable portion of his thought. He
was not a man easily influenced by feminine
charms, although in his way something of a society man; yet there had been a something in
Miss Pitcairn's manner of speaking, a depth in
her eyes, a strength in her manner, that had
more than riveted his attention,—it had made him
bow in instinctive homage. His acquaintance
with her was not a recent one, for the two families had been for years on terms of intimacy;
but in the past, while he acknowledged the young
lady, beauty and accomplishments, there had
been lacking the broad charity that is the chief
glory of the perfect woman. Now it had come.
Suddenly slipping from girlhood into womanhood, fair, talented, beloved by all, this crown
had been laid on her brow, and the Professor
in his day-dream even while driving up the avenue saw her not in the window looking down
upon him, but saw her in his mind's eye, a
vision of beauty.

As he drove on, turning out mechanically for

those whom he encountered, the vagrant dog attacked first his horses, and then snapped frantically at the slender wheels. The spokes were flashing faster than he knew, for, poor fellow, the fore wheel caught the rope, and before he could free himself the hind wheel passed over him, leaving him writhing on the pavement, while the Professor, immersed in happy dreams, drove away ignorant of the catastrophe.

The little creature lay in agony, and Belle, full of sympathy, was about to hurry out to its aid, when Armitage, who had been coming from the opposite direction, sprang from his horse and throwing the bridle over his arm, stooped over the muddy little heap. The rope had knotted itself round the fore-leg, and he knelt right in the dust and cut it carefully away. As he did so the dog licked his hand and tried to get up, but fell back moaning. A moment later, just as two gorgeous footmen had been despatched to his assistance, by a wildly horrified dowager whose carriage had been near at the time of the accident, Armitage rose and mounting his horse, the dog in his arms, rode away. He did not make a fine spectacle, with his riding-jacket smeared with mud, and the unkempt dog across his saddle, except to one pair of eyes, and it was for that pair that he did the deed.

Miss Pitcairn had seen it all, and the young man with his keen self-control had appeared un-conscious that he was any where near the Governor's mansion, or, indeed, that he was any where but in a country road with no one in sight; and skillful actor that he was, the impression that he desired had been produced. When he reached home he gave the dog in care of his hostler, with the charge that he have the best treatment possible. He considered him a valuable piece of property, for would he not be to Miss Pitcairn a reminder of the brutality of one ad-mirer, and the remarkable tender-heartedness of another?

The week after this episode Mrs. Armitage sat in the same room from which Belle had seen it, and both of the lovely women were looking again upon the passing carriages.

As before, the Professor drove by, and Mrs. Armitage, seeing him, bent her pretty brows into an indignant frown, exclaimed, —

"The brute!"

"Who, dear?" said Belle, in surprise.

"That cold Professor Buckingham. I always supposed that any *man* would feel badly over the sufferings of an animal, but he is perfectly heartless."

"Why, what do you mean?"

"Last Tuesday I went over to my cousin's and found him nursing a dog that was about the most forlorn specimen I have ever seen, yet it seemed to think the world of Stan. The creature had a broken leg, and was suffering terribly, and would allow no one to touch him but Stanley. I asked him how it happened, and he answered as savagely as possible that it did n't happen, — that it was done purposely; and that was all he would say, but I could see that he was dreadfully angry. I supposed one of the hostlers had done it in a fit of brutality, and as he would n't talk I went home again."

The lady paused and looked out of the window, interested, for the moment, in a passing "tally-ho."

"Go on, dear," said Belle, in a low voice.

"The next day Mrs. Van Brunt called and described the whole scene to me. It seems that she was driving down the avenue and saw Professor Buckingham coming, his head in the air with that cold reserve that I fancy he prides himself on. As he came opposite her a little dog sprang at his team and snapped at the wheels, just in play, and that cold-blooded creature drove calmly over him and left him with a broken leg. Stanley came along just then and took him home."

"It was very shocking, I saw it all," said Belle. "I am sure the Professor did not intend to hurt the dog, but I do n't see how he could drive away and leave it suffering. I was so glad that Mr. Armitage came along then, and took pity on the poor little creature. It was a very manly act, and I was proud that I knew him."

"His heart is as tender as a woman's," said Mrs. Armitage, with a gratified look.

XVIII.

Mr. Diffenhoffer's Lease.

BIG TOM had set his fire, where, according to his belief, there could be no doubt of its destroying the hated Faith Mission, and thus affording him a measure of revenge for his many fancied wrongs. When the flames first began to curl through the pile of "bundle-wood," that comprised the stock in trade of the humble fuel merchant, it did indeed seem as if the wooden building known as the Betteredge house was the only one in danger, and yet, in God's Providence, it so happened that this was far from being the case. The single fact, overlooked by the incendiary, that changed the aspect of affairs so materially, was that in the brick wall of the brewery was a window. It was not apparent to the casual observer, for in papering the wall, the wood-dealer had covered it over, yet there it was, the lower sill flush with the floor, the upper sash reaching almost to the roof of the shanty.

When, therefore, the pile of kindling had got fairly started, it began to topple and finally fell with a crash against the hidden window, and breaking through, precipitated a mass of firebrands into the basement of the brewery. Thus in an instant the whole aspect of affairs was completely changed, — the most of the fire was in the brewery, for what remained in the kindling shop burned weaker and weaker until all that remained of it was a few smouldering brands.

The heap that had fallen through the window fared almost the same and would doubtless have burned itself out without harm, had not a portion of it come in contact with a small pile of hay thrown there for the team horses. This it ignited and consumed, and then began again to die out. When little was left but a heap of ashes, hiding a few glowing coals, a single slender tongue of flame reaching out caught at a wisp that lay farther along the floor, and from this to another, flashing up for an instant and then dying out, it crept nearly the length of the room to the foot of a small elevator made of dry pine sheathing, and there it paused and settled.

With a soft, caressing movement it licked the smooth face of the boards, creeping from the front round to the back, stealthy, cat-like, feeling for a spot where it might catch a death-hold. At length its seeking was successful, for on the farther side was a wide crack, and here the flame entered, and catching on the dry pine shelves, feeding on the pitchy knots, it at length, growing strong and bold, climbed to the next story. Once there it spread out, and slipping under the office door, lapped the varnish off the chairlegs, consumed the straw matting, multiplied itself and climbed the shellacked partitions, spread into other rooms, reached the top story, and by the time a frightened watchman rang in an alarm it had so strong a hold on the whole building that nothing could save it.

The splendid fire department responded to the alarm on the instant, and as if by magic the streets were filled with engines, hose carriages, ladder trucks, and all the paraphernalia of the modern city fire.

When the ax-men sprang up to open a way for the hose, the strong gusts of wind almost swept them from the ladders, and entering the burning building flung the flames to and fro in waves that were irresistible in their fierce heat. Stream after stream was turned in the blazing mass from engine and water tower, but without apparent effect until the roof fell, and then they had all they could do to keep the neighboring tenements from sharing the fate of the brewery.

Among the excited spectators at this fire was a German, who waddled about the engines, whenever the police would permit, wringing his hands and offering unlimited beer if only his place might be saved. It was Dittenhoffer, the lessee of the brewery.

"Great himmel! vy don't you been at vork," he exclaimed to the chief engineer, who was standing watching with keen eye the progress of the flames. "Mein seven tousand bushels of malt vas in dere already. It vill get burned up all. Ach, I vas ruined! I vas ruined!"

Another in the crowd who stood apart with frightened stare, the perspiration gathering in great drops on his forehead, was "Big Tom." This was his work, but how it had miscarried! Dittenhoffer was his friend, and had "backed" him, resisting the aggressions of the temperance faction, and now he had been the means of ruining him. Was there ever such ill luck? As he glanced uneasily about, he saw the missionary standing near an engine, looking at the fire with a face so full of peace that he could not stand it, but with a curse fled the scene.

The news of the conflagration came to Belle in the morning paper, and it was without great sorrow that she announced it at the breakfast table. The Governor looked grave.

"I am afraid it will be a serious loss to Crittenden, unless he has lately insured the building, for he told me not more than a month ago that he was carrying but a light insurance on every thing."

"O, I hope not," said Belle, at once sobered. "But at all events he will not think of putting another brewery in its place, will he?"

"Here he comes up the walk; he can best answer that question," replied the Governor, who occupied a position that in the breakfast room gave him a view of a part of Fifth Avenue, and also of the street that ran by a side of his mansion. Coming so early in the day, it was in order to sit down to breakfast, which Mr. Crittenden did, saying over a cup of coffee, —

"Your friend's last argument is a clincher, Miss Belle. I am ready now to treat with your manufacturer."

"And you won't put up another brewery?" asked Belle, delightedly.

"No, I'm afraid it would burn down," said the other, with a roguish look.

"One moment, please," said the Governor. "What do you call the last argument?"

"Why, last night's fire!" said the gentlemen, jovially. "I told my wife when the messenger came to me that I had been expecting a real knock-down argument from some of Thomas' crowd."

At this juncture Mr. Crittenden suddenly paused, aware that he was confronted by a young lady whose flashing eyes were more terrifying than any thing he had recently expected.

"I — I beg your pardon," he stammered. "But no harm has been done. The property is more than covered. No one loses any thing, and I assure you I have nothing to say."

"Papa, will you excuse me," said Belle, very pale, as she swept from the room, leaving Mr. Crittenden overwhelmed with mortification.

"Well, I'm sure, what have I done now?" gasped the man, appalled by visions of domestic storms, should there be a break with the Governor's family.

"You have accused my daughter's friends of being the instigators of the brewery fire," said the Governor, with a calmness in which there was the least shade of contempt.

".But all is fair in war," said Mr. Crittenden, weakly, and at once aware of the enormity of, his offense. "I am sure Miss Belle must have known I was merely joking."

"Certainly," said the Governor, with the same icy blandness. "It was but a jest, — a poor one, of course; but only a joke, for no sane man could conceive of earnest Christians in any way countenancing the crime of incendiarism."

"Certainly not," assented Mr. Crittenden, wiping the perspiration from his brow.

"And as you are evidently in a hurry, I will take it upon myself to tender your profuse apologies, that the unfortunate joke should have been attempted," continued the gentleman.

"Thank you, thank you, I'm sure I fully appreciate your kindness," ejaculated the other, bowing himself out, and hurrying off in a fever of conflicting emotions, the most prominent of which was that he had hopelessly "put his foot in it," when he had called simply to say that he would now let the manufacturer have any sort of building that he might need.

"Papa, how could any one conceive so cruel a charge?" said Belle, her beautiful eyes full of tears as she met the Governor in the hall after the departure of the guest.

"My darling, only a man who would stoop to wrong doing himself would think of such a thing. Even he does not believe it now, I am assured. I am sorry he called, for he has made you unhappy."

To turn again to the scene of the fire. There remained of the brewery only a steaming, smoking mass of timbers, vats, barrels, and machinery. By degrees the heat died out of the smouldering beams, the warped and twisted iron, until it was possible for any who did not fear the contamination of the blackened wood to venture about in search of salvage. Many there were who availed themselves of this opportunity to get a stock of fire-wood, such as they had not possessed for many a long day. Almost all of the children in the vicinity of Bruges Street, who had homes of any kind, could be found here tearing off half-burned clapboards, and even combining their strength to secure planks and some of the smaller rafters. Their occupation during the week proclaimed itself on Sunday, for there were few in the Mission classes but had a suspicious line of grime under their eyes, or a darker-complexioned neck than cheek.

In one way their industry was a general advantage to the "Wedge"; the great unsightly heap was diminishing, and the time would soon come when there would not be left enough kindling for an ordinary bon-fire.

Mr. Dittenhoffer, after the fire had swept his

business away, appeared to be completely discouraged. He made no attempt either to induce his landlord to rebuild, or to transfer his interests to other fields. Most of his days were spent in walking up and down Bruges Street, smoking a long, German pipe, and gloomily watching the wood gatherers as they carried off the remains of his brewery.

It was during one of these walks that he encountered Mr. Crittenden, who had slipped over there from his office to have a look at the debris, and to plan for a new building.

"Good morning, Dittenhoffer!" ·

"Goot morning," was the gloomy response.

"I suppose you are anxious to have a new building put up here, that your business may go on, — as soon as the insurance is adjusted?"

"I don't dink I vill do any more peesiness already."

"What is the matter?"

"I vas most blayed oudt. De oder brewers has got mine beesness, and mine gustomers vas all gone," said the German, puffing sadly at his pipe.

"Well, but you have a lease of this place."

"Yes, and I vas going to give it oop to you already."

This suited the other so well that he proposed

that they go at once to the brewer's home and have that part of the business settled without further parley. On his way back, the good man in a moment of enthusiasm over the thought that he might thus gain a friend, imparted to Professor Buckingham, whom he met, the fact that the place was again in his hands, adding earnestly, —

"My next tenant shall be one whose business is clean and respectable, one that can be under the fear of the Lord,"

"I think you can find such a tenant in the person of the manufacturer of whom Miss Pitcairn spoke to you," remarked the Professor.

"Very well," replied he, somewhat surprised that the other knew of the affair. "Very well, I will put up a factory that shall be a model of its kind, and it shall be pushed right along, too, as soon as the papers are drawn.

"If you wish, I will bring the agent of the manufacturer down for an introduction at once, and have the affair arranged.

"I should be delighted, I am sure," was the answer, as he took his leave, his face suffused with gratified smiles.

That afternoon as Mr. Crittenden returned from lunch he found waiting for him in his outer office a powerfully built man of rough ap-

pearance, who introduced himself as the representative of a Liquor Dealers' Federation, whose
headquarters were on Van Alstyne Street.

"What can I do for you, sir?" asked the
church treasurer, in a tone of deep reproof that
such a man should presume to call upon him.

"Let me see you alone for ten minutes?" was
the gruff reply.

Mr. Crittenden, after a moment of thought,
motioned him to enter his private office, where
the stranger flung himself into an easy chair,
saying, directly, —

"I have come about Dittenhoffer's lease of
your place on Bruges Street."

"That lease was cancelled and destroyed this
morning," was the reply.

"I know all that, but what I want is a lease
of the land to erect a building that shall be
pretty near what the old brewery was, only
better."

"What is your offer?" inquired the other, dallying with temptation.

The man named a sum that made Mr. Crittenden's eyes sparkle with longing, but he said,
reluctantly, —

"You are too late, my word has been given
that a factory shall have the place."

"Well, sell us the land. We will give you

more than it is worth, twice over, just for the sake of defeating those total-abstinence fools that are spoiling the business in that section. Hark you, old man. It was through that Pitcairn faction that I was beaten out of the finest piece of property in the 'Wedge,' and I'm bound to have my revenge for it."

"Is not your name Betteredge?" was the interested query.

"That's just my name, and I can put a hundred thousand dollars of good, lively rum money into the fight, so you had better get what you can!"

"I can't sell the land, it belongs to my children," acknowledged the other.

"Well, grant a lease then. When that lease is signed and delivered, I will make you a present of a thousand dollars myself. Come, is it a bargain?"

"I shall be forever disgraced," groaned Mr. Crittenden, looking with hungry eyes at the roll of bills that the rum-seller held in his hand.

"O, hang the disgrace! Lie out of it. Swear that you were sick, and your son drew up the papers without knowing that you were opposed to the plan. Say what you please, that we tricked you, lied to you, any thing, but sign, and sign now!"

With trembling hand the tempted man took up a pen, when the office-boy announced, —

"Somebody to see you, sir!"

"It's Professor Buckingham and his friend!" gasped Mr. Crittenden. "You must not be seen here, — wait a minute, boy. Here, Betteredge, step into this room and stay until they leave, they wont be here long. Boy, where are you? tell the gentlemen to come in."

The burly guest was hurried very unwillingly into the cramped, closet-like room, and bowing and smiling, although with white lips and tembl'ng knees, Mr. Crittenden received his callers.

XIX.

Satan's Record Examined.

BUZZ — BUZZ — BUZZ went the busy throng of scholars at the Faith Mission, in that curious, undulating monotone that betokens forgetfulness of self and interest in some common topic. To many, in fact to most, who entered this place to study the Sabbath lesson, there was in it a genuine novelty. In the hands of the faithful teachers who had been secured it was fresher, and newer, and more pleasing even than the theatres that had so often absorbed their hardly-earned money. To be sure there were uneasy and restless children in the school; there were boys who would drop every thing for a fight, and swear a big oath from habit, but little by little these firebrands were placed among the less combustible material, and oftentimes by the side of a muscular, young Christian teacher, who did not scruple at once to stop trouble by an iron grasp, or even a kindly shake.

Conlon had in due time become a teacher, and strangely enough was the meekest of the lot, and possessed of the most patience with the wayward ones. Perhaps he felt that if justice had been meted out to him when he was so aggressively inclined that he would have never reached his present stage of happiness, and so thinking, had not the heart to be severe with those who were simply doing in a less degree what he had so long indulged. Be that as it may, he was patient and long-suffering, and the boys who made up his class loved him more than they could express.

This school being Miss Belle's particular project, and so carefully ministered to in a monetary way by her, was likely to be her objective point on many a Sunday afternoon. The teachers and scholars although not aware how much they owed this lovely young lady, one and all liked her, and it was admitted that no one who had ever been within the doors had her faculty for so gently and thoroughly subduing refractory children.

On this Sabbath Miss Pitcairn, who had come down and occupied the visitor's seat until the opening exercises were over, went up the narrow aisle toward the desk to speak with the superintendent, a young grocer, who was a recent convert, and a fine, honest, young fellow.

As they talked Conlon left his class, and joining them held out his hard hand, saying, —

"Miss Pitcairn, you gave me such good advice when I first came to the Mission that I have come for more."

The bright smile that greeted him emboldened him to continue, —

"Praps you do n't remember it, but when I was wild I was a leader among the men in your mill, — knew them all well, and had their confidence, — but since I 've made this change it seems as if they avoided me. They are pleasant, to be sure, but I can't get them to come down here if I died for it, and as for making them talk on the subject of religion they won't do it, and that 's all there is about it. Now I 'm just burdened for these men. I 've prayed, many 's the night, pretty nigh till morning, and seems as the Lord meant to answer, only the matter was with me. I do n't doubt but that He is pointing out some course of action fur me, and I 'm so blind that I jest pass it by and go on my own blundering way."

Conlon's eyes filled with tears, and his broad chest heaved with emotion.

"Have you tried walking home after work with any one of them, and talking till he was interested?" inquired the young lady.

"That's just what I have done. I've laid
for them in all directions, and made excuses to
see them alone, and all that. I did n't want to
talk on the subject before the crowd and make
'em ashamed, but it ain't no use, they dodge
out of the way and do n't give me no chance
at all."

"Perhaps," said Belle thoughtfully, "the Lord
wants you to speak to them when they are
all together. Certainly we are not commanded
to wait till we can find one soul alone before
we speak of Christ's love. It may be more
natural many times to hesitate about speaking
before a company, but it may do more good
in the end."

"I'm not sure but your right, Miss," replied
Conlon, a look of distress coming over his
face. "But I am so awkward a speaker that
I'm afraid the boys will laugh at me. If I
could talk like Mr. Thomas, now, they would
listen and enjoy it, but for me to try to
teach a half-dozen of 'em at once, why, it
makes me shiver."

With a thoughtful face the engineer went
back to his class, and sitting down among the
boys took up again the lesson of the day.
After the session was over he went home, took
the keys of the engine-house from their hook,

and started for Harlem. It had been his custom
when he wished to be alone to lock himself in
the engine-room, and to pray himself into a
proper mood for doing his duty. Since the talk
with Miss Pitcairn he was well assured what he
ought to do, but the trouble was he shrank
from it with an unaccountable dread.

On gaining his oily sanctum he locked the
door, and kneeling by the side of the engine,
his forehead resting against the cool, steel cylinder, he prayed long and earnestly.

While he knelt, thus struggling for victory,
there came to the window back of him a white
face that gazed long and passionately at him,
and then disappeared as suddenly as it came.
Unconscious of the woman's face, or her strange
look when she saw him keeling, Conlon had at
last risen full of peace, and strength, and calm
exaltation, and gone quietly home.

The next day he did not haunt the solitary
workers, with yearning looks that they did not
comprehend, but was bright, cheery, and chatty
to all, and by his ordinary behaviour made himself more of a companion than he had been
for some time past.

At noon, when most of the men took their
dinners into the fire-room, instead of sitting
alone in his sanctum and reading, or striving to

talk with his reluctant assistant, he took his dinner pail out with the rest. His old place had been on a short piece of timber that, protruding from the foundations of the building, afforded a good seat. This he took without a word, and it was yielded as his right.

"It beats the devil how natural it seems ter have you out here, old chum," said one cordially.

Conlon laughed with satisfaction.

"My feelings have always been just the same toward you fellers," he said, "only it does seem kinder queer to hear Dick say, it beats the devil, for that's what I've been trying hard to do for a long time past."

"Do you believe that there is such a man as him?" inquired Dick, boldly, feeling a sort of security in the presence of the crowd.

"Certain I do, I think he's just as much of a person as I be," said Conlon, decidedly, "of course he ain't exactly a man, but he —— "

"Gits there jest the same!" interrupted one of the younger men.

"Yes, he does get there pretty often without any doubt, and its a mighty pity too, ain't it, now, boys?" continued the engineer.

"Praps so," said Dick, "but I'm not sure that there is such a person at all. It seems ter me that the things a man does are jest the

natural deviltry in him — that is working out.
It 's as the feller said, 'only the froth on the
beer.'"

"Well, I do n't know as there is any way
but for you to prove what you say from out
the Bible,"

"Me ?" said Dick. "I do n't own such a book,
— but I usted to hear my old father say, either
that there was, or else there was not, a pussonal
devil — I disremember which, but it 's my belief that it 's only an idee, and when it. comes
ter that, I would n't be afraid ter bet that yer
Bible would back me up in it."

The speaker looked triumphantly about as he
went on eating his lunch, and the other men
nodded in solemn acquiescence.

"I do n't know as much about the Bible as I
mean to some day," replied Conlon, modestly,
"but I kin rec'lect one place where it says
something that makes it look as if. the devil
was real — it says he goes about like 'a roarin'
lion seekin' whom he may devour.'"

"Wal, now, there ye are ! Who has seen him
goin' round ? And who has heard him roar ?"
asked Dick.

This wakened the argumentative disposition of
an old Scotchman, who said, —

"Roor ? I heard him roor but last neet. Did

ye not hear the twa fules that were roorin' and
fighting over nathing at all, back of the gas
house? Sure the deil was devouring them,
and making them do his roorin' at the same
time."

The sentiment, odd as it was, struck the fancy
of the audience, and was grimly applauded.

"There's a trouble in getting at the facts,"
said Conlon, "when you have to hunt through
a big book like the Bible, for little verses that
are scattered in hither and yon without regard
to order. I've often thought if such things
were all in a lump so that we fellers that
do n't get much time could get right at the
bed-rock at once, then we would know more
about these things."

"You're right, Con.," said Dick. "More than
once, before I left home, I have taken the old
man's Bible, but there wuz so much to it that
I got discouraged and dropped it before I got
fur."

"There's a man, I forget his name," said
Conlon, "that made a little book that kinder
lumps the facts in the Bible, and helps a feller
out a heap. You see his idee was to take such
a word as the devil for instance, and begin at
the beginning of the Bible and hunt carefully
till he found it. Then he took his little book

and writ down the place where it was — then
he went on careful like till he found another
place and noted that down. In jest that keer-
ful way he went clean through the book and
took jest about every name and word that you
could think of. Then he hed the book printed.
I seen one in a store down town the other
day and I thought I'd get it."

"Now that's what I call sensible," exclaimed
Dick, mightily interested, "if we had that book
here, we could tell at short notice whether or not
there was such a thing as a devil. We could
finish it up in one hour's time. Say, what did
the book cost, old man?"

"About a dollar and a half, I think," was the
sober reply, although it veiled a most delighted
heart.

"Come, boys, copper up, ten cents a piece all
round will fetch it, and tomorrer noon we will
have a Sunday School," said Dick.

With so enthusiastic a collection the money
was not long forthcoming, and when the whistle
blew for one o'clock, Conlon had in his hand
the price of the book, and in his heart a great
prayer of thankgiving that the "the boys were
already so much interested in searching the
Scriptures."

The next noon the book was produced, and

was passed from hand to hand, and admired for its "common sense." Few of them cared to call it a concordance, for it seemed better to do as did "old Murphy": label it a "kay." And the name clung, although not always spoken with the Murphy brogue.

It took two noons to settle the question under discussion, and by that time they had learned much about the great enemy of mankind. Jury like they sat and waited until the evidence was all in, and then one and all, through their foreman, Dick, announced that Satan was a real, living power, and one that was capable of doing a vast deal of harm. The way in which the knowledge of this fact sobered the men was amazing, and the gratification with which they noted what Conlon pointed out, that the devil was to be finally overthrown, was like a prisoner securing the news of his pardon.

This question settled another was started, and ere long several Bibles belonging to the boiler-room library were in use, and every noon saw the majority of the men crowded in there with earnest air and listening ears, to hear the passages read and comments from the readers.

A couple of weeks of this preparation being indulged, it seemed but a natural thing for Mr. Thomas to be invited in to be examined in his knowledge of Scripture by the new students. Very gladly he came, and acquitted himself so well, and was so genial, bright, and interesting, that the men voted for him to come in again. He came, and the day being Saturday, and the discussion not being finished, he adjourned to Sunday, when he promised to have seats for them all at the Faith Mission and to finish the question.

At first there was some slight demur at this, but in this democratic crowd the majority always ruled, and it was decided to accept the invitation, and to march in a body and occupy the reserved seats.

Thus it was that workers in the machine room were being led in the right way, and were finding to their surprise that it was bright, pleasant, and peaceful.

Of course the questions of temperance and morality and others came up, and were handled without gloves. Many hard hits were given and taken, for the most part in a manly way. Some could not stand the pressure long, and slipped out and away; but others staid, and among them was Dick Whitman, who surprised and alarmed his companions one day by announcing that he had found the Saviour.

The shock to them was not, however, so great

as it might have been some months before, as all were more or less softened, and the Gospel truth, the sword of the Spirit, seemed to be piercing the armor of indifference that had covered many hearts.

As for Conlon, he was very happy in his trust in God these days, most of the time; yet occasionally, when his face was at rest, it betrayed a sadness that spoke of a secret heartache. With this hidden trouble, whatever it was, he did as with all others — rested it upon the Lord, and while he did not know it, in this instance, too, li ht was to break in upor. him, and his soul be filled with gladness.

An episode, better spoken of as a specia. providence, that occurred in connection with the work in the stock room of the box factory, and that would have been very disastrous had it not been for the change wrought in the heart of Dick Whitman, was this: Moses Cohen, in his bitter disappointment at being removed from his office as private persecutor for the trust, had not given up all hopes of yet doing substantial damage to the enterprise he so hated. The officers of the trust, knowing his feelings, threw him a tip in the shape of a permission to enter in his mill any of the help that their agents could coax away from the Van Alstyne Co., their wages to be largely paid from the general fund. This, however, did not satisfy him, for he wanted a sudden and sweeping revenge. To this end he had secured the reckless and dissipated Whitman to precipitate a series of "accidents" that should strike terror into the breast of the "vooman boss." It was to arrange the details of this evil system that Cohen called at the house where the young man lived, and ascending the stairs to his room, knocked confidently.

"Come in," called a hearty voice.

"Goot evening, mein friendt," said Moses, entering briskly.

"It's *you*, is it?" was the quiet answer.

"Of course it vas me; an' midty glad to see mein friendt, Dick," returned the caller, seizing Whitman's passive hand, shaking it warmly, and then holding it while he looked with fawning admiration into the calm face and deep-set eyes.

"Just return that, when you get done with it," said the young man, finally.

"Return whadt?"

"Why, my hand; I have to use it every day."

"You young feller," said Cohen, archly, "I nefer know what jokes you vill say next; but ledt us gedt to peesness. Is all ready for the first smash to-morrow?"

"No."

"O, I forgot; you vant the money first?"

"No."

"The mill aind't shut down that day, is it?"

"No."

"Goot goracious! why do you say dot 'No,' to me as if you shoot it oudt mit a gun? Vot was the droubles? Say somedings except no! no! no!" suddenly broke out Moses, unable to control himself longer.

"Listen!" said Dick, suddenly. "When I agreed to your rascally proposition I was a reckless fool, that did n't know who my friends were, and did n't care, and was wishing to do any thing for money; but now it is different. I shall have nothing to do with the plan."

"Ah! you vant more money, but you do n't get idt. I know anoder man, with twice your grit, what will be glad to do the jobs," returned the Hebrew, his face crimson with rage.

"Understand me; if any tricks are played in that mill, Conlon and I will make it hot, not only for the fellow who plays them, but for you as well!"

"Does dot Conlon know?" gasped Moses.

"Not yet; but I shall tell him if any thing is attempted."

"You are a drator!—a turrn-goat! Dere ish

not a leedtle bidt of a man aboudt you! I
know joost what is der matter midt you : somebody has boudt you; likely that vooman-boss,
what will fail in tree veeks, — in a month. She
has boudt you, but you will be oudt of a job
soon, and no box factory vill gif you vork. See,
you do what I say, undt I vill gif you steady
job?"

"No," said Dick, firmly.

"Vell, I'll tell you aboudt dot Mees Pitcairn; she's ——"

"Stop!" thundered Dick, reaching the door in
a stride, and throwing it open with a crash.
"You *git*, lest I lay hands on you, and don't
ever show your face. here again!"

XX.

McFadden's Boomerang.

AT the corner of Van Alstyne and Midnight Streets stood a large, square wooden house, in the lower story of which was a saloon and "beer garden." The upper stories, used as flats, contained a mixture of Germans, Irish, Swedes, and others of foreign extraction, who patronized the beer industry to all appearance more than they did the bakers or grocers. The garden was open night and day, with the exception of Wednesday evenings, when its shutters were up, and to the ordinary drinker it was closed. At the same time there were those who on this same night, when there were but few onlookers, knocked in a peculiar manner, and were instantly admitted. These exceptions were for, the most part, workingmen by their gait and general appearance, many of them brawny fellows, with the broad backs and deep chests of foundrymen. Certainly there were fifty of them, and perhaps more, who knew the "open sesame" to this darksome entrance, and who on this particular evening of the week stayed until the ordinary honest laborer had long been enjoying his slumber.

It was in very truth the club that McFadden had formed after certain socialistic ideas of his own, and which he believed would one day stand far ahead of the "Knights of Labor," or any of the many brotherhoods that have within the last four years been so popular among workingmen. At the meetings, which were always well attended and were more than animated, it was customary to begin by a species of "love feast," when in place of the bread and the water used at that primitive and excellent ceremony, were substituted pretzels and beer. This had been introduced by the German element in the first place, but by degrees had grown in favor, until it was an open question if some of the members did not come to enjoy the preface rather than the succeeding chapters of the meeting. When the beer flowed freely the discussions were very vigorously sustained, but if for any cause the supply was limited these exercises dragged.

There were among the members many who were honestly exercised about the condition of the working classes, and who would sacrifice much

to benefit others, and it was for this purpose
that they met and weighed "Land Theories,"
"Anti-Poverty Societies," Socialism, and even
Anarchy. None of the movements seemed to
this little company just what was needed, or
rather all of the well-known plans for the amelio-
ration of their condition had supporters among
them. McFadden was the leading spirit, partly
because he had started the club, but more perhaps from the fact that he was a clear reasoner
and a man of indomitable will, — beside which
he contributed largely of his money to pay the
running expenses.

One evening, after calling the meeting to
order, and disposing of one or two minor questions, the Scotchman had called upon any who
had a word to say on topics of interest to feel at
liberty to speak. At this a man who from his
appearance might belong to almost any of the
nations of northern Europe, but who spoke
English without accent of any sort, and in a
voice that was so harsh and loud that it filled
the room with its brassy clamor, said, —

"Brothers, when we look around us what do
we see? Monopoly! monopoly! monopoly!
Here a gigantic Oil Trust; here a Sugar Trust;
a Match Combination; a Rubber Trust. On all
sides are the capitalists combining that the

laborer, the real producer, shall pay double price for his goods. The Coal Barons live better than the Kings and Queens of Europe, and their help are more wretched than are the poorest peasantry of the Old World. Who is going to stop this systematic oppression of the poor, if not the poor themselves? Brothers, let us band ourselves together by even stronger oaths than those of our order, not to rest until we see the laborer in the full enjoyment of his rights, and the capitalist and his slave-drivers swept out of existence by a vengeful people."

The sentiments of this speech were much more enthusiastically applauded than was the resumé of certain land theories, that a stout gentleman in spectacles, and of an apologetic air, presented to the audience, — the first speaker glancing at him meanwhile, and gulping his beer as if it were draughts of capitalistic blood.

Two other speeches followed, somewhat in the vein of the first, and the gratification of the audience was showing itself in vociferous applause and cries of "Good," "Give it to them," "Our time will come some day," and similar phrases. When the president rose to his feet and, asking O'Toole to take the chair, began to speak, it had been noted by some of the observant that he had not that evening taken any liquor, — a most unusual thing for him, — and also that he had not shown whether he approved the sentiments of the various speakers.

"I've been warkin' over a new phaze of Socialism of the labor question," he began.

"Good!" shouted several voices.

"However the hyprocrites an' capitalists may deceive themsel' or fule themsel', we want the truth!"

"Yes, we're bound to have it," called one.

"Druth vos midty and vill brevail," grunted a huge foundryman, after which he took a long drink.

"Wherever we see oppreesion we raise our hoot agin it, an' whene'er we ken ain that's opprecsed we strive to relieve him."

"Yes! yes! every time," came the answers, with increasing enthusiasm.

"Our seempathies are wi' all those that wark for the buildin' up o' the puir and doon-trodden, and the stern rebukin' o' them that breek the laws o' reet and joostice."

"That's it, go on."

"Noo, if I tal ye that you all hae been halping an enemy destroy the warking mon, though ignorantly, will ye quit e'en if it does bring self-denial?"

"We will," came in quick chorus.

"Every mon that means that stand up," said McFadden.

Instantly the whole company rose to their feet, and the speaker continued, —

"At the bottom o' the Labor Question is, to the best o' my belief, the Temperance Question. It is liquor that is putting us doon more than any ither thing in the world. I didna use to think so, but o' late, sin' I luked up the matter it frightened me. I hae struggled agen the feelin' day by day, but it hae keppit comin'. I tal ye, lads, if we can but get shut o' the rum-curse, we will be a' reet and prosperous."

At first his words had been received in astonished silence, but recovering themselves, the men had stamped, and hissed, and shouted, until the old man's voice could no longer be heard, so he was forced to stop and wait until the storm subsided. O'Toole in his position as chairman strove long to bring about order, but failing, sprang down into the crowd, and seizing the fire brand of the enemy, the first speaker, by the throat, choked him till he closed his mouth, at which the whole assembly became quiet. With a red face the energetic "Moderator" picked up his dignity and his office again, and said, —

"If yez think that the freedom av speech is to be drowned by the yellin' av a pack av forrinners, yez are mistaken. The gintleman had the flure, and still has it, and I, as shairman av this matin', say he shall be heard."

"Mr. Chairman," said the fire brand.

"Mr. McFadden has the flure," said the chair.

"I will gie way tae the mon," said McFadden.

So the other stood up, and looking impressively about, said, —

"Gentlemen, there are those who are ever working to promote liberty by *taking away* from the laboring man, while common sense says *give*, as the rule for the enjoyment of liberty. As a rule, we are hard workers; we have few comforts; we grow old before our time. To use a pipe and a glass o' beer are comforts that I will not give up. They may be small things, but the man who says I shall not sit down at my table and drink a glass of beer, would soon have the right to say that I must not drink coffee, or eat bread of certain kinds. McFadden has been to me as a brother; to-day, by his words, he makes himself a stranger, — an enemy."

The Scotchman rose, when the vigorous applause that had followed his opponent's speech had died away, and said slowly, —

"A glass o' beer sarves tae change a mon frae a brither tae an enemy! Here is a mon sworn in every way tae halp the laborin' man, an' when he hears that liquor is spoken o' as a deetriment tae them, he oop an' wishes tae kill some ain for speakin' disrespectfu' of his favoreet drink. He is nae mon eneugh tae swear enmity tae what destroyed his ain hame."

"You lie!" roared the angry man.

"Eh, do I lee? What slew yeer wife but French brandy? Where are yeer twa lads that suld be here tryin' tae halp a gude cause, rather than rottin' in preeson for crimes commeeted in drunken fits?"

Another man flushed with drink suddenly sprang to his feet, and pointing a long finger at the speaker interrupted him with withering sarcasm.

"And it's you that tells us this, is it? You that formed this club, and furnished the first keg of beer? You that run a bar-room across the street, where more drunkards have been made than in any other in this part of the city? You think that rum is a curse, do you, and want us to stop drinking?"

The Scotchman held up his hand with so impressive a gesture that the angry tirade stopped for a moment.

"Jeems," he said, "I'm a' that ye hae said, ev'n more. I drave my ain son tae his death, but noo I see my wrong, which I dinna before. Noo I am conveenced that I am in the wrong, an' hae deescharged my bar-keeper to-day, an' stopped the sellin' o' all that's hurtful."

"Bosh!" was the impatient exclamation of the other. "Why didn't you find this all out before you made twenty thousand dollars out of it? Do you hear? *You*, a Socialist, are said to be worth twenty thousand dollars, made from your brethren. I tell you, brethren, we have nursed a viper in our bosoms. This man is a spy, a minion of the capitalists. Down with him!"

Inflamed by liquor and angry prejudice, the listeners swept forward, and despite O'Toole's muscular protest, caught McFadden by the coat, the hair, anywhere that a hold could be obtained, and with brutal roughness, — with curses, blows, and kicks, — threw him out of the door into the darkness. Soon after, the lights were extinguished, and the rest of the assembly departing the back way, left the hall in sullen silence.

Half stunned by the rough treatment, blinded, and dizzy, McFadden picked himself up from the street, where he had been thrown, and limped painfully away. He had been amazed at the sudden anger developed by the members of his club, and even now could hardly believe that the choice spirits whom he had selected could turn on him with such murderous intent. With bitter reflections he made his way across to the Cosmopolitan, and entering by a side door, went at once to his own room, where he bathed his head, and summoning the man-of-all-work, ordered a bottle of brandy.

"There's none in the 'ouse, sir; but I can fetch some from —— "

"Hoot, mon, I maun be daft. I dinna want any thing o' the sort. I am sae bruised that I dinna believe I ken my ain name."

The next day the hotel proprietor was very sore and kept his room, but on the day following he was around at his usual tasks, and to all appearance as well as ever. The guests of the house looked at him with more or less curiosity, for the story of his ill-treatment and its cause had leaked out, and was going round with substantial additions. O'Toole, also, had suffered that night, and advertised it by a particularly conspicuous black eye.

"Eh, but I was a fule tae try tae help those men," said the Scotchman to his friend, in private,

"They wor most av thim drunk," was the reply. "An' ye talked a thrifle strong, anyhow."

"Na mair so than I meant," was the positive reply.

"O, now, you'll let the boys have a drop av the crathur now an' thin?" said O'Toole, with wheedling tone.

"Not a drop! I'm dune wi' it for evermair, an' wi' the Britherhood, too! Any cause that's rootid and groonden on beer is bound tae be fause tae the verra core. Did ye ken that when I proposed to stop furnushine the liquor, the Britherhood deed? I've a mind tae teck oot a patent for suppressin' anarchy by confiscatin' a' the beer."

As McFadden said, the Brotherhood died. There were one or two more meetings, at which there was wrangling and quarrelling, and then the association went out like a quenched candle. The Scotchman watched the dissolution of his pet project with a glum sorrow, and consoled himself by preaching his new solution of the labor question, which was total abstinence.

XXI.

Wall-Street Wiles.

MR. STANLEY ARMITAGE was sitting in his elegant office in deep meditation. It was not business that engrossed his thoughts, else his amanuensis would have been at his elbow, ready to put down in shorthand the dictation of the great man. From the outer office came the sharp clatter of the type-writers and the musical tinkle of the "line-bell," ringing often and proving that the operators had skill in using these necessary adjuncts of office-work. No need had he to worry over his business affairs, for every thing was moving smoothly. The various roads in which he was interested were earning largely, and others that he hoped soon to absorb were gradually swinging round where the majority of stock could be secured, and the management either changed or made subservient to new masters. Aside from these interests, others in which he had a hand, either by investment or inception, were in a prosperous condition, and keenly looked after by men in whom he had the fullest confidence.

The fact was, the young man was not happy this fine morning, and Miss Belle Pitcairn was responsible for his dissatisfaction. With all of his confidence in his ability to secure his own ends, this autocrat was not sure that he was to be successful in winning the daughter of the Governor. There had been a time when he felt almost certain that she cared for him; but since she had spent so much of her time among the people at the East Side it seemed as if there was no opportunity to be near her. She had indeed appeared at the notable gatherings that season, and was as beautiful and brilliant, — nay, as was universally acknowledged, more charming than ever; still there had been an invisible barrier between them. He could not complain that she had been less cordial, nor had she appeared to take less interest in him than before; but there was a lack of the charming half-willingness with which she had listened to the tale of the Fate Flower, that kept him in a state of uncertainty as to whether she would be content to entertain the sequel of the tale.

On the other hand, his cousin, the charming and clever Mrs. Armitage, told him decidedly that the young lady loved him; she was sure of it, and it was his own timorous delay that kept him from plucking so rare and sweet a blossom. She had, moreover, with a woman's keenness, warned him against the influence of Professor Buckingham, who was quite a lion in society this season, when he could be prevailed upon to appear, and whose new book had at once made him especially distinguished in his learned profession.

The warning given by his gentle cousin was not lost upon the anxious wooer, and if his thoughts had been read, they would have shown that he was racking a fertile brain for some plan to put his rival far behind in this eager race.

Once, during one of his many reveries, he had struck a bell and dispatched a clerk with a slip of paper to the commercial agency that he patronized, and when the messenger returned, it was with a complete statement of his rival's financial standing, together with many minor details that none but a customer of his stamp would be likely to secure.

With this paper in his hand he sat and thought a while longer, then figured a few minutes, looked his work over, reluctantly saying half aloud, —

"It will cost me several hundred thousand if

I am not careful, but it's too good a plan to give up."

That evening he visited Mrs. Armitage, and found her alone, her husband, Jack Armitage, who was known as "one of the best-hearted fellows in the world," being off at the club, where he spent much of his time.

"Ah, Bess, alone?" he inquired. "Just as I hoped, for I have a good plan for getting further ahead of my learned rival, John Buckingham, PH. D."

"You speak plainly about your love affairs," smiled the lady.

"To you, — yes, — but to you only."

"Such flattery is very sweet to a woman, even if she be a relative; pray tell me your plan."

"In the first place, Belle Pitcairn would never marry a poor man, even if she did a hard-hearted one?" he interrogated, with a subtle smile.

"I should say decidedly not, although she has a large fortune in her own right, and the Governor is immensely wealthy. My belief is, that even if she cared for a poor man, her parents would interfere, as they are possessed of exceptional good sense," was the lady's reply.

"Very well; now give me your attention. I

have it in my power to make Buckingham a poor man," said the financier.

"Another scheme?" laughed the lady. "If I am not mistaken, you were going to close up the box-factory by means of the trust before three months, but it is still in existence, and then, too, the dilapidated dog that accompanies you everywhere was to be a constant advertisement of your worth, and Buckingham's unworthiness ——"

"The Van Alstyne Manufacturing Company barely exists. The other mills have secured the best help, and are doing the work that the money is in. The Harlem mill is alive, but so near death's door that any day it may be numbered among the city's defunct firms. My scheme is working exactly as I planned, and as for the cur, he has his influence," returned Stanley, with a shade of annoyance.

"Possibly, but I have a feeling that in attempting to defeat or hoodwink Belle Pitcairn you are meeting one who has as much cleverness as almost any one I could name. The end has not yet come ——"

"Well, let it come when it will, my plans will not miscarry," said the young man. "But about this one that is to put the Professor entirely out of the race. It can be done!"

"In an honorable manner?"

"In a way perfectly — commercial," was the half cynical reply.

"Explain, please, if it is any thing that I can understand," said the beautiful woman, leaning back in her chair and fanning herself languidly.

"It is easy of comprehension, in fact quite simple, yet it took time to perfect the plan so that there could be no miscarriage," returned the other. "The case stands something like this: the Professor is a large holder of a certain stock that is at present sold at a good round figure. He purchased it, not as a speculation, but an investment, and means to retain it, for it is constantly increasing in value and paying excellent dividends. I also hold large blocks of this same stock, bought at about the same price that he paid. My plan is to give to the papers for some time rumors that it will take long to discredit about certain parties who manage the affairs of this company, which will at once lower the market price of the stock. When all is ready, I will throw the whole of my holding upon the market, which will run it down to its lowest peg. If it does not, my partner has a large quantity to unload, and that certainly will knock the price down where it would mean a dead loss for any one to sell. Then I mean to 'squeeze' my doughty rival."

"But can he not hold his stock until it goes up again?"

"There is just the point," replied the gentle man with quiet enthusiasm. "Buckingham bor rowed a large sum of money not long since, to secure an estate on the Hudson that formerly belonged to his grandfather. This loan, which was negotiated by one who, unknown to him, is an agent of mine, will be suddenly called in, when the stock reaches its lowest point."

"And then?"

"Then he will be obliged to sell his stock at a dead loss to raise cash enough to pay that loan, and it will about eat up his little fortune. What do you think of the scheme?" inquired Stanley, leaning back with an air of satisfaction.

"I do not like it in the least!" replied the lady, boldly. "I would much rather you would win in a fair fight."

"Bless you, dear, isn't this a fair fight? Listen until I tell you the rest of my plan. As soon as the Professor unloads I shall buy up the whole of his stock, and shall also, through agents, have much of our original holding. Then soon after it is known that he is ruined, I shall press my suit, and when successful I will put

Buckingham in the way of getting back his money, if he wishes it."

"I very much doubt if he would accept assistance from you in any case," returned the lady. "However, you must do as you see fit. I suppose it is considered all right in business, but it does seem cruel, and I wish you had not told me about it."

"Not even for the sake of securing so lovely a cousin as Belle Pitcairn?"

"Indeed, I hope you will win her, but do it by fair means," was the reply.

"All means are fair in love and — Wall Street," murmured her cousin, sauntering out to have a quiet smoke.

Bent upon crushing his rival financially by one master stroke, the financier could think of little else, and even allowed his business to get somewhat behind as he watched this certain stock, keeping careful note of all who held it, and getting ready for the final moves. His partner held a seat in the Stock Exchange, and during the time previous to putting the deal into execution had purchased all of the stock offered, and had even looked for some among the yelling crowd of well-dressed men who occupy the pit of this famous enclosure.

Ordinarily cool, this keen man of business

was so wrought up by the combination of love
and jealousy that his own employes noted it,
and wondered what had happened in the railroad
world that could make Mr. Armitage so restless
and irritable. It had been his intention to stay
away from the Governor's until after the Professor was fully disposed of, but such a resolution
was more than he could keep, and the following day found him there, as ever a welcome
guest.

"We feared that you had gone on another of
those long 'inspection tours,' Mr. Armitage,"
said Mrs. Pitcairn, graciously, for the good lady
was justly pleased with the attentions that this
desirable young man paid her daughter, and, indeed, half suspected that his regard was returned.

"Business has been pressing of late, or I
should not let it interfere with the most valued
pleasure I have — my calls here," returned he,
with a graceful bow.

"Mamma and I were feeling almost neglected,"
said Belle politely, "and are you aware that
Bessie has not been near us for two long
weeks?"

"She is the sufferer, then, for there is no
family in New York with whom she feels so
much in sympathy, and whose social converse

she enjoys, as she does yours. She frequently tells me so, and Bess is not one given to flattering statements," replied Stanley.

"I am so glad," replied Belle earnestly. "She is so sweet and lovable, and comprehends one with such quickness, that she has seemed like a sister to me. Do you know, Mr. Armitage, I have a new heresy, which is to secure Mrs. Armitage, and papa and mamma, and slip out of society and enjoy country life, not for a short summer, but for both summer and winter. There are so many new phases of life coming up before me, that I want time to think."

"Extremely bad for a lady to think, Miss Pitcairn," said Armitage, in a tone of gentle but delightful irony; "none of the elite do it. My cousin is, I believe, an exception, and her brooding over domestic problems has brought a wrinkle between her pretty brows. Do n't do it, let me beg of you; on the contrary, enjoy constantly, but never question. The fact that you have a pleasure should be a patent of ownership to it."

Mr. Armitage had begun to banter, but had ended in earnest. In a word he had expressed his idea of the life of a woman, — one of graceful enjoyment of the present, with no thought of the future, no regret for the past, — and he continued, —

"I think oftentimes that the American girl is possessed of an impatience to do something that is entirely unnecessary, and that it may be unwise to attempt. The impulse comes from the best of motives, but is none the less out of place. Perhaps one is religiously inclined, — she is all aglow to do something, perhaps to spend a lifetime among the destitute. It would be a beautiful sacrifice, but is it the best she can do? I should say no, and prove it by an illustration, if you will pardon it, from my own life. I am full of energy to do something in the business world. Now to have my affairs attended to, many letters must be written, books kept, calls made, and even tickets punched, brakes set, and engines fired. There are none of those things but what I could do, and doubtless do well. But is it practical for me to undertake this drudgery, in person, when I can hire so many idle hands to attend to it? Further than that, have I a right to withdraw myself from my associates, where I am a power, and bring down a broad influence to the narrow one of a clerk or an engineer?"

The caller paused, feeling that he had said almost too much, but so full had his mind been of an energetic protest against the constancy with which the object of his affection

clung to her new ventures, that it took the form
of words before he knew it.

Belle smiled mischievously at the gentleman's
earnestness, and said, —

"Are these American girls whom you depict,
works of the imagination, or do you know
some such self-sacrificing maidens?"

Mr. Armitage flushed a little, and then said
with his rare smile, —

"To be honest, it is a protest against your
robbing us of your society to go among the
people at Harlem, and the East Side. If you only
will consent to come among us again, as in the
times of yore, we will employ a half-dozen able-
bodied missionaries to evangelize all of your interesting heathen."

What a picture came up before her vision,
as this fascinating friend spoke with eloquent
emphasis of the "times of yore"! How the
quiet dinner parties, the enjoyable evenings, and
the host of minor recollections crowded about,
summoned by the simple phrase! The mischief
had left her mobile face, and for a moment her
eyes took on a soft, dreamy look that sent the
blood bounding through the caller's veins as he
noted every change of expression. He felt that
his star was still in the ascendant, and that as
soon as his "deal in stocks" was finished, he

could indeed speak boldly and successfully to this peerless woman.

"I am not quite prepared to defend the restless American girl to-day, but shall be very soon," said Belle, awakening from her reverie. "Her friends would be amazed did they know how practical this same visionary personage has become. She will examine what has been done by results, and if her general usefulness has been impaired, or her influence in any manner narrowed, the experiment will not be considered a success."

"Perhaps my cousin, and may I add, I myself, are more than usually selfish, but we have felt that we were being partially robbed of a most helpful friend, and if we transgress in trying to hold fast her friendship, it certainly will not be through evil intent," rejoined Mr. Armitage.

"Indeed your friendship is greatly valued," returned Belle, earnestly, as he took his leave. "You will come again, and soon?"

"Gladly," was the reply, and he was gone with the quick, vigorous step and erect carriage that stamped him the gentleman of business.

Belle watched him as he passed down the avenue and out of sight, then turned with an inscrutable air to a tiny desk, and unlocking it, began to look over the last report of her business in Harlem.. As she read a crowd of thoughts surged over her, and she paused to ponder. Was she injuring her influence? Should she drop this work or delegate it to hired servants? It had thus far meant self-denial of a kind that ladies in the world of fashion most dislike. The magnificent diamonds that had been selected by the Governor for her birthday gift were still at Tiffany's, although the day was long past when they were to be given, while their price had gone into new machinery. Was the investment foolish? Was well-bred Stanley Armitage, with his knowledge of the world, after all, in the right?

XXII.

Won Without Wooing.

THERE was a mystery at the Harlem mill, and Miss Pitcairn was the only one to note its presence. Exactly when it was that she began to feel that Miss Jessie, one of the box makers, was the possessor of some important secret, she could not tell; but at last the conviction had become so strong that she had determined if possible to fathom it. Right in the line of her suspicions came an item in the report of the superintendent of repairs, to the effect that this young lady had been observed following Conlon to the Faith Mission on several occasions, and then remaining outside with bowed head, as if silently weeping.

Now Miss Jessie was the last person who would be suspected of a sickly sentimentality, for she was quiet, self-poised, and a genuine lady in manner and in speech. She was, to be sure, but a box-maker, but a good one, and as free from petty affectation or ill-breeding as if she had been brought up in the most cultured society.

With her steady self-possession, it seemed strange that she should flee in sudden panic whenever Conlon came through the " making-up " room on his way to the office ; or that under plea of too strong a light, she should place a rampart of boxes so that they partly hid her from view.

Another incident deepened the mystery. Mr. Thomas bustled into the Harlem mill one afternoon, and seeing her at her table, said, —

"You are always ready to help in a good cause, are you not ?

"I think so," was the quiet reply.

"Very well, come down to the Mission next Sunday, and take a class of boys."

"I do n't know about my talent lying in that direction," began she, but the missionary cut it short by saying briskly, as he went out of the door, —

"Then you will come? Very well, I will be on hand to introduce you to the scholars and to the other teachers. You will find yourself at once among friends."

"That is the way he captures many an unwilling worker," said Miss Pitcairn, smilingly. "And his energy is so infectious! You had better go, and if you get over-tired get another assistant for your pattern work."

Thus it happened that before she fairly knew it, Miss Jessie was made a teacher at the Faith Mission, and on the following Sabbath was on hand in good season, with the lesson well learned, and the same quiet determination in her eyes that made her so successful in box-making.

"I knew you would come," said Mr. Thomas, taking her hand. "Now for the introduction. Here is Miss Rutgers, one of our best teachers; this gentleman is Mr. Follansbee, our first assistant superintendent, — and O, yes, you must know Mr. Conlon ; excuse me for a moment, and I will fetch him."

Hurrying up to the desk Mr. Thomas took the arm of the engineer, and started back to where he had left the new teacher, but to his amazement she had gone.

"Almost ran out of the door," reported Miss Rutgers.

"Probably she had forgotten something important and had no time to explain," said the missionary. "No doubt she will be here next Sabbath, and possibly will return in time for this session."

In spite of this kindly interpretation of her

strange flight, the lady did not return to the
Mission school that day, nor the following week,
nor would she vouchsafe any good reason for her
singular conduct. Mr. Thomas called again at
the mill, but this time his quick intuition told
him that a brisk assumption that the young lady
would come down to the Faith Mission would
not do, and a bit puzzled, he left her for the
present, to do as she saw fit.

To Miss Pitcairn this action was a curious
outbreak, in one who heretofore in every thing
good had been eager to lend a helping hand.
The lady argued that there must be some
strong reason for so positive a stand, and more
and more did she connect Mr. Conlon with it.

There was the possibility that the quiet box-
maker might be in love with the sturdy disci-
ple, but why should that lead her to flee from
him?

A circumstance that strengthened Belle's belief that it was Mr. Conlon whom she dreaded
to meet, was her manner at a certain evening
meeting where both happened to be. The service occurred a little out of the usual line, and
was held in one of the lower rooms of the old
warehouse. It had not been expected that
Mr. Conlon would be present, but when the
meeting was about half-over he entered, and be-

fore long rose and gave an earnest testimony to the helpful influences of Christianity in the daily life. That it came from a heart full of love, and was supplemented by a life devoted to the Master's work, none could doubt. As he spoke Miss Jessie shook with sobs, so that it was impossible to conceal it from those near her. The speaker even noted her agitation, and spoke more earnestly of the Saviour's love, and of His readiness to accept those who put their trust in Him.

At the close of the service Mr. Conlon started down the aisle toward the seat where the young lady sat, but she slipped out of the door and away, leaving her companions to think what they pleased.

The next morning Miss Pitcairn, entering the mill at an unusualy early hour, found her sobbing as if her heart would break.

"Why, my dear," said that warm-hearted young lady, "what is the matter; are you ill?"

"Oh, no, no!" was the reply, with but a feeble flutter of resistance, as she felt a loving arm slipped round her. "I suppose I am nervous and foolish."

"Do you think it right to keep from your best friends a secret that will do no harm to tell, and may do great good?"

"A secret?" gasped the other.

"Yes, about Mr. Conlon. I could not but note your interest in him, and did not think it wrong to watch, as it was only with the idea of being helpful to you."

The girl rocked herself to and fro in hopeless agony, wailing, "O, if I only knew that he loved me; if I only knew!"

"Poor child," thought Belle; "I am afraid he hardly knows of your existence, and that you are cherishing only a hopeless affection." Then aloud she said, "I am so sorry for you! Mr. Conlon is a good, earnest Christian, and I am sure is worthy of your love, but we women can only live on and suffer when we bestow our affection on those who do not return it."

The words ended in a sigh, and the beautiful face was for the moment shadowed by a look of pain. "There is one refuge, I sometimes think the only one — prayer. Have you prayed the Lord to guide you in this matter?"

"Yes," was the faint response.

"Well, if you have placed it in the Lord's hands you can not do better. It is sure to be for the best in the end. There, the whistle is blowing; good-bye, and may God bless you and help you. I shall pray for you."

Among those who had interested themselves in

the meetings at the Mission, was Mr. McFadden, who had also more than once sent to the Young Women's Christian association some little token of his appreciation. The fact is, he had taken quite a fancy to Miss Jessie, although he scarcely knew her. The matron of the association, who was a wide-awake, practical lady, encouraged the friends of the girls to call on them in the large common parlor, and many did so.

McFadden had been able, further, to join a Bible class, the very one to which the young lady belonged, and when he could do so he, with great courtesy, showed her the places for the evening reading, and neglected no opportunity to make himself agreeable.

What she thought of him it would be difficult to say, but at all events she smiled gratefully when he paid her little attentions, and appeared not to distrust him as she did most of the masculine gender.

Her smiles finally completed the conquest that her quiet demeanor had made, and McFadden, bursting with the important secret that he was in love, resolved to speak with his bosom friend, O'Toole, about it.

"Jock," he said, impressively, "I canna sleep neets."

"Ye ate too much," was the reply.

"Na, it's na that. I mauna as weel tal ye, I'm aboot to marry."

"Phat is there extraordinary about that?" inquired O'Toole, slightly disgusted.

"Much," was the dignified answer. "This young person is a leddy, an' how I can adorn mysel' so as to luke well in her eyes and win her consent?"

"Oho, ye hain't axed her yet?"

"Na, it would be premature, but I ken this weel, that she smiles on me and dinna luke at another mon," was the satisfied answer.

"Thin you are all right," said O'Toole, with conviction. "Without doubt, she is a deal more anxious than ye are yerself, but what have ye done to fix yerself up?"

The Scotchman produced a paper collar and a large blue necktie, and carefully put them on before the glass.

"Noo, hoo do I look?" he inquired.

"Splindid, splindid!" ejaculated his friend.

"Ye see, it's na verra expensive to dress up," said McFadden; "a collar o' this kind lasts a long time. When it gets soiled it can be rubbed in chalk, and when that does na good it can be turned."

"It makes ye 'ook splindid," returned his friend.

"Aweel, I'm going doon and try her as soon as I think it weel to do so, an' gin I hae gude luck will come back an' tell ye aboot it," said McFadden, after another long look in the glass and a fresh adjustment of the tie.

Like a wise man, he allowed the news of his change of base on the temperance question to go over to Faith Mission, and also to the association, before he attempted to do any thing about the matter that was so near his heart. When a week had elapsed, he called, and being shown into the large parlor which was used for a sewing-room during the day, he asked to see the matron.

That excellent lady came in at that moment with Mr. Conlon, who, being an engineer, had been invited in to locate the trouble in the kitchen-boiler, which, in spite of "new water-back" and hot fire, refused to furnish the house with hot water. As the lady turned to speak with McFadden, she asked Conlon to seat himself, which he did on the sofa partly behind the great hall door. The Scotchman made known his wish, and, as it happened, the one he wanted to see just then entered the parlor, and the matron turning to her, said, —

"Mr. McFadden wishes to speak with you."

The lady looked surprised, but walked across

the room to where he sat and said, pleasantly, "Good evening," and waited for him to announce his errand. But the ardent wooer had none of the courage that he possessed when with O'Toole, and all he could do was to stammer out, "Gude evening."

When she had entered, Mr. Conlon was deep in his thoughts, and not aware that any addition had been made to the party, but he was immediately awakened from his reverie by the sound of the new voice, and at once an eager, startled look swept over his countenance. Her back was toward him, but he leaned forward, a hungry light in his eyes, and surmise deepening into certainty as he scanned the lines of the trim, shapely figure and the graceful, well-poised head. At last he could stand it no longer, and breaking into the conversation that McFadden had at last with difficulty started, he said, in a low, impassioned voice, "Jessie."

Like a flash she turned, and seeing Conlon, with face full of joy, his arms outstretched, ran straight into them, and lay sobbing and quivering, overpowered by sudden gladness.

McFadden, who had just begun a long peroration on the fact that "it wasna gude for mon to be alone," felt its truth more than ever before, and was about to stalk off bursting with outraged dignity, when Conlon stopped him, and addressing the few that the parlor contained, said, —

"Friends, this must seem a very strange scene to you, but I believe it is the Lord's doings. To explain, I must go back into my life — a thing that I do n't like to do, because it shows me little else but folly and sin. When I was a youngster I lived in a small village in Maine, and next door to me lived the minister of the place. I was a wild, strong, bad boy, and cared not a bit for any thing good, with one exception. Little Jessie, the minister's daughter, was the one person in the world that I cared for. As I grew older I liked her better, and although every one in the village recited my bad deeds and predicted my evil end, she never disliked or distrusted me."

The fair head pillowed on the deep chest was raised an instant, and the look of trust and confidence in the large eyes was beautiful to see.

"When I came home from a wandering trip and married her, in spite of the talk of the village gossips, and even despite her parents' wishes, I had no doubt but that I should make her perfectly happy. Rum, however, soon began to make me forget my good resolutions. While

I drank and abused her she stuck by me, until
I announced that I had bought an interest with
'Big Tom' in the saloon where the Mission now
stands; then she stood up and told me that she
would not live with a rum-seller.

"I was enraged, and, although I did not strike
her — thank God, I never did that — I talked as
ugly as I knew how, and finally went off down
to the saloon. When I came back at night she
was gone. O, how I missed her! Bad though
I was, I would have given all that I had to
get her back. I sent to her village home, but
no one had seen her. I employed detectives
here in the city, but it was of no use. Finally
word came that she had gone to an aunt's in
the West and had died. Then I went deeper
than ever into drink. You all know the story
of my reformation — how the Lord was willing
to save such a man as I was, but it grieved
me sore that I could not have been a Christian
while my wife was with me. And now she is
here. The Lord has given her back as from
the dead. It seems as if my heart would burst
with happiness."

"How very, very glad I am that you are so
happy," said Belle when Mrs. Conlon came to her
with the joyful news. "If my mill never pays
any dividends but such as these, it will be a

most successful venture. I presume you will leave me now, dear?"

"Not unless you discharge me," was the bright reply. "My husband," with a charming blush, "and I talked it over last night and decided to stand by you as long as you needed us. We shall board for the present, and maybe when every thing is prosperous again we will go to keeping house."

"You can not imagine how I am helped by your faith in me. The times will be better, and we shall prosper," said Belle, her eyes full of tears.

XXIII.

Could Not be Bought.

IT was Sunday afternoon, and McFadden had taken a line, hooks, and bait, and gone down to the wharves to fish quietly, and thus avoid, according to his ideas, breaking the Sabbath.

He was not an enthusiastic fisherman, and so often lost himself in thought that the finny denizens of the turgid waters of East River had ample opportunity to steal his bait without danger to themselves. For some time the Scotchman had been unhappy and could hardly tell the cause. When first he had given up the liquor business he had felt a spasm of real enjoyment, and afterward in the recognition that he received from the Professor, from Miss Pitcairn, and even from the stately Governor, had derived a deal of pleasure and self-gratulation. But now he was dissatisfied, and could hardly tell why; although when questioned by Mr.

Thomas, he had claimed that he was perfectly happy.

"I had hoped that you would give your heart to the Saviour when you gave up the liquor business," said that faithful missionary.

"I'm thinkin' aboot it," was all the answer that he gave, and the other went away to pour out his heart to the Lord, that this stubborn and influential member of the "Wedge" community might be shown his sin and brought to the foot of the cross.

It was the feeling that there was a void in his heart, an emptiness in his life, that had driven the hotel keeper to leave his chosen companions and wander off alone this bright Sabbath day, to sit, and fish, and think. There had been in his past life little of good that he cared to dwell upon. Since boyhood he had associated himself with a set of men who were rough, reckless, and hardened, and he had become a leader among them. With the true thriftiness of his race, he made himself useful to many of them, and exacted money for it. When he bought the Cosmopolitan Hotel he at once made the bar a most attractive place, and derived greater revenue from this than from the renting of the rooms. It was stated in the meeting of the Brotherhood that he was worth twenty thousand dollars, but had his accuser known it, the sum was far greater. This was much of it rum money, and unknown to others, that fact was ever painfully present with the Scotchman. Formerly he had secretly rejoiced that while his companions lived from hand to mouth, and were continually pinched for funds, he had plenty. It gave him an exalted idea of his own shrewdness and far-sightedness, to feel that his old age was prepared. for, while most of his associates knew not where the next day's meal was coming from. But now all was changed. He got no comfort from any thing, and he pulled up his line and rebaited his hook for the twentieth time, groaning, —

"It's na use, I canna give it up!"

Hour after hour he sat, and at last the lights began to twinkle from across the water on the Brooklyn side, and evening had fairly set in. Mechanically he rolled up his line and went home, pondering the while, and occasionally shaking his head, and ejaculating, "I canna do it." On one occasion O'Toole heard this expression, and asked bluntly, —

"What is it yez can't do?"

There was no reply, except a sad shake of the head, as the Scotchman walked slowly away.

"I'm bound ter belave that McFadden is goin' crazy," said the Irishman.

"He misses his licker. It's dangerous fur a man of his age to give it up so sudden," said a lodger, whose deep-dyed physiognomy implied a doubt as to his giving up liquor with any great degree of suddenness.

In the midst of these perplexing doubts the sufferer sought the Professor, and handing him a package of papers, said, —

"Professor, theer's the savin' o' a life time, the greater part o' it bein' rum money. I luve it as I do naething else in the warld, but I'm willin' to gie it a' that I may gain etarnal life."

"Forty thousand dollars," said the gentleman, slowly. "It isn't enough for the purpose."

"I suppose not; it's but a sma' sum after a'," was the discouraged reply.

"No, it's not enough. No man on earth has enough money to purchase eternal life. The gifts of God are not for sale, and eternal life is to be had for the asking. 'Believe on the Lord Jesus Christ, and thou shalt be saved.' That is all, — repent, believe, and then follow the Master's commands as closely as you can."

The other listened with an anxiety that proved his sincerity; yet to his sin-clouded mind, the way did not seem as plaim as it might.

"Yes, I ken a' that, but what 'll I do?" he asked.

"Nothing!"

"Naething? Hoot, mon, yeer mockin' me."

"Indeed, I 'm not; I am just trying to have you grasp the fact that all has been done. Christ shed His blood for you on Calvary. There is no penance to endure, no price for you to pay, because He paid the debt. All that you can do is to accept."

"I 'm willin' tae accept," murmured McFadden, the great tears gathering in his eyes.

Kneeling, the Professor prayed earnestly and simply that the Lord would come into the willing heart and abide there, and before the petition was finished, McFadden was sobbing and praising God that he had found salvation.

"The light hae coom!" he exclaimed, his face beaming with joy. "The deil had spreed a veil over my face, that I couldna see, but the Loord hae toorn it asunder, an' the light has streamed in till my hart is fu' of gladness. An' I thought that I could buy this happiness for forty thousand dollars, puir fule that I was; why, a million wouldna tampt me to part wi' it."

"I am very glad," said the Professor, wiping his eyes. "There have been many prayers sent up for you, and now they are answered. I hope you will be a true soldier of the cross, and that this neighborhood may be much the better for your presence here."

"Eh, theer's just the point. Hoo can I make mysel' o' use? My thought was to gie the money tae the Mission that I maun gain salvation; but I see noo that money canna buy joy like this. What can I do?" said the convert earnestly.

"I should hardly care to answer such a question hastily," replied the other. "But I will tell you of a thought that has occurred to me more than once. At the corner of Van Alstyne and Midnight Streets is a saloon that has connected with it the large hall used formerly by your labor club. Now that is just the place, cleaned and renovated, that could be made into a temperance garden for men. You comprehend, — a beer garden without the beer, — a room where they could congregate evenings and talk over the news of the day, read the papers, listen to good music, and enjoy temperance drinks and light lunches."

The listener leaped to his feet, clapping his hands together with an emphasis of gladness that proved his appreciation of the thought.

"It is the verra thing needed. I can see it a'. The hall noo is fitted for it. We'll hae a

place where instud o' selling poison, we'll sell
what 'll refresh.   Instud o' furnishing music
that 's a' for the deil, we'll hae an orchestra
that can play Auld Hundred and some o' the
sacred music o' the day.   It 's a grand plan.   I
hae a gude mind to apply for a patent on it."

"Suppose you see Miss Pitcairn, and tell her
your plans.   No doubt she could give you many
practical hints as to the best course of action.
In starting such an enterprise, it seems to me
most important that it should, as far as possible, be so managed as to pay expenses.   It is
a grand good plan to make any enterprise as
permanent as it can be, which end can not be
attained, unless it is established on a sound,
business basis."

The gentleman paused, his handsome face
lighted with interest, while his companion said, —

"Na doot ye are reet.   I will be lavish an'
yet carefu', an' will be glad tae lerrn a' I can
fra sae successfu' a warker as Miss Pitcairn.
I hae kenned lang that she was the ain wha
has dune sae much for this pairt o' the city.
It 's as grand a wark as e'er was dune."

Full of zeal in the new project that was to
utilize the liquor money in doing good, McFadden
promptly purchased the good-will and lease of
the saloon and beer garden, taking care to learn

the names and addresses of the best customers. He then set a force of men at work tearing out old partitions, painting, kalsomining, and generally renovating the whole lower floor.

While this was in progress he found opportunity to call on Miss Pitcairn, going to Harlem for the purpose. He was kindly received, and in his broad Scotch with infinite gusto related his plan for the "Garden."

"I must compliment you upon your originality in conceiving such a plan. It gives every promise of success, and will, I doubt not, be a source of much good," said Belle.

"Dinna compleement me, for it wasna my idea at a'. It was the suggestion o' a mon the tie o' whose shoon I am na worthy tae fasten," was the reply.

"Indeed!"

"Yes, a mon who has had it in his power for a long time past tae hae me arrested for conspeeracy, but wha has, wi' a nobleness a' his own, never said a word that could injure me," continued the Scotchman, his face lighted by a glow of honest admiration.

"That is quite remarkable," said Belle, with growing interest.

"It is. You see, I was the founder o' a Socialist order, and ain neet word came that a

mon who had injoored many o' our members
wus in the vicinity o' our lodge. We sent out
a spy and managed tae trap him and bring him
into our meetin'. Then we started tae try him,
an' it would hae gone hard wi' him — I do n't
say that we wuld exactly hae killed him, but he
would hae been pretty weel hammered. We were
about half through the trial, when in came a
brother wha recognized the mon as not being
the ain we thocht he waur. Then, you ken, we
were in a pickle. A' we could do wus tae
foorce this mon to take an oath that he wouldna
divulge what he had seen. When it kem to that,
however, he wus set as yer please, and would
do na sic a thing. Whate'er we said had nae
effect, for he stood cool and calm, and dinna
appear to fear the lot o' us, mair than if we
had been bairns. We threetened him weel, but it
dinna move him, and at last we decided to keep
him preesenor until he waur willin' tae do as
we bid."

The narrator paused and wiped his brow with
an enormous handkerchief, as if the story was
not entirely pleasant to him, and yet was forced
from his lips by a desire to unburden his conscience.

"He was certainly very brave to defy you
all," murmured Belle.

"Aye, he waur brave, an' he did this for conscience' sake. Weel, we keppit him prees-enor six hours, an' then I took the responsibility on mysel' an' let him go without any promise, for I believe he would hae had us a' by the ears if I keppit him much longer."

"What did he do?"

"Eh, he preached tae us, an' talked temper-ance, till I felt as if I were in the deil's own business in sellin' rum. I let him gang awa' wi'out promise, because in another day he would hae made a baby o' me, an' had me the laughin' stock o' the men, so I thought, fule that I wus. Sin' that he has been round mony the time, an has never failed to speak a word for the rect, an' neet before the last he it was who pointed me tae the Saviour o' the warld, an' I'm gloryin' in the sure knowledge that my sins are for-given."

McFadden paused and wiped his eyes, that were streaming with happy tears, and said, —

"You ll pardon an auld mon, Miss, but the Loord's luve for a reeprobate like me melts me a' to tears."

"I am very glad, Mr. McFadden, that you have found the Saviour," said Belle. "If you carry out plans in His strength there can be no failure for them   If it would do no harm, I wish you would tell me the name of the noble man who was the means of bringing you to the Lord."

"O, nae harm at a'. I had nae doot ye would at once recognize him. It was Professor Bookingham."

"Professor Buckingham," said the lady, in amazement; "why did he never let us know, I wonder?"

"He tal, Mem? He's ain o' them heroes what will do a great deed and blush to find that folk ken it. He spends nae time in blowin' his ain troompet, nor advertisin' his ain gude deeds," replied the other, with enthusiasm.

"You are right. He does not talk of himself or his own deeds, nor encourage others to do so. He is a noble man, indeed, and I am glad that you told me this," responded Belle, in a low voice.

XXIV.

On Demand.

WE left Betteredge in Mr. Crittenden's private office, in a surly mood indeed, that he should be set aside for callers, no matter what their errand might be. He heard the gentleman's dismayed exclamation that his caller was Professor Buckingham, but it did not occur to him at the moment that his advent would affect his special errand.

"Glad to see you, Mr. Buckingham," Mr. Crittenden had said, with a weak attempt at cordiality.

With courtly grace the Professor turned and introduced his companion, who was none other than Miss Murdock. Seeing the look of surprise on the real estate agent's face, the gentleman added, —

"Miss Murdock represents the manufacturer of whom I spoke to you, and wishes to consider the question of the lease of the brewery property."

"Very happy, I'm sure," murmured Mr. Crittenden, unhappily.

"No doubt you are ready to state exactly upon what terms you will erect the building for Miss Pitcairn?" continued the gentleman.

"Is the Governor's daughter to be the lessee?" inquired Crittenden, with a gasp, although it only verified a former shrewd guess.

"Yes, and she has given her representative full powers to close a contract with you."

"Miss Pitcairn knows how anxious I am to serve her, but — but — I find myself singularly embarrassed," said Mr. Crittenden. "The fact is, I find myself growing old, and I have bursts of enthusiasm that last for the moment, and then leave me completely robbed of nervous vitality."

"Will this loss of nervous vitality prevent your keeping your promise?" inquired the Professor, a trifle sternly, while Miss Murdock, keen little business woman that she had grown to be, sat silently weighing each sentence, and noting every look of the real estate man.

"I have about decided to put the whole matter into the hands of my son, and go away for a while to recuperate."

"You will at least give us the refusal of the land until you may return?" said Miss Murdock.

"I fear that would be hardly business-like,"

replied the other, with a sickly smile. "Suppose some other customer should come along who intends to put up a — a —— "

"Brewery?" interjected the Professor.

"A sugar refinery or a flour mill, and who would give twice the price you offer, what a loser I should be!"

"There is but one line of business with which I am acquainted that can afford to pay twice the rent that other industries pay," said Miss Murdock, sagely.

"I am only supposing a case," said Mr. Crittenden.

"By the way, Governor Pitcairn wished me to say that he should consider it a personal favor if you would settle this matter to-day," continued the Professor.

"I am not in a fit state to do business," replied the other, an obstinate look coming into his eyes.

The Professor sat back calmly watching him, and wondering if he had better push the matter then, or wait until another day. The man certainly did look ill, and who could tell but he might be suffering from a mild attack of nervous prostration, that made business an impossibility? At the same time a shrewd intuition told the young man that he had once failed when he had promised to renovate the brewery, and that it was quite possible the same means that had triumphed before were being again brought to bear on this pious lover of money.

"Governor Pitcairn also told me to say that he should be obliged to reconsider his promise to sell the Harlem property if you allowed the rum faction again to secure this piece of ground," said the visitor in the same even tones.

The last shot was effectual, for the gentleman turned white, and without another word opened a desk, and drawing out paper and pens began to write. Before he had finished, the door to the little room where the first caller had been sequestered burst violently open, and "Big Tom" strode out, his eyes flaming with fury.

"Look here, you hound!" he growled in a tense voice that was more appalling than a louder tone, "don't you dare to sign that paper, or I'll kill you!"

Mr. Crittenden, cowering in extreme fright before the wrath of the giant, almost sobbed aloud, while the Professor stepped quickly forward to prevent violence.

"Go on, Mr. Crittenden," said the young athlete, facing the bully, while his broad shoulders screened the other from his wrath.

"Stand out o' my way," said Betteredge, drawing back for a tremendous blow.

Quietly the other faced him, looking into the wild eyes with so calm a gaze, one so full of confidence and so utterly devoid of fear, that the aggressor did not deliver the blow, but dropped his hands, apprehending that the other "had science," and that he would fare badly in a set-to with him.

Meanwhile the boy had been dispatched by Miss Murdock for an officer, who stood not a rod away from the outside door, and who responded with alacrity, entering the room just as the enraged man, his courage returning, was about to spring upon the young Professor and risk a hand-to-hand encounter.

"Shall I put him out?" asked the officer, swinging his club suggestively.

"Not yet. Have you signed that document, Mr. Crittenden?" inquired the Professor.

"Yes," was the low response.

"Well, I will be glad to read it for the benefit of our friend, who is, I take it, a representative of the rum power," he continued; but Betteredge, with a muttered curse, strode out of the apartment, and shutting the door with a crash, was gone.

After his departure, it required but a few moments to finish the preliminaries of the business, and then, with all of his kindly courtesy, the Professor escorted Miss Murdock to her home and turned again down town.

" Professor, old fellow, how are you?" called a hearty voice, as he was passing rapidly down Broadway. At this hail he turned and saw his friend and college mate, Jack Armitage, a young man noted chiefly as being a "precious good fellow," and "husband of the lovely Mrs. Armitage."

" Glad to see you, Armitage," said the other, slipping an arm through his and moving in the direction in which he had been going. "What are you doing to kill time nowadays? Playing billiards at the club, or have you fulfilled your threat and reformed?"

"Well, I haven't reformed exactly, but I don't play as much as I did, 'pon my honor, I don't. You know, I always was a lazy chap, even at school?" was the good-humored reply.

" A man with your abilities ought to be making himself felt somewhere," said the Professor, a bit sadly, looking into the handsome face that was already lined by dissipation.

"O, I do some good," returned the other nonchalantly. "Now there is a friend of mine, a prime good fellow, who has always done all he could to help others. He is in danger of being wrecked financially by a Wall-street schemer, and I am on the watch to give him a hint of his danger."

"Good!" exclaimed his friend heartily. "You couldn't do better, although if he has dipped into speculation I doubt if your warning will be effectual. Well, I must hurry along. Shall I say good-bye?"

"Not quite yet until you hear a trifle more of my disinterested kindness in regard to this old classmate of mine. I want you to exactly understand in what danger he stands, and how obtuse he is about hints that are thrown out to him," said Armitage, chewing the end of a cigar reflectively.

"Very well, say on, Jack, but please remember I am in a hurry."

"To hurry away before I tell you all about this friend of mine would be costly economy," said the club man, looking straight into the other's eyes with an expression that could not be misunderstood.

"Go on!" said the Professor, suddenly all attention.

"This friend of mine owns certain stock, which has, during the past week, dropped a number of points, and is still steadily declining, although apparently without cause. When it reaches its lowest point a loan that he has negotiated will be called in, and to meet it he must sell his stock at so great a sacrifice that he will be practically a poor man."

"When is this loan to be called in?" asked the listener, a trifle pale, but with a calmness that won the admiration of his friend.

"To-morrow at ten o'clock. I wish I could have got you word before this, old man, but news only just came to me through a relative, and I have been hunting for you all day. I have a few thousand to spare if you need them, but not nearly enough. If you have any powerful friend, now is the time to test him."

"I can not tell you how much I value this expression of your friendship," said the Professor, grasping the other's hand. "You are right, if ever a man needed a powerful friend I need one now. How glad I am that I have such a friend!"

Jack's face lighted up with pleasure as he said heartily, —

"Then you will be carried through all right, and mighty glad I am too. Good-bye, old fellow, and good luck."

Had the gentleman been quick enough to explain that the Friend to whom he referred with such confidence was none other than he whom all Christians lean upon, it would have provoked a careless smile, or skeptical jest; yet the Professor was none the less in earnest. So strong was his faith since he had seen what the Lord could do, and was willing to do, in a place like the "Wedge," that nothing seemed impossible. It would be a great blow to him to lose his property just when he was fairly started in life. There were many enterprises that he wished to further by its aid; many a good cause that he planned to assist, and he did not believe that it was the Lord's will that a hidden enemy should despoil him of his patrimony, which had been won in honest business by a line of godly, industrious ancestors. He felt, indeed, that he had a powerful Friend, and hurrying home he shut himself in his library, and kneeling, asked fervently for the help that must come before the morrow at ten.

When he arose it was with a feeling of victory and peace such as he never before had enjoyed. It was as if a promise had been spoken. So sure, so definite, that he could no longer doubt, and thrilled with thanksgiving and happiness, he broke into song, his rich baritone filling the apartment with the melody of the hymn, "Jesus, Lover of My Soul." As he finished

the verse the door opened, and Governor Pitcairn came in with face radiant and eyes full
of tears.

"Bless your heart, my boy," he said, "I
could n't stop to knock, for your song filled me
with such great gladness. It seemed as if the
Lord was present with you, and I wanted my
share of His blessing."

"He is here and has blessed me," replied the
young man.

"That's grand; I came over to see you to
gratify a whim. This afternoon I was thinking,
and some way my thoughts centering on you, I
began to feel that you were in trouble. Now,
I'm not a bit superstitious, but do what I
would I could n't shake the idea off, so I sat
at the window and watched for you to come from
down town. As soon as I saw you I knew I was
right: your face, your walk, your whole bearing
showed it. So, as soon as I could, I came over
here, and behold, I find you glowing with happiness and singing with such joy in your tones
that it made a Gospel-hardened old soldier like
myself weep. Has the trouble vanished?"

"It will come all right, of that I am assured,"
replied the Professor.

"Tell me all about it. How do you know but
what I was sent to help you out?" said the Gov-

ernor, settling himself into a large easy chair, and completely filling it with his portly form.

Thus adjured, the other told the whole story simply and in a straightforward manner, and the Governor listened attentively, now and then putting a question. When he had finished, he said, with an air of paternal kindness, —

"Now, my lad, listen to me. The loan that you negotiated is to be the instrument that will do the damage. I will assume the loan if you wish, and you can hold your stock until it goes up again, which it is sure to do."

"It will be the salvation of my fortune if you will do so," said the Professor, with feeling.

"All right; to-morrow when the loan is called come down to the bank, and the money will be ready for you. Be sure your receipts are all right," said the Governor, rising and going as far as the door, then turning about and coming back, put his hands on the young man's shoulders, and said, —

"Buckingham, we Christians are a queer set. We find it very difficult to believe that God is leading us and directing our steps, and yet He keeps right on showing us the path. I believe that He sent me over here this afternoon to help you out of this scrape. And I am going to keep on believing it, and if, by-and-bye, I get a bit cold and worldly, and begin to think it is all luck, I want you to come ard remind me of what I am saying now."

True to the words of the friendly warning came the money-lender on the following day, and asked for the payment of the loan.

"But is this not a very sudden demand, Mr. Ashcroft ?" was the inquiry.

"Possibly, but when I let you have the money it was to be payable on demand, and the time has come when I must have it."

Unconsciously the man adopted an aggressive tone, that showed he expected to find his victim off his guard, yet one who would not yield without a struggle.

"You mean that your house is in need of this money at once?" said the Professor, with a piercing look.

"I mean," replied the other, doggedly, "that we shall collect this money, or force a sale of your stock held by our bank as collateral, as soon as the necessary steps can be taken."

"Do you realize that such a step would involve me in great pecuniary loss?"

The man gathered up his papers, saying coldly and impatiently, —

"I am to understand, then, that payment is **refused** ?"

"One moment, if you please. My grandfather, my father, and I myself have had large dealings with your firm. If I am not mistaken, during the panic of '57 my grandfather loaned your father a sum of money that enabled your house to stand while many others went down. It was but last week I came across your father's letter of gratitude. Perhaps it may not be in the best of taste for me to remind you of these facts, but now might be the time to repay that trifling favor."

The banker flushed, either with shame or anger, but set his lips only the tighter, until he had swallowed his feelings, when he replied harshly, —

"Mr. Buckingham, there were many things done in the past that I, as a business man, do not approve. At present, our house is run as a commercial enterprise, not as a charitable institution."

The Professor rose calmly, with a look of such lofty dignity that the money lender fairly quailed beneath it, saying in measured tones, —

"If you will meet me at the —— National Bank in one hour, with the necessary papers, your demand will be paid in full. Shall my servant call a carriage for you, sir?"

Mr. Ashcroft, bewildered by this promise, which

he was assured could not be bombastic, took his leave and was rapidly driven away. When well down the avenue he turned, and looking through the window in the rear of the carriage, saw the handsome bays belonging to the Buckingham stable following, with arching necks and stately step.

At the bank the Professor was on hand, exactly at the time named, where with a bow to the money-lender he at once proceeded to business.

The latter, however, seemed to be strangely agitated,—so much so, that he found it almost impossible to examine the securities that representing large sums were passed over to cancel the loan. At last he pushed them from him and said, —

"It's no use, I can not and will not go on with this. I don't want this money to-day nor until you are perfectly ready to pay it."

"Be kind enough to examine the securities, and sign this release as soon as convenient, sir. I am pressed for time," was the only reply, and for a few moments the work went on in silence. Then the man broke out afresh, meekly and penitently now, —

"Professor Buckingham, will you listen to me for a moment?"

"If it is a communication of a business nature," was the dignified reply.

"Well, sir, I wish to say that in all this infernal meanness, our house are simply agents. The telling of it will, perhaps, wreck us, but I can not have you believe that I willingly injure the grandson of the man who saved my father from financial ruin."

"This explanation comes rather late to be effective," was the quiet comment.

"I know it; I tried to make you angry at your house that my task might be more agreeable, but I failed, as I hope I may always fail where such deeds are to be done. Can you forgive me? Will you keep this loan?"

"What would you advise, Governor?" inquired the Professor, for that gentleman had come in from the directors' room and was listening to the conversation. After a moment's thought he said,—

"Do this: cancel the loan and accept mine; and you, Ashcroft, get some trusty broker to go into the market and buy up all of the stock that this hidden enemy unloads. If you can get two good men who will buy with apparent reluctance, perhaps it will be better. Understand me distinctly — I say *all you can get.* I shall be here at the bank all day. Now let me see if you can be trusted in this matter."

XXV.

The Combination Outwitted.

BELLE PITCAIRN sat in the almost deserted store-room of the Harlem factory waiting for her trusty helper, Sarah. Little by little the Box Trust had secured her customers,
coaxed away her best help, and placed obsta-
cles in the way of the purchase of materials,
until the business was practically dead. Only
the Governor's credit, and his fair daughter's
pluck, kept the concern from a sudden and in-
glorious wind-up.

"If my daughter chooses to put a half
million into the Harlem project, it is her business and mine," he was accustomed to remark
smilingly to advising friends. "Granting that
this a folly, it is no more expensive than are
many others that New York encourages. This
has lost perhaps a thousand dollars a week during the year past, about what a good yacht
would cost, and this is far more entertaining."

There was more than braggadocio in this, **for**

the Governor was exceedingly pleased with the progress that his daughter had made in reaching the hearts of the people, both at the mill and at the "Wedge," and he argued that even if this were a failure, in a monetary sense, the savings of a score or more of souls might be reckoned in with the assets.

In all of this time of trouble Belle seemed buoyed up by a steadfast faith that was delightful.

"I do not believe we shall be suffered to meet with utter failure, papa." she had said earnestly. "This enterprise was started that I might help the poor, and lead them to the Saviour, while I gave them easier work and better pay, and I claim the promise, 'I will never leave thee, nor forsake thee.'"

"The Lord is with your efforts I am convinced, and if he wants me to open my purse wider, I am willing," replied the Governor, with a look of affection, and his daughter felt strengthened and gladdened by his sturdy support.

At this somewhat critical period in the fortunes of our heroine, came a new burden, which was the completion of the great factory on the site of the old brewery. With all of his talent for "pushing" matters, Mr. Crittenden, once started in the right way, had hurried this along, until at length it was finished, and now awaited a tenant. Belle had in a measure directed the arrangement of the rooms, and the huge empty structure that she had leased and that seemed even to the Governor more than she could possibly use, now awaited ·her action.

"In case you wish to let the building until you need it yourself, I think I can find a tenant," Mr. Crittenden had remarked, with a keen eye for business, and in his narrow, faith-less little heart, sure that the Governor's daughter was "stuck."

"Thank you," Belle had said vaguely, and he had departed more than ever certain that she did n't know her own mind, or else was too proud to own up that she was fairly beaten.

And so the great building stood empty for several weeks, and the Harlem mill was almost "shut down," and about all the life there was to any of Miss Pitcairn's enterprises was the daily meetings at the Gospel Common, and the changes that were quietly taking place in the old warehouse.

Miss Pitcairn waiting in the store-room of the mill, which we mentioned in the first paragraph of this chapter, was rewarded by the appearance of Sarah in due season, and soon after by one after another of the old hands. Finally, when the number was complete, the doors were shut, and all with one accord knelt for a moment in silent prayer, and then rising were seated facing a tiny desk that had been moved in from the office. Belle was the first to break the silence, —

"It is three months now," she said, in a quiet, cultivated voice, "since we have met here twice a week to pray that if it is God's will we may have the victory over this wicked combination, and our prayers do not appear to be answered. Yet my faith has never been stronger. Indeed, I am sure God will hear and will help Sarah will you read us His promise?"

"'Again I say unto you, if two of you shall agree as touching any thing on earth, it shall be done,'" read the young woman, and the faces of the listeners assumed a fresh look of assurance.

"Are we not agreed?" asked Belle.

"Yes, yes," came the low, earnest responses.

"Then the victory is ours. There can be no doubt about it. What is it, Jessie?"

Slender, fair haired Mrs. Conlon had risen, and stood waiting to speak.

"You remarked at the last meeting that even while we prayed we should try and do all we could?"

"Yes."

"Well, last night as I prayed that your efforts to help the girls might not be frustrated by any thing, and that the work might start up, I kept thinking of the big piles of paper boxes that stood in the packing-room. At first it seemed wrong for me to let my thoughts stray, and I fought against it, and tried my best to keep my mind right on my prayer, but the more I tried the worse off I was, and finally I gave right up, and on my knees by the bed let my mind do as it pleased. And my thoughts stayed right in the packing-room with the big crates of boxes. It seemed so needless to have a few hundred boxes take up so much room. There they were empty, and yet taking up as much room as if they had been full. Then, too, I could see how it must trouble store men who had only a little space, and it seemed as if they were like square- egg shells all ready to smash."

"They are," said one of the old hands. "Lots of 'em git broken and thrown away."

"So I began studying how I could make a box that when it was empty would not take up so much room, nor break so easily, and I could n't fetch out any thing at all, till finally I just prayed God that if He pleased I'd like to know whether the thing could be done. Then I got a box and cut it to pieces and put it together, and pretty soon I brought out this."

Every eye was on her as she drew out what seemed to be a small square of card-board, and turning up one side gave it a smart rap in the centre, and behold a complete box.

"A folding box," exclaimed the girls.

"Yes, all you have to do is to let the sides down and it takes only about one-fifth as much room, and is much stronger," replied the little lady.

"I believe our prayers are answered," said Belle, reverently. "This certainly will take the place in a host of cases of the ordinary box. If we can secure the invention before the trust know about it, we can fill the new mill with hands at good wages, and defy any combination."

That very evening the whole party, full of this secret, repaired to the Governor's residence and took him into their counsels. He was less enthusiastic until he knew there was nothing of the kind in the market, and then he allowed that it was of great value. At his suggestion patent papers were drawn giving the Van Alstyne Manufacturing Company the right to make it, and allowing Mrs. Conlon a good royalty.

By the time the papers were drawn all was

ready to move the machinery of the Harlem mill down to the "Wedge," and set it up with several new machines designed to partly make the folding boxes. When the first-named mill prepared to close its doors, there was great rejoicing among the other box manufacturers, and Moses Cohen, in the fullness of his joy, called all of the help he had stolen from Belle into his office, and made this characteristic speech, —

"Say, maybe you dinks I vos goin' to bay you doze big wages now anymore. Vell, you vas mistakened! I don't got any use for you at all. You kan get oudt, und ven you see dot Governor's daughter, you may tell her dot a voomans aindt no goot at peesness."

"We were going to leave to-night, anyhow," spoke up one of the most independent of the girls.

"Hey! what's dot?"

"Miss Pitcairn has already hired us for a better job," reiterated the girl.

"What job?"

"Well, you see when she advised us to come here ——"

"Advise you to come! She didn't do dot. It vos our detective dot coaxed you here. She vas craazy mad when you left her blace!" screamed Moses, excitedly.

"O, no, she told us that the summer time was sure to be dull, and that to spite her you would pay us good wages, and she said she was much obliged to the trust for being willing to pay her help —— "

"It vos a lie!"

"And we all signed a paper promising to come back and work for her when she wanted us, and now we are going."

"What kinds of work?" demanded the Hebrew, curbing his wrath to give his curiosity a chance.

"Boxes, of course. I think there is a new trust formed, but I do n't know. At any rate, the new mill on Burges Street is fitted up, and we are all going down there, and shall take the best of your help with us."

In the meantime as the reports of the success of the box trust were brought to Stanley Armitage, he felt a masterful sense of victory, and as the weeks passed and the detective brought in the names of fewer and fewer Harlem customers, he concluded that the end was near, and despite his apparent obduracy, decided as soon as the crash came, to help settle matters as satisfactorily as possible, and to console Belle as best he could.

In pursuance of this plan, when news came that the Van Alstyne Company were doing al-

most nothing, he prepared to put his plan in
execution, and to that end called at the Harlem
mill, timing his visit so that it should fall on
the morning hour, when he was sure Belle would
be there.   It was with a feeling of affectionate
condescension that he stood in the doorway of
her sanctum, and waited for recognition.

"This is an unexpected pleasure, Mr. Armitage," said Belle, with surprise.

"I felt that, being in Harlem, I could not
deny myself the treat of seeing you," he replied,
beamingly.   "Lie down, Calamity, lie down, sir.
If you can not behave better I shall not allow
you to come with me."

"Did you wish to see me or my methods of
doing business?" asked Belle, with a smile, pat-
ting the dog pityingly as he limped up to her,
his bright eyes full of friendliness.

"Both," he answered with a charmingly frank
manner.   "You know that I have been jealous
of your being thus absorbed, from the first, because it has in a measure kept you from us,
and when a friend told me that you had concluded to retire, I was selfishly glad."

"But did you consider that if this mill stops
it throws more than a hundred girls out of
employment?" queried Miss Pitcairn, gravely.

"Hard-hearted as I am, even that occurred to

me, and I came prepared to offer them all good places among different manufacturing concerns with whom I have dealings. One house in Cincinnati will take fifty, and pay them wages while learning, while I will send them over the road for nothing."

"You are very kind," she said, turning to Mr. Armitage, "the more so as you think I am wrong in running this factory, but you are mistaken; I do not contemplate shutting down."

"Surely you do not intend to go on at a positive loss?"

"Mr. Armitage," replied Belle, "there is a conspiracy among the manufacturers to crush this enterprise, and to drive me out of the business. I entered into this work that, with God's help, I might lift the girls and women who were little better than slaves up to a higher, nobler womanhood, and am at once opposed by a trust. Every known means have been brought to bear to insure my defeat, but all have failed. My trust is in the Lord, and I shall be successful. At this moment I would not exchange my business for the whole of the holdings of the trust."

"I am pleased that you are so courageous, and only regret that I can be of no use," said Armitage, taking his leave with a look of chagrin

and disappointment that he tried in vain to
hide, followed by the limping "Calamity," who,
like his aristocratic master, looked very much
cast down.

On his way home, baffled at the turn of affairs, he could not help wondering what it was
that the future held in reserve that could over-
come the combination.   He did not discover
what it was until a week later, when Moses burst
into his office, his face aflame with rage, and
throwing a neat folding paper box down on his ·
desk, said, —

"Look! See vot that voomans has got oop!
The ceety is flooded with them. The gustomers
must have notings else! Dey say dey can put
a hoondred of them anyvheres under the counter, in the drawers, anyvheres.; but ours, dey
say, tooks oop all the room."

"Very likely.   It does not interest me," was
the cold reply.

"But you vas manufacturing, like the rest of
us?"

"I have sold my interest."

"Sold oudt, hey? unloaded? Vell, I pelieve
you vas knowing this all the dimes," was the
angry response, and Moses rushed off to find
somebody who would answer wrathfully when he
railed, that he might enjoy a quarrel.

As Mr. Armitage had stated, he had disposed of his trust certificates. A feature of this sudden sale, which he would not readily acknowledge even to himself, was that he had been led to this action by a strong presentiment that the Van Alstyne factory had, in some mysterious way, not only escaped the clutches of the combination, but would be its most dangerous and incorruptible rival. In addition to this, he was far from anxious to have his name in any way brought into prominence in connection with this matter, as he naturally felt that it would be liable to injure him in Miss Pitcairn's estimation.

As had been foreseen, the box was an unprecedented success, and the new mill could not fill the orders. To satisfy the customers the old mill at Harlem was refitted and crowded with help, and turning out goods by the thousand dozen, and even then the books were filled with lists of orders, dated months in advance.

The trust was wholly taken by surprise by this sudden turn of affairs, and after a hurried consultation, made a feeble attempt to infringe on the patent that controlled the folding box, but was met by swift and sudden punishment that effectually frightened others from following their example.

With this success came the culmination of another plan, the changing of the warehouse into a model home for the employés, and in fact any reputable girls who wanted good food, clean lodgings, and home comforts for a small sum. The plans had long been matured, but the partial failure of the Harlem project had seriously interfered with their consummation. At one time Belle had gone so far as to order all of the merchandise moved out, which had been done, and off and on had made some alterations. Now, however, as soon as her factory was going well enough to spare her for a brief time, she visited the old warehouse with her father and mother, the Professor, and Sarah.

"This is to be the girls' home," she had said, by way of introduction, as old Jefferson let them in.

"A free home?" inquired the Professor.

"I think not, rather a home that will furnish a neat, clean room and substantial board for the sums they now pay for poor attics and baker's bread," was the reply.

"In mercy to the girls do not call it a home," suddenly spoke Miss Murdock. "Every infirmary, hospital, or charitable institution in the city is a 'home.' If the girls are to be independent and self-supporting they want the

name of it, and not even an implication that
they are objects of charity."

"Human nature," murmured the Governor.

"Then we will not call it a 'home,' whatever
else it is named, but when we know just what
it is to be and to do, we will try and name
it accordingly," said Belle.

Leaving this decision for some future date,
the plans were brought forward and carefully
gone over, each floor receiving its proper attention, and provoking much discussion. When
the building had been "done" on paper from
attic to basement, old Jefferson showed them the
place that now looked desolate enough, all of
the merchandise having been removed.

"I have shown you this that. when you next
.ook it over the constrast may startle you,"
said Miss Pitcairn.

The very next day a large force of men
were put at work upon the building, tearing
down old partitions, rebuilding the weakened
wall, sheathing, relaying floors, and doing a
score of things that were necessary before the
place could be made attractive and useful to
the working girls of the East Side.

When after a time the work was finished,
and the building ready for occupancy, before
even the matron, who was also superintendent,

had taken possession of her room, the Professor,
Miss Murdock, Governor Pitcairn and wife, by
special invitation from Belle, again came down
and were shown over the edifice from basement
to attic by the enthusiastic lady. And what a
beautiful house they saw! Light, airy, cheerful,
furnished substantially, and yet simply, and of
so inviting an appearance that the Governor declared his intention of selling his Fifth Avenue
property, and taking a suite of rooms in it.

"How much did you run over the apppropria-
tion, dear?" he said in an aside.

"Not one penny, papa. I have nearly a
thousand dollars left," was the complacent reply.

"Good, my little financier. Make it pay. It
will if it is managed right, and will do all the
more good for being self-supporting."

The problem of filling the home with the
girls, for whom it was built, came next, — those
of the working girls who were struggling to get
a living, and yet were daily running behind, —
was at first not so easy of solution; but the
practical Mrs. Thomas being appealed to was
at once able to furnish a dozen names, and by
suggesting an amendment to the plan for con-
ducting the dining-room, to bring the management in contact with many more. Her plan
was to offer a free dinner to all women or

girls who could not pay for it. In a city like New York, of course it was not wise to advertise this, and the capable little lady took it upon herself in her calls to inform the neighbors of the advantages that this place offered.

To appreciate the hopes and fears that an announcement of such a nature produces upon a half-starved sewing-girl or box-maker, it was only necessary to see one of this thin, overworked sisterhood hurrying up Burges Street, at dinner time, on the occasion of her first visit to the place. With timid knock she gains admittance to the waiting-room, just off of the side entrance, and meets a comfortable, kindly looking woman, who says, —

"Dinner is all ready in the next room."

"How much?" falters the hungry girl.

"Not a cent, dear. There, there, never mind the thanks — go in and enjoy your dinner. When you are through come into the office a minute and see me."

This free dinner eaten, the ice was broken, and the overburdened girl found it natural to tell the nature of her struggles and disappointments, and the usual result was that a comfortless attic was abandoned, and one of the rooms in the new institution found a most thankful and industrious tenant. Small sums

were paid for rent, and for breakfasts and sup·
pers, which were as simple as they well could
be.

In three weeks' time every room was full, and
still applications came in. All of the box-makers
who lived in that vicinity had gladly taken rooms
there. As the new lodgers gained in health and
spirits, as they almost invariably did, almost
without exception they were able and preferred
to pay for their dinners, and it so happened
that at the end of ten months there were none
in the house who were not paying their expenses, and were proud and happy so to do.

Professor Buckingham had watched Miss Pitcairn's enterprise with keen interest, and had
been very glad that it was signally successful.

"One thing has occurred to me," he said, meeting the lady as she was coming out of church
one Sabbath morning. "How do you prevent
gossip in a place where so many persons of
limited resources are gathered together?"

"We *were* sadly troubled by it at first," she
answered; "but we made a rule, that no one
should speak against another. Then we have
somebody reading aloud in the general sitting-
room evenings, while the others are working,
and it gives them subjects to think of other
than their own petty jealousies.'

"Miss Pitcairn," said the gentleman, "I have vainly tried to suggest something that would .be of value in your good enterprises, but you have forestalled me on every occasion. It is rather hard for me to feel that my wit is slow, and my inventions so trite. Is there not something that I can do?"

Belle smiled at the sadness of the tone, and looking into the handsome face with a glance of especial favor, replied, —

"You have helped me wonderfully already in your suggestions, your work, and your moral support, and as a token of my appreciation I ask you to name the institution."

"Has it not yet a name?"

"They call it the 'Corner House' now, but we want something more dignified than that. I confess my own brain has been ransacked till I am weary, but without avail, for the proper appellation."

"Suppose it be called the 'Industrial League,'" said he, after a moment of thought.

"Capital! Indeed, that is just what is wanted to give it dignity, and to make the young ladies feel that they are workers together with us. How can I thank you?"

The young man had no chance to state in what form the lady's gratitude would be most acceptable, for Mrs. Armitage rustled up at that moment and carried the Governor's daughter away, after a keen, questioning glance at the Professor, who looked extremely happy. Man-like, it did not occur to him that there was a covert opposition in this glance, and that, while in not the least danger of being defamed by this lovely woman, her faint praise might do him injury. Possibly he would not take it much to heart were he appraised of this hostility, for he was a busy man, and loftily ignored the petty strifes of modern society.

XXVI.

A Coward's Blow.

WHEN a determined man makes up his mind to injure another, and is defeated in his attempts, his desire for vengeance is likely to become a monomania.

It was so in the case of "Big Tom." His dislike of Professor Buckingham had commenced when he learned of the influence he had with McFadden, and especially had it grown when the young man secured the lease of the brewery property. Through him, as he believed, his saloon had been turned into a mission, and prayers and testimonies were as frequent as had been curses and ribald songs. Then again, his friend Conlon had been transformed into a veritable lamb, which was alone cause for the most serious grievance.

The petty annoyances that had been inflicted on the people at the Faith Mission and at the Gospel Common were hidden blows at the Professor, or at Miss Pitcairn; for Betteredge believed that to injure one would be to trouble tne other. All of his plans had signally failed, and this was so apparent that Betteredge gnashed his teeth in fury. The more he brooded over these affairs, the more incensed he became against the Professor, and the greater was his longing to do him harm.

Just what he could do to injure him was not yet plain, for several reasons; first, because the Professor's visits to the "Wedge" were not confined to any particular time, and second, because he felt that the people of the vicinity had learned to love him so much that it would be dangerous openly to assault him.

The devil helps his own, so it is said, and certainly he must have entered into "Big Tom" when he conceived the plan that was to "make him square" with the Professor.

With her usual keenness Meg knew that "her Tom" was meditating extra ugliness toward some fancied enemy, and felt that it might be her duty to warn the unfortunate person. She dreaded to face her master, and yet, when a question of duty was broached, she had a certain Scotch stubbornness that in her case was akin to conscience.

It was for the purpose of learning what she could that she knocked at his door and stood waiting to be let in. After a long silence, he said, coldly, —

"Come in."

With trembling step she entered, and gently closing the door faced the occupant of the lounging-chair, who was regarding her with a fierce scowl.

"Well?" said Betteredge, finally, finding that she was not going to be the first in breaking the silence.

"I thought I hae served ye long years enough to be told what ye are aboot to do."

"Do! Do!" returned he, passionately. "What do you think I'm going to do?"

"Some hairm to somebody," said Meg, resolutely.

Betteredge gnawed his heavy moustache for a moment, then said, in a tone of cynical indifference, —

"I am about to harm an enemy as much as possible."

"Wha is it?" demanded Meg.

"None of your business."

"Thomas Betteredge," said Meg, slowly, "it's my business to look out for your interest. It's best for you not to be too cross wi' the auld woman. While ye gi'e her yeer confidence, she's a' right and a host o' strength toward yeer protection, but 'gin ye deceive her ye are a ruined mon."

Betteredge raised himself in his chair, and grasping its oaken arms sent the whole energy of his intense evil nature in one look, but apparently without effect, for Meg muttered doggedly,—

"It's na use, that dinna trouble me, noo."

With a baffled look he sank back.

The woman maintained her waiting attitude, and even the spark of triumph in her eye was instantly extinguished, lest it should offend.

"What do you want to know?" he said at last, with an attempt at roughness.

"Who is it ye intend to hairm?"

"Professor Buckingham," said he, savagely.

The old woman raised both hands with an expression of despair and sank into a chair, shaken as if with the palsy. One by one the great tears coursed down her cheeks. Her master gazed uneasily at her, and finally said,—

"Well?"

"Ye'll not do sic a thing. Ye daur not. He is a mon wha' is keppit of God. It's not for the likes of you to try to hairm him, else 'gin ye succeed the vengeance that falls on ye will be manifold worse. Listen, laddie, tae an auld woman that's seen muckle of the warld. Dinna try to injure one o' the Lord's annointed.

I tal ye th'rs na mither as jealous o' the safety o' her bairns as the Lord is o' them wha' are ever busy servin' him."

The man rose, and grasping Meg by the shoulders, turned her out into the hall, whispering through his set teeth, —

"Hark you, Meg, I 'll have my revenge, whatever happens. I hate that canting Professor, with his proud step and sanctified smile, and he has got to feel my hate."

The door shut with a slam, and Meg withdrew to weep and pray for "her laddie." Betteredge going to the sideboard, drew out a case of liquors and drank. In an hour he was crouching in a corner, and sending up frightened calls for Meg. She came, as ever, and soothed his insane fright, bathed his head, and at length got him to sleep.

For several days Meg watched to see if, on second thought, he gave up the idea of taking vengeance on the Professor, but for once she was puzzled by the behavior of her master, and knew not what to think. It is possible that he knew he was watched, and purposely assumed the careless air that revealed nothing, or it may be that the plan was fully matured, and gave him no further uneasiness until it was time to put it into execution.

At last the eventful evening in which he was

to "get square" arrived, and clad in heavy
coat and his favorite slouch hat, Betteredge
started for the Professor's residence. He well
knew where it was, having carefully reconnoi-
tered it, and approximated the location of the
lower front rooms with remarkable skill. He
knew just where the study and library were
situated, and was familiar even with the general
habits of the household, of whom the gentleman formed a part. He was therefore upon no
uncertain venture when he rang the bell, and
mentioning the name of the missionary at the
"Wedge," obtained instant admittance. The
Professor was hard at work in his study when
the visitor was announced, and rose somewhat
reluctantly to see who it was. When he found
that it was a messenger from the "Wedge" he
was more interested, and though the message consisted only of an urgent request for the Professor
to be present at the meeting on the following evening, as an important communication was to be
made, he did not grudge the time already taken.

"Very well, I will try and be there," said
he, perfectly willing to excuse the messenger
then and there, but the latter standing in apparent awkward indecision did not seem to be
able to get away.

"Are those the books that I have hearn tell

about?" finally inquired the man, pointing toward the library.

" Yes."

" Well, now would you allow a man to have a look at them?"

" If you will come when I am not busy I will show them, and lend you any books that you may need," said the other cordially, but with a longing look at his unfinished work.

" Aye, sir, but it's a long way up here, and I am often obliged to work evenings. All my life I have had glimpses of books from a distance, but no one could spend time to show me any," sighed the man, with a resigned pathos in his voice that won the day.

A trifle ashamed of his selfishness the Professor led the way into the spacious library, and began indicating its contents. From one side to the other he went, showing what the shelves contained, spending the most time over the illustrated works, and doing the best he knew to give the ordinary intellect before him an idea of what was to be found there.

As the Professor talked, and his visitor answered, there was a something in his tones of voice that sounded familiar. So strong did the impression grow that he had seen the man before that he finally faced about and said,—

"I am sure that I have met you before, might I inquire your name?"

"Tom Betteredge, usually called 'Big Tom,'" was the cool reply.

A glad light was in the Professor's eyes as he held out his hand, saying, —

"Ah, now I know. You have come over on the right side, at last ——"

The sentence was never finished. "Big Tom" had taken the extended hand, and grasping it firmly, had drawn a sand-club out of his pocket and struck the other a heavy blow on the head. Without a groan he sank down in a heap, and his assailant taking his purse scattered part of the money on the floor, pocketed the rest, left the room locking the door behind him, and let himself quietly out.

He was about to slip through to Madison Avenue and take a carriage down town, when he saw a sight that almost made his heart stop beating. An old woman was climbing the steps to the Buckingham mansion. There could be no mistake! It was Meg! It would not do for him to tarry, and yet if she reached the door and rung the bell it was all up with him. Quick, as a cat he darted back, and springing up the steps two at a time said, hoarsely, —

"Meg, follow me!"

Without a word or an exclamation of surprise, she turned and came after him. A few of the passers-by noted the strange proceeding with a mild curiosity, but with no attempt at interference, and the strange couple hurried around a corner and out of sight. When they reached Madison Avenue there was found a carriage waiting, and both got into it and were driven rapidly down town.

"Meg," said Betteredge, with an oath, "what were you doing up there?"

"I was aboot to warn the mon agin ye," replied the old woman, boldly.

"And you would then peach on me, and have me arrested?" inquired Tom, gripping his sand-club and looking at his companion in the dim light with a most malevolent glance.

"Na, I sud not hae gi'en yeer name. Do ye take me to be a fule? But I 'd pit the mon on his guard."

"Well, you are too late now, Meg. To-morrow's papers will tell of a burglary at the Professor's, and of his — his ——"

"Weel, what? What did ye do to the mon?" questioned Meg, seizing his arm convulsively, "sure ye dinna gie up to yeer evil impulses and harm him? Ye wouldna du sae fulish a deed." The old woman's tone was agonizing, and she had fallen on the floor and was clasping the strong man's knees, as if in entreaty. Her agitation seemed to communicate itself to her companion, for he dropped the club, and leaning back against the cushions, ghastly and shivering, muttered, —

"It's too late, Meg! Too late! Why did n't you get there sooner? I tell you I have done it, and to-morrow all the city will ring with it, and I shall be hunted down like a mad dog. O, what a fool I was to put myself in such a place just for the sake of revenge!"

At this Meg woke to the dangerous situation, and assumed the reins of power.

"Hush, laddie, dinna speak sae loud," she cautioned. "The driver may hear ye. Dinna fear, ye needna be caught. Auld Meg 'll protect ye, and, if need be, they may think it's she killed the mon, but you, laddie, shall gang free."

At a friendly saloon in the lower part of the city Meg and Tom got out, and the latter assumed his ordinary habiliments, while the former went home to mourn over the terrible event, and to set her sharp wits at work to throw detectives off the track, should there be inquiries in her vicinity.

XXVII.

A Fearful Harvest.

THE strain that had been upon Belle for so many months was gradually being lifted by the growing success of her plans, and the satisfaction that this was to her had furnished new life and spirits.

Every morning, when the weather permitted, it had been her custom to take a gallop in the park, sometimes alone and sometimes attended. For this especial ride she had a spirited little horse, known among the stable fraternity as Dandy Jim, and called by his fair mistress simply Dandy.

As she returned from a morning's ride the air seemed so fresh and pure, the world so lovely, that her heart filled with thankfulness.

"Belle, darling, how happy you look," said her mother, as she kissed her good-morning.

"It agrees with Dandy and me to be up early," she said, gaily. "He went like the wind, and once he acted so ridiculously that every body laughed. Up in the park there was a squirrel running along beside the drive, and Dandy threw up his head and snorted as if he had seen an elephant, and then he danced around and pretended to be dreadfully alarmed, till I spoke to him, when he cantered off as if he had been behaving properly all the time."

At breakfast, on this eventful morning, Belle learned that her father had taken an early train for Albany, and only Mrs. Pitcairn and herself were left of the little family. The daughter's brightness awoke in the mother a responsive chord, and they chatted cheerily of things that were of mutual interest in society, as well as in the home-circle. A stranger would hardly have thought the two ladies occupied the respective relations of mother and daughter, either from their looks or from their entertaining ways when talking together.

At that time, when the world was so bright and every thing was apparently so prosperous, Bridget entered, the bearer of evil tidings.

"Sure, mam," she said, "did yez know that there was a murther in the house next beyant yez, lasht night?"

"Why, how shocking!" exclaimed Mrs. Pitcairn, turning pale. "One of our neighbors?"

"Yis, mam; Perfesser Buckingham was killed

by a tramp — howly murther! look at Miss Belle; she's faintin', she's faintin'; what 'll I do?"

Quick as a flash the mother slipped round to the daughter, and caught her as she swayed back in her chair.

"Bring my bottle of salts," she commanded, and the domestic hastened away, wondering that the "'Merican" girls could n't hear of a murder without falling into a faint. By the time Bridget returned, Belle was so far recovered that the salts were not needed: but she sat with a look of such hopeless misery on her face that it brought tears to the mother's eyes.

"Come to my room, darling," she said, "and lie down. This shock has been so sudden that I fear it will make you sick."

With her mother's arm about her, Belle suffered herself to be led to the luxuriously furnished apartment, where peace and quiet reigned, and pale and wan, reclined on a lounge. By her side knelt the mother, who attempted to reassure her, not dreaming how deep the wound was.

"I fear that this is the result of his work among those people at the 'Wedge.' He was doubtless martyred by some whom he was attempting to save from a life of sin. How very, very sad; and, dear, how he will be missed in your Mission school!"

Belle made no reply, but buried her face in her hands, and with aching head, tried to think that it was all over. Never again should she see that princely figure, nor hear the tones of that helpful, manly voice. How the work at the East Side had been brightened by his presence! Could it go on, now that he was dead? Dead! The word made her turn cold and faint, with a desolate loneliness that the mother-love could not banish. Dead! The hopes never before acknowledged, the heart-flutter, the sweet maidenly imaginings now all blotted out, and in their place was only a dull pain. As the realization of the blow that had fallen upon her became more acute, she could no longer hold her peace, but moaned aloud in her agony.

"My darling, what is it?" murmured the mother.

"O, mother, I loved him," sobbed Belle, the tears coming at last.

"Poor little one! it is very hard. He was a noble man, and worthy of your love. God has taken him, darling, and in the midst of his usefulness and his labors. He knows best," whispered the mother.

"O, I have told suffering women and girls so many times to be resigned, to feel that God's hand is in their affliction, that it is but for the moment; and now, when I have need of such comfort, it seems a mockery. How can I be resigned to the death of one so noble as he was? How can I bow submissively when the man, for whom I would lay down my life gladly, — willingly, — is laid low?"

At this instant Lucy burst into the room, and in spite of a warning gesture from the mother, broke out excitedly, —

"O, Miss Pitcairn, did you hear the awful news?"

"Lucy," said Mrs. Pitcairn, with more sternness than had ever before appeared in her dove-like nature, "leave the room instantly."

Much abashed, the child slowly retraced her steps until she reached the door, when she said rapidly and half defiantly, —

"Professor Buckingham is almost killed," and then darted off down-stairs and out of sight and hearing.

"Almost!" The word had possibilities of hope that amounted to an instant blessing. Belle started up with a look of joy in her eyes, and cried, —

"He is alive! He is not dead! O, thank God! thank God!"

With this good news to cheer her, Mrs. Pitcairn lost no time in hurrying over to the Buckingham residence, which was but a short distance away, to discover the exact truth, while Belle sat in the window, counting the minutes till her return.

As a friend of the family, Mrs. Pitcairn found no difficulty in learning all that was known of the strange affair. It seems, soon after the man called on that evening, there had been another caller, who had insisted on seeing the Professor, although he was locked in his study. After waiting some time, the servant had tried the door again softly, and then had knocked. As there was no answer, and as an absolute silence reigned in the room, the man became concerned and knocked again much louder than before, and, listening, was sure he heard a slight movement and a groan.

With this for an incentive, he went outside, and standing on a short ladder looked into the window, and saw his master lying unconscious on the floor. At that sight he sprang down, and running inside, burst the door open and found the Professor just opening his eyes, but too weak to raise his head or even to speak.

The best medical aid was summoned, and the wounded man removed to his room, where he was soon raving in fierce delirium. The surgeon arriving, found that he was dangerously ill; indeed, that so savage had been the blow, that there was small chance of his recovery. ·

That the motive for the deed was robbery, no one seemed for a moment to doubt, and at once the "Inspector" was made acquainted with the meagre details of the crime. With his customary sagacity he put men looking for clews, and they were able to discover that the assassin escaped in a carriage down Madison Avenue, and that he was accompanied by a woman. At the saloon, however, where he had left the cab, they were thrown off the track and could not follow the trail further.

Meanwhile the Pitcairns had bulletins from the patient many times a day. When the delirium that followed the terrible shock was at its height, Belle sat in her room at the window next to the Buckingham mansion, and hidden by the clinging ivy vines that covered the outside of the house and drooped gracefully over the casement, watched and prayed. Not for a moment had her faith wavered that his recovery would be complete, nor be long delayed. Even the mournful news that Bridget was continually bringing in about his not being able to "lasht much longer, poor crathur," produced no effect. When she met the genial surgeon and asked his opinion of the case, and he had shaken his head and said simply that it was still "doubtful if he would pull through," she had not despaired, but waited hopefully for better tidings.

At length word came that he was out of danger and would live, and who can describe the joy of that true heart when this announcement was confirmed? She felt it an answer to prayer, and now that her petition was thus answered, she took up again the duties of her former life, and if now thoughts came of the few inconsistencies in his otherwise noble nature, she put them aside, thankful that he had again the gift of life and the promise of long years of strength and usefulness.

When the Professor was able he received a visit from the "Inspector," a man well known in New York for his acuteness and singular faculty for tracing crimes. Ushered into the sick room, he had said, after a word of greeting, —

"Do you feel able to make a statement regarding your assailant?"

"I have reasons for not wishing the matter carried further," said the Professor.

"Personal reasons?"

The other smiled and said, —

"To a gentleman of your astuteness, Mr

B——, it might be dangerous for me to say, that to apprehend my assailant would be to disgrace a relative of his, in whom I take a deep interest."

"Hum," said the Inspector. "Let me see. You are interested in a waif named Jack. Her relative is Tom Betteredge. How would his arrest injure her? Few of those with whom she will come in contact will ever know that he is her uncle."

It was a shrewd guess, and the gentleman was keen enough to see that it was, so he said smilingly, —

"Do you consider it wrong not to revenge one's injuries?"

"It is my business to bring criminals to justice. In this case we have almost no proof except what you could furnish us. My judgment would advise that this man Betteredge — for I am convinced that it was he — be brought to justice. You may see it differently. If you change your mind, let me know."

With these words the Inspector was gone, and the Professor left alone to wonder if he was not wrong to allow so desperate a criminal to remain at large when he had an opportunity to put him behind the bars for so long a time.

In the meantime, Betteredge had been suffer-

ing some, at least, of the torments of the
damned. Although he knew that he was not a
murderer, he was aware that his victim, as
soon as he recovered, would tell who it was
that assaulted him. Determined to hide himself,
he instructed Meg to still keep their home as
if he were ready to return to it at any time,
while he, in the disguise of a laborer, sought a
place in one of the city factories; engaging a
room where he could see what passed in his
former home.

In the room in which Betteredge worked
were two monster machines called "kneaders,"
made after the fashion of huge cylindrical
quartz crushers. One of these was assigned to
him soon after he came, because of his strength
and size. This same machine had an uncanny
reputation; the men called it the "man-eater,"
for if report could be trusted, two men had
been sacrificed to its rapacity when it was in
another mill. It had been dug out from beneath the ruins after the burning of that factory, bought by the present owners, and moved
to the works here. Workmen have deep-seated
superstitions about unlucky machines, as well as
unlucky men. There was not one in the room,
with the single exception of "Big Tom," who
would not have been thankful if it were hope-

lessly injured. Had they been asked to formulate their thoughts, they would doubtless have presented some curious reflections upon haunted "kneaders" in general, and the man-eater in particular. As a rule, however, laborers are reticent about such matters, judging it ill luck to talk much concerning uncanny things, lest by mentioning them they, like human eavesdroppers, hear no good of themselves and be angered. One or two, nevertheless, warned Betteredge of the dangerous work that he was undertaking, — spoke in lowered voices of the whispered tradition, that in the dead of night the man-eater had been seen noiselessly running at full speed, while the engine was still, and that it was fed by two men who, dreadfully mangled, stood over its fluted rolls as they had in the days past in the distant factory; that the machine was haunted, and always would be, till it was taken and buried beside those whom it had murdered. While it remained above ground, the awe-struck narrator had concluded, it would not want for victims.

Betteredge had received this information with an expression that might mean contempt or indifference, — his informant could not tell which, — but he noticed that the Scotchman, as he was called, did not refuse to tend the machine,

but went about it with the same dogged cool-
ness with which all his duties in the mill were
performed. His companions shook their heads
gravely, and predicted the one dreaded accident
that made every heart stand still ; and with fore-
boding waited till the hated machine should
claim its third victim, and prove that their
knowledge of such matters was not guess work,
but the result of long experience and gathered from
the unimpeachable testimony of men who had
grown gray in the grinding-room, whose obser-
vations and escapes were worth more than all
the theorizing that learned men might bring to
bear upon what they would call foolish super-
stition.

Betteredge was a man of unaccountable fancies. In the short · time that he had been a
laborer in the mill, he had formed no friend-
ships, had encouraged no familiarity. The workmen tacitly acknowledged the superiority with
which the dignity of silence invested him.

He had, from the first, taken a deliberate
survey of the employes, and estimated them very
nearly at what they were worth. There was not
the least companionship there for him. As a lonely
man often turns to a horse or dog for sympathy, so in the hours when his disguise required
hard labor, under which he secretly chafed, he

imagined the mighty machine to be endowed with intelligence, and with a feeling of kinship gloated over its reckless destruction of all that came in its way, and its stubborn energy. He felt that many of those attributes were his, and consequently better than any other could he appreciate the machine.

The forenoon had nearly passed. Swiftly the wheels were turning, the whole room was breathing an air of intense activity. The rattle of the machines, the jar of the kneaders, mingled with the shrill calls of the calendar boys, made incessant din.

All at once, in spite of the noise, everybody seemed to be looking at a group in the rear of the room. It was the foreman, two men in the uniform of police, and a stranger in citizen's dress. The foreman pointed towards Betteredge, while the man in citizen's dress stepped in front of the others and started in the direction of the machine. As he did so, " Big Tom " glanced up, and for the first time saw the uniform of the police. A fierce look lighted his eyes for an instant, and he half turned and looking through the window at his back, and saw a third enemy in the yard. A second of irresolution succeeded, and then he stood regarding the alert-looking stranger. The latter advanced quickly, till he was facing him, but on the other side of the machine.

"Tom Betteredge," he said, "I have a warrant for your arrest. You will fare better to give yourself up quietly."

A sneer came to the death-white face of the defeated man, and the liquor which still held him in thrall made him desperate. He looked so fearful, with his brilliant gaze fixed on the officer, his sharp teeth showing through the parted lips like the fangs of a wolf at bay, that the speaker retreated a step and motioned his subordinates to be ready.

Behind the police the operatives were crowding in from the other rooms, and in excited groups watching the "Scotchman," as they still called him, although every one there now knew that he was the former owner of the "Wedge" saloon.

With head thrown back, heavy brows bent in a frown, yet with defiant smile, stood Betteredge, holding his pursuers back by a look. The workmen shuddered as they beheld him; the women and girls that were forcing their way in despite the efforts of the foreman, were sobbing hysterically.

"Look here," said the head officer, at last, "there has been enough of this. Stetson, go

down that line of machines and around to where
he is. Doddridge, come with me."

As they pressed near, this time to take him,
Betteredge gave one quick, farewell glance around
the room, and with a deepening of the triumphant smile, flung himself into the jaws of the
" man-eater."

.   .   .   .

The great engine was standing still. The
grinding room was full of men. On a low, zinc-
covered stock table lay a form concealed by wrapping-cloth, the white of the fabric dyed in places
with spots of blood. The kneader, its mighty
driving-wheel shattered by an iron-bar that had
been thrust through it, stood blood-spattered,
silent, wrecked. The men gathered in groups,
fairly dumb with horror, and with white lips
whispered of what they had seen, of the terrible
death of their hunted comrade.

There was a slight stir at the door.

"You can not go in," said a firm voice.

"Eh, but I will go in!" was the reply.
" Dinna ye ken that it's my lad? Stand aside,
mon, and let a puir, hairt-broken creetur see her
laddie!"

It was Meg. With eager steps she entered
the room, her grey hair disheveled, her withered cheeks covered with tears. Kneeling

by the shapeless figure, she gently drew down the sheet and showed the dead face with a history of torture written on the drawn lineaments.

With a look of anguished love, the faithful servant-mother gazed upon her boy, kissing the lips, smoothing the contracted brow.

" O, my bairn!" she sobbed, in a whisper, as if the dead alone could hear, "ye dinna ken who it is that greets for ye; ye dinna ken it's auld foolish Meg, wha luves ye mair than all the world beside! Eh, but I'm sair, sair stricken!"

The quiet sobs ceased, and she fell anew to caressing the passive form. Suddenly turning to the crowd of men, she said, —

" Dinna ever ain of ye all daur to call yersel' men! Ye drove to his death ain wha's shoon ye were na fit to dust. Eh, ye'd stand like a pack o' cooards and let him gang to his death, and ne'er a hand raised to halp him! May the pain and anguish fa' double on ye all!"

Then again clasping her dead she sobbed, " O, my bairnie, would that ye had deed in Scotland, when yeer wee baby fingers used to stroke my face and dry my tears. O, hoo can I bear it that ye suld be sae torn, sae mangled — would God I were deed beside ye! O, it's rum! rum! rum! It killed yeer father, and now it's killed thee, my puir lad. It made ye a criminal; it wrecked yeer happiness; it stole yeer life! Cursed be they who make it, and twice cursed they who sell it!"

XXVIII.

The Roof Meeting.

"HAVE we not dwelt in tents long enough?" said Miss Pitcairn to Mrs. Thomas one afternoon, as they were waiting for the Gospel common to fill with the regular Sabbath audience.

To make her question fully understood, we must preface it by the statement that the common was no longer the "open lot," but was roofed with canvas. When first the meetings had been started, there was no covering for the audience, nor were there seats, but all stood under the bright rays of the sun, or were wet by sudden showers, neither of which, however, had yet served to disperse these enthusiastic gatherings. It had been the suggestion of an old sailor that enough sail cloth be purchased to form an awning as a protection against the elements, and this had been done, the people themselves paying for the luxury. Very proud were the members of this primitive church, of

their new roof, and most constant in their at-
tendance upon the services held under it. Many
of them had the shyness that comes to those
long unused to worship, which so effectually
keeps them from ever entering a church. No
doubt had these suspicious ones at first been
invited to come to a tent meeting, they would
have fled away; but when the services were begun in the open air, and they themselves wanted
the canvas covering, it seemed the most natural
thing in the world, and very far removed from
any "religious trap." In addition to all this,
very many had been converted during the out-
of-door meetings, and no longer feared Christian
people, or the places of their gathering.

"Have we not dwelt long enough in tents?"
said Miss Pitcairn, looking up at the weather-
stained canvas and out over the faces of the
gathering multitude.

"I think we have," replied Mrs. Thomas; "the
people are more prosperous than I ever saw
them before, and are eager to work. I will ask
my husband to talk it over with some of the
brethren."

At the close of the service a few of the
workers gathered about Mr. Thomas, as the custom was, and he, without delay, spoke right to
the point, as his wife had suggested.

"Brethren, our roof is growing old," he said.

"Canvas is plenty," spoke up one.

"And money to buy it is plentier," said another.

"Suppose we make a change and put up a more durable roof of wood," said the missionary.

"A grand idea; gude for ye, parson," said McFadden, who took a prominent part in all church affairs.

"Then a little more money would suffice to build side walls that would keep out the cold," continued Mr. Thomas.

"Aye, so it would."

"And then we could have the ground covered with boards, and seats put in for the women and children."

"Eh, but you'd hae a whole church on yeer hands," was the astonished comment.

"That is it, exactly. There are enough of us to form a church and build a chapel. We can not afford to let our precious flock scatter during the cold season. I believe it is the Lord's will that we should have right on this spot a temple to His name."

"Amen!" came from the lips of the listeners.

"Now, brethren, let us get up a circular that shall call for a 'roof meeting,' for we won't frighten the timid by talking too loud at first," said the minister, and all agreed.

An adjournment was made to the Faith Mission, where the committee seated themselves and drew up a brief circular, to be sent to all whose addresses they had, and who were interested in the meetings. These were printed the next day, and by Wednesday of that week few of those who were in the habit of attending the Gospel common meetings were ignorant of the proposed assemblage. The unusual call provoked varied comment among the people, but the majority were pleased that they had been honored by an invitation, and resolved to attend and do what they could.

The Sabbath that was to inaugurate this unusual effort on the part of the people of the "Wedge," opened bright and fair, and by ten o'clock, which was the hour set, the common was packed with people as it had never been before. At the Industrial League the young ladies had opened the parlor windows and filled them full of bright, cheery faces. In the tenement to the east of the common every window had its listeners, although many could not see the speakers because of the canvas roof.

Promptly at the hour named, the volunteer choir struck up "Nearer, my God, to Thee."

The audience joined, the voices gaining in number and strength, the chorus swelling in volume,
till the waves of sound rolled out over Van
Alstyne, Bruges, and Midnight Streets a grand
benediction of praise.

Then came a prayer from the one-legged
sailor, whose energy and industry had resulted
in the canvas roof. He prayed, —

"Our Father in Heaven, we are so full of
thanks that we are like a water-logged bark,
able neither to sink or swim. We are loaded to
the water's edge with Thy mercies. We were
poor, miserable wrecks, and Thou didst save us,
and now we sail into port this fine Sunday
morning with every thing calm and fine about us,
and our captain says, Let go the anchor, for this
is the house of the Lord, our haven of rest. O
Lord, this isn't much of a house, with only a
canvas roof and no pews, but Thy children are
in it, and they love Thee ——"

"Amen!" rolled out a deep, nautical voice.

"We haven't got much money, but what we
have belongs to Thee, and we will divide just as
soon as you show us the right cause ——"

"Yes, we will!" "It's the truth!" came the
voices of the crowd.

"Now let Thy light shine into our hearts.
Give us Thy Spirit, and make us full of love,

and take every bit of stinginess out of us.
Amen!"

"Amen!" "Amen!" said the deep bass of the
listening assemblage.

"Brethren and sisters," said Mr. Thomas, raising his clear voice in vain attempt to equal the
trumpet tones of the old sailor, "many of you
no doubt received our circular, but to those
who did not, I will explain the cause of this
meeting. When first we gathered here we were
few in numbers, and did not know whether it
would please the Lord to have us continue our
meetings or not; but our numbers have grown
From one or two who loved the Lord we have
increased to more than a hundred. Besides those
who have already acknowledged their faith in the
Saviour, are others with whom the Spirit is
striving, and who, please God, will come out on
the right side."

"Yes! yes!"

"We have been together so long that we
wish to stay together; we wish all the other
churches well, and will help them all we can
to save souls, but right on this spot is the
place where most of us found the Saviour,
and we love the place as none other on the
earth."

Tearful cries of assent, of thanksgiving, and

heartfelt amens, acknowledged that the speaker knew their minds. He went on, —

"There was a time when we could afford only the blue sky as a covering for our heads ; then as we prospered we were able to purchase the present canvas roof; but at last has come the time when we can afford a good, substantial wooden roof that shall not leak in any storm of rain, nor blow to shreds in the strongest gale."

"That's the talk! We can afford it," called the crowd, with gaining enthusiasm.

A burly stevedore, who had been a constant attendant upon the meetings for weeks, suddenly .eaped upon the platform, and with an apologetic bow to Mr. Thomas, shouted, —

" Fellows, let's take this bull right by the horns, and do what we'd orter. Let's build more 'n a ruff. Let's put up a buildin', a good, clean one, where we kin gether an' hear the minister say his say, and if it's rainin', keep dry, an' if it's cold, keep warm. Now just so you need n't think I'm givin' ye guff, there's jist a hundred dollars in this pile, and — here goes. Parson, collar the dosh, and look alive, for the boys will swamp ye with it."

At once the audience bristled with hands and arms in which there were purses, bills, and silver, and a general collection was taken up, a record being kept of every one who contributed to the fund. After the first excitement had begun somewhat to subside, a short, fat man, who had been wedged up against the fence in the rear of the crowd, began by dint of pushing and punching to work his way forward, until he was quite near the platform; then he took off his hat, and raising it to attract attention, said, —

"Meester, can you told who I vas?"

"Your name is Dittenhoffer," was the reply of the missionary.

"Yah, yah, you vas right. Dittenhoffer the brewer is what I vas."

"Yes."

"Vell, I ain't him any more, already. I vas Dittenhoffer de Ghristian. Mine sins vos forgiffen, I vas so happy. Bleeze bass de gontribution box. I vant mein share in dis buildings."

The box was passed, and the little man pulled bills out of almost every pocket and stuffed them in, uttering grunts of joy, and telling those about him of the "leedle German girl" from the League, who had shown him and his "vrow" the way of life.

While Dittenhoffer had been talking, a thin, scantily clad woman slipped up to the platform, and drawing from under a faded shawl a little packet of bills, thrust it into the treasurer's hand, and tried to hurry away. Mr. Thomas, however, always on the alert, saw the movement, and stepping down into the crowd, took her hand and said, —

"We want your name, sister."

"It ain't worth putting down, sir. I can't come to many of the meetin's and orter be home now seein' to the baby."

"If you can not come to us we can come to you, and no doubt some of our young girls would gladly drop in an evening or a Sunday afternoon, and look after the little one while you go to church," said the missionary, with instant comprehension of the genuineness of the excuse.

A little kindly questioning brought out the woman's story. She was a washerwoman, a widow with six small children, the youngest of whom was less than a year old. All day long she worked down town scrubbing the marble floors of palatial stores and elegant offices, earning hardly enough to cover rent, food, and fire. By the most careful saving she had gathered ten dollars, the surplus of a year's labor, and that with thankful heart and streaming eyes she had now given to the Lord.

His own eyes full of tears, Mr. Thomas again mounted the platform, while the woman hurried off to her waiting family, and with the story for a text, he preached a sermon that reached many a heart present. In the midst of it came a package from the box-makers at the League, containing fifty dollars and a promise of as much more as soon as they could save it. With this came promise after promise from the audience. Men, women, and even children who had no money, then pledged themselves to self-denial in many ways, with an eagerness that showed they appreciated the benefit the church would be to them, and they were moved by God's Holy Spirit to lend a hand just where it was needed.

McFadden now rose and said, in a quiet voice that still could be heard throughout the large audience, —

"Brethren and sisters, I'm a brand pluckit frae the burnin', and I neer forget it. Many's the wrong thing that I've dune in the past, but the marcy o' the Lord hae made my crooked paths straight. It is a pleasure tae me tae gie a sma' sum for the building o' this hoose o' the Loord."

Turning, he laid a bit of paper on the table and sat modestly down. The young man who had been elected to the position of treasurer

opened his eyes in astonishment as he read the
amount, leaned over and whispered to McFadden,
who nodded that it was all right, and then wrote
on the books the name of the Scotchman, and
opposite it the sum of two thousand dollars.

After this, the missionary's hundred, Conlon's
hundred and fifty, and various sums from workers
and friends, may for the moment have seemed
small, but they were given just as heartily, and
the audience seemed to appreciate the fact that
in one case the self-denial might be even greater
than in the other.

The missionary had for a last surprise reserved
a paper which he now read, it being a deed of
gift of the land known as the Gospel common,
from Miss Belle Pitcairn.

This reawakened the enthusiasm, and now that
the money was all collected, the crowd fell naturally to singing and giving testimonies.   Glowing
ones they were, full of fire and consecration, and
empty of egotism.   This general meeting was kept
up until the missionary announced the amount of
the sums given, which was enough to begin the
work at once, the money for its completion being furnished by a rich man " up town."

With one voice the people joined in the grand
old hymn, " Be Thou, O God, Exalted High,"
pealing it forth till man, woman, and child were

thrilled with the grandeur and beauty of the worship of God in song.

"Mr. Thomas," said a hearty voice after the meeting was over and the people had dispersed, "do you not think it would be better to let me give at least half of that sum to be loaned?"

"No, Governor, I do not. The people here, poor as they are, have helped build many a rum palace, and they will be blessed in building one church. If they can not swing this I will let you know and ask for help, but it is best for them to do all they can."

"Well, I suppose you know best, but my heart was full to overflowing when all were paying out their hard-earned money so freely; it made me feel like a stingy old miser."

"You wrong yourself, sir," said Mr. Thomas, his eyes filling with tears. "Your generosity saved me from death, years since, and in hundreds of cases has it been felt. But I am glad that you saw and heard all to-day. Where were you?"

"In the directors' parlor at the League. Every word could be heard there, and as for Belle, she was as uneasy as a fish out of water, until she was sure that you understood that the building was to be put on the land that she had given, not loaned."

"What a noble woman your daughter is, sir! She has been the prime mover in all of the good work done in this section. It is marvellous how she has seemed to appreciate the needs of the people, and in one way or another supply them," exclaimed Mr. Thomas.

"She is a noble girl, and will, I hope, grow into a fine woman some day," said the Governor.

Just then a messenger stepped up, and touching the missionary on the shoulder, said, —

"Mr. Thomas?"

"Yes."

"Message for you, sir. Sign here, please."

The gentleman broke the envelope and read, his eyes lighting with pleasure. Soon he broke out, —

"Governor, listen to this : —

"'No. — FIFTH AVENUE.

"'MR. THOMAS, —

"'Sorry that I can't leave to join your love-feast. Draw on me for one year's salary for the pastor.

"'JOHN BUCKINGHAM.'"

"Bless the boy," said the Governor, wiping his eyes. "His heart is in the right place. I'm proud of him, the son of my old college chum; bless his big, honest heart!"

"I wish I could tell you what a power for good he is among the people down here," said the missionary. "The people fairly worship him. He has gone into the hardest parts of the 'Wedge,' and by his Christian manliness has won the hearts of old and young."

"He does not know what fear is," said the Governor.

"Except that fear which is the beginning of wisdom," was the reply.

The "after-meeting," attended by the Governor and his daughter, was little else than a praise meeting, even the exhortations and prayers being full of thanksgiving. Just before the close of this service a slight young man, clad in a faded blue suit, wearing linen much soiled, arose and said in a voice in which there were tears, —

"My friends, I am always, as you might say, glad to meet with Christians. Although a stranger to most of you, I feel that I am not, as you might say, a stranger in the truths you believe. I have wandered far away from the fold, and now I am anxious to return. Pray for me."

Hardly had he seated himself when, to the surprise of everybody, Mr. Chick arose and said, in an embarrassed yet determined way, —

"This young man has, as he has said, wandered far away, and before we pray for him it seems to me that he had better acknowledge that he told a great many lies about persons connected with this Mission."

"I'm sure I am willing, as you might say, to acknowledge that I lied when I said I was Professor Buckingham's valet, for I never worked for him; and when Mr. Chick took pity on me and hired me, I stole his clothes, and went and lied about him, as you might say, to a club man down town. I can't remember all the things that I've done, but I think I've lied about 'most every body of prominence down here, and I'm sorry, and hope you will forgive me."

Of course he was forgiven, and put on a long probation, and finally really seemed to become a Christian. He never became a bright and shining light, but, as he used to say of himself, "If the Lord could convert a backsliding hypocrite like me, that lied all the time, and that hadn't one honest feeling, why, He can convert any body!"

XXIX.

A Voice from the Chimney.

STRONG, energetic, and vigorous, the Professor, fully recovered from his illness, was walking "'cross town" toward the Third-avenue Elevated Railroad, when he saw in front of him a trim, stylish figure that caused him to hasten his steps.

There was no possibility of mistake, it was Miss Pitcairn out for a walk, and by great good fortune going in the same direction that he was. So fortunate a circumstance would be taken advantage of by most young men, and the Professor hurried, as if bound for the Promised Land and a trifle late, and ere another block was passed was by the lady's side.

"I am more than glad to see you," she said, when the usual greetings were exchanged, "for I was just feeling that I needed your counsel."

"I wish you could realize what happiness it

gives me to hear you say so," was the response, spoken gallantly, and in a more lover-like tone than he had ever before used.

Miss Pitcairn flushed slightly, and a shade of sadness showed itself for a moment on her expressive face, a look that her companion caught and utterly misunderstood. She went on, —

"Lucy wants to take the attics of her house and make a gymnasium for the news-boys and boot-blacks — a place where they can be kept from the theatres and streets evenings. What do you think of the plan?"

"I think it well to give them some kind o₁ evening recreation, but whether the attic of that house is fitted for it is a question that I do not feel competent to decide," was the answer, in a tone that had in it a certain disappointment that caused Belle to look suddenly and anxiously into her escort's face.

"It was my doubt on the same points that led me to wish so earnestly to consult with you. When could you come down and look at the place, as you did the League building?" asked Belle.

"I am on my way to the 'Wedge' now," was his reply.

"Are you, indeed? So am I, by way of the Third-avenue Elevated. How fortunate it was that you saw me," said the Governor's daughter, with every manifestation of pleasure.

Under the magnetic influence of her voice, the Professor's feeling of disappointment over the way in which he fancied his gallantries were received, melted rapidly away, and, by the time the long stairs leading to the mid-air station were reached, he was his old cordial self. What a delight it was to him to help the beautiful girl up the steep, rubber-carpeted stairs, and to show her into the small waiting-room, and sit by her side until the train came!

With a rattle and prolonged hiss the tiny engine drew up alongside, and halting its long train of cars, gave the waiting passengers a brief moment to hurry on, — a moment improved by the gruff guard, who, standing with one hand on the signal-rope, and the other on the gate-crank, called: "Step lively, there!" as if the Metropolitan Elevated Railway were his private property, and the passengers a pack of nuisances who abused his generosity by waiting at every station to catch a ride.

It is hardly necessary to state that the train was crowded, — so much so that the aisles were filled, and even the platform black with passengers. Room was made for the lady, however, and her escort, who were wedged into the mass of people so tightly that they could hardly breathe. Just within the door stood the Professor, and in front of him, so close that the feather tips on her hat brushed his cheek when she moved, stood Belle. At the next station more people got on, and the crush was even greater. With one hand the Professor held to a resting strap, and with the other holding the arm of his fair charge, steadied her when the train lurched from side to side, or when some frantic passenger forced his way through to the door, in an endeavor to get off. Never before had he stood so near to Miss Pitcairn, nor had this calm, self-controlled man ever in all his life been so supremely wretched. Happy and unhappy, he was at one and the same moment, — happy that the woman that he loved, and at last he knew it, was with him, was by the pressure of the crowd forced into his very arms, —unhappy because he believed that she had no feeling toward him other than a platonic, sisterly regard. What would he not have dared, to drop the strap, — to brave the world and clasp this fair woman to his heart, and tell of his consuming love? Why had this affection grown so quietly in his heart, that now to uproot it would be like death?

"Are we nearly there?" inquired Belle, turning her eyes up to his face and starting at sight of his paleness.

"I'm afraid we are," he replied, desperately. "It will all be over soon, and we shall be where there is more room."

His voice had in it a trembling tenseness, which might sound like suppressed passion, or frigid weariness, that brought a crimson flush to the fair cheek of the lady, who, to cover the look, gazed steadfastly out of the windows at the second stories of the tenements that made up the scenery of the ride. The Professor dropped his hand from the strap, and it fell by the side of hers, — a touch — a thrill — but he drew it resolutely away, and set his lips with an expression that meant absolute self-abnegation.

At length the station was reached, and the vigorous shouldering of the Professor opened a way for the pair to get safely out upon the platform, and from thence to the street, where a short walk brought them to the Faith Mission.

"If you will wait for me one moment I will show you over Lucy's former house, the upper rooms of which are to be used as a gymnasium," said Belle, leaving him and hurrying away to the missionary's office, a little room to which she had a key. Slipping in, she threw herself into a chair, the picture of hopelessness.

"No, I can not be mistaken," she half sobbed. "He does not love me! He touched my hand, and drew back as if it hurt him! He stood by me, kept me from falling, almost held me in his strong arms, and cared not a whit that my heart was bursting. And at last he spoke in impatience of the length of the ride, that was to me the shortest and sweetest of my life. O, how could mamma have been so blind as to think that he could care for me? Why am I so tried? Why should I so suffer?"

A few moments later Belle rejoined the Professor, her eyes, perhaps, a trifle bright, but her whole bearing calm and friendly. Together they passed out of the mission room, and opening the door that led to the tenements above, ascended the stairs. Since Betteredge had been dispossessed there had been numerous changes in this building, prominent among which were the clean, light stairways. On all of the floors were lodgers, except on the lower and the top. Aside from this, as is well known, Lucy had one room on the second floor, for her news-boy and girl class. Up to the great attics climbed the Professor and his companion, the latter stopping often to exchange a word with some neatly dressed lodger, and once there, looked about to judge the capabilities of the apartments.

In the meantime in Lucy's Sunday-school room three floors below sat the young missionary herself, and her friend, Mr. Chick. They were to meet certain of the waifs that afternoon, and teach them verses for a concert. While they waited for them and the ever-helpful Mrs. Thomas, Lucy, leaning against the huge fireplace, began to open her heart to Chick upon a topic that had long troubled her. Very earnestly did she talk, and after his usual manner of receiving her assertions he at first contradicted and finally fell in with them.

The Professor and Belle having examined the room quite thoroughly, approached the fireplace to decide upon the system of heating, when up the chimney, in Lucy's childish treble, came the startling sentence, —

"I tell you, Professor Buckingham does love Miss Belle."

There was a moment of embarrassed silence, and then the gentleman said, in a strained voice, —

"It's the truth. I love you better than my own life."

Belle turned as white as a sheet, and swayed as if she were about to fall, and he continued, —

"I had thought to spare you this, but fate is against me, and, perhaps, if we never can be more to each other than friends, can not it be with the old trustful friendship of our first acquaintance?"

"I shall always be your friend," said Belle, in a voice scarcely audible.

"The trustful friend of three years ago?"

Belle shivered and whispered, —

"We can not go back to the past. It is your own act that raised the barrier. Sometimes I forget it and remember you as you were, but then again it comes between us."

"My act? What is this barrier?" exclaimed the Professor.

"Stanley Armitage's dog," replied Belle, in a husky voice.

A flash of anger came into the gentleman's eyes, and then, as he saw the drooping figure, his look changed to one of pity. She was not mocking him; it was simply some weak feminine caprice that, at the supreme moment of his life, was to rob him of happiness. Belle glanced up and catching the pitying gaze broke out in sudden energy, —

"You should know what I mean. I was looking out of the window when you so heartlessly turned away from the animal that your wheels wounded. Mr. Armitage dismounted and knelt in the dust, raised the creature and took him home

That is the barrier, — your cold cruelty to a dumb animal. O, don't look at me that way! I have tried to forget it, — tried to excuse it, but can't."

"Miss Pitcairn," said the Professor, his voice full of sweetness. "Had I known this before, it would have saved me many a weary hour. I did not know that it was I who injured Armitage's dog. The story was told me, and it thrilled me with indignation, but it never occurred to me that I was an actor in it. In my drives I have often lost myself in thought, — many times the thought has been of you. A man indulges fancies sometimes that are hopeless." This last was said with a wan smile that went straight to the heart of the maiden.

"Is it so hopeless?" she said, shyly.

The Professor stepped quickly forward and said, hurriedly, —

"Tell me that you are not engaged to Stanley Armitage."

Belle lifted her true eyes to her lover's face and said, —

"I have never loved Stanley Armitage, nor am I engaged to him. You have not questioned me, but in atonement for my unjust suspicions I say, I have cared for none but you."

A moment, and the arms that had so yearned

to clasp this fair woman had their wish, and the strong man said, chokingly, —

"Thank God, my darling, my darling! This is reward for all my suffering."

"Have you suffered? So have I," said Belle, softly.

"When I thought you loved another, it was agony," said the Professor, kissing her brow, cheeks, and lips, until she was rosy with confusion and shy protest.

"How strange it is, but I too was perfectly miserable. It does not seem possible that a half hour ago I was in the mission office, my heart aching, and aching because you showed such dislike when you touched my hand," confessed Belle, pillowing her shapely head on the broad breast.

"Dislike?" echoed the other. "O, blind little woman! It was all that I could do to keep from gathering you right to my heart then and there, and defying Stanley Armitage to steal you away."

"But, we are forgetting the gymnasium," said Belle, at length disengaging herself with some difficulty.

"How can I help it when I look into your eyes, and remember that you love me?" said the young man.

Belle looked grave, and to her lover more beautiful than ever, as she said, earnestly, —

"Dear, my love for you began when I saw
how unselfish you were, and the more I knew
of the good you did to others, the greater grew
my affection. Now, let us have no selfishness
in this love of ours. We have both been workers together to uplift this community. Can we
not now, with stronger faith and closer sympathy, do even more?"

"Right you are, you blessed little woman,"
said the Professor heartily, giving her a look of
such admiration and love, that she blushed and
stole into his arms to hide her face again, till
her cheeks stopped burning. "Right you are.
I won't be selfish. Give me the note book, and
I will put down the rest of those dimensions
and have carpenters here to-morrow."

This work finished, the young couple left the
great, bare apartment, and descending the stairs,
retraced their steps to the elevated station. Once
in the cars, they found seats, and the Professor,
to his regret, had not the opportunity to stand
and support his now betrothed wife, as he had
fondly dreamed; yet the ride was full of happiness to both, and the gentleman was in danger
of being carried by the proper station, so absorbed did he become in the lovely woman by

his side. Once at the Governor's residence, the young man had rather felt that he must go, but his reluctance was so evident that Belle, smiling and happy, invited him in to dinner.

As he sat alone for an instant, while Belle was absent removing her wraps, who should come in but the Governor, portly and cordial?

"Ah, Buckingham, how do you find stocks?" he asked, with a smile, for the good man had been so pleased at the deal in which he had bought Stanley Armitage's stock and cleared a half million, that he liked to chuckle over it.

"I have n't done much in them lately, although I see that mine is worth more than it was before the depression, but I should like to ask you for another loan," was the reply.

"How much, now? Glad to accommodate you!" said the Governor, heartily.

At this moment Belle returned, and the young man took her hand and standing up in the full pride and strength of his splendid manhood, said, —

"Governor, I wish to negotiate for the permanent possession of your daughter, whom I love and whom I will cherish all the days of my life."

The old man rose, his face full of emotion, and advancing to Belle, said, in a tender voice that brought tears to her eyes, —

"Little one, shall I say yes?"

"I love him, papa," came the low response.

"Then it's all right. I would rather you would have her than any man I know, Buckingham, but it gives my heart strings a tug to think of my little Belle belonging to any one but mother and me," said the Governor, blowing his nose with suspicious loudness, and soon after leaving the room.

"Poor papa, he will feel lonely enough, now," said Belle, sorrowfully.

"Lonely! O, no, he will in a little while feel that it was the very best thing that could happen. Has he not many times told me that he wished he had a boy? Did he not even once tell me that if he had a son like me, and a daughter like Belle, 'bless her heart,' that he would be the happiest man in the world? Now, his wish is to come to pass. I will be to him a son. We will not allow ourselves to be selfish, dearest, but will, as you have advised, make all those who have been benefited or helped by our presence in the past, twice as happy in the future, by our combined helpfulness and love."

"That's a sentiment worthy of you, my son," called a hearty voice from the doorway, "and you may consider yourself from this moment adopted into the family under the name of John.

Now, as my foot is a bit troublesome, suppose you go up and escort your mother down to dinner, and, by the way, she does not suspect the truth, so you may as well tell her. She is in the 'Bible room.'"

Very obediently the newly elected son went to the "Bible room," a small octagonal apartment, where the family had always gathered for religious study. It was beautifully fitted with reference books, maps, and other helps, and was one of the lady's favorite retreats.

Ten minutes later the Professor appeared with Mrs. Pitcairn on his arm, and the way in which she kissed her daughter, and her proud and affectionate glance toward her escort, showed that she had no word or thought but would add to the happiness of the newly adopted son.

XXX.

Unwillingly Convinced.

A BACHELOR party of four were gathered in a luxurious private parlor of the Hoffman, before a table furnished with costly plate and magnificent china. The occasion was a quiet birthday dinner to the popular club man and railroad king, Stanley Armitage, and occurred two years after the events narrated in the preceding chapter.

It was just such a gathering as that aristocratic gentleman enjoyed, where the ingenuity of the *chef* was taxed to its utmost to provide rare and palatable dishes, where the table service was without flaw, and the few guests those whom he had long known.

The wine flowed freely, and the conversation was varied, but always pleasant and gentlemanly. The sallies of wit were greeted with laughter that had in it no element of boisterousness, for it was one of the articles of faith of these feasters that a gentleman was always such, drunk or sober,—not that any of the party were given to intoxication, but the champagne had loosened their tongues for the moment and made them a trifle more confidential than usual.

"I say, Redmond, I saw Buckingham last night, and he is off for Europe next week for a short vacation,—going to take his wife and the boy."

"O, no, the boy is to be left at the Governor's," said the gentleman addressed, with a lazy intonation. "I dropped into the Professor's last night and learned all about it."

"You gentlemen appear to be well versed in Buckingham's domestic affairs," remarked Armitage, accepting a light from the ready waiter and smoking with luxurious air.

"I consider myself a lucky fellow to be in vited there, and so would you, old man, if you were acquainted with them. They are the most charmingly hospitable people in New York; and as for the baby boy, he's a beauty,—a big, black-eyed, knowing chap, who can be seen it you are intimate enough to ask for him," replied Redmond, warmly.

"A bachelor raves e'er domestic bliss," returned Stanley, with pronounced sarcasm, which, however, passed unheeded.

"Well, if I could be as happily settled as the 'Prof.,' I would forsake the vanities of this evil world, especially as represented by the Hoffman, and be an ornament to society," said the gentleman, more than half in earnest.

"It is easy enough to be so settled," said the railroad magnate, with an acidity of tone more marked than before. "Just take a deep interest in some mission in the slums of the city, bribe some of the hangers-on to be ever ready with benedictions, then talk it up to the prettiest girl you can find, and make her think that she has a call to assist these people. When she is interested, propose that you and she join hands in this glorious work. She will at once accept. Then when you are married and nicely settled, and family cares accumulate, you and she will begin to let the mission take care of itself, and will finally agree that it is your duty to go abroad, and will pack up and start for Europe."

Redmond listened to this half-sarcastic speech with a flush rising to his cheeks and fire in his eye, but his answer was as calm as if he were discussing the color of the other side of the moon.

"You have evidently been grossly misinformed concerning the Buckinghams, for your reference to their work can not mean any thing else but a belief that it is a pretense from beginning to end."

"O, perhaps so," said Stanley, "but people may rave all they please about city mission work. The 'Wedge' will always be the 'Devil's Wedge,' and no one can really change it. A few converts may be made, but I very much doubt if it pays for the effort."

"You have been there?"

"Been there!" exclaimed Armitage. "When I was a 'blood' and worked all day in the office, I used to run round town nights with a couple of detectives that I knew, just for excitement I have been into Conlon's many a time, and all through the Cosmopolitan, kept by an old Scotchman —— "

"McFadden?"

"Yes, that's the name. Is he still there?"

"O, yes, he still runs the old hotel," replied Redmond.

"Then there was the beer garden on the next corner to Conlon's. Why, I got knocked down and robbed there one night, in spite of the detective that I had with me, and then both of us were hustled out into the street with the clothes nearly torn from our backs and our stiff hats crushed all out of shape. O, yes, I know the place, or did, when I was fool enough to 'do the town.'"

"How long since you were there?"

"About three years ago was my last visit, and then I vowed I would let the slums alone and be satisfied with the more respectable sights of the city."

"Say, gentlemen, let's go over to this 'Devil's Wedge' and have a look at it," broke in young Stockbridge, who, fresh from college, had not seen as much of the darker side of city life as his companions.

"Your eloquence has fired him with an ambition that is my own in part," said the fourth member of the party, a stout gentleman, bald, florid, and fast, yet eminently respectable by reason of high birth and wealth.

A carriage was called, and the four were soon seated in it and rolling toward the portion of the city that had been under discussion. During the ride Armitage laughingly showed a handsome silver-mounted seven-shooter that he had borrowed from the hotel clerk, saying, —

"I do not propose to be handled as roughly as I once was, for I feel that I am older and could n't stand it as well. With this in my overcoat pocket I can take care of myself, and not spoil the set of my collar in so doing."

"Say, old man, let's take in every public building in the 'Wedge,' no matter how danger-ous the thing looks," said Redmond.

"Very well," was the half-reluctant reply.

"I will bet a fifty that you back out."

"Done," said Armitage. "Of course this means only such buildings as are open to the public? No tenements are to be invaded."

"Only places for the accommodation of the public," was the reply.

On rolled the *coupé*, and the gentlemen, leaning back against its luxurious cushions, smoked and chatted until the driver drew up in front of Conlon's as the first place of interest to be visited. -

"Faith Mission," read Armitage in amazement. "Why, Conlon must have moved from here. Say, boy, where is Conlon, nowadays?"

The youngster addressed said respectfully, —

"I think you'll find him inside o' the Mission, sir. He wuz there a few minutes ago."

"Yes, but where is his saloon now?"

"He don't keep no saloon. He's superintendent o' the Mission an' ingineer down ter Dowd's Factory."

"Whew! Sorry, boys, but this was one of the places where things were kept lively. They had a fight 'most every night, and when it got too noisy, 'Big Tom' would pound with the butt of a revolver and yell, 'Less noise, thar!' and if all was not quiet at once, would shoot. But

now the whole place is changed. Why, the
upper part of this building was the roughest
kind of a tenement, and now, by that sign, I
see it's a Newsboys' Home. No object in going
in here now."

"Not unless you are willing to lose your bet."

Armitage halted at this reminder, and then,
throwing away his cigar, stepped quietly in, and
followed by his three friends, found a' seat. The
room was fairly full of persons of both sexes,
who were almost all welcomed as they entered
by a quiet-appearing gentleman, who now came
forward to speak with the visitors.

"Won't you come further to the front and
help in the singing?" he said, holding out his
hand, which was shaken by Redmond only.

"Thanks, we are not singers, but are only off
on a quiet lark and are looking for a man named
Conlon," said Armitage.

"That is *my* name," said the stranger, looking
keenly at the speaker.

Stanley was for the moment embarrassed, then
he said, —

"It was the old Conlon we sought, — the man
who kept the hardest 'dive' at the 'Wedge.'
You may have been the man once, but you certainly are not now."

"Thank God, I'm not," was the grave reply.

"More money in this?" inquired the other, easily.

"I made a hundred dollars a week clear, out of my saloon, and loafed at that. Now I work sixteen hours a day and get twenty dollars a week as engineer," said Conlon, with a happy smile.

"Why don't you go into the business again?"

"Because the Lord Jesus Christ has cleansed my heart from sin, and instead of leading my fellow-men to perdition I am trying to save them from it."

Armitage moved uneasily under this answer, and was about to suggest an adjournment, when a question was asked that led to the story of Mr. Thomas' first visit to the place, and of the impression that his prayer created.

"Do you mean to say that he knelt and *prayed* in the face of one of your crowds?" asked Stanley, in amaze.

"That's just what he did, and 'Big Tom' all ready to shoot him any minute," said the other.

"Well, he has got grit, at any rate," murmured the millionaire.

"And grace, too," responded Conlon, as his guests, refusing to stay until the meeting opened, departed in search of the beer garden.

It was but a step away, and a moment later Armitage, in a tone of relief, saw the great gilt sign that read, " Workingmen's Garden," and said, —

" Here we are at the place that I told you of when I was robbed and 'bounced.' They have polished it up a bit, but it's probably none the less lively for that."

Pushing open the green door they stepped in and found themselves in a large hall, dotted with tiny round tables and beautifully decorated with foliage plants and pictures. Before they had a chance to recover from their surprise a polite waiter had shown them to a table, and they were seated.

" Can I serve you with any thing?" asked the waiter.

" Bring some bottled beer," said Stanley, after consulting the tastes of his companions.

"Ginger or spruce?"

" Lager," said the other, shortly.

"Only temperance drinks here, sah," was the polite reply.

Armitage flushed with angry amazement and said, —

" Do n't bring any thing. Gentlemen, this place is evidently not what we are seeking. Let's get out."

As they left, the really fine orchestra on the platform struck up "What a Friend we have in Jesus," and the crowds at the tables joined over their lunches and temperance drinks.

"Not a very hard-looking set of men in there," said Stockbridge,—a sally to which the leader made no answer.

Turning up Van Alstyne Street, Armitage remembered a little German saloon that was a door or two above, and mentally resolved to step in and get "a glass of beer," for he was really thirsty. Remembering former failures, however, he said nothing about it until he reached the door, when, to his disgust, he saw not a saloon, but a grocery. Involuntarily he looked up and down the street opposite him for the familiar liquor dispenser's sign, but saw not one. Without saying a word he walked along by Redmond's side until the latter attempted to turn into a building that had every appearance of being a church, when he remonstrated.

"'Every public building,' so said the bet," was the statement, accompanied by a jolly laugh, and the others joining in the idea. Armitage was forced to yield and enter with the rest.

A very neat little chapel the edifice proved to be, and here, as at the Mission, a service was in progress, and the audience, neat, well dressed, and respectable, were so intent on the words of the speaker that they did not note the entrance of the strangers.

"What I wish tae reiterate is the fact o' our individual responsibility for the wickedness o' this great city," he said.

"Why, it's old McFadden," ejaculated Armitage, under his breath.

"Noo, here is this chapel that, except for the gift o' the land to pit it on, we hae built an' paid for ourselves. There suld be five hundred just like it in the slums o' this wicked city. We hae been greatly blessed. The rum curse has been almaist driven from this section. We that aforetime were idlers, brawlers, and droonken wretches are, by God's grace, sober, honnust, and happy. This place was aince the 'Deil's Wedge,' but noo it is God's Wedge, and by His halp we'll use it tae split the poors o' unbelief, corruption, and eentemperance, till the auld, tough tree tae which they belong is reduced to chips and spleenters."

"Have we been here long enough?" asked the millionaire.

Again on the street Redmond said, —

"The next building, that fine one on the corner, is the 'Industrial League,' Mrs. Buckingham's pet project, but as it is for young ladies only, perhaps we had best save the blushes of our bachelor friends and not attempt to visit it."

"As you please," was the reply, but with a look of relief at the suggestion.

The ordeal, however, was not quite over, for at that instant an elegant carriage rolled up, and a lady and gentleman alighted so near at hand that the strolling party were close upon them before retreat was possible.

"Why, Redmond, happy to see you," said the pleasant voice of Professor Buckingham, as he bowed to Armitage and the others. "Were you on your way to our reception?"

"Do n't say no," said Mrs. Buckingham, as beautiful as when they had known her as Miss Pitcairn. "You and Mr. Armitage and your friends will, I am sure, be much interested. It is only, after all, an informal affair. A few charades and tableaux that the girls have arranged in the parlors."

"I should like to come," said Redmond, turning to the others, all of whom were more than willing, with the single exception of Stanley, who stood with a dark frown that showed through his polished smile and chewed the end of his glove savagely. Too polite, however, to demur, he went in with the rest, and sat through the entertainment outwardly calm, yet inwardly so

full of a variety of emotions, none of them cred-
itable, that he heard hardly a word of the pretty
speeches, nor knew what was done in the charades. In spite of his pre-occupation he could
not but see that the denizens of the institution
were well dressed, bright, and happy, and that
what they did was well done. He saw, also, that
the whole company loved and respected the Professor and his charming wife as few people in
this world deserve.

At length the ordeal was over, and the gentlemen bade their gracious hostess good-night and
went back to their carriage. Instead of returning to the Hoffman, Armitage pleaded a head-
ache and was driven to his home. As he stepped
out of the carriage Stockbridge said, —

"Say, Armitage, old man, will you take me
up to the Buckinghams' some time next week
with you? I heard her invite you and Redmond."

"No, I won't," was the answer, as the millionaire hurried into the house.

"Well, I must say, that's short," exclaimed
the young man, much hurt.

"Never mind him. He is in a huff, and if
you won't tell any one, I will let you know
why. He was sweet on Miss Pitcairn himself
once, and she preferred the Professor."

"You do n't say?"

"Indeed, I do, and my idea in getting him to come down to the 'Wedge' to-night was to forever stop his sneering remarks about the work done there."

"Well, I guess you have done it."

"I guess I have. Why, old boy, sceptical good-for-nothing that I am, when I see what that good, true woman and her noble husband have done right in the heart of one of the wickedest cities in the world, I just take off my hat and stand uncovered with a feeling that I am in the very presence of the Lord."

That evening, on their return from the reception at the League, Mr. and Mrs. Buckingham found the Governor seated in their drawing-room, listening with his old amused smile to Lucy, who, grown to quite a young lady, was detailing her trials with the boys and girls at the Newsboys' Home, and the wonderful advantages they enjoyed.

"Lucy thinks that Harold ought to be put into the Home for a year or two, that he may have no false estimate of life," said the Governor, teasingly.

"Why!" exclaimed Miss Betteredge in amaze.

"At least your remark, that 'if all of the children on Fifth Avenue had their excellent training they would grow into more useful men and women,' led me to think so, especially when you further stated that if you had your way they should each and every one of them have a year or two of it."

"I doubt if Lucy's democratic ideas are so advanced as to include our baby, Harold; indeed, I believe they would embrace every other infant in christendom first," said the Professor.

"Papa, why were you not there to-night?" asked his daughter, sitting on the arm of his chair and running her fingers through his iron-gray hair.

"Could n't leave Lucy and the baby."

"Ah, but we had such a pleasant evening, and Mr. Stanley Armitage and three of his friends visited the League."

"You take my breath by such startling assertions, dear. Did the gentleman come willingly?"

"Not very," laughed the lady. "His friends wanted to come, and he was too polite to refuse, but he did not enjoy it at all. I was very glad that he could hear the financial statement of the League read, however, and understand that it is more than self-supporting."

"I took occasion to tell him that real estate had advanced more than a hundred per cent.

since the church was built and the saloons closed," remarked the Professor.

"Why was I not there?" exclaimed the Governor. "How I should have enjoyed showing him over the 'Wedge,' and explaining things that he has so persistently sneered at!"

"Why, papa, that would be a very wrong spirit," laughed Belle.

"Even if real estate had gone down, and the enterprises were not self-supporting, it would be a success," said Lucy, her large eyes full of earnestness.

"You are right, dear," said the young wife. "The fact that souls have been saved makes the work a grand success, and one that should not be lost sight of."

"And to my mind it is a long step toward the evangelization of the heathen in our midst, the hundreds of thousands that dwell in our great cities," said the Governor, earnestly.

. . . .

A few more words and our story is finished. The great box factory and the numerous philanthropic institutions that were the outgrowth of its wise administration, grew year by year and did incalculable good. To the factory was added an art department, where the most delicate souvenir boxes were made and decorated by young ladies, who, at the expense of the Van Alstyne Manufacturing Company, were thoroughly educated in drawing and painting. From the mill went forth a host of young women fitted for higher places, while a host remained — contented, industrious, useful.

The most conspicuous example of a happy graduation from the active duties of the factory was the often-quoted case of Miss Murdock, who surprised everybody by falling in love with and marrying Mr. Chick, after he had wooed her for nearly two years. The wedding was a fashionable one, and the bride was lovely. To-day Mr. and Mrs. Chick, — the former grown into a capable business man and still retaining the grand good qualities that his "dudishness" never wholly hid, the latter a bright, cheery helpmeet, — are among the most popular young people in Gotham, and live as befits their wealth. If I should mention the plan that they are maturing for a hotel on the Sound, a half-hour's ride from the factory, with a special steamer to carry the workers to and from the city during the heat of summer, it might be thought premature, and I desist.

John Conlon is still a power at the "Wedge," and has risen to be general superintendent of the box factory. His wife, still young and fair, is wealthy from the royalties paid on her folding box, and very proud John is of her success. They own a pretty place up the Hudson, where three little Conlons, with a full share of their father's energy, "keep things moving."

Mr. and Mrs. Thomas, bless their kind hearts, are the wealthiest of all, not in money, — for they find a thousand uses for their surplus, — but in the heartfelt benedictions of the poor and the knowledge of many souls won to Christ.

Teddy Timmins, the little pie-eater, the coolest, most audacious of all the "Wedge" gamins, adopted by Professor Buckingham, secured a good education, and is nearly through West Point. He has grown tall, straight, handsome, and pays marked attention to Miss Betteredge, and it is whispered —— but we are getting gossipy and must stop.

As we write this last chapter, there comes the news from the "Wedge" that the building known as the Cosmopolitan Hotel, which Mr. McFadden resigned when grown too feeble to manage it, had been given over to carpenters, masons, and decorators, and at length had come out of the ordeal a technical school for girls and yonng women. A splendid institution it is said to be, with a fine corps of teachers, no lack of valuable apparatus, and the dignified name — "**The Buckingham School of Useful Arts.**"

www.ingramcontent.com/pod-product-compliance
Lightning Source LLC
Chambersburg PA
CBHW022018110726
47901CB00006B/1578